ANARBIA
THE JOURNEY

CHRIS VANDENLANGENBERG

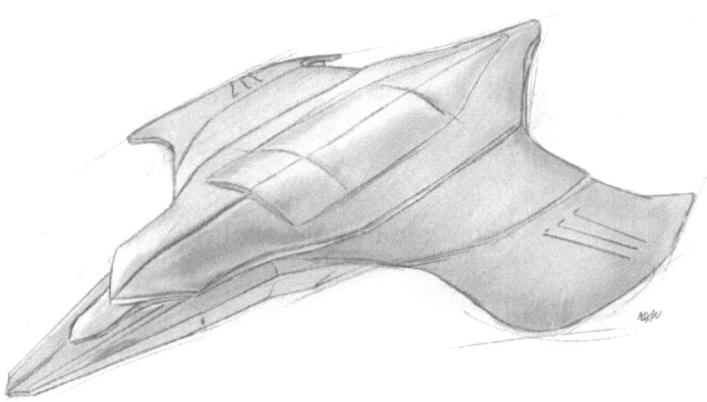

Published by Long Mountain

Dedication

To my Father, who put up with my need to watch every science fiction TV show that came on. Now that I look back, some cf those shows were pretty bad. And to my Mother, for getting me interested in books. Each book opened a new world in my imagination and I learned so much. Without them, this book would not be possible.

Table of Contents

Acknowledgments

I would like to acknowledge the people that helped me the most with this book.

Dwight Bell - Dwight is a coworker who let me bounce ideas off of him and graciously read sections of the book to help clarify the ideas presented.

Jeff Brown - Jeff is a retired Air Force Weapons Systems Officer. We worked together during 9/11 and stayed in touch with each other over the years. He helped me with the military jargon for the in-flight radio traffic, which I would not have gotten correct without his help.

Phillip (Eric) Pearson - Eric is a friend who did the initial edit for me and gave me the idea to write this book.

Evan Petty - My nephew Evan performed a critical review, and I truly believe his efforts made for a much better book.

Mary Wright - for her artistic skills that made the cover come alive. She can be reached at www.fiverr.com/mary_k_wright

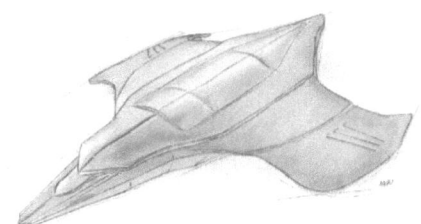

Chapter 1: EXPERIMENTAL

The massive bomber YBV-92 effortlessly slipped through the Earth's atmosphere with test pilot James Norgas at the controls.

The craft got its nomenclature from its design and purpose. The "Y" signified an experimental prototype intended to go into full production, as opposed to an "X" model that was purely experimental. Its basic mission was designated by the "B" for bomber. The "V" indicated the craft was capable of vertical or short take-off and landing.

As the YBV-92 approached the Karman Line, Jim began to level off the ascent. The Karman line was the unofficial separation point between outer space and Earth's atmosphere.

He keyed the bomber's internal comms and announced to his crew, "At my mark, you are all officially astronauts." He counted down as they approached the altitude of 100 kilometers, and keyed his mic as the altimeter ticked, "Three, two, one, mark."

He heard cheers come over the speaker on the bridge and fondly remembered the hazing ritual he went through the first time he crossed the Karman line. He caught himself subconsciously rubbing the groove in his scalp he received during the hazing from colliding head-first into a bulkhead. He started to watch the gathering in the cargo bay on a display in the console before him.

He said over a private channel, "Chief, is everything in place?"

"Yes, sir. You should see them. Some of them are already turning green."

"As green as I was my first time?"

Chief laughed at the memory, "I don't think a toad alive could turn that shade."

Jim was actually weightless but did not notice. The uniforms the entire crew wore were woven with special fibers that were also embedded in all the tools and equipment the crew used. These fibers allowed the scanners embedded in the floor plates to identify and pull the various objects toward the floor and allowed the crew to move around as if they were in gravity. The gravity plating pulled on each object to simulate what the crew's mind would normally expect from that object. Liquid had to be kept in special containers. The only visual clue that they were in a weightless environment with the gravity plating turned on was the way the long hair of a coworker floated about their head.

The gravity plating was an adaptation of the YBV-92's drive which used force fields and magnetism to push and pull objects at the atomic level. The drive was named after the physicists whose theories made the drive possible – The Faraday-Maxwell drive.

Jim watched the video as the chief and the crew members that had previously crossed the Karman line got the rest of the crew ready.

Chief Besch bellowed, "Line up and strip. Everything but your underwear. Ladies, you have been told not to wear your dainty frillies and gentlemen, you were warned to make sure your tighty whities are white. Keep your boots on so you don't float away – yet."

The crew started to taunt those lined up with comments and laughter about their underwear. One crewman thought it would be funny to wear underwear that had a clown face and a long nose, and a crew-woman had on the back of her panties the words "Enjoy the view." Everyone wore the funniest they could find.

Filthy-looking buckets and equally filthy mops appeared. Soon each person in line was lathered up with a foul-smelling liquid they called 'Slickery Sheeit'. A combination of engine grease, used cooking oil that was way past its expiration date, and lard.

A fire extinguisher was placed approximately 15 feet in front of each person, which just floated in the air. The tag was removed so the gravity plating did not pull the fire extinguishers toward the floor.

Chief Besch explained the rules, "There are no rules. When I say go, you will remove your boots, find your way to a propulsion device, and race to the finish line. That's one lap around the second floor then back here."

Without any prep or fanfare, Chief yelled "Go!"

Jim activated a simulated alarm, which caused the lights throughout the ship to go out, replaced with sporadically placed beacons that pulsed a red glow, and klaxons began to wail.

Each of the greased-up crewmen fought to reach a fire extinguisher. Some were pushed the wrong way as others used them to move toward the extinguishers. Each drifted with the momentum they obtained till they were able to interact with something to correct their direction, or add speed. The 'Slickery Sheeit' made it difficult to grab onto anything and many missed the handholds they reached for.

The other crewmen stayed well out of their way, yelling encouraging criticism.

The first crewman to reach a fire extinguisher was actually the first person pushed out of the group in the wrong direction. When he reached the back wall, he used his legs and propelled himself as hard as he could. When he crashed into the extinguishers, he sent several flying and tried to grab the closest one but failed thanks to his greasy fingers. The second one he reached for, he circled his hands around the neck and wrapped his legs around the base. He discovered the extinguisher had a coat of grease of its own. He could not rely on friction, only his grip to hang on. When he squeezed the trigger, he was sent into the wall in front of him. The impact caused him to lose his grip on the extinguisher, and they both floated in different directions.

Jim subconsciously felt the groove again as he watched. 'Six stitches' he remembered, 'and blood. Oh man did that bleed. In zero-G they had a harder time than usual to get it to stop bleeding'.

The next person to reach an extinguisher saw what happened and used quick, short squeezes. This worked till he tried to turn and discovered he could not change his direction.

One of the women was next to gain any momentum. She discovered the nozzle could be moved in different orientations and was soon heading down the hall one floor up.

It did not matter who won. What mattered was having fun, and in the process, they all learned more than they expected about zero gravity. They learned they could still function if the gravity plating failed.

When the race was over, Chief Besch told the contestants to return to their quarters to get cleaned up, "Hurry up, the rest of us want to have some fun, and we will turn off the gravity plating soon."

The rest of the crew helped the contestants back to their boots and then to their quarters in the nose of the ship.

Approximately an hour later, the navigation computer indicated the ship was approaching the optimal position to begin the descent to reach its primary target in central Asia.

Jim said over the ship's comm, "Chief, prepare for reentry."

"Copy that. Avoid the chop this time would ya? It took the ground crew a week to get this bird ready after our last orbital flight."

Jim felt the gravity plates gradually come back on as the chairs' straps loosened and his arms felt heavier. The Chief brought the power up slowly so anyone that was still floating did not get injured.

Chief Besch was a crusty lifer, pushing 28 years in service. He said things the way they were and didn't care who heard it, and one damn good mechanic. Jim enjoyed pulling his chain at times, and Chief always had a witty comment ready.

Jim said over the comm, "It's not all creamsicles and unicorns up here, I take what I get. Tighten the whatsits tighter next time," and waited to see what the chief came up with this time.

"So you want creamsicles and unicorns do ya? I'll make sure I tell your nurse and the guys with the butterfly nets. And the only 'whatsits' I know of on board hold the captain's chair to its pedestal. Sorry I forgot that adjustment tool at your mother's house. Did I tell you she sent me a birthday card this year?"

Jim had a smile on his face when he keyed the mic to talk with ground control at the classified base he took off from in North America, "Bomber Two – Home Plate, commencing reentry." He angled the nose up slightly and slowed the forward momentum. Gravity took care of the rest.

"Home Plate – Bomber Two, Roger that, initiate handoff to local control." Engineers monitored every aspect of the flight; the YBV-92 was completely experimental. This was not the first time the ship was in outer space, but the ship on an actual combat mission was a first.

The software engineers did not know how the AI (Artificial Intelligence) would react in combat since they did not write the AI, and did not know where it came from. This was typical of "black projects." The people who should be informed are kept in the dark until something goes wrong.

"Big Watch One – Bomber Two, descend to angels five zero," came the initial contact with the AWAC (Airborne early Warning And Control aircraft) circling outside of the area Jim was briefed to attack.

An AWAC was an aerial version of an airport's control tower but had many more responsibilities. It controlled all friendly aircraft like a ballet. It timed each action of the aerial portion of combat moments before friendly ground forces moved in. This kept them out of harm's way and the enemy's heads down. The next inbound aircraft with a mission was marshaled on the heels of the departing aircraft. The screens inside the AWAC identified each aircraft with a different color for friendly, hostile, and unknown. Interceptors were sent in to destroy or identify any aircraft that were not already identified as friendly.

Jim radioed, "Bomber Two – Big Watch One, roger, angels fifty." He confirmed the directions the AWAC gave him. He was to enter the area at an altitude of 50,000 feet.

"Big Watch One – Bomber Two, proceed on vector two eight zero, initiate your run, heavy AA (Anti Aircraft) in area, Coyote Five and Six loitering." The AWAC informed Jim to initiate his planned attack run on a heading of 280, and Coyote Five and Six were two friendly interceptors in the area in case he ran into trouble. Lastly, he learned the intelligence was correct. The target was still protected by anti-aircraft guns and missiles, and this was not going to be an easy swoop-and-drop mission.

"Bomber Two – Big Watch One, copy that, IP in sight." Jim informed the AWAC he had a visual on the hospital he was briefed to use as a navigational aid. This was the last identifiable object in the area for him to use to line up on his target, a mere 100 meters beyond. "Starting bomb run."

His target was an airbase nestled among gently rolling hills. The base appeared to be abandoned. On closer inspection it was discovered the hills were being used as natural blinds to shelter aircraft hidden between them.

He pushed a control on the panel before him. A slit under each wing nestled next to the fuselage opened. A moment later a bomb appeared, fed by an auto-loading rail system with more munitions behind it.

A variety of weapons were available, each were loaded in sequence. For this run the majority were anti-personnel bombs, known as 'Daisy Cutters', mixed every third bomb with incendiaries and a few low-yield EMP (Electromagnetic Pulse) bombs.

The initial bomb was an EMP bomb and would silence all the automated guns in the area, making the area safe for the friendly aircraft behind him. The bomb would not do any damage to the hospital itself, but the EMP generated would destroy any electronics inside including life support equipment. The planners determined the collateral damage was acceptable. They thought the hospital would be partially shielded by the hills, provided the EMP bomb landed on the other side of the first set of hills. It had to be a precision drop, but Jim felt confident he was up to the task.

The bomb release was programmed to alternate release from port to starboard every bomb. At his current velocity, each bomb should have a spacing of 50 meters upon impact.

The approach became littered with AA fire, nearly a solid black wall of metal fragments Jim had to fly through. Any other aircraft would be severely damaged if one of the fragments entered an engine or ripped the aircraft's skin.

The YBV-92 manipulated matter to propel itself, and so the metal fragments never touched the ship and actually boosted its performance.

He flipped a switch to activate internal comms, "Grab onto something, this might get rough." Everyone in the engine room took a seat and strapped in. The engine room was basically just a power plant since the skin of the ship provided the thrust.

He heard the chief reply, "As if the chop wasn't enough. Looks like no 'Boom Boom Room' this weekend." The Chief referred to a run-down strip joint outside the base.

"Bomber Two – Big Watch One, bombs away," Jim transmitted as he set the bomb release switch to automatic.

Almost immediately the ship was rocked by an AA missile, which impacted the belly of the ship near the aft section and exploded. Shrapnel ripped through the interior of the ship and caused a nose-down attitude.

Internal comms came alive with casualty reports from the engine room. "Chief, what's going on down there?" Jim asked over the comm to get one report on the entire situation instead of multiple while he struggled with the controls.

Thanks to the propulsion system, the ships orientation did not effect the direction of flight. It was merely more efficient. To his surprise the YBV-92 righted itself to its orientation before the explosion, all on its own.

"Major," Jim heard Chief's voice over the comm, "I got three injured back here. One with a few cuts, another caught some shrapnel in an artery in the upper thigh. He lost a lot of blood before we could get a tourniquet on. The third, I don't think is going to make it. She has a sucking chest wound and trouble breathing."

"Damn it," Jim said to no one in particular. There were other seats and stations available, but he was alone on the bridge. "Do what you can Chief. Can you cover the wound with plastic or something to stop air from getting in there?" He flipped a switch and began to transmit on the radio, "Bomber Two – Big Watch One, AA silenced, took damage, three injured onboard, one, possibly two critical," Jim relayed to the AWAC.

Chief said, "I got some tape that will stop the fuel leak on a tractor, but it's far from sterile."

"Do you have enough to seal a trauma pad? That'll keep the wound sterile."

"Roger Bomber Two, Coyote Five and Six en route your position," came over the radio. Jim knew the two interceptors were on the way. They could not assist with the internal issues but they would help take some of the pressure off him.

Over the internal comms he heard Chief say, "Reminds me of a flavor pack at a pig roast. Modesty is out the window but she is breathing easier. Ma'am, with a pair like that you should be working at the jiggle palace."

Jim yelled, "Chief!" He couldn't believe the chief would say something like that. "Do what you can and keep her calm. And no more comments like that. We're almost done here."

Chief said, "Aw shucks, just trying to keep her mind off it. I'm sorry ma'am."

Jim heard a woman's voice, "Don't worry. I know you're trying to keep my mind occupied so I don't..." she paused to fight off a spasm of pain, "go into shock. A bit unorthodox but I know."

Chief said, "Exactly. Now do what you can to stay awake. Don't you fall asleep on me."

"Why does everyone say that?"

Chief said, "I don't know."

Jim continued the bomb run and saw several secondary explosions as munitions and fuel on the ground ignited. The push button controls were a bit sluggish to respond but manageable. Soon the inbound friendlies would tell him the extent of the damage.

A red blip showed on the HUD (Heads Up Display). The blip closed from a higher altitude, behind and to the right. A few short seconds later Jim received the warning of the new threat from the AWAC. "Big Watch One – Bomber Two, hostile inbound on your four."

"Coyote Five – Big Watch One, hostile in range, got a lock, fox one," came over the radio from one of the interceptors as he fired a missile.

Jim knew a missile was on the way, targeting the hostile aircraft on his tail. His display showed the hostile fired a missile of its own and he launched decoys. Chaff and flares were jettisoned from the sides of the YBV-92 as counter measures to the missile – both, because Jim did not know what type of targeting the missile had. He hoped the missile would lock onto something other than him.

Jim said over the internal comm, "Hang on everyone. We got a hostile inbound. Chief are you able to secure – what's their names?"

"For crying out loud, would you stop getting us shot at?"

"Creamsicles and unicorns Chief, just keep thinking creamsicles and unicorns."

"Yea well that unicorn is about to ram us up the ass with that big honking horn of his if you don't start doing some of that fancy piloting shit." Chief felt he got his point across and said, "Eric and Amy, Sir. Yea, I can rig something up." Then Jim heard, "Crewmen get me some straps," as the comm channel ended.

The missile passed through the sea of aluminum strips scattered by the chaff canisters he launched. The missile's computer determined that its distance from what it was tracking had expanded, and so it detonated its warhead in the event it was still close enough to do some damage.

Luckily, the missile switched its target from the bomber to the chaff. The explosion was still close enough to force Jim to steer into the shock wave to stay on course.

The hostile aircraft had drawn close enough to switch to guns, and the pilot began to fire. To the bewilderment of the pilot, all his shots went wide. He began to rock his aircraft back and forth but saw his tracers fly in wild directions.

Moments later, the missile from Coyote Five slammed into the side of the hostile aircraft. A ball of fire, followed by a black splotch in the sky, marked the location where the enemy fighter ceased to exist. Its remains rained down and added to the carnage on the ground.

Jim heard Coyote Five's wing-man warn, "Coyote Six — Coyote Five, got another bogie climbing from three five five," almost due north. Followed by the AWAC giving the same warning.

The bogie closed and immediately went guns on. The pilot aimed at the belly of the bomber and chewed gaping holes where damage was already done. The bullets ripped deep into the bomber and did additional damage as they impacted internal parts.

The YBV-92 began to roll to the right, and when Jim tried to correct it, the controls fought him and seemed not to respond to his touch. The control panel began to vibrate under his hands, and a display showed a representation of the damage to the aft section grow as the ship suffered more damage.

He continued to attempt correction to the roll, but the ship began to yaw to the right. He began to fight the new change in attitude. Despite the direction the nose of the ship faced, it remarkably continued to hold its course. Jim did not understand how, and it felt completely unnatural to him.

"Coyote Five – Big Watch one, fox two," came over the radio to Jim's relief, followed by an orange glow in his right peripheral which also reflected off the surfaces of the bridge. "Coyote Five – Bomber Two, you're in the clear."

The controls Jim had been fighting moments before began to respond to his touch. "Bomber Two – Big Watch One, bomb run complete, secondary explosions witnessed. Climbing to angels fifty. Controls sluggish."

"Big Watch One – Coyote Five, assess damage Bomber Two."

"Coyote Five – Big Watch One, already on it," The pilot of Coyote Five maneuvered his craft below the bomber and crept up to it gradually. Aircraft smaller than the YBV-92 had been known to suck fighters into their wake when they got too close. The pilot of Coyote Five was aware of this and proceeded cautiously. "The aft section on Bomber Two's belly barely hanging on. I'm able to see damage inside Bomber Two through the missing pieces."

Upon hearing the status of his ship, Jim knew it would not survive its return flight to the States if it went into low Earth orbit again. "Bomber Two – Big Watch One, request exit vector to nearest friendly base."

After several moments of silence on the radio came words Jim did not want to hear. "Big Watch One – Bomber Two, negative,

Home Plate wants that asset returned unseen."

He started to get frustrated, "Bomber Two — Big Watch One, inform Home Plate intercontinental flight impossible and casualties on board. I got two souls in critical condition."

Several moments later, he could not believe his ears, "Big Watch One — Bomber Two, last transmission understood. Return to Home Plate."

Chills ran down his spine, and he became noticeably upset. His palms began to sweat and his forehead creased in wrinkles as he narrowed his eyebrows. He thought about how the developers were willing to risk the lives of his crew to protect a secret that would be revealed in a press conference soon. Everyone on board knew the risk, but the combat phase of this flight was over; they were now flying for themselves. He switched to internal comms and asked for an update on the injuries.

Chief replied, "Not good sir, Amy is unconscious, breathing labored. Eric is awake but his skin is pale and clammy. I think he lost too much blood."

"Bomber Two — Big Watch One, request exit vector, Diego Garcia," he pleaded. He knew the YBV-92 could not withstand an orbital reentry, and feared Amy and Eric would not survive long enough to fly to the States while remaining within the atmosphere. That would more than triple the flight time.

He waited several agonizing moments of silence till the radio began to crackle, "Big Watch One — Bomber Two, adjust course one eight seven." A wave of what felt like cool air ran across his scalp.

"Bomber Two — Big Watch One, copy that, thanks Big Watch One, I owe you," he said with gratitude in his voice, and he wiped the sweat off his forehead with the sleeve of his flight suit.

"Coyote Five — Bomber Two, we will escort you all the way."

"Bomber Two – Coyote Five, thanks for the company, sure you can make it?"

"Coyote Five – Bomber Two, look out your wings."

Jim looked to his right and left and saw he was in a "V" formation with what looked like miniature versions of the YBV-92. He never saw this variant before and did not know a fighter sized version of the YBV-92 was developed. The only notable difference was that the interceptors had a laser cannon mounted on their belly, whereas the bomber had a cargo ramp. The interceptor looked small enough to fit inside the YBV-92's cargo bay. Jim did not dwell on that thought for long.

When he was able, he set the autopilot and went to check on Eric and Amy. The amount of damage surprised him. A huge hole with several smaller ones peppered the rear wall of the engineering room. That wall was not the outer hull of the ship, and he could only imagine the extent of damage beyond the wall and the fear that everyone in engineering must have felt as it happened. Upon seeing the extent of the damage he had to ask, "Chief, what's the status of the core?"

"The outer casing got a few rather deep gouges, but nothing serious."

Jim approached Eric, who was lying on his back with his legs propped up in an attempt to have more blood go to his brain. Eric was clutching his left leg just below where the tourniquet was applied. Jim asked, "Hang in there Eric, almost there. Think you can do that?"

"It hurts sir," Eric said, referring to the tourniquet cutting off the blood to his lower leg.

"I know, it has to be tight or it will start bleeding again."

"It feels like my leg is dying."

"I'm getting you help as soon as I can. We will be landing in Diego Garcia in a few hours."

Eric asked, "Oh God, a couple of hours? Why not the States? Won't that take less time?"

"The ship is too badly damaged. We'd never make it. I'm sorry Eric. As soon as we land, help is waiting."

Chief Besch, out of ear shot of Amy, told Jim, "Amy has been in and out of consciousness. I'm really worried about her and I don't know what else to do."

When Jim looked her way she was conscious again, just looking at the ceiling, and she looked scared. It was obvious she had difficulty breathing, which was shallow and appeared painful for her. Chief Besch looked at Jim and shook his head.

Jim got a feeling of dread and tried to fight any visible sign of it in fear it may send Amy into shock. He sat on the floor and cradled her head in his lap. "How are we doing Amy?" He said in soothing tones and fought back the quiver he felt migrate to his throat.

She struggled to speak between labored breaths, "Not so good sir. My boys – who will take care of my boys?" Her voice was barely over a whisper.

"Don't you start thinking like that. I need you to concentrate on your breathing. We will get you through this. Wasn't that you that won the fire extinguisher race?"

"Yes, Sir." She tried to manage a smile.

"I'm sure the person I saw, with that kind of determination, can get through anything. Including this." Jim brushed the hair off Amy's face that stuck there in dried tears.

"But sir," she gasped, then he noticed all movement left her eyes.

"CPR," he shouted as he slid out from under her head.

The Chief and Jim worked on Amy taking turns till both were exhausted. After what seemed an eternity they had to stop. Both men looked defeated and physically drained.

Jim reached over and closed Amy's eyelids with the palm of his hand. It was not as easy as they show in movies. He figured it was because she no longer produced tears and her eyes were now dry. He had to pinch the eyelids away from her eyes to close them.

Amy was new to the crew and he did not know her yet. He still couldn't fight back the tears and stuffy nose as a wave of emotions flooded over him.

He stood, feeling like he failed her, glanced at Eric and ordered, "Don't you quit on me."

Eric said, "No, Sir."

Jim left engineering, not wanting anyone to see his emotional state. When he got to the hall and the door closed behind him he wiped the tears that formed in his eyes.

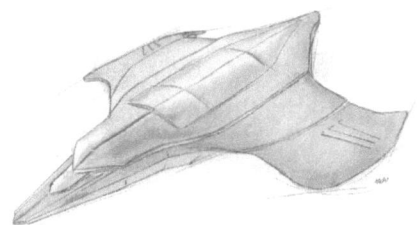

Chapter 2: DIEGO GARCIA

The three aircraft were immediately marshaled into a hangar barely large enough for the bomber. The interceptors easily nestled under the bomber's wings. As soon as the last aircraft entered, the massive doors closed behind them.

Jim noticed a couple of ambulances and a larger than usual security contingent gathered around the back wall of the hangar.

His chair began to vibrate, which indicated to him the cargo ramp was lowering. Everyone in the hangar started to make their way toward the bomber. He suspected the extra security was there for him. Despite this, he continued the shutdown procedures.

The Lieutenant in charge of the security detail began when he passed through the bridge door, "Major Norgas, under the Manual for Courts Martial, and the Uniform Code of Military Justice I place you under arrest. You are to come with us."

Jim asked, "Lieutenant, can you give me a few minutes to finish shutting this thing down? I'm not going anywhere."

"Yes sir, take your time." The Lieutenant said as he gazed in awe at the spacious bridge and its clean consoles devoid of the controls he expected to see. Instead, he noticed Jim manipulate glass touch screens as he went through the checklist in his hand.

Jim saw an occupied body bag at the base of the ramp when he was escorted from the bomber. Anger came over him as the events that led to this moment flooded his mind. He was comforted by the thought Eric was getting the medical help he needed. He believed there would have been another body bag if he had followed the orders he was given and had flown halfway across the planet in a partially crippled ship.

Less than an hour after the shutdown checklist was complete, he found himself seated between two Security Police officers in a military cargo plane headed for Barksdale Air Force Base – A place where several high profile court's martial and the investigation into the space shuttle Challenger explosion took place.

A security detail led him to a private room in the base VOQ (Visiting Officers Quarters), and guarded the door from the outside so he could not leave. The gravity of his career ending hit him when the door slammed shut.

He saw a phone next to his bed and decided to call his parents. He did not know if any news reached them and he wanted to let them know he was okay. He picked up the phone, and on the second ring the receptionist at the front desk answered.

"I'd like to place a long-distance call."

"Sorry, Sir. We have been instructed that your room is not allowed outside calls. If you would like to order food or something, I'll be glad to help you."

He was disappointed and tried not to let it show in his voice, "Thank you but that won't be necessary," and hung up.

He knew there was always a hearing after an incident like this, but he felt they were taking it to the extreme. Security Police were known to take the extreme, but he wondered if it was the Air Force who ordered the lockdown.

He wondered if his parents knew anything about the mission and if they were worried. He heard of other pilots who were shot down. The Air Force notified the family the pilot was dead, only to discover days later he was very much alive.

A particular incident came to mind when he was in junior varsity football. There was a player on the opposing team who looked like he was held back several years due to his size and the amount of growth on his face. He seemed to delight in causing injuries and was nicknamed 'The Hulk'.

When Jim was called in to replace an injured teammate he found himself lined up across the scrimmage line from The Hulk.

Jim knew his size would have no effect, so he tried to outsmart The Hulk. Instead of going head to head, he ducked and stayed low. He waited for The Hulk to pass over him, and then rose up catching The Hulk's legs against his shoulders and knocked him off his feet.

The next play, he was lined up against The Hulk again. This time The Hulk looked pissed, "Don't think you're going to get away with that this time, shrimp."

Jim thought The Hulk looked like a bull ready to charge, which he did seconds before the play. The Hulk slammed into him as if he was a tackling dummy and pounded Jim's head into the ground with all his weight.

Smelling salts were used, but that's all Jim remembered till waking up in the hospital.

The worst of his injuries was a mild concussion, but as the story was passed from person to person the injuries grew. When his parents were notified, they were told he suffered a broken collarbone and was in a coma.

The following Monday when he got to school he was treated like a hero by his classmates. Because of his injury, The Hulk was ejected from the game and Jim's school won, which put them in the running for the championship.

Jim's parents understood he could not talk much about his job but he wanted to let them know he was okay.

He had a lot of time on his hands to sleep and think. He thought about how he got here.

Traditionally, a pilot's first unit after flight school has the honor of giving him a call sign. That call sign will follow the pilot for his or her entire career, for better or worse.

His first unit was going through an ORI (Operational Readiness Inspection). An ORI is a very big deal for a unit. It tests a unit's war readiness and can make or break the career of the commanding officer of the units involved and the base commander. These inspections can also set the budget till the next ORI.

A unit under this pressure usually does not give newly assigned personnel any tasks that may affect the outcome of the inspection. Jim was assigned administrative duties in the orderly room till the inspection was over.

The inspectors noticed the wings on his uniform and asked him to be an aggressor. This meant he would attack his own unit, so they would have a live target to fly against for evaluation.

His first day as an aggressor did not go so well. That night he laid awake and analyzed in his mind every move that was made. The next day he got a kill shot on everything sent up against him.

Unknown to anyone, Jim knew where gaps existed in radar systems used by different aircraft. These gaps caused blind spots for the pilot. He discovered this purely by accident in flight school and researched various aircraft radar systems and what aircraft had what systems. He also studied where these blind spots overlapped with the pilot's inability to see.

he tried to take advantage of the gap on his first day but made mistakes and drifted in and out of the pilot's view. The next day was a completely different story. By the end of the day he was sole survivor. With permission from the ORI commander Jim began strafing the runway.

The weapons used were all either inert or simulated. The ORI commander used this as a pretense for other scenarios on the base, which involved medical, fire, and EOD (Explosive Ordinance Disposal) personnel.

Jim volunteered to take part in a ground attack on the base headquarters building. During the preparation for this, he learned different tactics, including 'bounding with cover', concealment, and how to study a structure to find its weaknesses against ingress and quickest egress with hostages. He learned quickly, and his team pulled off a flawless mission, taking the base commander in tow.

The base commander took it all in stride. He never revealed the word, or color of the day. What upset the commander the most was when his blindfold was removed, and he discovered his aid, who was also taken hostage, was sitting across from him eating a nice juicy hamburger with all the fixings. In the spirit of the exercise, he had been eating MREs (Meals Ready to Eat) and from a field kitchen for the past week. Some joked MRE stood for Meals Rejected by the Enemy.

In the end, the unit failed it's inspection. Because how well he did his job working with the inspectors, Jim was given the call sign 'Stinker'.

His unit commander was extremely excited to learn Groom Lake wanted Jim for a special project when they heard about his accomplishment. The commander practically packed his bags to get rid of him.

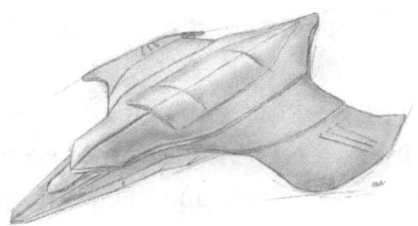

Chapter 3: HEARING

Several days passed before Jim was brought in front of the panel, which was comprised of fellow officers. The judge presiding over the hearing asked, "Major James Norgas, in your own words, what happened?"

He stood and cleared his throat, "Sir, my craft was struck by a surface-to-air missile, causing damage to the aft section."

He heard the doors behind him open and the shuffling of three people enter the room. his supervisor, an engineer that helped develop the bomber he flew, and a third person he did not know.

The judge asked, "You were saying?"

"I received casualty reports from my maintenance chief," Jim said exchanging glances with his supervisor. "An enemy fighter descended on my craft and fired a missile that was decoyed by chaff I launched. A friendly fighter, Coyote Five, fired a missile which intercepted the enemy fighter as it closed within range for guns. Coyote Five's wing man reported another hostile fighter climbing to intercept, which began chewing my underside with his guns. At that time my craft became difficult to control; it started to roll toward the right. I tried to correct but the controls began fighting me."

"How the craft performed should not be discussed in an unsecured area," the unknown person interrupted, now seated at the table to Jim's right with the others.

The judge said, "In order to ascertain any wrongdoing these

events need to be addressed. I have not heard anything that may allude to classified information. Would you care to elaborate?"

The person who interrupted Jim looked at his colleagues and said, "Due to the sensitive nature of the craft itself and national security we are not at liberty to discuss it at any length in this –" the man looked around the room, "...setting. No your honor."

"Major, you may continue."

"Then the craft began to yaw the same direction and again fought me to bring the nose back on course. Coyote Five shot down the second enemy with another missile. That was when I regained control of the craft and was able to finish the bombing run," Jim explained and noticed the engineer appeared uncomfortable with what he said. The third man looked angry, which bewildered Jim.

The judge asked, "Then what happened?"

"I began climbing, but the craft felt sluggish, which I reported to the AWAC. Coyote Five moved closer to assess the damage and reported the aft section may fall off, and he saw interior damage through the holes."

"Your honor!" Came a protest from the table on Jim's right.

"Again, nothing classified has been said. Please continue."

"At this point, I knew the craft would not be able to –" Jim paused and looked to his right, "...reach the U.S. safely and requested coordinates for the closest friendly base."

The judge asked, "Knowing the craft is classified?"

"Yes, sir."

"Were these coordinates given?"

"No sir, the request was denied."

"Then what did you do?"

"I asked for a casualty report from my maintenance chief."

"What was the report Major?"

Jim poured a glass of water from the pitcher on his table, took a sip, and wiped his left eye with the side of his hand. "I had two critical from the initial missile strike." His voice fluctuated and he took a deep breath. He felt the quiver creep into his throat, the same as when this all unfolded.

In a sympathetic tone, the judge said, "Take your time Major."

"One lost a lot of blood and had his leg in a tourniquet. The other had a sucking chest wound. We did not have the medical supplies to deal with either." It was clear by the expression on his face that he was still pained by the memory, and he blamed himself for the injuries of his crew. He looked as if he would jump out of his skin if someone were to slam a door, and he also appeared a bit shaky as evident by the water in the glass he held. When he noticed, he set the glass down. "I then requested directions for Diego Garcia."

"Were those directions given?"

"Yes sir," Jim said as he wiped his left eye again.

"Then what?"

"When I was able to set the auto pilot, I checked on the crew. Amy, one of the crew, died in my arms. Chief Besch and I tried CPR but..." Jim's voice trailed off, shaking his head.

"And the status of your other crewman?"

"I don't know your honor. I saw one body bag as I departed the craft, but I received no information since then"

"Do you have anything else to add?"

"The other crewman, Eric. The one with the tourniquet. He looked pretty pale from loss of blood the last time I saw him. Do you have any information about how he is doing?"

"Sorry, I do not." He turned to address the men at the table to Jim's right. "Do you have anything you want me to consider?"

"No your honor," came the response from the unknown man.

"Court is in recess while we deliberate." The judge slammed the gavel, which caused Jim to jump.

Everyone left the room, leaving behind Jim and the three men from Groom Lake. Even the security detail exited the room, closing the doors behind them.

Jim's supervisor and the engineer stood and offered their hands toward Jim, which he accepted. The third person remained seated and indifferent.

Jim asked, "What is going on here?"

His supervisor replied, "There is always an inquiry after an incident involving loss of life and extensive damage caused to an aircraft."

"Yes I know, but why the courts martial?"

The engineer said, "When the incident first happened, a courts martial was on the mind of the higher-ups. When the data was downloaded from the ship and testimony from your crew started to arrive, Groom Lake backed off and let the military handle it. In the end, cooler heads prevailed."

The third man in the group spoke up and said, "Unfortunately, Groom Lake does not want you back, and you have been reassigned. Your belongings have been packed for you and are waiting at your next base."

Jim asked, "What? Where am I going?"

His supervisor glared at the man that spoke out of turn and turned his attention back to Jim, "It's not as bad as all that. We want you for a project starting up at Langley using the YBV-92."

"Langley? What do they need a ship like that for? Langley falls under the First Fighter Wing. It's not a bomber base.

The engineer said, "I don't know, but it looks like you won't be flying any more combat missions. They ordered a transport variant."

"A transport? That makes no sense," Jim laughed. "You're kidding, right?"

"I wish I were. They got that thing packed with special requests we won't have finished for a month. Once you sign off on what they want to be tested, they are ordering three more for the initial purchase."

"What would they possibly want a transport capable of space flight for?"

Jim's supervisor said, "You would think Groom Lake would know what our projects will be used for, but we are in the dark on this one."

"You said you got the data from the ship. Have you been able to analyze it? What happened up there? Why did the ship fight me?"

The engineer asked. "Do you know how the drive system works on these birds?"

Jim shook his head, "Not a clue. I just love flying it. Every time I fly that ship I learn something new about it. It's really an amazing craft."

The engineer said, "Let me try to explain. The drive system is called 'The Faraday-Maxwell drive', because it uses principles theorized by those physicists, James Maxwell and Michael Faraday. Maxwell's theory creates waves at near-light speed using vibrating Faraday force fields. Coupled with engineering we obtained from a classified source we were able to adapt."

"I understood none of that. Classified source, huh?"

His supervisor budded in, and said, "Rumor has it, it's not of this planet."

Jim laughed, "Doesn't the public think that of all our projects?"

"Yea but this time, I don't know."

The engineer said, "Gentlemen, please."

Jim asked, "Then you explain why I have not seen an intake or an exhaust. What makes it move?"

"The entire skin of the ship is the drive. It's completely electric. It identifies matter ahead of it in the direction the pilot wants to move, and does this down to the atomic level. The computer adjusts the skin's polarity, drawing the matter toward it. Then the drive manipulates the electromagnetism for each atom, alternating polarity, causing the matter to accelerate till it passes over the entire skin of the ship and is thrown in the opposite direction."

Jim was still confused but tried to simplify what the engineer explained and put it in terms he understood, "So it's like a rail gun?"

"Well, in simplistic terms, yes."

"How can it do this in space?"

"That implies space is empty and completely void of matter, which most people believe," the engineer said with a finger raised, "Space is not empty. Matter is farther apart, but it is out there. In fact, it's estimated 5 to 300 tons of interstellar dust enter the earth's atmosphere daily."

Jim raised his eyebrows in bewilderment and asked, "Daily?"

His supervisor said, "I'm curious about this myself. You said up to 300 tons?"

The engineer said, "Yes really, and that does not include the meteors that enter the atmosphere. The earth is expanding – well actually all planets are. How do you think ancient civilizations got buried under meters and meters of sand, rock, you name it, and were totally forgotten?"

Jim answered, "Volcanoes."

"That does some but does not account for all of it. Anyway, as long as we are able to manipulate what's there, we can move the ship, and in any direction."

Jim asked, "What do you mean any direction?"

"We analyzed the data and believe it or not, your ship's drive helped shoot down that first fighter."

Jim's jaw fell open and all he could muster was, "What?"

"The ship's drive manipulates matter, right?" The engineer

asked. When Jim acknowledged his question he continued, "The computer controlling the drive identified the bullets the attacker fired as a danger and caused them to be thrown back at the attacker."

Jim countered, "No, Coyote Five got it with a missile."

"I'll admit the impact was at the same time, but the drive did do this to the bullets. The data is there."

"Okay," Jim said not believing what he heard, but he had no proof of what actually shot it down. "Why did I lose control when the second one attacked?"

"Actually, you didn't. You continued flying the direction and elevation you were and the bombs continued to drop. However, the attacker was in a position that the drive was unable to manipulate the bullets coming at it, due to the damage it sustained from the missile. The computer first tried a roll to protect the belly, and more drive coils that were still on-line could redirect the bullets. When that failed because of your interaction, the computer tried again by rotating the ship on its Y-axis, which put the ship into flying sideways."

"It can do that? Why was I not briefed on any of this before I took off?"

"We didn't know. The computer is constantly learning. We have no idea of its full capabilities. It's not our design, and to be truthful with you, I have no idea where it came from."

Jim and his supervisor smiled at each other, and Jim asked, "Well why did the control panel vibrate?"

"Interesting," the engineer said out loud while he took notes. "Have you ever driven a self-driving car?"

"Who hasn't?" Jim asked, since self-driving cars had been around for years.

"Have you ever tried to correct it?"

"Of course not."

"Well if you had, the steering wheel would have done the same thing, vibrate to warn you of something. The data says it activated a display on the console. What did it say, or show?"

Jim thought for a few seconds and said, "It showed a 3D image of the exterior hull. The area behind the cargo ramp was red," Jim paused for a moment thinking, "Are you telling me –"

"Yes," the engineer interrupted.

"The dead and injured on the ship were my fault?"

The engineer backpedaled, "That is not what I meant. You couldn't have known that is what the ship was doing under the circumstances."

"So what else can that thing do?"

"To be honest with you, we really don't know. We suspect – I mean, I suspect – It's capable of even traveling underwater."

"You have got to be kidding."

"It only makes sense given the way the drive works."

The door to the judge's chamber opened. The panel of officers filed into the courtroom and took their seats, and security reentered the room.

After a few minutes of the judge shuffling papers he said, "Major James Norgas, please stand. In light of the information presented and the developers of the aircraft you were flying not being forthcoming on the nature of the aircraft, we are unable to determine if there was any wrongdoing on your part. All injuries to persons, damage to the craft itself and loss incurred by the United States Air Force are of no fault to you, the pilot and officer in charge. Any charges that may result from the aforementioned incident are dismissed." The judge struck the gavel and relief washed over Jim like a flood.

Jim's supervisor and the engineer came over to his table and congratulated him.

His supervisor said, "You've got two weeks before reporting to Langley. Take this time to do what you need to do, to put this behind you. That death was not on your hands. You understand me? Don't keep dwelling on this. It will eat you up and prevent you from moving on if you do. This is over and there is nothing you could have done to make the outcome any different."

"Yes, sir. Thank you." He accepted his supervisor's hand but ended in a hug with each slapping the other on the back.

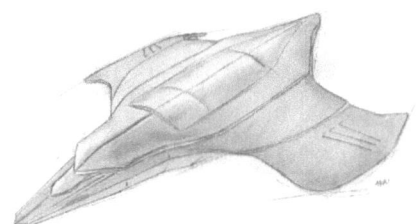

Chapter 4: NEEDED BREAK

Jim had not seen his parents, Elsa and Harold, in over a year due to his busy schedule and his being stationed in Nevada. The military was eager to get the YBV-92 into production, the testing of which was Jim's primary focus.

He arrived at his parent's house in a car he rented at the Charleston West Virginia International Airport.

Upon recognizing him in their driveway, Elsa ran out of the house and gave him a warm embrace. Harold came from the garage, and after greeting Jim, began inspecting the car he drove.

Harold said, "Damn foreigners are ruining this country," referring to the make of the car.

"Dad it's just a rental."

"That's the problem. A fella fighting for this country should rent American."

Elsa said, "Oh Harold, just let him be. Come inside, I need to call everyone and let them know you're home."

"Please Mom, don't make a fuss. I just want to relax a bit before I have to go back."

"Nonsense, it's not every day my boy comes home. Lord knows I need a good excuse to have everyone over. Ever since that Madeline, I've been dying to outdo her."

"Is that feud still going on?"

"Not after today." Elsa wandered off, planning the party.

Jim yelled after his Mom, but his father stopped him, "Don't even bother; when she gets this determined all you can do is accept it. Then wait for the bills to come in."

Over the next couple of days, all of his cousins, distant cousins, and cousins he didn't know were cousins stopped by.

All of them wanted to know what he was up to and were not satisfied with, "I'm testing an aircraft for the Air Force."

They would always respond with, "Oh, you can tell me."

National security aside, Jim did not want to discuss his last flight. The memory of Amy kept creeping into his brain.

He decided he had to get out of there and try to spend some time alone thinking about nothing. Escape, reboot, recharge.

He grabbed his old camping gear and told his folks, "I'm sorry but something happened, and I need to get my head clear. I think I'm going to go for a couple of days on the Appalachian Trail. I'm surprised the fall colors are still looking great this late in the year. I'll try to stop by and see you again before I report in at Langley."

"Oh my boy, what did they do to you?" Elsa said as she fussed with his hair.

Harold said, "Elsa, let him be. I had a feeling something was wrong."

Jim looked at Harold and saw something he never noticed before and knew his Dad understood. "Thanks Dad."

Elsa looked at Harold questioningly, and he said, "A lot of my buddies and I joined the Army right after high school. When some of them came back, they weren't the same. I suspect the same kind of thing happened to him." Harold thought when Jim joined the Air Force, he would not experience the same kind of thing as front-line troops, so he did not bring up his concerns at the time.

Jim got the food and water he would need for the hike at a

roadside grocery store. Around noon he parked the car where he did several times before when he was a senior in high school, and he headed out on the trail.

He kept a leisurely pace; he was in no hurry and he had nowhere to go. After several hours, he knew he needed to start preparing for the night and he began gathering a few things off the forest floor and putting them in his pockets. Some dry pine needles here, dry skinny sticks there. He kept looking in the trees as he walked till he found the prize he was looking for: 'Goat's beard'. He knew that with this, building a fire would be easy.

The light in the woods began to diminish as he got to the next camping area.

There were already two tents set up, but there was enough room for another without crowding them. Jim did a quick check of the tree tops around him to ensure there were none dead that could fall on his tent.

After getting his tent set up and situated, he began preparing to build his fire. He found a suitable flat piece of wood for his base, then emptied his pockets. He arranged everything from the skinniest to the thickest.

He fluffed up the Goat's Beard a bit and put it in a pile in the center of the flat board. He then began to build a teepee with the pine needles, then the thinnest twigs he had. He continued making the teepee larger with thicker and thicker sticks, but made sure plenty of air could still get to the Goat's Beard.

With one match, some gentle blowing, and feeding of larger sticks, he had a good fire going.

A man from one of the other tents asked Jim, "How did you do that? I used half a bottle of lighter fluid and it still wouldn't light."

That night everyone at the camp site gathered around Jim's fire, shared what food they had, and swapped stories.

The next night was much the same with few exceptions. This camp site, Jim was alone and he could not find any Goat's Beard that day. Instead, he dug in all his pockets and pulled out what lint he was able to find. It took more care to get the fire to flame up and ignite the pine needles and the smallest twigs, but soon Jim had a nice fire going.

He stared into the fire. His mind drifted from one thought to the next. He knew what happened on his last mission would follow him to his next assignment and wondered how that would affect his duties. Would he have to prove himself all over again, or was it done with?

On the third day of hiking, Jim heard a ruckus around the next bend and he picked up his pace. He saw two coyotes stalking a baby deer tangled in some barbed wire.

Jim screamed, picked up rocks and threw them at the coyotes as he ran. The coyotes were startled, but quickly recovered and pounced toward him. The coyotes ran away when Jim continued toward them.

It looked like the baby deer had tried to jump between the horizontal strands of a barbed wire gate. The gate fell open, trapping it. There was blood in spots where barbs pierced its skin. The deer tried to remain motionless. Every move it made aggravated the wounds. Thanks to the coyotes, blood covered the ground.

Jim looked around and did not see the deer's mother. He dropped his backpack and took off his shirt, which he used to cover the deer's eyes. He learned this from some high school friends who raised sheep – covering their eyes would help calm them. He hoped this worked on deer so he could work on freeing it.

He sat under a tree with the deer laying across his ap. He cleaned its wounds with whatever he could find in the remains of his medical kit.

Jim could feel the deer's heart slow the more he soothec it. The baby let out a call, and Jim uncovered its eyes. To his amazement, it remained laying on his lap.

For a while, in Jim's mind, it was not the deer laying across his lap, it was Amy. He did not know how much time passed as he sat there with his eyes closed. Tears ran down his cheeks as he petted the deer.

Eventually, he heard a rustle in the grass next to him. He opened his eyes and saw the deer's mother checking on her baby. Jim slowly moved his arms off the baby's back and the baby remained there for a few moments. The baby slowly stood, looked at Jim, then joined its mother.

The mother was so close, Jim could feel its hot breath. He did not know what the deer would do to protect her baby. Several moments passed and he began to worry, but he knew not to make sudden movements. To his surprise the deer nuzzled him, then mother and baby walked away, seemingly taking his grief of Amy with them.

He felt a weight lift from his shoulders, leaving behind calm. He knew what happened to Amy was a tragedy, but now, her memory would be accompanied by that of the deer he saved.

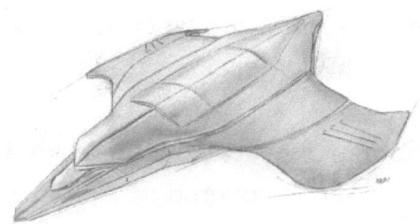

Chapter 5: LANGLEY

Jim arrived at Langley AFB's west gate on a Friday in time for lunch. He asked the gate guard for directions for his gaining unit's orderly room and the VOQ. After giving him the directions, the gate guard snapped to attention and saluted. Jim returned the salute and drove through the gate.

The salute made Jim feel good to be back at a regular base, till he saw the scruff on his face in the rear-view mirror. "Hmm, I sure don't want to meet my new commander looking like that," he said to himself.

Walking toward the entrance of the VOQ, he heard a lone fighter streak across the sky. It was low, barely clearing the treetops. The fighter pulled up quickly, rolled to its right, and feinted a stall only to race off like a madman in the opposite direction.

While checking in at the VOQ, he asked the receptionist about the lone fighter.

"They have been doing that as long as I worked here. Every Friday around lunchtime a fighter from the 1st Fighter Wing will put on a show. I think it's a tradition or something."

Refreshed, clean-shaven and now in his class B uniform, he walked to the BX (Base Exchange) for something to eat. The screech of the lone fighter punching holes in the sky was still going on ahead and to the right of him as he walked.

Less than an hour later he sat outside General Long's office. After several boring minutes, the phone on the aid's desk buzzed. The aid said "General Long will see you now."

He entered the general's office, stood at attention, and saluted. "Major Norgas reports."

General Long was leaning back in his plush leather chair. He continued reading the last few pages of the file he held and casually returned Jim's salute. This allowed Jim to lower his arm but remain standing at attention. "Looks like you had a colorful career," General Long said. "Care to explain why you attempted to disobey orders on your last mission, twice?"

"General, I had crew members severely wounded who needed medical attention."

General Long took his reading glasses off and began to nibble on one of the tips as he studied Jim. After a few moments, he asked in a condescending tone, "How many times did you rehearse that answer?"

Jim was taken aback by the attitude, "Sir?"

"'My crew, my crew!' while risking national secrets? Does that help you sleep at night?"

"No sir," Jim got defensive, "I wake up in the middle of the night, seeing their faces and wondering if I could have done anything different."

General Long glared at Jim with clenched teeth, "All I want to know is, while under my command, will you pull a stunt like that again? Before you answer you need to think this through."

Without hesitation Jim said, "Yes sir."

General Long bellowed, "I don't think I heard you right."

Jim said clearly so there was no mistake, "Yes sir. My crew comes first." He thought *'This assignment is going to suck,'* and started to dislike the man seated at the desk.

"That is exactly what I wanted to hear," General Long stood and offered Jim his hand. "Our people come first. The rest we can deal with later."

The top of Jim's head suddenly felt cooler as he realized that was all a test. He accepted General Long's hand.

General Long said, "I don't want someone who will blindly follow orders. I want people who will think and stand behind the choices they make. There is no time to show you around today and I still have a lot to do before I leave. How about I see you in my briefing room next door, Monday at 0900? A briefing that will interest you will be going on. No need to come any earlier. Just walk in and take a seat till I introduce you."

"Yes sir," Jim said and gave General Long a salute.

General Long returned the salute and as he turned his attention back toward his desk said, "Welcome to the project, Major."

Jim thought for a moment to ask about the project. Seeing the mountain of papers piled on the general's desk he decided he had better not. He performed an about-face and left General Long's office.

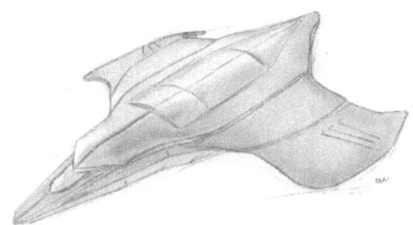

Chapter 6: A FEW DRINKS

Leafing through pamphlets in the lobby of the VOQ, Jim decided to check out a bar not too far from the base called "99 taps on the wall" that advertised micro-brews from all over. He knew the name was a cliché, but the photo made it look like all the taps worked.

He ordered transportation rather than driving himself. He did not know how eager security on this base was.

He sat at the quiet end of the bar and noticed a few bottles of his favorite beer in the cooler behind the bar. Fond memories of his time stationed in Germany flooded over him. He had not seen this beer in years. He ordered a Maisel's Hefeweizen with coke. The bartender poured the beer into a glass and brought him a glass of coke with ice along with the beer. "Next one, can you let me pour, and can I get the coke without ice? It's for the beer"

The bartender looked confused and asked, "What's wrong? Isn't that what you ordered?"

Jim explained, "The wheat settles in the bottle along with much of the flavor. The last bit of beer needs to be stirred before finishing the pour. The coke is to be added to the beer, blending the flavors just right."

The bartender apologized and offered to bring Jim another beer, but Jim joked, "No, that would be a waste of good beer."

An embarrassing memory came to mind. While stationed in Germany Jim observed a bartender pour a bottle of Weizen by placing a glass upside down over the bottle. The bartender flipped both over and gradually pulled the bottle out as the glass filled. The result was a perfectly poured glass of beer with a beautiful head of foam on top.

Jim asked if he could try and did it exactly the same way, but his attempt resulted in a slightly different outcome. He got nothing but foam in the glass, which spewed all over the bar.

He cleaned up the mess and the bartender showed him where he went wrong. The glass had to be wet or the friction of the beer flowing over the glass would do exactly what it did. The bartender let him try again, and this time, most of the beer fit in the glass.

Letting his thoughts drift back to the present, he sipped the beer but it just did not taste the same as his memories. On his next beer, the bartender was true to his word and allowed Jim to pour the beer himself. This time, the beer had the flavor he remembered. The bartender was intrigued, poured one for himself, and fell in love with a new favorite.

Jim sat at the bar nursing his beer. A few tables away he noticed a group of women. He figured they were colleagues by the way they interacted with each other. They enjoyed themselves but were not as loud as old friends would normally be.

But then, a few moments later a particularly loud high-pitched squeal drew his attention. The women at the table jumped up to greet a woman that just walked into the bar.

He was in awe of her. She was the most beautiful woman he has ever seen on any continent. He first noticed her slender build, then the curly dishwater blonde hair that cascaded past her shoulders. A flash of her big brown eyes as she surveyed the room made him swoon.

Everything disappeared but her. He enjoyed watching the dainty way she maneuvered the room. He felt a tingle over his entire body and had to remember to breathe.

Pilots have a type A personality, confident, a take charge kind of person. Nothing fazes them, and they're always in control of the situation. Until now.

He caught a glimpse of a slight dimple on her cheeks when she smiled. All he could think of was how he wanted to be the reason for those smiles.

One of the women at the table asked what she wanted to drink and headed toward the bar where he sat. She ordered refills for everyone and a 'Sex on the Beach' for the new arrival.

Jim asked the woman, "Who is that?"

"Who? Sarah? Oh, she's some brainiac that works on base. We have been trying to get her to join us but all she wants to do is work."

He kept glancing at Sarah, now seated toward the middle of the table. She engaged in conversation with the ladies around the table, but he was unable to hear any of it over the noise of the bar.

The woman standing next to him asked, "You new here?"

"I just got here today."

"Well I hope you enjoy your stay. I'm Joyce."

"Thanks, Joyce, I'm Jim."

The way Sarah carried herself reminded him of Western European women – refined, a bit reserved, and beautiful, but not acting like it. As if she didn't know how beautiful she was.

When the drinks came he said to the bartender, "I got this round."

Joyce cocked her head and asked, "You like her?"

He glanced at Sarah and raised his right eyebrow. He did not realize he was nodding his head.

Jim did not have time to form a response before Joyce said, "I'll put in a word for you, Hot Stuff. Thanks for the drinks."

The expression on his face must have told her all she needed to know. Joyce walked away with the drinks and said over her shoulder, "Good luck."

"No wait –," but it was too late. Joyce began to talk with Sarah and pointed in Jim's direction.

Sarah looked his way, and he felt a sudden flash of perspiration reach his scalp. She curled her lower lip into her mouth and scraped it along her upper teeth, tilted her head forward, and started walking in his direction.

"My coworker said you paid for this round. I'm Sarah," she said with a smile that flashed her dimples.

"It's a pleasure to meet you, Sarah, I'm Stinker." Not thinking straight, he used his call sign and mentally kicked himself after saying it.

"Stinker huh?" she flashing her dimples with a giggle. Her face gained a mischievous look. "Do you clean up well?... Stinker?" Sarah licked half her upper lip and gave him elevator eyes. She turned to rejoin the women at the table, who were all watching. Squeals quickly erupted from the table. Jim knew he was the cause but didn't care.

Sarah stopped halfway to the table, "Hey Stinker," with a giggle and turned his direction, "Come join us."

"Girl?" said one of the women at the table.

As he approached the table, Joyce said, "Hey, Hot Stuff."

Jim mouthed "Thank you," in her direction, and she responded with a *'who, me?'* innocent act.

Sarah noticed the tall glass Jim set in front of him as he sat next to her and asked, "What are you drinking, Stinker?"

"I'm sorry, my name is Jim. Stinker is like a nickname. This is a beer I discovered while I was stationed in Germany. Its called a Hefe

Weizen Gespritztes."

"I don't particularly care for beer, Stinker," she teased with a giggle.

"Cute, your dislike for beer might be because you've only had American Lager. You can find beer with all different kinds of flavors. There's even one that tastes like banana bread. You're drinking Sex on the Beach, right? So do you like fruity drinks?"

"I rarely drink, but I guess I do."

"I can't remember the name but there's one that tastes like raspberries." He wished he could change the subject. He did not want to come across as if he drinks all the time and thought he was making a bad impression by talking about beer.

Sarah said, "Raspberries, really?" She studied his beer; it did not look like the beer she usually saw. The deep brown matched her eyes. She saw little specs floating around but could not see through the liquid and noticed a layer of foam on top that did not seem to want to dissipate. "What does that taste like?"

"Do you want to try it?" and he handed her the glass.

She took a sip and her eyes lit up, "That's good," then took another drink. She tipped the glass up and took a healthy drink, several swallows worth, and that put a smile on Jim's face.

When she set the glass down he said, "You have a mustache."

Sarah defensively said, "Excuse me?"

It took a moment for Jim to realize what he said. "No, no, I'm so sorry. I meant the foam from the beer is on your lip."

The shock on his face told Sarah he was embarrassed and his words were sincere, but she wanted to play with him a bit. She cocked her head to the side and just looked at him. A few moments passed, and she said in a scolding tone, "Stinker!" She tried to be ladylike, but her body betrayed her as she let out a belch. Now the embarrassment was on Sarah as she covered her mouth, and they both laughed.

Joyce yelled, "Hot Stuff." The conversations around the table wrapped up and Jim discovered all eyes were on him. "So what do you do?"

Being asked by all his cousins a few days ago what he had been doing, Jim had learned how to respond without offending anyone or revealing anything he shouldn't say. "That's a boring story, and I'm sure we could talk about something more fun."

Joyce asked, "You said you just got here. Where from?" Her speech showed she had a bit too much to drink.

"I just got here from Nevada."

Joyce said, "Ooh, Las Vegas. You must have some good stories."

Sarah touched his arm to get his attention, "You said you were stationed in Germany. Military?"

"That was before Nevada, but yes, Air Force."

She asked, "And now you're stationed here? Doing what?"

"I honestly don't know. I met my commander earlier today and he said he will brief me on Monday. How about you? Joyce said you're a brainiac? You working on some cutting-edge technology?"

Sarah said, "I hate this because it always ruins the conversation, but there are some things I can't talk about."

The two sat nursing their drinks trying to think of something to say. Sarah jumped up and said, "Stinker, dance with me."

She delighted in calling him by his call sign throughout the night. It made her giggle every time she said it. Jim enjoyed seeing the flash of her dimples and was glad she was enjoying herself.

Before tonight, Sarah's coworkers only saw her buried in her work. They invited her every Friday for a 'ladies night out', but she preferred to work instead. They enjoyed seeing this side of her and hoped they would see this more often. They could tell she liked Jim by the way she played with her hair when he spoke with her.

When last call was announced by the bartender, Jim asked Sarah, "Can I see you again?"

Sarah said, "I had a really fun time but I'm way too busy at work."

Her coworkers were disappointed and tried to encourage her, "You've got to have fun sometimes or what is it all for?" "Work can wait, you come first." Other comments were made but in the end, she wouldn't budge.

She said, "I'm sorry Jim, I had a great time but I really don't have the time and it wouldn't be fair to you."

"It's been a pleasure Sarah." He gave her a hug and walked away. Jim was devastated; he had met the girl of his dreams and lost her all in the same night.

Joyce said to Sarah, "Girl, there is something wrong with you."

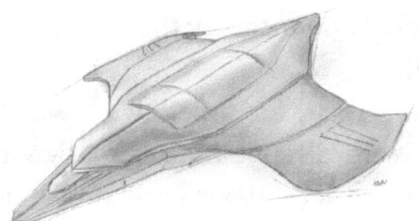

Chapter 7: SARAH

One day a guest speaker to Sarah's school, Dr. Kovonich, gave a lecture on Physics.

He used these lectures to encourage high school students with an interest in science to consider physics and to see if there was a budding physicist in one of the area schools. He found most of the recommendations he received from teachers who thought they had a gifted student were a waste of time and preferred to find them on his own.

He started his lecture with simple equations and formulas, then progressively got more challenging in his presentation until the audience appeared to be confused.

Usually at this point in his lecture, he would lower the difficulty of his talk for everyone to understand again so next year he would be invited back. But this time, one student, Sarah, did not look confused. To test this, he introduced an error in the formula he was writing on the overhead projector, and continued as if nothing was wrong.

She caught the error right away. She pulled out a notebook and started writing in it with quick glances at the stage.

This was the first time a student caught his eye. He wondered if she had the aptitude, or if she would be a waste of his time.

Even after he moved on, she continued writing in her notebook. She would glance at the ceiling for a moment, then write some more.

After the lecture, he approached the teacher who invited him and asked about her. "She did something during my lecture that I'd like to talk to her about."

"What did she do? If she was disruptive, I'll take care of it."

Dr. Kovonich shook his head, "No, it's nothing like that. Do you remember how I got more difficult in the equations I presented?"

He looked confident, "Yes. You do that every year."

"Did you notice if there was an error in the equation?"

The teacher shook his head and shrugged his shoulders.

"She did. Or I think she did."

The teacher was in disbelief, "I doubt that. If I didn't catch it —"

"I got a feeling, she might surprise you.

"Doctor, with that one I think you will be disappointed. Her grades are mediocre and she is antisocial." At a young age, her teachers labeled her as someone with a learning disability, when in fact she was gifted and school was boring for her. Without a challenge, her grades suffered.

"Maybe she just hasn't been properly motivated."

The teacher defensively said, "Doctor, I —"

"I did not mean to offend. I'm just saying, state sponsored academics puts everyone in a mold and sometimes, the mold does not fit. Those few may blossom in a different environment. May I meet her?"

"You're right, I wish we could actually teach and not just follow a script. Wait here, I'll be right back."

Despite his skepticism, the teacher asked at the school office where her next class was, pulled her out of class, and made the introductions in the hallway. "Doctor Kovonich, this is Sarah Burnett."

"Hello, Sarah. Before today did you know of me or what I do?"

She shrugged and said, "No."

"Then why did you attend my lecture? Are you interested in physics?"

"I don't know, I just figured it would be a good way to skip an hour of school. Am I in trouble or something?"

The teacher said, "See what I mean? She has no interest in being here in school. Skipping classes."

Dr. Kovonich shushed the teacher, which brought a smile to Sarah's face. "Partway through my lecture, you started writing something. May I see it?"

She handed Dr. Kovonich her notebook. He flipped through it till he came to the last written page. He saw the formula he presented, several assumptions in scribbles around the page, and the correct formula toward the bottom of the page. He had not revealed the correct formula during his lecture, so he was impressed. He asked the teacher, "Is there somewhere Sarah and I can talk?"

The teacher, surprised Dr. Kovonich was still interested after seeing her notebook, suggested the cafeteria.

Dr. Kovonich asked her, "Is that okay with you?"

She said, "Sure."

The three sat in the cafeteria. Dr. Kovonich asked, "How did you know this was not correct?" He pointed to his formula in her notebook.

"I don't know, the pattern on the board. I saw the numbers and – it just didn't look right."

"I've been doing this lecture for years. You are the first person to notice the mistake. Not even a teacher has caught it."

The teacher looked at Sarah's notebook and still didn't see the error.

Sarah asked, "Really? Then why do you do it?"

"I do the lectures to encourage students toward a career in physics and hopefully find someone like you. Normally I don't get far enough to introduce the error. I already lose everyone in the audience before I get to it. But you, how did you know there was an error? You said the pattern, what pattern?"

"When I see calculations on a big screen, like you had, the numbers leap off the screen and make like – I can't explain it. But when there is a mistake, like yours, they don't – well there is just a hole and I know something is missing. And I don't mean where you changed '68' to '86'."

The teacher took a closer look at the formula and still did not see a mistake. He found the '68' and it still looked correct. To him, '86' would make the formula wrong.

Dr. Kovonich was impressed she caught that. Then asked, "There was something missing? It wasn't just wrong? What's missing?"

"Right here." She showed him in the margin of her notebook what was missing and where it should be in his formula.

Before the school year, the teacher read the records of the students he would teach that year. He based his opinion on what the student's former teachers said about the student. On the first day of class, the teacher was already biased against certain students. Sarah was one of them. The teacher wondered how many other students could have done better if he had not let his bias get in the way.

Dr. Kovonich asked, "May I?" He spent over an hour go ng over the formula. She made comments here and there. All these years he thought the formula was wrong by a switch of just a few numbers. A formula he wrote. Now to find out from a fifteen-year-old girl an entire section was missing. The formula was correct with switching the '68' back, but her addition changed what the formula imp ied. This put him on the edge of a breakthrough. He knew she was destined for more than a public school could offer.

He wanted to sponsor Sarah for a program he ran at a university. It was difficult to convince her parents that she would be taken care of and be in a safe environment. Eventually Dr. Kovonich became Sarah's mentor. Several times he felt like she was mentoring him.

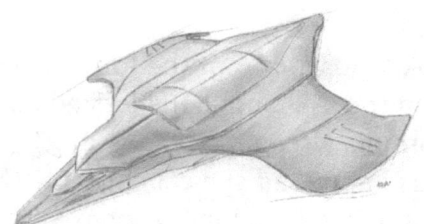

Chapter 8: PROJECT ANARBIA

Monday morning Jim approached General Long's briefing room. Recessed into the wall was a red illuminated sign that read, "Classified briefing in progress."

He approached the security guard and said, "General Long asked for me to just walk in at 0900."

"May I see your ID card, Sir?"

Jim fished his military ID out of his wallet. The security guard used a radio to verify Jim's access to the room while he waited.

After a few moments the security guard said, "Major, you can go in," and gave his ID back.

Jim opened the door to the briefing room and saw a faint glow come from the room at the end of a short corridor. As he got closer to the room he heard a female voice describe a power plant, but she used terms unfamiliar to him.

The room was occupied by three people who hovered over a brightly lit table in the center of the room, which was covered with schematics, charts, and stacks of paper. The rest of the room remained dark, where he found a chair and sat down.

Facing him, he recognized General Long on the other side of the table. Across from the general was an older man with disheveled white hair wearing a lab coat. Next to that man was the woman Jim heard when he entered, also wearing a lab coat.

He could only see the back of her. The hair color looked the same as Sarah's but from his position, that's all he could see. He had a bit more to drink Friday night than he had planned and had a hard time remembering her voice. He remembered she worked on base, probably in some think tank, but he had no idea where.

He was lost in thought with a slight smile on his face when he realized General Long called for him.

General Long said, "Let me introduce you to our primary pilot for the project. He has been flying the combat version in Operation CAMPFIRE, testing your power plant and drive system in real-world missions."

"General, I must protest our work being used to kill," the man in the lab coat bellowed.

"I know," General Long said pushing his right hand down in a gesture for him to calm down. "Under the circumstances we had to expedite testing. There are no quicker ways to find flaws in a system than to put them in the fight. Major James Norgas, call sign Stinker," he said as Jim entered the ring of light surrounding the table. "His last mission had a few setbacks, and as a result, we gained a pilot already familiar with its flight characteristics."

Jim approached the table, finally able to see the woman's face. He felt his pulse quicken when he recognized her. He couldn't believe his luck and inadvertently blurted out, "Sarah."

She appeared to be in shock seeing him and was unable to continue with what she was briefing the general on. In her stead, the man beside her continued for her.

She looked up at Jim and gave him a quick elevator look, taking all of him in. She admired his uniform and the chest full of medals. She didn't know what they all meant, but they looked impressive. She ended her gaze on his eyes and asked, "Stinker?"

He enjoyed her reaction. The gaze she gave him caused him to subconsciously puff his chest out. He did not want to prolong her embarrassment so merely smiled, and nodded his head toward her.

Several minutes passed as the man described their progress with tests in the lab and expressed their desire to ramp up the project to full-scale testing.

General Long knew Major Norgas had no clue what was going on, and the look on the major's face confirmed he was lost in the technobabble. "Sarah Burnett and Doctor Kovonich, let's catch Major Norgas up. We haven't let anyone know what's really going on that didn't need to know, Major Norgas included. It's time to bring him into the fold."

Dr. Kovonich looked at Jim as a parent looks at a child and began a fantastical story. "In short, we have been in communication with an alien species for years and learned from them all life on earth will soon cease to exist."

Jim asked, "Wait, what?"

"And what made the ship you were flying possible is technology we learned from them."

"Slow down a minute. What?"

"That reaction never gets old," Dr. Kovonich said with a smile to Sarah.

She smiled but it quickly faded as she thought about the way she acted Friday. She sympathized for Jim and felt terrible about herself.

"Doctor," General Long scolded, "Please behave."

"Fine. You know what SETI is right?" Dr. Kovonich asked and turned his attention toward Jim.

"Of course, the Search for Extra Terrestrial life forms."

Dr. Kovonich corrected, "Search for Extra Terrestrial Intelligence. Well, they found it. The information we obtained enabled the creation of the ship you were flying and caused the war we are fighting."

"We're fighting against terrorism."

General Long said, "That's what they told you to keep it a secret."

"Wait, what do you mean *'caused'* the war?"

Sarah said, "We came up with a plan to save humanity –"

Dr. Kovonich added, "But for that to work the entire planet had to work together –"

Sarah said, "To get the materials needed to build it."

Jim asked, "Can you back up a bit? So far I got aliens and a plan."

Dr. Kovonich said, "A couple of years ago SETI started an exchange of information with an alien species. One day SETI received a warning followed by a constant stream of data as if they were sending everything they knew. Then suddenly all communication stopped."

"What do you mean stopped?"

Sarah said, "SETI tried to regain communication till linguists deciphered a section of the data that contained a warning."

"A warning?"

Dr. Kovonich said, "We believe they were under attack by a force roaming the galaxy. The warning said we're next."

"Possibly next," Sarah said glancing at Dr. Kovonich.

General Long said, "A big summit involving most of the United Nations followed these events. Soon after, Operation CAMPFIRE began, which you were a part of. Everything concerning the true nature of what was going on was held under 'close hold' level of classified information."

Jim asked, "Why such a high level of secrecy?"

General Long said, "Most that were involved felt if the general public found out, 'life on Earth may soon end', chaos would follow and any hope of finding a solution may not be possible." He studied Jim's face and saw he was trying to sort out the info. To speed up the conclusion, he decided to help it along, "If all hope is lost, society breaks down. Very few will go to work anymore and crime will skyrocket, till those trying to work can think of nothing more than defending their home or family and how to feed them, resulting in even more crime." He paused and waited for that to sink in a bit before continuing. "How will the scientists working on a solution be able to concentrate in the middle of that?"

Jim began to nod his head, "Yes, I understand that, but linguists? And 'that part of the message'? I think I'm missing something here."

Sarah said, "The language, or data stream, SETI received was more pictograms than a language. Every image had to be deciphered. Only a small percentage of what was received has been interpreted. They are so beyond us in science and technology, we will spend years figuring it out."

Dr. Kovonich said, "Well, that's not hard to believe. If their civilization started at the same time as ours, the dark ages alone would let them pass us if they didn't have one of their own."

Sarah said, "That's true. Considering intelligence doubles at an ever-increasing rate. Any interruption in that..."

Dr. Kovonich interrupted, "Then Einstein, as brilliant as he was, indirectly caused scientists for decades to be shunned if they tried to disprove his theories."

Jim asked, "What do you mean?"

"Einstein's theory of relativity had so many scientists believe that the closer to the speed of light you got, the more energy you needed to go any faster, and infinite energy was needed to break the speed of light. Any scientist who said the contrary was shunned and never published another paper, which caused a mini dark age in itself."

"I can see that."

Dr. Kovonich looked at Jim surprised, "You understood that?"

"I know a little about physics, so the part about Einstein and the dark ages, yes, but this whole thing about aliens and messages and..."

General Long said, "Guys we're getting off track. Operation CAMPFIRE was sanctioned not only for the 'War on Terror' but mostly to open borders, allowing access to rare materials needed by the scientists to put their plan into action."

"That's the second time I heard there is a plan. What is it?"

Sarah said, "Thanks to discoveries we learned from the data stream, time travel is possible."

Dr. Kovonich corrected, "Theoretical."

She defended, "No, we made successful shots in the lab."

"Those were so small they were impractical."

"We need a bigger facility, and that's the reason for this meeting."

General Long stopped them, "More to the point of why you are here, Major. Project Anarbia was created to send humans into Earth's past. Their goal is to increase technology and weapon systems beyond what is currently imaginable. So when the day comes that Earth falls under attack, we will be able to defend ourselves."

Jim asked, "So you want to change the past? Doesn't that cause a paradox?"

Dr. Kovonich said, "I'm starting to like this guy. That's not what we're doing. We will create a city isolated from the inhabitants so we don't contaminate the timeline. We will advance our technology, not theirs."

"How will you do that?" Jim started to get confused again.

General Long said, "That's where the ship you were flying comes into play."

Jim asked, "Excuse me?"

Sarah said, "We plan to build a city beneath the ocean floor and are shooting for the mid-1400s. To go back in time, one of the things you have to know is where the Earth was at that time. Since the Earth is moving faster than two million miles per hour, to keep a margin of safety, we decided to send any live, or human shots into near-Earth orbit. Using your ship, we just fly down, and there you go."

"And you can do this?"

Sarah said, "Yes."

Dr. Kovonich said, "That's a little premature."

Sarah said, "With a ramped up version of the power plant and the coils we're here to request, I remain confident."

General Long said to Jim, "Sarah designed the power plant of the ship you flew."

Jim looked at her and couldn't believe someone near his own age could design such a revolutionary device. He had no reason to refute it and congratulated her, "That power plant changed everything. I heard they made different sizes depending on the application, and it's powering cities. What are you doing here?"

She blushed and said, "Thank you. I'm here because, who knows when, but those cities might not exist anymore. I've been working with Doctor Kovonich for a couple years now, and I think this is where I need to be."

"How come I have not heard any of this before? I have a Top Secret compartmentalized clearance."

General Long said, "You did not have the need to know, till now. You know as well as I do you need the proper clearance, permission, and need to know."

"I forgot that part. The engineers at Groom Lake were wondering why you were ordering transport versions of a bomber. I guess they don't need to know either."

General Long said, "Probably not." He then turned his attention to Sarah and Dr. Kovonich and asked, "Do either of you know where the base golf course was? I've procured that site for our Project. There are steam tunnels not far from there on the NASA side of the base, which we can tap into for some of our needs. We will break ground this week."

Dr. Kovonich said, "That's good but till we get a working model, full scale is just going to complicate the issue."

General Long said, "Doctor, I've gotten somewhat used to your... unusual behavior, but this entire meeting, you have been nothing but pessimistic. What's going on? Isn't this your brainchild?"

"Well yes, but... every time we do a test in the lab, a coil blows and we spend hours tracking down the problem and rebuilding all the fried circuits. We have yet to be able to do two tests in a row."

Sarah said, "Yes but it does work."

General Long asked, "Why does it keep breaking?"

Dr. Kovonich said, "It's what we're using as insulating material in the coils. It just keeps turning to a liquid, or gel. So far nothing holds up to the power needed."

General Long asked, "Is there an alternative material you haven't tried yet?"

Sarah said, "I heard about a promising new composite, but it will be difficult to get."

Dr. Kovonich said, "They won't have enough for what we need, and no one has gotten enough to actually test."

General Long said, "The majority of the United Nations is behind this project. If it's needed, we can get it."

Sarah said, "It's made by hand in Bhutan."

General Long said, "Bhutan? Do they even export anything?"

Dr. Kovonich said, "Now you know part of the problem. Apparently, Bhutan's entire society is wrapped around 'happiness for the people'. We might start getting shipments of the composite and..."

General Long said, "Nice, is there anything else I can get you?"

Sarah said, "Mech-Bots. We can use them for the construction of the new coils."

General Long said, "You got it. In fact the requisition sheet is waiting for my signature to build the facility. I'll just add a couple more items to the list. As far as this stuff from Bhutan, I'll do what I can." He adjourned the meeting.

Leaving the meeting Sarah said to Jim, "You clean up well." She walked away with Dr. Kovonich, looked over her shoulder at Jim and smiled.

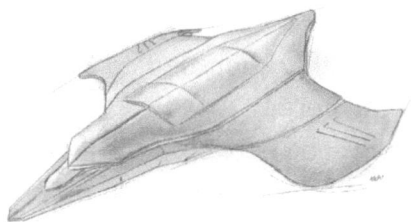

Chapter 9: QUESTIONS

After learning what was really going on, Jim found himself in conflict. He wanted to warn his parents, but he knew that would be a huge mistake. Not only would it be a violation of national security, Elsa would probably use this as an excuse to outdo Madeline, and before nightfall the entire county would know. There would be no way for him to hide where his mother got the information.

He understood why Sarah put her work first and told him she had no time. He wondered how long till Earth was attacked, and decided to talk with Dr. Kovonich.

It took some time to find Dr. Kovonich's lab. To be more specific, it took longer to find someone who knew where his lab was. Jim was amazed at the history of Langley. Neil Armstrong had his office in the very building where Dr. Kovonich's lab was located.

Jim stood in the hall and looked through the open door. He saw Dr. Kovonich and Sarah buzzing around a table covered with equipment he could not identify.

He thought she looked exquisite. She had her lab coat on and oversized eyeglasses that made her look so sexy. She leaned over to adjust the alignment of something on the table. A curl of hair slid over her shoulder, caressed her cheek and flowed on the slight breeze from the cooling fans in the equipment on the table.

"Stinker," he heard Dr. Kovonich bringing him back to reality. Sarah looked at him and lowered her glasses toward the tip of her nose as she stood.

"Doctor, when is all this supposed to happen? I mean, do we know when they will be here?

"Who? When who will be here?"

Sarah scolded, "Doctor, you know who. Sorry, he likes to play these games. At least I think they're games."

"Of course they are. Can't I have some fun? I'm not some senile codger."

"I don't know," she said jokingly.

Dr. Kovonich said, "Oh you two. Sarah, why don't you take him somewhere and answer his questions. I know you are dying to talk to him."

Sarah scolded, "Doctor!"

"Well he is the only thing you talked about all day."

She scolded even louder, "Doctor!"

Jim smiled and saw her blush. He was thoroughly infatuated with her. This revelation made him think '*I might still have a shot. Don't screw it up*'. He wanted badly to convince Sarah to go on a date with him, but first, he had to find out why everyone was so sure, what he heard in the briefing was true.

Sarah Burnett was an accomplished scientist and mathematician who worked as one of the leading scientists on Project Anarbia. She was the brains behind the development of the power source that gave the Faraday-Maxwell drive the massive amounts of power needed. She mostly kept busy with Project Anarbia. Both of which used the same power plant, but on a different scale. Project Anarbia required a power source so great, it could only be described as a micro star.

She took him to her office, where she showed him on her computer the message from SETI and the part that gave her the idea for the power plant she developed.

"How did you come up with that, from this? It's nothing but pictures, or Japanese, or something."

"It wasn't what it said, but what it looked like." She turned on a projector and the image was displayed on a wall. "You know those 3-D images where you have to... kind of... cross your eyes to see them?"

He said, "I've never been able to see those things."

"Just sit here, look at the wall and relax your eyes, let them go out of focus a bit and..."

Jim exclaimed, "I see it! What is it?"

"That is what gave me the idea. In essence, its self-sustaining cold fusion taken to the next level. Completely clean and never needs fuel."

"But that's impossible. How did you – where does it –Sarah, you are way smarter than me."

She blushed and said, "I don't fully understand it myself."

He asked tons of questions. Instead of just answering, she showed proof not just from the SETI message, but also from video clips from the United Nations meeting where scientists from all over the world gave testimony.

It was late in the evening when all of his questions were answered. Sarah was very patient and explained everything.

He asked, "I know it's late, but could I interest you in dinner?"

"Jim, you're really sweet, but I got to be back here early tomorrow."

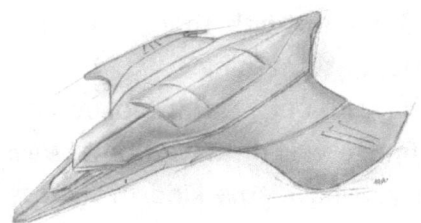

Chapter 10: PURSUIT

Jim remembered seeing a florist in the BX complex. On his way back to the VOQ every evening, he stopped at one of the restaurants for supper and purchased flowers that fit his plan for the next day.

Early in the morning with no one around, he set his plan for the day in motion and placed the flowers somewhere in her office. The first day, Monday, he put a single white rose in the stack of books on the corner of her desk, with the blossom sticking out.

On Tuesday, he put a corsage in the top pocket of her lab coat.

Wednesday, he wove the stems of a variety of flowers through the slats of the wooden chair-back at her desk.

Thursday, he attached a yellow rose to a pen on the center of her desk.

On Friday, he put a single pink lotus in her water glass.

He ran into her several times that week in the halls of the building they worked in. Him acted as if nothing was unusual. The look on her face told him she knew it was him, but she did not say anything about it.

He would say, "Good morning Sarah."

She would nod and say, "Stinker."

Friday night, he went to '99 taps on the wall'. When the bartender saw him, he brought the ingredients for him to pour his beer.

He sat there slowly nursing his beer and thought. '*The flowers should be telling Sarah I'm interested. She's got to know I'm interested. How do I convince her a relationship will not take time from her work'?* While contemplating the dilemma, Joyce sat next to him.

"What's up, Hot Stuff?"

"Oh, hi Joyce."

"Why so glum?"

"I just don't know how to convince Sarah she has time for a relationship. I know her job is important and all, but... I don't know, maybe she is just not interested."

"Oh she's interested. Trust me."

He said, "She doesn't act like it. Sometimes she looks like she's flirting, then shies away."

"What do you know about her past?"

He shrugged his shoulders and said, "Well, nothing."

"She was some king of child prodigy. Doctor Kovonich recruited her during her freshman year in high school. You're probably the first man to show any interest in her."

"Come on. With the way she looks? How could I be the first?"

Joyce said, "Most men are intimidated by a smart woman. From what I hear, when it comes to Sarah, smart is an understatement. Men just slither away shortly after meeting her." She looked at him with a raised eyebrow. When the look on his face showed he finally started to understand, she said, "She is probably trying to figure out how long it will be till you leave. Just keep doing what you're doing. She'll come around."

The following Monday, he placed a ring of flowers woven together surrounding Sarah's computer display.

For Tuesday, he purchased an entire drum of flowers and scattered them randomly in the blinds of her window.

Wednesday, he taped a pin to the top of her office door to pop a balloon when she opened her door, showering her in a cascade of pedals.

For Thursday, he used a mouse trap to snap a flower upright when she opened the center drawer of her desk.

Friday, the final day of his plan, he removed all the thorns from a single red rose. He weakened the spring of another mouse trap so it would not hurt her, and he rigged it to tape a note to the back of her hand, with the rose attached, as soon as she turned on the light switch just inside the door of her office.

Later that day General Long called for a meeting.

Jim overheard Dr. Kovonich tell Sarah, "It's strange – I went to your office this morning and a rose stuck to my hand with a note that said '99 taps on the wall, tonight 8pm'. I think I have a secret admirer."

Sarah said, "I think that was meant for me." She looked at Jim, smiled and nodded her head.

Dr. Kovonich said, "That makes more sense." He looked at Jim and said, "You? Good, it's about time."

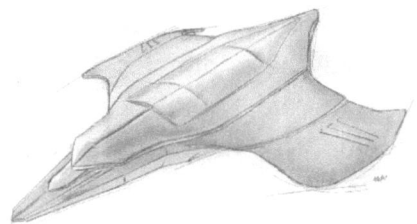

Chapter 11: TIME TO KILL

Until the ship could be delivered for Jim to start putting it through its paces, he did not have much to do and found himself in Sarah's lab on many occasions. He learned her mind was as bright as she was beautiful and it was apparent she enjoyed his company. Her work was not hindered by his presence since further testing was unnecessary till the new facility was finished and new insulating materials were procured.

Sarah found she had more and more free time available, and they began seeing each other outside of work.

A few weeks later he suggested, "How about we go away for the weekend? How long has it been since you had a down-home country dinner?"

"I don't think I ever did."

"It's settled then. After work tomorrow we take a road trip to my folk's place in West Virginia."

"Your folks? Oh no no no. I couldn't. It's too early for that."

He said, "Nonsense, they will eat you up and love you like I do."

"What did you say?"

"Oh come on, like you don't already know."

"Yea but you never said it. A lady likes to hear it once in a while, even if she knows it."

"Well then, I love the way your hair caresses your face and flows over your shoulders. I love your big brown eyes, I love the way your mind works, and I love these dimples," and began kissing her cheeks. Between kisses he said, "And I love you."

She giggled and said, "Not here, Stinker. So, your parents are going to love my dimples?"

"Of course, but if my Dad starts kissing you, you better stop him."

"I don't know. Is he as cute as you?"Sarah said jokingly.

The two got off work early and were on the road by noon. Jim called his mother and had his phone on speaker so Sarah could listen in, "Hi Mom, we're on the road and will be there around six."

"What do you know about that girl?"

"Well she is a Christian, I think. You're a Christian right?"

Sarah said, "Yes, I am."

Elsa said, "Is that her? She can hear me?"

"Yes Mom, you're on speaker."

"Well hi Sarah. It will be a pleasure having you here. Now don't you worry about a thing. Whatever you need just ask. I can't wait till you get here."

"Thank you Missus Norgas."

"Nonsense, you call me Mom. Now Jim, get me off this speaker thing."

Jim turned off the speaker call and said, "Yes Mom. But Mom. She's a nice girl. Mom! Okay, I love you too," then hung up the phone.

Sarah started to feel uncomfortable, but Jim said, "Don't worry, she is just protective. She is probably calling the neighbors saying her daughter-in-law is coming to visit."

Sarah screeched, "What?"

"Don't worry, she always exaggerates. Mom and one of the neighbors are always trying to outdo each other."

"You just remember this when you meet my folks. I doubt they will be calling you son any time soon, and don't even think of calling my mom, 'Mom.'"

Jim said, "Yes Ma'am."

The last hour of the trip, Jim drove slower because it began to snow. Fifty minutes later than expected, they pulled into his parent's driveway. Sarah looked relaxed but Jim knew she was nervous. He took her hand in his, gave it a kiss and said, "Don't worry." He started to get out of the car and added, "I just hope she hasn't invited all the cousins over, yet," and got out of the car.

She jumped out of the car and said, "Hey Stinker!" and caught him between his shoulder blades with a freshly packed snowball. She screamed when he bent over to make one of his own.

His parents came outside to see what the commotion was all about. They saw Jim and Sarah running around the car, throwing snow at each other. Jim faked an injury, and when Sarah came close to check, he grabbed her and fell into the snow. He cushioned her impact with his body and they both laughed.

Elsa yelled, "You two clean yourselves off. Supper is on the table getting cold."

Jim said, "Yes Mom."

Sarah covered her face in her hands and laughed. When his parents went back inside she said, "Do you think they love me yet?"

"I guess you will find out if they make you sit at the kid's table or not."

She found his parents were a delight. They were so warm and made her feel right at home. All her worries about meeting them were forgotten. Until it came close to bedtime.

Elsa came into the living room with a large white heavy sheet that reminded Sarah of a sleeping bag. She said, "Sarah, have you ever heard of a 'Bundling bag'?"

Jim said, "Mother, no!"

"Oh it's not for you. It's for her." Sarah looked confused. "It's an old tradition some of us out here in the country still use. You get ready for bed, get in this bag and Harold and I will stitch it closed so Jim can't, well, you know. We will let you out in the morning."

Sarah looked in shock and Jim said, "Mother!"

Harold said, "Our house, our rules."

When Sarah was about to comply, Elsa said, "We were just having some fun. Sarah, you can sleep in Jim's room. Jim, you get the couch. Good night."

As Elsa and Harold headed toward their room Harold said, "Did you see how big her eyes were? That was classic," and the two laughed.

Sarah turned to Jim and said, "Now I know where you get it from."

It snowed all night. The snow on the back deck looked two feet deep.

Over breakfast Jim asked Sarah, "Would you like to go skiing?"

"I don't know how."

Elsa said, "Why don't we make a day of it? Jim is an excellent teacher." She yelled at Harold still in the bedroom, "Harold, we're going skiing. Pack up the truck when you get done in there."

As Harold walked toward the kitchen he said, "Did we get that much?" When he got to the kitchen and looked outside he said, "Yup, come on Jim, you can help get the skis down. Good morning Sarah. What's your shoe size? Elsa, get her some extra socks, we got boots that will fit."

When the group got to the ski slope, Elsa and Harold got on the chair lift, and Jim took Sarah off to the side to give her a lesson.

Jim helped Sarah put her skis on and set her feet in a slight 'V', "Okay, just keep your feet like that so you don't go anywhere and balance yourself on the poles." He got in front of her, facing her and held her arms. "The way your feet are is called 'Snowplow'. It's the easiest way to steer and stop." He let go of her arms and backed up a couple of feet. He saw she was nervous and said, "You're okay. When you're ready, just straighten your skis a little and come to me."

He caught her when she got to him, and she started to laugh. "This time, before you get to me I want you to make the 'V' bigger, and stop before you hit me." He backed up about ten feet and she slowly began to move. When she got close to him she crossed her skis and fell over.

Jim was quick to catch her and help her to her feet, "Whatever you do, don't let the tips cross or that will happen every time. Let's try it again."

"This is hard."

"It will get easier. Before you know it you won't even be thinking about it."

"Yea right. Alright, let's do this."

She got the stopping and starting down. He then showed her how to steer by straightening the ski on the side she wanted to turn.

Before long Sarah did not need coaching and Jim asked, "Are you ready to move to a steeper hill?" He saw she was nervous, "Just use your snowplow to slow down and you don't have to go straight down the hill. Zigzag and you will go slower."

Sarah was nervous but said, "Okay."

The two rode the chairlift up the next leg of the mountain and spent the next hour on that slope as Sarah gained her confidence. When she started 'free-styling', turning without his instruction and relaxed, he asked, "Are you ready to go higher?"

Sarah looked up the mountain and asked, "Where are your parents?"

"They are on the top run. We're supposed to meet them for lunch at the bottom of it. The top of the next run."

"Where we're going next? Let's go."

This part of the hill was steeper, and when Sarah saw it from the top she got scared. She saw a building with tables outside and several people milling around to her right. "Is that where we're meeting your parents? Why don't I wait over there?"

"Sarah, you're doing great. It's no different than you've been doing. It's just a little faster."

"Okay, if you really think I can do it." A few minutes later, with a little encouragement, Sarah pushed off. She was not prepared for the vertical drop right at the top. It was only a few inches tall, but tall enough to make her go faster than she expected.

She was not looking where she was going. Instead she concentrated on the tips of her skis. She was afraid of what would happen at this speed if they crossed.

When Sarah did look up, she saw she was headed for a pile of snow made into a jump. She had no time and lacked the experience for her mind to process how to turn quickly enough.

Jim's heart was in his throat when he saw what was happening. Sarah left the end of the jump and sailed through the air.

She was scared and knew there would be an inevitable impact with the ground. When she landed, she kept her balance and kept skiing. She looked behind her, saw the height of the jump, and yelled, "Yes!"

Jim caught up to her near the chairlift and asked, "Are you okay?"

Sarah was beaming, "That was great, let's do it again."

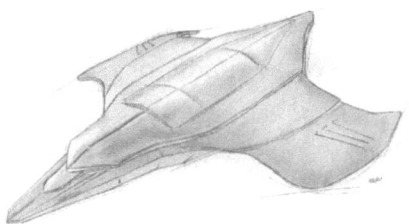

Chapter 12: BUILDING AND TESTING

One week later He was summoned to General Long's office. Jim was told to enter by the general's aid and saw someone standing at attention in front of the general's desk. "Just what makes you think I should give you a chance?" He heard General Long ask, and snickered to himself remembering the grilling he received. "Major Norgas, allow me to introduce you to your copilot, Captain Scott Dixon, call sign Gumshoe."

Scott turned toward Jim to shake his hand, "Nice to..." he began but changed mid-sentence upon seeing Jim. "Last time I saw you, you were being led away to a transport by Security Police."

"Do I know you?"

"We never met but we've shared the same air space. I'm Coyote Five."

Jim's eyes grew, and instead of shaking Scott's hand Jim gave him a hug, "I owe you one."

General Long asked, "You two know each other?"

Jim said with a smile, "General, Scott is the reason I'm still walking. He got two bogies off my back on my last mission."

"I'd say you owe him another. He just delivered your new ship, and he brought along someone who requested this assignment because of you. Lord knows why."

Jim was curious who that could be and asked, "Who?"

"A Chief Besch. He came highly recommended. I spoke with him earlier. A bit crusty and I'd say ready for retirement but he wants to fly with you. Do you have any idea why?"

"We flew together for a while, and he was my maintenance chief at my last assignment. He knows more about these birds than anyone I know. Why anyone would request reassignment for me, I don't know."

General Long said, "I'd say either he trusts you, or has a score to settle."

"With Chief Besch, it's definitely not a score to settle."

"Whatever it is he's your problem now. You guys be gentle with that bird, it's the only one we have to test. From the brief time I spent with Chief Besch, I'm sure he will have a few words with you if you do so much as scratch the paint."

Jim laughed, "General, you don't know the half of it."

"Good, so I got some help keeping an eye on you two then. I need you and Captain Dixon to test everything. The sooner you get that done the sooner we can order some more if it will suit our needs."

"Sir, I'm not completely sure what those needs are."

"Talk with Doctor Kovonich, he can fill you in. I understand you and Sarah Burnett are becoming an item. I do not have a problem with that, but this project needs her. If this – whatever you're doing – interferes with our mission I will have no choice but to intervene."

"Yes sir. I assure you my intentions are genuine."

"I'm not her father. Dismissed."

In the hallway Scott asked, "Is he always that intense?"

"Only when he wants to make a point, and as far as I can tell, always with a new troop."

"I think he enjoys it."

After Jim introduced Scott, Dr. Kovonich explained what the ship will be used for. Jim and Scott had a better understanding of what to look for as they began preflight of the new ship. Jim knew this procedure like the back of his hand, but because this ship was fresh off the assembly line and so many specialized systems had been added, he took extra time to check everything that could pose a flight risk before they left the ground.

"What brings you to leave fighters and take this thing on?" Jim asked as he slapped the fuselage of the new ship.

Scott said "After escorting you, the higher-ups didn't think too kindly of me leaving the conflict area and I was reassigned. I guess the Air Force is hurting for pilots right now, or this could have been worse."

"You have no idea."

"What do you mean?"

"It's not my place. General Long will give you the scoop when he's ready. But I will tell you, it's nothing like you have ever done."

On the way to the bridge, Jim stopped by engineering to see Chief Besch. Upon seeing him, he said, "Chief, what brings you here?"

"When I found out what they did to you, I requested a transfer. Groom Lake started spouting all this mission-critical crap. My tour was up over a year ago, and since they refused to accept the transfer, I dropped paperwork to start using the over ninety days of leave I got saved up."

"You didn't."

Chief said, "Oh, you better believe I did. And it wasn't just me. Pilots were aborting test flights because 'something didn't feel right', where they would previously just muscle through.

Maintenance slips on aircraft were growing. They were almost out of aircraft not in status code 'Red X'."

"You're kidding. Because of me?"

"Not just you, but also what they did to your crew."

"What did they do to my crew?"

Chief said, "Oh it's not that, it's what they did during the mission, risking your crew's life like that. The company is mostly civilian. You know they don't understand military culture, rules and unwritten rules. When faced with 'Military Regulations' they cave."

Jim said, "I see what you did, you used the military against them. Because of how much leave you had saved up, they risked losing their maintenance chief for three months and couldn't replace you while the billet was still full. So they pushed your transfer through instead. But if they had approved your leave, what would you have done for three months? Fish?"

"Something like that. You don't think I could afford to live at the jiggle palace for three months, do ya?"

"With you there the bouncers would be out of work."

Chief laughed, "So you're saying I missed a career opportunity? It's probably for the better. I'm sure those girls would drive me nuts. Anyway, being on a controlled tour, I had a B.O.P. (Base Of Preference) so here I am."

"But why?"

"You showed me you care about your crew, to the point of risking your career. In my book, that's someone I want to work for, and that's someone I respect." Chief snapped to attention and gave Jim a salute, "Sir!"

Jim shook his head, returned the salute, and shook the chief's hand as the chief lowered his salute. "Thanks Chief. Hey, what happened to Eric?"

"I visited him before they transported him to Landstuhl. His doctor said he was lucky. Apparently, he slipped into something called 'hemorrhagic shock'. His heart stopped from blood loss just as they got him to the Operating Room. He lost his leg but he survived."

"Good to hear. Well, not that Eric lost his leg, but I'm glad he pulled through. Thanks, Chief."

Jim met Scott on the bridge and helped him finish the preflight checklist. Scott sensed a change in Jim's mood and asked, "Are you okay?"

"Yeah, I just got some good news from the chief is all." He then keyed the mic, "Heavy Six – Tower, request vector for shakedown."

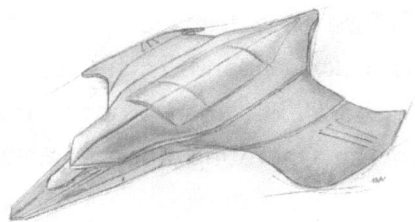

Chapter 13: SCOTT

Captain Scott Dixon, call sign 'gum shoe', graduated from the Air Force Academy at Colorado Springs.

Scott quickly adapted to flight training, which made him a candidate for fighter pilot training. To reduce the washout rate, only the top of the class were offered the opportunity to train as fighter pilots. The washout rate was still high.

Near the beginning of training, each student was strapped into the back seat of a jet with an instructor at the controls. Upon landing, each student was barely able to stand and looked completely miserable, with their faces covered in their own filth. A few walked funny because something else decided to leave their bodies.

All students heard stories about this phase of training and put their game faces on, but they were not prepared for the real thing. The visual of the first student as he departed the aircraft and required assistance from an ambulance caused realization to set in. Being a fighter pilot is serious business even with no one shooting at you.

Some students were overwhelmed and dropped out while the ground crew strapped them into the back seat, long before the engines were ignited. The students knew if they dropped out, the only thing they would fly for the rest of their Air Force career was a desk.

The students thoroughly believed the instructor's sole job that day was to get the students to throw up and spend the rest of the flight completely nauseated. They were barely able to breathe with the mess stuck to their face, and it sprayed into their nose and mouth as fresh oxygen was pumped into their face mask.

Each student was given clear instructions prior to the flight not to remove the mask, as oxygen was required to keep from blacking out.

A quick turn, then a barrel roll, was followed by an inverted loop, and halfway through the maneuver, the jet hurtled at breakneck speed straight down, just to pull out at the last second so as not to break the hard deck. The hard deck was an imaginary horizontal line in the sky the pilot was not allowed to fly under for safety reasons. The students did not know that, however, and it didn't matter. The students' inexperienced eyes thought they were going to plow into the ground any second. Their screams seemed to encourage the pilot to be even more aggressive.

Whatever the instructor thought of to make the student think twice about pursuing a career as a fighter jock, that's exactly what he did, one maneuver right after the other in quick succession. The instructor completely ignored any sounds of discomfort that came over the intercom from the back seat. The smile on the instructor's face was obvious even with the oxygen mask covering his face. He wasn't ignoring the students; he just didn't care. The screams helped him enjoy his job all the more.

All throughout, the students tried to remember what they were supposed to do with their breathing, clenching of muscles, and everything else they had been told to keep from blacking out. These exercises were needed to keep the flow of oxygen to the brain and to prevent blood from pooling in the lower extremities. The inexperienced students eventually failed and blacked out anyway.

At that point, the pilot heard nothing but silence from the student. He stopped the aggressive maneuvers, radioed the tower, and requested to land.

Upon landing, the students thoroughly believed the instructor was Satan himself. They wanted to kiss the earth but didn't want to give the instructor the satisfaction. Each tried to walk as dignified as possible back to the group of students.

Those who had already flown laughed as each student got out of the jet. The rest were nervous about their flights and didn't want to be last. Rumor had it the last flight was longer than the rest.

The maintenance crews also hated these orientation flights and tried everything possible to have the day off, which never worked but didn't deter them from trying. Each aircraft had to be swapped out when it landed. The cockpit needed to be cleaned of any foreign matter and the oxygen supply system completely gone over.

The normal way to test the oxygen supply system was to attach a hose to the pilot's oxygen mask connector. And then, by mouth, test the baffles by alternately blowing and sucking on the hose.

Fighter pilots have a Type A personality and do not like to admit when they mess up or have an accident. If a pilot does not put in the flight log that he got sick and threw up, then the maintenance person gets a mouthful during the oxygen supply test. At these first-day flights, it was a given that the students would get sick, so the test required complete disassembly and rebuilding of the oxygen system.

Unfortunately for the maintenance crews, vomit was not the only bodily substance that needed to be cleaned from the back seat before the aircraft could be used again. Every new maintenance person assigned to the squadron would ask if the back seat and its controls could be covered with a plastic sheet for these flights, but this was always dismissed as a safety concern.

Cadet Scott Dixon came out of his first flight unscathed, to the complete disappointment and loss of pride of the instructor, who tried everything short of going below the hard deck to try to rattle him. In return, the only sounds the pilot heard over the intercom were grunts during high-G maneuvers as Scott performed his stomach clenches, then howls of "Wahoo" or "Yee-haw," as if Scott thought it was not much more than a high-speed roller coaster ride.

From that point on, Scott was at the top of his class and was thrilled to push whatever aircraft he was allowed to fly to its limit.

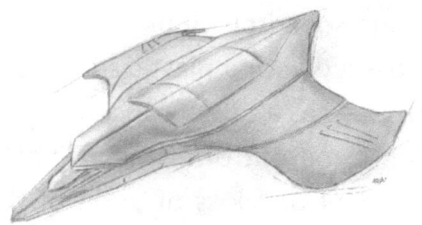

Chapter 14: GOING LIVE

Jim purchased a house in Newport News and asked Sarah to move in with him, which she accepted. She was eager to spend more time with him; she was not seeing him in her lab as much as before due to his increased work tempo.

In the evenings sitting on the couch snuggling with her, he learned what had been going on at the new facility being constructed. He was busy doing shakedown flights in the Atlantic east of Langley, testing everything on the ship. He hardly knew what was going on at Langley except what he could see while landing.

Once the new facility was finished, he saw her at home less often. She had so many things to check before the first test shot that she often came home exhausted. her job was not physical, but mental exhaustion was just as tiring.

As their jobs grew more demanding, they rarely had time to spend together. Jim was glad Sarah came into his life. Any chance he had to help her, he welcomed the opportunity. He gave her foot rubs in the evenings as she read telemetry data. He looked at the sheets she studied but had no clue what he was looking at. Most nights Sarah fell asleep on the couch, which resulted in Jim carrying her to bed.

General Long had so many things he wanted tested on the ship, it was hard to tell who was more tired some evenings, Jim or Sarah.

Jim felt like Sarah gave him more than he gave her. Sarah felt Jim gave her more than she gave him. Neither asked for a thing from the other. What was freely given, caused their relationship to strengthen and grow despite their busy schedule.

"We finished testing and did our first real shot today," Sarah said, excited one night when she got home and saw Jim cooking. Usually food was delivered. Occasionally, one of them finished work early enough to try their hand at making a balanced meal.

"What do you mean, real shot?"

"Well, a couple days ago we coordinated with Groom Lake to keep an eye on Area 52 and make sure no one entered the area."

"You mean Area 51?"

"Do you know how Area 51 got its name?"

Jim thought for a moment and said, "You know I used to work there and... no I don't know."

"There were several plots of land for sale and the government purchased most of them. They were originally surveyed and recorded as "Area" with a number designation at the courthouse. The names stuck. Area 51 is not the only one the government still owns. It's just the one that gets all the attention."

"Are you serious?" Jim asked.

"You worked there and you didn't know? Since Area 51 is in the public eye it does make sense you don't know about places you're not cleared for," Sarah teased which caused Jim to tickle her till she let out a squeal.

"So what happened at 'Area 52'?" Jim asked, stressing the words 'Area 52'.

Sarah said, "We planned a shot one day into the past," The look on Jim's face told her he did not realize the difficulty, "The Earth moves roughly 2.3 million miles per hour."

"Oh come on. What? Never mind, I learned not to question you on science stuff."

"That's cute." Sarah said with a smile which flashed a dimple. "In order to go back in time, you not only need to know when, but you also need to know where."

"What do you mean?"

"Movies make it look like, if this couch was a time machine and we go back in time, we will end up right here, in this living room. But that's not true because this room used to be over there."

Jim said, "So you have to figure out where this room was at the time you want to go?"

"Exactly. Today, to make sure the computers are calibrated correctly, we chose a shot for one day in the past in a location no one should be. To see how accurate our calculations are, grid marks were painted in the desert."

"How did it go?"

Sarah said, "We sent a test container containing several objects."

"And?" Jim asked now caught up in it.

"I heard the champagne tasted great." Sarah wore a huge smile, flashing her dimples.

"That's wonderful. We have to celebrate."

The following weeks consisted of Jim and Scott finishing the tests directed by General Long. Sarah began shots several hundred years into Earth's past to create what will become the city Anarbia.

One night Jim asked Sarah, "How is it going with the shots you have been doing to create the city?"

"They're not building the city – well not exactly," she paused and used her hands to help explain when she got her thoughts together. "When a shot forms in the past it creates a void," Sarah held her hands as if holding an imaginary ball. "Anything in that void is destroyed and replaced with whatever we had on the shot pad. We are sending building materials and supplies. We will also send

Mech-Bots to assemble everything and help us when we get there. Everything we can think of for comfort and recreation, we're sending. Not just work facilities."

"That's good," Jim said. "Inspiration comes from weird places sometimes. Not to mention if everything is so sterile, people will go nuts."

"Inspiration?"

"We're sending people into the past to come up with and build better weapons. The idea for something revolutionary —who knows where it might come from?" Did the message you looked at from SETI tell you how to make that power plant?"

Sarah said, "No, but it…"

Jim said, "It got your creative juices flowing, and your genius took over."

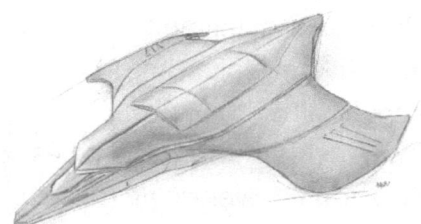

Chapter 15: GOT LUCKY

The following day Jim met Scott for more shakedown flights. Today's flights were more for the crewmen to get familiar with the ship under the guidance of Chief Besch.

Most of the checklists given by General Long were complete, and four more ships were already under construction for the project. Jim decided to let Scott pilot the ship. Scott had only flown fighters in the past and was nervous about taking the controls of such a big ship. While the ship was still on the ground, the pilot sat so high it was like looking out the window of the fourth floor of a building.

The ship handled like a dream, and acceleration seemed faster than the fighter variant. Once in the sky with nothing around, Scott began to relax and wiped the sweat off his forehead with his sleeve.

The flight lasted several hours, flying circles over the Atlantic off the coast of Virginia. When Chief Besch had enough, Jim contacted the shot pad control for a practice landing. The shot pad was a confined space with scaffolding surrounding the entire pad, with the control building on the southwest side.

"Shot Control – Heavy Six, you're clear," came the reply on the radio. "The next shot will be in two hours, pad is clear till then."

Jim said to Scott, "Alright, just take it nice and easy, you already know how to fly this thing."

When Scott was able to see the shot pad in the distance on the northwest side of the runway, he began to sweat. "Are you sure this thing will fit?"

"It's tight, but it will fit. The pad was made for this ship. Just center the ship using the displays and come straight down."

Scott flew the ship toward the pad, slowed to a hover, eased it into position, and began to decrease the altitude. Warning buzzers squealed and a display showed a proximity warning.

Scott quickly pulled up and tried again. It took several attempts before he finally got the ship even with the top of the scaffolding with no warnings going off, and then he slowly bled off altitude.

When the port wing got just below the roof line of the control building, the ship listed toward the building. Scott over-corrected and crashed into the scaffolding on the starboard side, which caused the coils on the scaffolding to fire arcs of electrical energy between them and ripped huge holes in the starboard wing. The arcs worked their way over the body of the ship and ripped a hole in the bridge glass as the ship fell the remaining distance to the tarmac.

Jim found himself waking in a hospital bed and heard Sarah's voice yelling, "Doctor!" as she ran out of the room.

He heard another voice to his left croak, "Keep it down." He looked and saw Scott on the other bed in the room with his eyes bandaged.

Shortly after, Sarah returned with a doctor in tow, who introduced himself as Dr. Stevens.

The doctor checked both their charts, then looked over Scott a little closer. "Captain Dixon, you'll have to stay with us a bit. We want to make sure we got all the glass out. Major Norgas, we're waiting for your lab work to come back. Any questions?" Dr. Stevens asked and Jim shook his head no.

Sarah said, "I want to know. What happened to him? How

serious is this?"

"Well, he had a mild concussion and was unconscious for quite some time. Let me check on the lab results."

Sarah asked, "What will lab results tell you for a concussion?"

"A concussion is caused by a blow to the head and can cause brain swelling. Not to mention you guys experimenting with some weird stuff over there. I want to make sure everything is normal and get a baseline in case he comes in later complaining of something." Dr. Stevens excused himself as Sarah apologized.

She scolded Jim, "You scared the hell out of me. When I saw that bolt go through your ship, then the crash, I thought —"

Jim interrupted, "Oh, it didn't even touch me."

She pointed at the other bed and asked, "What about him?"

Scott said, "Didn't touch me either," which caused Jim to chuckle.

In an attempt to calm her, Jim introduced Scott. "Sarah, this is Scott Dixon, my copilot."

Scott asked, "Even after today?"

"You saved my neck once, and the jury is still out on today. So we'll see."

"Fair enough. Nice to meet you, Sarah. Just call me Gumshoe." He held up a hand to shake a hand he couldn't see.

"Nice to meet you," and she shook Scott's hand. "What is it with you two? Stinker and Gumshoe."

Scott said, "They're our call signs."

She said, "I get that. Couldn't you come up with something better?"

Jim said, "We didn't get to choose our own."

Scott added, "The members of our first active squadron vote on it."

Jim said, "And they follow us for the rest of our career."

Sarah asked. "And they thought of you guys this much to stick you with names like that?"

Jim said, "I actually like it. And you would too if you knew why they chose it."

She rolled her eyes and interrupted him, "I can only imagine, Stinker. How about you, Gumshoe?"

"In part, it has to do with my last name, Dixon. Someone said 'Sounds like one of those trashy detective novels'. Someone else said 'He does have an uncanny knack for finding things the unit needs' and Gumshoe won the vote."

Sarah said, "Hmm." Then looked toward Jim who started to speak only to be cut off, "I'm not talking to you. I'll probably get gray hair out of this."

He kept quiet but Scott couldn't help but laugh.

She said, "I thought you were a better pilot than that."

Scott said, "I was flying."

Sarah asked, "And that's supposed to make me feel better?"

Jim looked at Scott to warn him to quit while he was ahead, but with Scott's eyes bandaged, he couldn't warn him. Jim thought, '*Verbal communication may anger Sarah more, leave it alone*'.

Scott was saved from any further wrong steps by Dr. Stevens's entrance. The doctor cleared Jim, and Scott felt sorry for Jim having to ride home with Sarah, considering the mood she was in.

But later that evening at home with Sarah, Jim knew she was more worried than mad.

The day after Scott was released from the hospital, a hearing was held. It was determined that due to the size and proximity of the control building and the amount of time Captain Dixon hovered in the area, the engine created a vortex of air which caused the port side of the ship to no longer produce lift. This type of event is called 'ground effect'.

As a result, the shot pad was moved fifty yards farther from the control building and the scaffolding holding the coils was placed farther apart and modified to accommodate the distance.

Later that day, Jim and Scott were called to General Long's office. Upon entering, a young man stood in front of the general's desk and was being dressed down by the general. The man still held his salute and waited for the general to return it so he could lower his arm, which started to shake under the strain.

Scott glanced at Jim and smiled. Jim nodded in agreement. The two knew General Long enjoyed putting newly assigned members of the unit on the spot and decided to go along with the fun.

"Gentlemen," General Long motioned for Jim and Scott to step forward.

"Major Norgas reports as ordered," Jim belted out as he snapped to attention and saluted.

Scott followed suit, "Captain Dixon reports as ordered."

General Long turned toward the two, returned the salute and said, "This lieutenant thinks he is worthy of joining our team."

Jim glanced at the lieutenant still straining with the hand salute, forehead covered in sweat.

"We've got four new ships arriving this evening. I need you two to do a preliminary check. This is Lieutenant John Anders. Fresh out of OCS (Officer Candidate School). He thinks he can change the world. See what you can do with him. Dismissed." General Long returned the salute which allowed the Lieutenant to finally relax his arm. In unison, the three men performed an about-face and started for the door.

General Long took on his normal tone of voice and said, "Gentlemen hold on a minute. I've got something serious to discuss with you that, until now I took for granted. Stand at-ease lieutenant. Major Norgas and Captain Dixon, do both of you understand what is going on around here?"

Both Scott and Jim glanced at each other and in unison said, "Yes, sir."

"I assumed the two of you were on board with it, but I never asked. This is a voluntary mission. I will not order you to do it, and I want both of you to understand, this is a one-way mission. There is no coming back."

Lt Anders started to look nervous but remained silent.

General Long continued, "I thoroughly understand if you would prefer to stay behind, but I ask you to stay with the project to train the pilots that will go. Gentlemen, you are the most experienced pilots we have in those birds. The success of this endeavor may depend on what you can pass on."

Jim started to say, "General, if I may?"

"You may not. I understand you have a stake in this now, and if you're going for a girl, that will probably be a mistake. I want you to remember, if you go through with this, you're going to be seeing Sarah for a long time, better or worse."

"I already know I want to be with Sarah."

"I'm glad for you, I really am, Sarah is a good girl. You know you will be leaving everything else behind. Your parents, brothers and sisters. I don't know if you have any or if they are still alive, but you need to know that all of them, and everyone you know, will be gone." The general paused to let that sink in, then said, "The two of you, fill in Lt Anders on what's happening, all of it, in a secure area. I want your answers in two days. Dismissed."

The three left the general's office and made their way to the hangar where the ship was being repaired.

John nervously asked, "So what's really going on, and what did he mean, everyone will be gone?"

Jim said, "Not here Lieutenant. Wait till we're in a secure area."

John said, "Yes, Sir."

Before entering the hangar Jim briefed John on the proper flight line procedures. If he does not follow those procedures, Security Police would know he didn't belong in the area, and John would end up on the ground with a rifle barrel pressed against the base of his skull. Jim and Scott would not be able to help him if that happened.

When the YBV-92 came into view John was awestruck, "I have never seen anything like that. It's huge, and it looks fast just sitting there. What is it?"

Walking toward the ramp in the ship's belly, Jim said, "This variant, I'm really not sure. I piloted basically the same ship but a bomber, and Scott flew a fighter version. It was teeny tiny compared to this."

"Hey, that teeny tiny saved your butt."

Jim said with a smile, "Whoa, don't get your feathers ruffled. I didn't know size mattered so much to you. I do thank you for that. It would have ended badly without you there. What is the nomenclature of this? Is it still YBV-92?"

"I don't know. The fighter I flew was..." Scott thought for a while, then said, "I honestly never asked. They had me in something different almost every day, but it should have been a YFV. And this should be YCV."

Jim asked, "Why YCV? That implies its primary role is cargo, but isn't this more... Hell if I know. Do they have a YJV?"

John asked, "What's 'J'?"

Jim said, "Jack of all trades."

Scott laughed and said, "I don't think it works that way. They do have an 'S' for space plane."

Jim said, "Won't that replace the 'V'? So it would be 'Y' something 'S'."

John asked, "What do you mean space plane?"

Jim said, "So YJS-92?"

Scott said, "We have to get some clarification on that 'J' and I bet they used 'V' instead of 'S' to hide its true nature, even though 'V' does fit."

J"Well, let's get inside."

Jim and Scott started walking up the ramp, and John ran after them asking, "Wait, what did you mean by space?"

When the three got to the bridge of the ship and were alone, Jim and Scott, to the best of their ability, explained what Operation CAMPFIRE and Project Anarbia were all about.

John did not know if he could believe them and thought this was one of those 'pick on the new guy stunts'.

Jim could not provide proof of the alien message or time travel, but as far as space travel, he showed John the telemetry stored in the ship's computer of its previous flights.

John said, "This can't be right." He looked through the flight logs and searched their faces for any sign of a joke. When he couldn't find any, he said, "Okay, assuming I believe all this, what do you guys think about what the general asked?"

Jim said, "No one living today will know what we did, but I'm used to that, most of my career I can't talk about. I think it's the right thing to do and I'm making the trip, but not being able to tell, or bring my parents, that's rough."

Scott said, "I hear you there. If you are not on some list, you're 'SOL' (Shit Out of Luck) and have to fend for yourself. Do you think the government will at least tell everyone what is going on?"

Jim said, "I doubt it. If you knew what was coming, would you keep working? Allow whatever goods you produce to keep getting to market for others to have a chance? Or carry a gun, horde, and shoot anyone that got in your way?"

Scott said, "That's a tough one that I don't think I can answer till

I'm in that situation."

Jim said, "I sure as hell don't want to be here when society breaks down. I just wish there was something I could do for my folks. They live in the hills so will be spared the brunt of it, but eventually..."

John asked, "Will we need money where we are going?"

Scott said, "Come on Lieutenant, didn't you hear what's going to happen here?"

John said, "Well, if we can't tell our folks, can we at least help them?" Jim and Scott looked at each other and John could see the possibilities going through their minds. "Like buy them nonperishable food and such."

Scott said, "We could turn them into survivalists overnight."

Jim said, "Yeah but without being able to tell them what it's for, my Mom will probably have a big block party and invite the whole county."

John asked, "What else can we do for them?" Both Scott and Jim shrugged their shoulders. "And I take it by the direction of the conversation, both of you are making the trip?" He looked overwhelmed, like he just needed a direction to be pointed and would follow what Jim and Scott decided. Both nodded their heads.

Later that evening Jim told Sarah his plan to spend all his money and help his folks.

Sarah said, "That's fine for your parents. What about mine? Even if I could send them stuff, they live in a city. Cities will self-implode and I can't even warn them to get out."

"I wish there was some way to get them to my parent's house. Trouble is to get them to stay there without telling them why."

"Yeah, my mother in the country? She would lose it without her barista."

"Do they know what you do? If you told them 'Don't ask any questions, just leave'. would they?"

Sarah thought for a moment then said, "I think Dad would understand, but Mom?"

"Can you let your Dad know to get to my parent's house as soon as things don't seem right? And I'll let my parents know to expect them."

Sarah said a bit unsure, "Yeah, I think I can."

"Do you want me to talk to him?"

"That might be better. I might slip up and say something I'm not supposed to. Why don't we do it over speakerphone so both of us can convince him?"

That night Sarah and Jim set their plan in motion and scoured the internet for survival-type food and whatever else they thought would help their parents. They learned that anything labeled 'survival' was expensive. Jim knew from backpacking and survival school that dry goods like beans, rice, and grain would keep for a long time, and canned food was good for at least five years.

For some time, Sarah and Jim toyed with the idea of marriage. They attended mass together at the base chapel where they met Chaplain Green. The chaplain suggested they attend the couples bible study to test the waters, and began coaching them toward the sanctity of marriage.

Sarah's parents were totally against the idea of their daughter marrying a military man. Her Mom felt he was beneath her and feared he would take her little girl to some godforsaken armpit of the earth on his next assignment.

Jim felt like he had to prove himself to her parents and never quite measured up to their expectations. This was difficult for him considering he had a type A personality — a typical unwritten requirement for military pilots.

Jim's parents warmly welcomed Sarah into their family and home. Sarah felt completely at home in his parents' house, especially after the practical joke they played on her on her first night in their home.

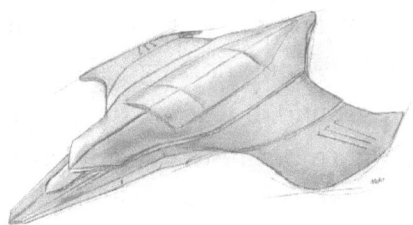

Chapter 16: JOHN

"Lt" is short for Lieutenant and interchangeable for both Second and First Lieutenant, the first two ranks for an Air Force officer. Lt John Anders was fresh out of OCS (Officer Candidate School), a school enlisted personnel must attend if they wish to become an officer.

John's first assignment after graduation from OCS was at Langley AFB. Upon arrival, his commander did not know what to do with him. As an enlisted man, John worked in communications. As an officer, John was more in the way than helpful, and with Operation CAMPFIRE in full swing, no one had time to train him. His commander caught wind of a special project on the other side of the base that needed bodies. Since John still retained the security clearance needed from when he worked in communications, it was an easy way for the commander to get John out of his hair. All John had to do was take a polygraph and sign the nondisclosure statements during his in-processing, and the job was his.

John was assigned to the maintenance department for X-projects within Project Anarbia. Being prior enlisted, he gained the respect of the enlisted personnel in maintenance, now called crewmen.

Chief Besch gave no one a break, regardless of rank. 'Pull your weight or find another job' was his philosophy. Chief had no time for lazy people and would not allow it from anyone.

John was a go-getter and did not have a problem rolling up his sleeves, getting dirty, and helping out. He came from a communications background, but some things were common sense, and he was able to figure out how things worked. The things John was able to help with got him some approval from the chief. He learned later that the little approval Chief gave meant he did pretty darn good.

Enlisted personnel found it easier to speak with officers that were prior enlisted, and John found it difficult at times to distance himself from the enlisted. He had to ensure friendships did not form, or his superiors might think fraternization was going on. OCS graduates were never assigned to the base they just left for this very reason.

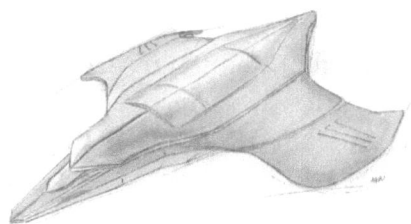

Chapter 17: RECALL

Jim, Scott, and John were kept so busy over the next week doing shakedown flights and assisting new pilots that they barely had time to hear about the progress of the project. Upon return from a test flight of the YBV-92, they were ordered to report to the general's office at noon. Upon arrival, the general's aid told them to go to the conference room next door.

In the conference room, Jim saw his entire crew was already seated, and a medical group, evident by the orange bags they were carrying, were setting up tables.

Chief Besch asked, "What is going on?"

Jim said, "I don't know, but it looks like they're getting us ready for a deployment." He noticed other groups filtering in from C3PO (Consolidated Base Personnel Office) and OSI (Office of Special Investigations). The latter always gave a brief introduction of what to expect at the deployed location they will be going to.

"I think you're right, but where?"

"It doesn't make sense. The YBV-92 can strike anywhere on the planet in just a few hours. There is no reason to deploy it."

Chief Besch said, "Since when did the military do anything that made sense?" He noticed General Long enter the room, stood, and said, "Looks like we're about to find out." Then bellowed, "Room ten-hut!"

General Long said, "As you were," and proceeded to the center of the room. He looked about him at the gathered group. "Chief, has your crew been briefed about Project Anarbia?"

"Yes, sir."

General Long looked about him and said, "Good-good. If anyone is unsure about their desire to participate, please leave the room." Everyone glanced around at each other, but no one got up to leave. He said, "You understand this will be a lifelong commitment; your families will be notified you died in service to your nation. If you can't handle that or have any reservations, this is your last chance. There will be no repercussions if you leave."

No one left, and a few moments later, a sergeant stood and said, "Sir, we trained hard for this and are committed to it."

"Thank you sergeant, Sergeant White, right?" General Long nodded his head as he surveyed the faces around him. "From this point on, all enlisted personnel are confined to base."

Chief Besch stood and protested, "General!"

General Long tried to quell the chief and the grumbling that started in the wake he created. "Tomorrow will be the first shot with live – I don't know what to call you – travelers? Passengers? Cargo? Major Norgas, your ship and crew along with a hand-picked group of scientists and engineers will be the first to go. Because we are dealing with time travel, be aware, that you may not be the first to arrive."

Chief Besch, still standing, said, "General, I can understand your concern for security and some of the crew not showing, but thus far there have been no leaks, and I think my crew has shown their commitment. At a minimum, those of us living off base should be given the opportunity to gather our possessions."

"You're right, but anyone who does not show will be considered a deserter. Last chance."

A young female airman said, "I'm sorry General, Chief, but I can't handle this," and walked out."

General Long asked, "Anyone else?" Two more walked out. "Okay, we can begin. Immunizations are here because there are some exotic diseases you may be exposed to. CBPO is here to ensure everyone's SGLI (Serviceman's Group Life Insurance) is properly set up. Legal if you need a last will in testament, and OSI to let you know what to expect."

Chief said, "What to expect? 'Last of the Mohicans', 'Dances with Wolves', what's more to know? Salem witch trials?"

An OSI agent stepped forward and said, "Well there goes my briefing. Actually, that does sum it up. We really do not know what you will encounter from the indigenous residents, so we created this primitive wilderness survival guide. Please everyone take one. We took things you might need from several books, including the "SAS survival guide" and "Edible plants" just to name a few."

General Long finished with, "Okay, if no one has any questions, line up for your immunizations."

Jim stood and asked, "What time are we to report?"

"Thank you, Major, zero nine hundred."

That night when Jim got home, Sarah greeted him wearing her best evening gown. She informed him, "Get ready, we're going out." He had wondered if he would have to break the news to her and was glad she already knew. This was to be their last night together until Sarah could join him with her own time-travel transit. She wanted to spend this evening with Jim at the finest establishments the area had to offer.

The next morning, he woke to a louder-than-normal commotion of breakfast being made – the banging of pots, and a bit more hushed swear words than the normal chaos when Sarah cooked. He cleared the cobwebs of sleep away as he thought, '*No matter how brilliant Sarah was as a scientist, she just can't quite get breakfast together*'. He loved her all the same.

This particular morning Jim entered the kitchen and saw Sarah's back turned toward him facing the stove. He came up behind her, brushed her hair to one side, and gave her slender neck a long kiss, beneath the jawline, right in the spot he knew sent shivers down her spine.

"Mm, good morning to you too, Stinker," Sarah said, giggling as she turned to face him, spatula still in hand. "Now I don't want to hear it, today is going to be a very long day for both of us, sit down and eat. Not your usual grabbing something and running out the door."

"Yes Ma'am," Jim said as he saluted Sarah, then looked at the spread she prepared on the table. "Wow, you outdid yourself. I'll have to call for help to finish all this. Just what time did you wake up?"

"My mind was racing and I couldn't sleep," Sarah said as tears started welling up on her bottom eyelid, and threatened to spill over. "It might be the last time you have a decent meal in some time."

Jim took Sarah in his arms for a warm embrace, "It won't be long, and we will be back together again. It's going to be a whole new beginning." Jim, being half a head taller than Sarah, kissed her forehead, and she laid the side of her head against his shoulder.

"I know," Sarah stared at a random pattern on the opposite wall and focused her thoughts, "I just hope my math is right. Doctor Kovonich has not got back to me on my calculations."

"You are the smartest person I know. You pored over those numbers more times than I can count. I trust you."

Sarah practically yelled, "With your life? If I'm off the slightest – just one decimal point in the wrong place –?"

"What's the alternative?" and squeezed her in a tight hug to comfort her. "We have no choice; time is running out. If we stay here we're doomed. We go, we have a chance."

"I know. But we have no proof on a living subject being sent that far," Sarah returned Jim's embrace, calmer now. "I just don't want you to be the guinea pig."

Jim said with a slight grin, "That's why I'm not worried about it. With me going first I know you did everything to make sure it was right. Someone has to keep you science types in check."

Sarah squeezed out of his embrace and said sarcastically, "All right, fly-boy. Sit down and eat before I throw it out."

They enjoyed breakfast together and made small talk. Both dodged what the day would bring until an urgent call ordered both of them to report for duty immediately.

General Long initiated a recall for the entire unit. Civilians were not usually included in recalls but these were extraordinary circumstances.

Sarah had never been briefed on what to do in a recall. Jim explained, "All we do is get dressed and report to work as fast as possible."

Sarah demanded, "I am not leaving this house without taking a shower. And you, your shot is scheduled for today. This will be the last time you are home. Don't you want to at least clean up?"

Jim tried to reason with her, "We're supposed to get there as fast as possible. The general would not have initiated it if it wasn't an emergency."

Sarah put it in terms that gave Jim no room to negotiate, "I am not kissing you goodbye without you brushing your teeth. Now get in there and get cleaned up."

He said sheepishly, "Yes ma'am."

They rushed to get cleaned up and ran out the door. Jim grabbed the bags he packed earlier.

Soon after Jim backed the car out of the driveway, the car was flanked by armored military vehicles. "What the hell is going on?" he asked as they were surrounded and escorted to the base.

Sarah shouted, "Look!" and pointed toward the base. A green glow could be seen on the horizon as transformers on the power poles began to burst in the distance. The transformers burst consecutively, radiating out from the base. The only light to be seen afterward was a green silhouetted skyline in the direction of the base, and smoke began to rise from that direction.

When Jim and their escort got closer to the base, mobs of people were running toward the base while others, bloodied, were walking away.

Sarah looked at the chaos and asked, "What is going on?"

"Word must have gotten out. It was only a matter of time. I'm surprised we were able to keep it quiet this long."

"Yeah but what do they expect to accomplish?"

"I'll bet a newscaster blurted some dumb idea, everyone thought it was a good idea and here we are."

Sarah looked surprised and asked, "Don't these people know the military won't let them in?"

"It doesn't matter, when fear takes over, people don't think. They believe the person next to them knows what to do and they follow. The military tries to train this out of troops." Jim pointed around their vehicle at the crowd.

"What do you mean?"

Jim could tell she was scared. Even with the escort, he was busy dodging debris and the occasional rioter and was not able to comfort her the way he wanted so he just talked. He talked about the military and knew that was not what she wanted to hear. It was easier to talk about what he knew while he concentrated on the road. He also tried to let her know the people escorting them were perfectly capable of dealing with the situation and keeping her safe.

"You do something enough times, it becomes muscle memory. When fear creeps in, muscle memory takes over. If a soldier gets scared, he reacts because of training, not by the suggestion of some idiot. Don't worry, you will be fine." Jim reached over and took

Sarah's hand and smiled. "You're safe and soon this will all be behind us. See? There's the gate."

Sarah cradled his hand in both of hers and smiled. She did not flash a dimple and Jim knew she was calmer but still scared. He wanted to hold her but could not do anything more to comfort her while driving.

The column of vehicles passed through the crowd that was held back by security outside the west gate of the base.

Sarah screamed when the window behind her shattered from something a rioter threw.

Security began to strike rioters with batons and the butts of their rifles. Several rioters fell and were walked over by the first line of security, only to be swooped up by the second line. Security took no chances and pushed the rioters back.

A fire truck used to put out aircraft fires took up position inside the fence. The water cannon on the roof trained on the crowd as firemen ran hoses to the nearest hydrant.

Jim saw more security come from inside the base. They were being handed live ammo from wooden crates as they passed.

The fresh troops took up position to repel any in the crowd that pushed past the security that were already at the gate. From the looks on their faces, they appeared a bit uneasy about being given orders to fire on their own citizens, and were surprised by what they saw when they came through the gate. Jim knew they were prepared and if needed would open fire to protect their team.

That's the way of war, or conflict. You do it for your teammates, to keep them safe, regardless of the mission. Watch your buddy's back, he's watching yours.

"Are you okay?" Jim asked. "Did you get hit?"

"No, I'm okay," Sarah said nervously.

"Check yourself," Jim said as he looked in the back seat to ensure whatever was thrown was not on fire. "Make sure you're not bleeding from a cut you can't feel right now."

Sarah looked at Jim oddly at what he just said.

"With your heightened adrenaline you may not know you're cut. We will pass by the base hospital on the way to headquarters. Please check yourself." Jim turned on the interior lighting as Sarah ran her hands over her head and back of her neck, then checked her palms for blood in the light. To his relief, she was untouched.

Sarah said, "You're bleeding, your cheek."

"It's just a scratch. I've cut myself worse shaving."

"Here, let me look at that," Sarah said as she dabbed a napkin at the cut. Jim let her; it distracted her and seemed to calm her down.

Jim suggested, "Why don't you call your folks? Get them moving if they're not already."

"Oh yes. Good idea."

The escort vehicles led them past the guards, through the gate and across the base to the driveway leading to the front door of Project Anarbia's headquarters building. The security outside the headquarters building ushered Sarah and Jim out of the car with a constant eye on the sky and hurried them inside.

Jim asked the closest person, "What happened?"

"I'm not at liberty to say, sir." The young man, barely in his twenties, almost jumped out of his skin when asked the question. His mind was elsewhere and was suddenly pulled back, but he was able to maintain his composure, "I heard a briefing will begin as soon as everyone is there. I think you two are the last ones we are waiting on."

The briefing room was on the second floor of the four-story building and looked more like a small theater. The room was packed, all seats to be seen were taken and the aisles were filled with everyone who was anyone on base. Jim knew most of the faces that turned their way as they entered from the back of the room. Jim and Sarah were ushered toward the front and onto the stage where a table was set up. Four chairs sat empty along the back side of the table. They took two of the seats.

"General Long will be right in," the young man who ushered them said in a hushed voice. He quickly disappeared only to return a moment later with a bottle of water for Sarah and Jim, and he placed two more in front of the empty chairs.

Jim asked in a whisper, "What happened?"

The young man replied as General Long entered the room, "All I know is a spaceship was spotted heading this way. It's got everyone jumpy."

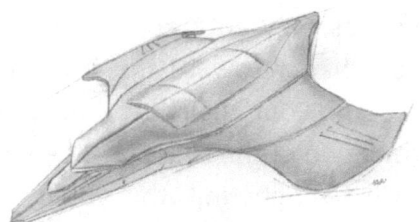

Chapter 18: BRIEFING

"Room ten hut!" came from somewhere in the crowd and everyone briskly stood up. Complete silence enveloped the room except for the footfalls of General Long as he approached the stage.

In a nonchalant manner General Long said, "As you were." He had said it so many times before, he was bored saying it. "Dim the lights and bring up the first slide. Will someone get Doctor Kovonich?"

The lights dimmed and an image of the night sky was displayed on the screen behind the table. The moon was in the upper left corner and a red arrow pointed to a white speck just below and to the right of the moon. If it was not for the arrow, the speck would blend in perfectly with the stars.

"Next slide." The first image was replaced with another. This time the speck was larger, and the shape of a spacecraft was more distinguishable against the round white dots of the stars splattered in the background. "As you can see, we are out of time. Most of you here have no clue what I'm talking about, and for good reason. Ah Doctor Kovonich, care to enlighten us on what we're looking at?"

Dr. Kovonich entered from a side door carrying a stack of computer printouts he was studying, talking to no one in particular as he made his way through the room.

"This can't be," Dr. Kovonich mumbled. "Um, what? Oh yes, yes, it's a ship."

"We know that," General Long said with a slight irritation in his voice followed by a chuckle from the audience. "Care to expand on that?"

Dr. Kovonich said defensively, "It's not one of ours!"

Sarah asked as she started to rise from her seat, "May I take this?"

General Long was shaking his head and replied, "Please do."

Dr. Kovonich glanced up from the papers long enough to smile at Sarah, "Oh, Sarah. Impressive work my dear, impressive work. There's one calculation that's not quite right. Don't tell me after all this you're using the chaos theory with..." Dr. Kovonich paused and looked at Jim. "What's your name, Stinker? With Stinker's life."

Jim looked at Sarah a bit uncomfortable. Sarah scrunched her forehead and squinted at Dr. Kovonich as angry as Jim was uncomfortable.

Dr. Kovonich laughed, barely able to contain himself, "Ha! You should see the looks on your faces. A joke, Jim. In my field, there's not much room to have fun, but the look on your faces – oh, that was good." Dr. Kovonich took the last empty seat at the table between Jim and General Long.

General Long said, "This is not the time, Doctor."

Jim looked slightly perturbed for being the butt of his joke

"Your math checks out, and I think we are ready. Go ahead and explain to these good people what we have here." Dr. Kovonich pointed behind him to the screen. "And what we plan to do about it." Dr. Kovonich reached over and grabbed a hold of the back of Jim's hand, shook his arm and smiled at him. "We're counting on you," he said, loud enough for only Jim to hear.

Sarah said, "Thank you, Doctor," slightly sarcastically due to his joke but still respectful.

"Judging by the unexpected phone call this morning, this briefing, and that photo... they're early?" Sarah asked General Long who just nodded his head yes. "And this photo was taken last night?" General Long held up four fingers in front of his chest, "At four A.M.? Oh boy."

She turned her attention to the audience and began to explain the situation. "As incredible as this may sound, several years ago SETI began communicating with an intelligent race on a planet near Alpha Centauri." A bunch of rustling began as members of the audience changed their seating positions in disbelief. For years they were convinced such stories were only spoken by conspiracy nut jobs, but Sarah continued, "A few years ago a warning was received and believed to be completely genuine. Soon after, all communication from them ceased," She paused for a moment to let the audience digest this. For some, a far-fetched story, now being spoken by a respected scientist, was still hard to believe. "Operation CAMPFIRE and Project Anarbia were a direct result of that warning. In short, an armada of spaceships hell-bent on conquering all inhabitable planets in their path, wiping out the indigenous life, and making the planet theirs, is now on our doorstep."

Those who heard this for the first time began talking among themselves, which caused Sarah to stop.

"At ease," bellowed General Long as he stood, leaned on the table with straight arms ending in fists on the tabletop. With quiet restored, "We have a lot to cover and less time to go over it! Now please, this briefing is more of a courtesy to you than a necessity. You all know your jobs, but I'd like for you to know why you're doing them. I've learned people perform better when they understand the gravity of the situation instead of just doing their job." General Long paused, glanced around the room, and made eye contact with each person present, which gave everyone reassurance that what was being said was the truth. "Please, Sarah, continue," General Long raised a hand in her direction as he sat and took a drink of water.

"We have known for some time Earth cannot defend itself in a battle against what's heading our way," Sarah continued. "The planet we were communicating with was further advanced, and as far as we know, they have been wiped out." She paused, debating what to say next. "But we have a plan. Today we will send our first settlers, with Major Norgas piloting the ship."

She pointed at Jim sitting at the table in front of her. "We are sending Major Norgas and as many people as the ship will hold – engineers, historians, scientists. People that will give us the best chance at a new start. I will remain here monitoring this firing and go on a later transit. Major Norgas will be sent into Earth's past, hidden from all those living there, or were living, with the hopes of raising the technology level to the point where, when this day comes again, they can rise up like 'Dragons Teeth' to defend Earth and destroy these invaders."

The room exploded in cheers and applause but faded away soon after with just a look from General Long.

The audience began talking among themselves as Sarah asked General Long, "Are my slides in here?" and pointed at the screen. He nodded his head and gave her a thumbs up, "Next slide," she said loud enough to be heard over the crowd and the picture on the screen changed to a picture of Earth. The audience quieted back down.

"Time travel is possible, but all the movies you may have seen have one major mistake. The Earth is not stationary." Sarah started. "If you want to go into the past, you also have to know where the earth was at that time." She signaled for the next couple of slides.

"If you add the speed of the earth around the sun, the speed of the sun around the Milky Way, and the speed of the Milky Way, the Earth is moving approximately 1.3 million miles per hour," Sarah explained.

"This raises a problem. We don't really know how fast we are moving. Speed is based on a fixed object. Space does not have fixed objects. The best we can do to calculate Earth's speed is to base it off background radiation. We do this because background radiation is ever-present and was formed when the universe was created. The radiation is the closest thing we can find to stationary, but it is not absolute."

Sarah could tell she was starting to lose the audience and moved on to the next slide in her presentation. "We have decided the best places to hide in Earth's history are where anomalies are frequent. Earth has three. Most people only know of the Bermuda Triangle. But there is also the Great Lakes Triangle and the Dragons Triangle." The slide changed to a map showing the three locations she just mentioned. "We have decided to build underwater bases in these locations in an attempt not only to hide from the indigenous people but also just in case we are followed. The history of these locations should help hide us."

She said, "We have been doing what we call 'shots' into these locations for several weeks now. The shot it creates a spherical void on the other end. We have been hollowing out a large area in the shape of a diving bell in the rock beneath the ocean floor in which our base will be built. In addition, we have been sending supplies, building materials, and Mech-Bots to make our new home. Everything should be ready for us when we arrive."

Sarah signaled for the next slide, which showed a diagram of a large cavern with structures in it, then signaled for the next several slides showing much of the same.

"For safety reasons, we will not send people directly to the base. Instead, they will be shot to near-Earth orbit. From there, they will fly down unseen. The Great Lakes are too shallow to stay hidden.

The Chinese have claimed the Dragons Triangle for themselves. We will be using the Bermuda Triangle. We have also carved out an area in the Great Lakes and put some supplies just in case a backup is needed. Well, that's the plan," Sarah finished.

Several people raised their hands and wanted to ask a question. Sarah acknowledged one at random, who asked, "What year are we sending these people?"

Dr. Kovonich stood to answer, "Due to the sparse indigenous humans in North America in the mid-1400s – so we are able to hunt and gather food relatively unseen – that is what we are shooting for."

Dr. Kovonich called on another person with a hand up, "Why stay hidden if we will raise their technology?"

"We will not raise the indigenous technology. I want to make that perfectly clear," Dr. Kovonich paused for effect. "If we alter our past we risk the present. I mean, if we do something as simple as introduce Velcro the ramifications are unknown. We know a company called 3M invented it, but who at 3M? If we give it to the wrong person at 3M, how will that affect that person's family or anything else invented by that person? We intend to only raise our technology. Events will play out as we all know they did."

The next person called on asked, "So the descendants of those you will send are down there now? Have we looked or tried to contact them?"

General Long stood and took control of the briefing once more, "Alright, that is the best plan our scientists and elected officials have been able to come up with to ensure the continuation of the species. It is apparent we cannot simply leave the planet and go elsewhere. We will eventually be found. We were planning to only have two shots today, but with the appearance of that, thing, we need to speed things up and get as many as we can. I know this is an extremely stressful situation. Do your job as you were trained. That's all we can ask of you. If our paths do not cross again before this is all over, it has been a pleasure working with each and every one of you. Chaplain Green, can you please give us a closing benediction?"

Chaplain Green did his best to pray for God to watch over his flock in the face of what he just heard. In the end, he was satisfied with what was said and ended with, "Amen."

"Room Ten Hut," was shouted and everyone in the room snapped to attention as General Long made his way to the exit. The general had always given the command to carry on as soon as attention was called, but this time he had to make a quick exit. There were other briefings he had to attend, and he could not be tied up by people stopping him to ask questions when he did not know the answer.

"Carry on," General Long said when he got to the door. He hoped Sarah and Dr. Kovonich were able to extricate themselves quickly and get to the control room, without him having to send an escort for them.

Even with the door closed, General Long could hear the audience bombard Sarah and Dr. Kovonich with questions. He reentered the Auditorium and order was restored when someone shouted "Room Ten Hut."

General Long said, "Sarah, Doctor, come with me." Jim followed, knowing an escape when he saw one.

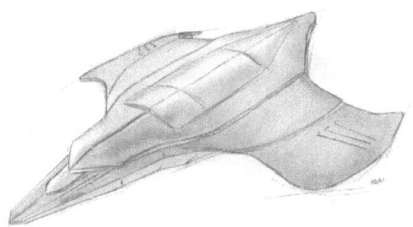

Chapter 19: DEPARTURE

After raising the question of the craft's nomenclature, the historians' office, of all places, had the answer for the proper naming convention. Since the craft was experimental, "Y" remained. This variant was a transport. To Scott's disappointment, a transport shared the designation of "C" with cargo, but to the entire crew's pleasure, the ship was finally listed as a 'Space Plane' and received the designation of YCS-92. However, the crew was disappointed when the historians, office informed them that, thanks to political correctness dating back to the mid-1980s, nose art was no longer allowed. Jim noticed doodling on bulkheads here and there, and some were quite good. But none were allowed to be painted prominently on the outside of the ship.

Jim settled the YCS-92 down onto the shot pad. The ship's needle-like nose protruded under the graceful curve of the bridge glass, all swooped back and seamlessly flowed into the wings. The wings formed the backbone of the craft and curved downward their entire length till the tips were nearly vertical. The back of the ship was angled as sharp as the front, giving the ship the appearance of speed even while sitting perfectly still.

The entire skin of the ship appeared to shimmer due to the way the ship manipulated the space around it to move. Nothing but a slight buzz and the whoosh of air could be heard coming from the ship. The ship settled with a slight compression of the landing gear and a ramp lowered from its belly, which lead up toward the back of the ship. Several land vehicles were loaded, one four-wheel wedge-shaped vehicle and two two-wheeled vehicles. These vehicles were specially designed to fit into the very back of the ship.

Jim appeared at the top of the ramp and observed the loading of the vehicles. When everything was secure, he walked around the outside of the ship and visually inspected every part as his passengers walked up the ramp. There were a lot more passengers than planned. Due to the urgency of the situation, as many people as possible were put on board. Some had to sit on the floor in the corridors, because the ship was not a passenger ship but a ship designed for war.

Jim wanted to check and recheck everything. Nothing like what they were about to do had ever been attempted, at least not with living people. The life of his passengers and crew may depend on his thoroughness.

He rounded the port side of the craft and could make out the silhouette of Sarah in the control room. The two exchanged a wave before she was pulled away by someone behind her. When Sarah returned she appeared frantic and waved at Jim, pointed to the sky, then to his ship over and over again. Jim realized what Sarah was trying to tell him when the base air raid sirens started to blare, and a chill ran down his spine. Jim had checked his craft before he had brought it to the shot pad, so he was confident enough not to finish the rest of his inspection and took off at a sprint toward the ramp.

The massive coils surrounding the launch pad began to come alive with an ever-increasing hum and hue of electrical energy. Even with Jim's sprint he could feel the concrete begin to vibrate from the coils buried beneath his ship as his feet made brief contact with the tarmac. The hum became so loud it was easily distinguishable over the blare of the sirens and still increased in volume and pitch. Huge scaffolding began to move the coils over-top the ship, which engulfed it as sparks resembling lightning began to shoot between the coils. These sparks encouraged Jim to run faster, and he felt the hairs all over his body begin to stand on end. If it hadn't been for the urgency of the situation, he would have found it an interesting sensation.

He made it to the top of the ramp and reached for the button to close the ramp door when he was sent flying by an explosion somewhere outside, which threw him and rocked the ship. Jim impacted and bounced off a bulkhead, leaving him on the floor of the cargo area unconscious.

"I don't know what to do!" Jim heard someone say as he slowly opened his eyes only to close them as rapidly as he could. An intense light shined in his face from above. He reached for the side of his head only to discover a large goose-egg-shaped lump.

Scott said, "Looks like he's starting to come around."

Dr. Stevens said, "That's ship two, Major zero."

Jim asked, "What, are you keeping score?"

Scott said, "You know the ship got me for one."

Dr. Stevens said, "I know. I'm just keeping track of personal scores."

Jim said, "Funny, where am I and what happened?" He slowly opened his eyes and began to sit up to discover he was in the ship's infirmary.

Scott said, "Major, you were out for three hours. We're in big trouble, and we need you."

"What's going on?" Jim said as he slid off the bed and

immediately lost his balance. Scott grabbed his arm before Jim hit the floor.

"It will be best to show you. Doctor, is he okay to leave if I help him?"

"Yes, but if he starts to feel queasy, bring him right back."

Scott said, "Thanks, Doctor." Jim put his arm over Scott's shoulders and the two of them walked together toward the door of the infirmary.

Passengers along the way to the bridge pulled their legs out of the way as Jim and Scott passed.

Passengers that were shoved on at the last minute did not have uniforms and were floating in the weightless environment. Some tried to hang on to something and pulled themselves out of the way. Others resigned themselves to float either curled up into a ball or, stretched out like a board. These passengers looked none too happy as Jim and Scott had to snake their way around them.

Jim asked, "You said I was out for three hours. Why haven't you landed the ship?"

Scott whispered not to be overheard by the passengers, "As I said, it will be best to show you." Scott was worried the passengers might cause trouble if they knew the situation.

The doors to the bridge slid open to reveal a spacious room with windows curved nearly 300 degrees around the bridge. This gave all stations on the bridge a clear view around them outside the ship. The pilot and copilot seats were in the front of the room. Four other stations were scattered around the edges of the room. The captain's chair was centered behind the pilot and co-pilot and in front of a table centered on the bridge.

Jim was able to see immediately they were not where they were supposed to be. Earth was nowhere to be seen, nor was the moon, sun, or any other familiar objects. The stars were not scattered about the sky but instead seemed to be on a single white p ane on the port side of the ship at an odd angle. The starboard side of the ship showed faint specs in various locations.

Jim walked toward the glass on the starboard side of the bridge, where another plane of stars was visible. "What the?" Jim asked no one in particular and then got an idea of their possible locat on. Jim leaned over the pilot's seat and reoriented the ship. The two planes of stars became one line that met in the distance before the ship.

Over the ship's intercom, Jim asked for Chief Besch to join him on a private channel, "Chief, I need you to prepare two recon probes."

"I hear there is not much to look at."

"That's why I need the probes."

"Okay, I'm game. What do you need?"

Jim said, "Program them to gain as much distance from us as they can till we begin to move. Then maintain that distance and move with us."

"You got it. Is there anything else?"

"Yes. Launch one straight up and one straight down from our current orientation. Run continuous scans and feed the data of both probes into the computer to analyze our position. That will increase our ability to map where we are."

Chief asked, "Where we are?"

Jim said, "I'll be down there in a few minutes to talk to you, but make this your first priority."

Chief said, "Yes, sir." and closed the channel.

Scott asked, "Major, what are you thinking?" He started pushing buttons on another console. "Where are we?"

"I have a hunch, but I'd like more facts before I make a guess. How many people are on board?"

"We have 35 passengers and a full crew complement."

Jim asked, "35? there should be a couple hundred. What happened?"

"When that air raid siren went off everyone ran for cover. I guess that's all that made it onboard."

"That just might be a blessing in disguise because if I'm right, 35 will still be to many."

Consecutive thumps were heard throughout the ship and the bulkheads vibrated slightly. Jim knew Chief Besch launched the probes. The computer started to display data on one of the displays toward the back of the bridge on the port side. Jim knew it was too early to confirm his assumption but he had to look anyway.

Scott asked, "What do you mean, 'too many'?"

Something Sarah said was stuck in Jim's brain, *'We not only need to know when we want to go but where the Earth was at that time'*.

Jim asked, "How long before the shot did the explosion happen?"

Scott thought for a moment and began shaking his head, "I'm not sure but I think it was at the same time. Why?"

Jim told Scott his suspicion, "What if that explosion caused the shot to go off course? We're 'when' we are supposed to be, but not 'where'."

"What?" Scott looked at Jim, trying to comprehend the idea. "Then where are we?"

"Were you in General Long's briefing this morning?"

"No, I was prepping the ship."

Jim said, "Well, the Earth is moving, well... really fast," the look on Scott's face still showed confusion so he tried to explain it using his hands like Sarah did for him. "The earth is moving around the sun. The sun is moving around the Milky Way. The Milky Way is not only rotating but it is also moving like this." Jim rotated his open hand in an upward direction.

Scott started to nod his head and understood what Jim described, "So, you think we were sent back to the 1400s, but the explosion sent us to a different spot than the Earth was at that time?"

"Now imagine if we are, at the same spot the shot took place. We never moved, only time did,"

"So we have what? Over six hundred years for Earth to get here?"

"Or we go to it." Jim heard the door to the bridge open and Dr. Stevens stepped through. "Doctor, we have 35 passengers and a full crew complement."

Scott said, "You still haven't said why that's too many."

Dr. Stevens said, "About that —"

Jim interrupted, "The air scrubbers can only handle 16," Jim pointed at what was visible outside the bridge glass. "We do not know how long it will take to find Earth or how long it will take to get there."

Dr. Stevens took a deep breath, thought for a moment to take it all in, then let his breath out audibly. "How many escape pods is the ship fitted with? They are equipped with cryogenic capabilities and can hold two people each. In an emergency three."

Scott said, "I'd say this is an emergency."

Jim said, "Eight pods to accommodate the crew of sixteen. Passengers were never figured in on the plans. So that leaves eleven people too many, using air and adding carbon dioxide, if we put three in each pod. Not to mention how much has been used and exhaled already."

"I think I have enough medications needed to induce artificial comas," Dr. Stevens spoke as he thought, "which will reduce the levels but not cut it off as cryo will, so," Dr. Stevens looked at Jim and said, "It might be enough, but I'm not sure."

Scott asked, "Enough for what?"

"To get our oxygen usage to a manageable level."

"If all the passengers are either put in cryo or artificial coma, they will not like it."

"No, they will not." He walked toward the glass of the bridge to get a better look outside. Having never been in space before, it was truly a sight to be seen. "Leaving only military personnel awake, the civilians might scream conspiracy and not see the urgency of the situation."

Jim asked, "Are any of the passengers able to take over the duties of the crew?"

Dr. Stevens said, "Oh, I'm sure of it. They are the best in their fields. I'm certain most of them will fit that bill."

Jim glanced at the screen displaying the compiled data from the probes. The data was a lot more than the last time he looked but still not what he needed. "Doctor, assemble everyone in the cafeteria in one hour. We should have enough data by then to figure out where we are. Also, will you inquire covertly about the best candidates to replace our crew and bring me a list with their areas of expertise to the meeting? I will talk with Chief Besch to find out more about what we need."

"Sure, but we still have a problem."

"What's the matter?"

"I said I have enough medication to induce the comas, but not to maintain them. From the looks of it, they might be under for a long time."

Jim said, "I hope it won't be as long as it looks. But don't you just put them under and, I don't know, just give them the antidote or something when you want them to wake up?"

Dr. Stevens laughed, "It's not quite like that. I have to continually give them medication to keep them in the coma and monitor it so I don't give too much, or too little."

Jim asked, "If you had the raw materials, could you make what you need here on the ship?"

"What do you mean by 'raw materials'?"

"Broken down to their basic elements. Like the periodic table."

Dr. Stevens asked, "Do you have that?"

"No, but I think I can get it."

"I will have to do some research but I should be able to make what we need. How are you able to get basic elements out here?"

"I think I have an idea. The ship's drive analyzes each molecule as it manipulates it. We can program it to deposit certain elements in collection containers."

Scott asked, "Really?"

Jim said, "Researchers built it into the ship to analyze what's up here. They wanted me to take samples as I did the 'up and back' flight tests that lead up to the strike during Operation CAMPFIRE. Those systems I think are still built into the ship."

A surprised "Huh," was the response from both Scott and Dr. Stevens.

Jim said, "I'll need a list of what you need."

"That might take a while. Like I said, I need to do some research to find out what I need."

"Will you have enough medication for the time being?"

Dr. Stevens said, "I think so. If not they will just start waking up." He turned to leave the bridge but paused, "How are you feeling?"

"A slight headache, but other than that, I'm okay. Thanks for asking. Scott, have you been able to inspect the ship since the shot?"

"Chief had a crewman complete a damage report and no damage was reported. He also performed a systems diagnostic and everything came back normal."

"Good, thank you." Jim was distracted by the data streaming in from the probes and he thought about multiple tasks that needed to be done. "Take a team and prep the escape pods. Lock them down so they don't accidentally eject. And I forgot to ask Doctor Stevens; Where is the most convenient place for him to use as the 'coma ward'?"

Scott asked cautiously, "I'll ask him that. How bad is it?"

"I'm not sure yet." He flipped through the data on the screen, "but I think we will make it."

"Thanks, because I was worried this would turn into a generational ship. I've never seen anything like that." Scott pointed at the scene outside the bridge glass.

Jim said, "Neither have I. Living with Sarah opened my eyes to things I never thought possible. You knew this was a one-way trip."

"Yes, on Earth. Not stuck out here in a tin can. I bet you didn't bet on this when you woke up today."

"No I didn't. We're not out of the woods yet but getting there." He finished what he was looking at, and followed Scott out of the bridge. "If you need me I will either be on the bridge or engineering. I have a few things I want to check. Where is John?"

Scott said, "I asked him to get some sleep while we figure stuff out."

Jim said, "I doubt he is getting any. I know I couldn't. Let him know about the meeting, please."

When they entered engineering, one of the crew shouted, "Captain on deck," and everyone not involved with a critical task stopped what they were doing and stood at attention. Engineering was located one deck down from the bridge in the strongest part of the ship, beneath the wing spars.

Jim said, "As you were." Then he asked a crewman, "Where is the chief?"

The crewman pointed toward the opposite end of the room and he said, "He is checking on the core."

Jim said to the crewman, "Thank you."

He found Chief Besch peering into the core with the inspection cover in one hand and a dark visor in the other. The visor resembled a welder's helmet. The core was essentially a micro star and could only be viewed using safety shields, and only for brief moments or the viewer risked singed retinas. Jim did not want to disturb the chief while he performed such a delicate task and waited for him to finish.

After Chief Besch put the inspection cover back in place, he noticed Jim. "Welcome back among the living. I heard our voyage didn't start so well for you."

"Not exactly as I planned. How does the core look?"

"We're in luck, everything is in order, and I got the probes launched as you requested. But that's not what brings you here, is it?"

"Can we go somewhere and talk?"

Chief Besch closed his eyes for a second and raised his eyebrows, "Sounds serious! Did someone use your personal lavatory and forget to flush again?"

Jim scolded, "Chief!" He told Chief Besch their situation and the two of them spoke at length about the capabilities of the propulsion system. If Jim was correct about their location, he would push the engine for an extended length of time to get back to Earth.

Chief Besch was confident the engine would do what Jim asked, but because the system had never been tested for the length of time and speeds Jim was suggesting, Chief said, "I know it will be like taking your date to a hotel after prom. I'm confident my team won't let her Daddy show."

Jim asked, "What?"

"We will take care of your girl, she will deliver."

"We're talking about the ship, right?"

"Of course! What did you think I was talking about?"

Jim knew he was about to drop a bombshell. He cautiously asked, "Which crewman can you do without?"

"Excuse me?" Chief could not believing his ears. "Do you not want your girl to cross the finish line?"

"Chief, I don't know how long till we reach Earth. The CO2 scrubbers can't keep up. If we don't do something soon we will be in serious trouble. Doctor Stevens said all the passengers need to either go into cryo suspension in the escape pods, or artificial comas. I have a feeling if only military are left on board we may have problems getting the passengers to cooperate."

"So to nip it in the bud you're offering..."

"I asked Doctor Stevens to find out who among the passengers could replace a crewman."

Chief got defensive, "Oh so my crew is replaceable? Do you know how long it took to get them to work as an effective team? I'm sure we could find someone among the passengers that's played a flight sim."

Jim said, "Chief, I didn't –"

"I'm just pulling your chain. I'll talk it over with my crew and ask for a volunteer. I'll get you the name in an hour. You should see the look on your face."

"You've got half an hour. We're having a meeting in the cafeteria in 35 minutes with everyone on board and need the name by then. I don't like making unreasonable demands but the longer we wait, the more dire our oxygen situation gets and that's all the time I can give you."

Chief Besch said, "I understand. I'll get it done."

"Thanks Chief. Be sure everyone comes to the meeting. Put the engine on idle, or whatever it is you do. I'll be on the bridge if you need anything." Jim left confident the ship would get them home.

When Jim returned to the bridge, the data screen on his left confirmed they were between the fingers of the Milky Way. Earth was either to their left, or their right, but it was unclear which way that was. As the probes got farther from the ship, the mapping got more precise, and hopefully, as soon as the meeting was over, he would have the direction for them to go.

He gazed out the window of the bridge at nothing in particular. Thoughts of Sarah entered his mind. He wondered what the explosion was and if she was okay. He got an idea, went to a console on the starboard side of the bridge, and searched video feeds for the right angle. When he found it he backed it up to just before the explosion.

The ship shown in General Long's briefing made a strafing run on the base. The shit was shot at by two pursuing fighters. It dodged a shot from a fighter and collided with a coil. The coil and the ship exploded, which triggered a chain reaction in the other coils and initiated the shot prematurely.

The control room Sarah was in appeared to be intact when the video turned completely white from the combination of the explosion and the shot. Jim backed up the video and watched it again and again. He noticed a shock wave from the explosion blew out the glass of the control room just as the video cut out. Sarah was standing near the window when the shock wave hit. Jim had no idea if she was okay.

He discovered the explosion was nearly simultaneous with the shot. What that meant to their predicament he didn't know, but maybe one of the scientists on board would know what to do with the data.

"Major," Scott's voice came over the speakers on the bridge, "we are assembled in the cafeteria."

"Sorry, I lost track of time checking on something. How are we on your end?"

"The doctor said the crew quarters in the nose of the ship will be easiest for him to monitor, and we were able to prep all but one escape pod. We will take care of that one after the meeting. Nothing is wrong with it, we just ran out of time."

"Understood, I'm on the way." Jim walked across the bridge and checked the mapping data one last time. He saw the computer put Earth on the port side of the ship. He was glad they now had a direction to go and darted out the door.

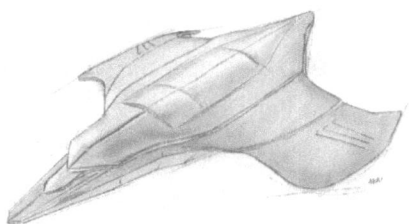

Chapter 20: NOT ENOUGH AIR

Jim entered the cafeteria and said "As you were," before anyone was able to call the room to attention. He tried to prevent the civilians in the room from being annoyed by military protocol and saved time by having everyone remain seated.

The tables were laid out perpendicular to the food dispensers on the left wall from the door. He walked toward the middle of the food dispensers and asked those sitting on the floor to move to the opposite wall, but when he turned and saw several people without uniforms floating weightless, he turned back and said, "Never mind."

Dr. Stevens handed him a short list of names he felt were best suited to replace a crewman. Jim looked for and spotted Chief Besch, who sat in the middle of the room. Chief Besch gave him a thumbs up to acknowledge he had a volunteer. He smiled and nodded at the chief. At least something today worked as planned. Hopefully, this meeting would also.

The civilians ignored protocol and bombarded him with questions all at once almost as soon as he said "Hello." His headache had faded some time ago, but it gradually began to make its presence known again. He pointed his nose toward the ceiling, pushed his head as far back as he could, and rolled it to each side to ease the tension in his neck. He hoped that would get rid of the last remaining tendrils of the headache, and he waited for the room to simmer down a bit.

Chief Besch, with a deep voice, bellowed, "At ease." The room became silent except for a light chuckle from the military members in the room.

Jim let out a deep breath. "Thanks, Chief." He knew *'why did we not land?'* was on everyone's mind.

"As you know, we were supposed to be sent to near-Earth orbit sometime in the 1400s."

The civilians in the room became loud again with questions about *'supposed to?'* but became quiet again when Chief Besch began to stand.

Jim said, "An alien ship collided with one of the coils and exploded. I think that initiated the shot prematurely. One thing is for certain, we are not where we are supposed to be."

Everyone glanced at their neighbor with confusion painted on their face.

"Just where are we?" asked one of the civilians before most were able to process what was said.

Jim said, "We were supposed to be in orbit around Earth and land shortly after. If I'm right, Earth won't be here for a long time."

The scientists in the room started whispering among themselves while the engineers looked bewildered.

Jim said, "Currently the ship's computer is gathering data to plot a course to Earth. In the meantime, we are using more air than the ship is capable of cleaning and replacing. We have to put as many people as possible in cryo. Several more will have to be placed into a chemically induced coma or we will soon run out of air. The ship simply was not designed for this many people. We will plot the quickest route to Earth."

One of the scientists sarcastically said, "Is this where you fold a piece of paper in half, push a pencil through it and tell us this is how we are getting home?" The outburst caused several chuckles among the civilians and just a few of the military. Mostly just those who felt a bit scared at the moment chuckled in a nervous response.

"Not exactly." Jim laughed at the scene that played out many times in popular movies years ago.

Another person toward the back of the room asked, "Why did they put so many of us on here knowing there's not enough air?"

Jim said, "For short-term space travel, like the near-Earth orbit shot we were aiming for, we would have been perfectly fine. This was completely unexpected, and the ship simply cannot handle this many people. Since the crew is vital to keeping the ship running, I need all passengers to report to the escape pods where you will be placed in cryo for the journey to Earth. Unfortunately, there are not enough escape pods to bring the oxygen consumption level down to a maintainable level. Those who cannot fit in the escape pods, please report to Doctor Stevens in the crew quarters, at the forward part of the ship. My crew is giving up their sleeping quarters for your comfort. Those people will be put into a chemically induced coma and monitored constantly by Doctor Stevens."

The cafeteria exploded with discontent among the civilians who felt they were being singled out as second class to the military. Jim tried to speak over the crowd in an attempt to explain what needed to happen for the survival of all that are onboard, but it was a losing battle. Even Chief Besch was not able to return order.

Someone near the door turned out the lights, only to turn them back on after quiet was restored. Jim looked toward the door and gave the crewman standing there a nod of thanks.

"Look, we are not in near-Earth orbit, and to be truthful with you, up until a few moments ago, I did not know where Earth was," Jim confided to everyone in the room in an attempt to drive home the severity of the situation they were all in. "Just before I left the bridge the computer finally found where Earth is. I did not have time to calculate how far away or how long it will take to get there. Regardless, our air supply and the CO_2 scrubbers will not last long enough at the current rate of consumption. This has to happen. We don't have a choice."

The civilians began to discuss options among themselves in a more civilized manner and at a volume easily spoken over.

Dr. Stevens said, "I understand your apprehension, and the more time we waste finding a solution, the more dire the situation gets. If we stand any chance of getting back to Earth, this ship must be maintained by an experienced crew. If the roles were reversed, I'd feel the same."

Jim said, "Doctor Stevens and I spoke about this and one of my crew volunteered to take the place of one of the civilians. He or she will go under chemical coma so you have a civilian representative awake and looking out for your welfare." He paused a moment and felt the tension in the room ease a bit. "Is this acceptable?"

The civilians in the room started looking at each other, not wanting to be the first to agree with the plan, but they all started to slowly nod their heads. The military started looking around trying to figure out who volunteered for such a procedure.

Jim continued when he saw he had the approval of almost everyone in the room. "Doctor Stevens compiled a list of five people most suited to help maintain the ship's systems and be your representative on board." He held a sheet of paper in his right hand and set it on the table in front of him. "Please stay behind for final selection by Chief Besch. Everyone else please go with Doctor Stevens."

Everyone started to move around and Jim asked, "Chief, who is our volunteer?"

Chief said, "Sergeant White," and pointed to the man who turned out the lights earlier.

Jim said "Thank you, Sergeant White." He smiled at the man, who appeared to be the same age as Jim. "Please go with Doctor Stevens. Before you know it, we will be back on Earth."

Sgt. White said, "That's what I'm counting on, sir." He shook the hand him offered, then followed Dr. Stevens.

The military personnel began to leave the room to go back to work. All the civilians walked past the table to see if their name was on the paper. Most were disappointed and followed Dr. Stevens. Those who did not have a uniform were pulled along like helium-filled balloons. In any other situation, the sight would be comical.

Chief Besch, Scott, and the five who were selected stayed behind and sat around the middle table. The five all knew each other, and after Scott filled them in further on the situation they faced, Chief Besch told them what was needed and expected. They all agreed Samantha Green was the best person for the job.

Samantha, who preferred to be called Sam, followed Chief Besch out of the cafeteria. Meanwhile, Scott escorted the four to the escape pods. Crewmen tried to ensure the occupants of each escape pod were comfortable, in an attempt to keep everyone calm before the door was closed and the cryo unit activated. Dr. Stevens checked the data display to ensure everything was in order.

The escape pods ran along the sides of the ship slightly below the bomb release doors, about mid-way up the fuselage and under the wings which gave them added protection. They were centrally located from all sections of the ship. The pods were canted to be jettisoned down and toward the back of the ship.

Each person got in the pod feet first. They laid on their back and were strapped down. The pod would rotate 120 degrees to allow the next person to enter. When full, one person was strapped against each side wall and the third was strapped to the floor, facing each other in a triangular formation.

The two strapped to the walls were weightless since there wasn't any gravity plating in the area. They felt a bit awkward as the pod rotated going from gravity to weightless, and back again as the first person passed over the top. With the straps tight they felt comfortable, if not claustrophobic.

Scott explained to each person how to get out of the pod in the unlikely event they woke. Scott knew no one would wake unless there was a leak in the system which allowed the gasses to escape, but it reassured the occupants.

When all the occupants of the pod were ready, Scott closed and sealed the hatch, knocked on the glass, and gave a thumbs-up to the persons inside.

Each would either respond with a thumbs up, smile, or just shake their head. Soon after, their eyes closed as they fell into a deep sleep. The pod filled with cryo gasses, and the glass frosted over.

Dr. Stevens checked the status screen for each occupant and gave his approval, then moved on to the next pod.

The pair worked together until all the pods were full, activated, and the occupants' stats were verified. Scott also verified the launch interlocks were engaged.

When all the escape pods were full, the two made their way toward the crew quarters, where the remaining eleven nervously waited to be put into a coma. On their way, Dr. Stevens asked, "The vehicles in the cargo bay – do they have CO2 scrubbers?"

Scott had a slightly puzzled look on his face. Dr. Stevens explained, "In case we land on a moon or something without an atmosphere."

Scott went to a communications panel on a nearby wall and paged Jim. He explained the doctor's question and Jim checked the vehicles' capabilities on the computer. Moments later, Jim's voice came over the communications panel. "I will send an engineering team and get those scrubbers going. That car can scrub the CO_2 of two people. Thank the doctor for me. Good thinking."

Scott said, "I see two of the people that were on the list. Should I send them to you for assignment?"

Jim said, "Just send them to the bridge for now. We will deal with the work details later. Finish what you're doing and head to the bridge. We have enough data now to plot a course and get underway."

"Yes sir," Scott said excitedly as he looked at Dr. Stevens.

Before Scott could ask, Dr. Stevens said, "Go ahead, the crewmen and I can finish this."

Scott approached the two he saw earlier, explained the discovery of the additional scrubbers, and asked if they would join him as he walked to the bridge two floors up.

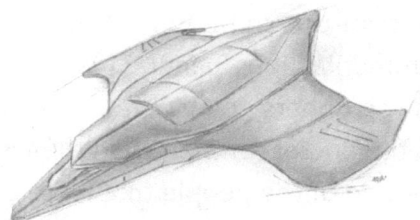

Chapter 21: HEADING – EARTH

The bridge had a buzz of excitement. Lt John Anders sat in the left pilot's seat flipping buttons as instructed by a crewman doing systems checks on the rear starboard side display. Jim poured over data being compiled on a display on the port side of the bridge. And a few crewmen that mostly just wanted to be a part of what was happening milled about out of the way and stayed quiet to avoid being kicked out. Everyone was excited to get the ship moving toward home.

The two civilians following Scott were Claire St Patrick and Steve Harris. Both Claire and Steve let out an audible exclamation of astonishment when they saw the view out of the glass.

With the distance the probes were from the ship, the computer was able to generate an accurate 3D image of the celestial objects that had been identified so far. Jim plotted a course on the display which showed their current position and the location of Earth.

Claire took particular interest in what he was doing, "I'm sorry, but you're looking at that wrong."

As Jim turned, he was drawn to Claire's intoxicating eyes; they made him think of the light blue water of the Caribbean. He took in the light splattering of freckles across her nose that faded as they crossed her high cheekbones. Soft reddish-brown curly hair framed the angelic face before him.

His distraction was interrupted when Claire asked with a smile,

"May I?" and pointed toward the display he was working on.

Jim stammered, "Uh um, sure," as he stepped out of her way. He saw Scott smile, which caused him to feel self-conscious and guilty about Sarah. He gave Scott a stern look and turned his attention back to what she was doing. He tried not to take in her other attributes as she leaned over to enter data.

"You're plotting the course to where Earth is, not where it will be when we get there. With the course you were planning, we will miss it, but if you go this direction," Claire pointed toward empty space, "you could shave quite a bit of time off our trip."

Jim looked at what she suggested and asked, "Are you sure?"

"I'm no expert, but I did dabble a bit in astrophysics back in college. Look at it like this, does a pilot flying from Los Angeles to Japan fly directly there?"

A military pilot would never fly that route. They would fly to Hickam AFB in Hawaii, then to Japan. Jim had no way of knowing the answer to Claire's question. He said, "I don't know."

Claire explained, "Pilots fly west only partway, then turn south. While the plane is flying, the Earth is rotating and brings Japan under the path of the plane, saving fuel and time. That is similar to what we do here."

Impressed, Jim said "Sounds like you have a new job," and pointed at the display.

Claire apologized, "Oh, I didn't mean to step on your toes."

"Trust me, you didn't. The job is yours. Obviously we need someone that knows more about navigation than I do." Jim stepped back and watched her work for a moment. He was grateful she came along when she did but knew she could be trouble. Shaking his head, he turned to find the next task that needed his attention.

Out of earshot of Claire, Scott asked, "What do you think?"

Knowing what Scott implied, Jim said, "Shut up."

The two walked toward the captain's chair. "She's got the

credentials," Scott said. "And what a package. I'm sure glad Doctor Stevens thought of the scrubbers in the car before we put her in the coma."

"You didn't."

"Oh come on. Like you didn't notice."

John looked over his shoulder and asked, "What are you two talking about?"

Scott said, "Just fly the ship."

John said, "But we're not moving."

Jim said, "Then make sure nothing hits us," and turned his attention back to Scott. "You'd better not have pulled her because of that. Did you?"

"What?" Scott looked defensive and tried to explain why Claire was not put into a coma. "No! She was one of the five we interviewed after the meeting, when Samantha Green was selected. After you said we can keep two more awake, I saw her and Steve Harris. Besides, you saw the way she stepped up and helped without being asked."

Jim said, "That might be true, but no more comments like that, or this just might come back and bite us."

"What do you mean? How can it bite us?

"When we get back to earth and wake everyone up. If anyone thinks we kept someone out of cryo or a coma just because they were attractive, someone is going to have to answer for it."

Scott said, "I swear that's not why."

"I hope so. We will be moving soon, so help John with the final checks."

"This is going to be a fun trip. You're not a player anymore, right?" Scott said with a smile. Jim shook his head and hoped he was joking.

Everything was being taken care of, and Jim was finally able to take a break and just observe everyone prepare the ship. The nose of the ship that was visible outside the bridge window started to shimmer as the core's energy began to reach the drive plates which encompassed the entire skin of the ship. The transit home would begin as soon as the navigation coordinates Claire worked on were transferred to the helm.

John said, "Major, all systems green, coordinates received and set. Ready for your command."

Jim said, "Take us home."

The acceleration was so smooth, the inertia was compensated by the gravity plating, and the nearest stars were so far away, it was difficult to tell if the ship was moving.

Claire compiled data from the probes launched earlier and sent course corrections for the probes to follow the ship at their current distance. She was able to see the ship move in relation to the background radiation. Using background radiation to measure speed was the accepted method. She relayed the data to the helm and sent course corrections as needed.

Several minutes passed and Jim said, "Any time now, Lieutenant."

John said, "Sir, our speed is already over 1600 miles per hour and accelerating fast."

Sitting next to John, Scott looked at his screens and nodded over his shoulder to confirm.

Jim heard the crewmen milling around the bridge doors comment, "Was that it?"

Those on the bridge who were not in view of the data were unaware of the ship's movement. This continued for several boring moments till a speck of light whizzed by the port side of the bridge glass, then another shot past above them. Other than sensors, the streaks of light were the only visible evidence the ship was moving.

The specks of light increased in number and intensity al around the ship as the ship's engine manipulated the interstellar dust it made contact with and used it to push itself through space. As the ship accelerated, it was able to make contact with more dust in greater quantity, and pushed the ship even faster till the entire bridge was awash with light so intense that the glass had to darken to allow the bridge crew to see what they were doing.

The glass blocked most of the light caused by the engine, but they only had to look toward the leading edge of the wings to see the intensity of it all. The dance being played out on the wing was mesmerizing and relaxing to watch, like staring into a bonfire.

Jim pulled a glass panel from the arm of his chair, which remained attached by a telescoping pole. He tapped buttons only visible from his position and checked various systems on the ship. Moments later a crackle came from the ceiling of the bridge and every deck of the ship, then Jim's voice addressed the crew. "Good job, everyone. All systems are green across the board and we are on our way home."

Everyone cheered at the news.

In the forward part of the ship where Dr. Stevens worked, he sensed the tension lighten and the remaining civilians being put into the artificial coma were not as reluctant. They were mostly apprehensive of what would happen while they slept and nervous about the needle being stuck into their veins. Jim's announcement made things easier.

Jim watched for a while until he began to yawn. He realized there was nothing he needed to attend to, and he stowed the panel. "I'll be in my quarters if needed," he said to Scott. "Have the department heads make a duty roster. Have those not on duty get some shut-eye, and you get some rest when you can. It's been a long day for all of us."

Scott said, "Some of the crew's quarters are being used by the doctor."

Jim asked, "Are there enough beds for now to let at least half the crew get some rest?" Scott nodded his head. "Tell them to use whatever is available and get some rest. We will sort out bunk space later."

"Mr. Harris," Jim asked of the last remaining person on the bridge without a job, "Will you please help Doctor Stevens? I know his work has gotten much harder, and I'm sure he would appreciate the extra hands."

"Yes sir, I'd be happy to." Steve did not like the idea of being put to sleep for however long it took to get to Earth and was eager to do anything useful to avoid the possibility.

Jim said, "Just till we find something more to your talents," as he left the bridge.

Jim did not go directly to his quarters, which was across the hall from the bridge. That placed the captain's quarters partially beneath the wing spars and above the engine room. He aimlessly wandered the ship and checked things over. He wanted to make sure everything was working correctly and that he could get some rest without tossing around the entire time, worried he forgot something.

When he finally did go to his quarters and lay down under the covers, he had trouble falling asleep, because Sarah was not beside him. He had been away from her before, but this time was different. His mind kept wandering to the last image he saw of her on the video.

Thoughts of Sarah began to flood his dreams, along with the predicament he and the crew were in. He did not understand why he missed her so much after only one day. But that explosion – is she okay? Will he ever see her again?

He dreamed about the two of them lying on the couch telling each other about their day. At the time, Jim didn't understand most of what she said; He just loved to hear her voice. Now in his dream, those words had more meaning and clarity. He understood more than when she originally said it. He knew he was dreaming and tried to focus on certain things Sarah said only to lose them when he woke. What little he remembered, Jim rolled over in his mind until he found himself asleep again.

Another dream but a different time from the last, and again Sarah told him about work and what she and Dr. Kovonich discovered that day.

Jim thought there must be a reason he was having these dreams and felt they might contain a solution to get back to Earth quicker. He stopped trying to focus on certain things and just let the dreams happen, which became a maze to navigate. Time began to lose dimension.

More time and information was presented in the dream than possible, considering how long he slept. It dawned on him that the lives of everyone on board depended on his command experience, and a heavy weight came over him.

The dream slowed and focused on the image of Amy and Eric and the tragedy that befell them, only to be replaced by Claire looking at him, studying him. She was wearing a long white sundress and appeared to be waiting for something. Jim felt guilty but walked toward her and stopped when she turned and looked out the glass of the bridge. He admired her backside till the blackness outside the ship exploded. Ribbons of light danced like lightning from the center and fizzled away in sparks along their path.

The glass of the bridge vibrated as shock-waves buffeted the ship. Claire looked over her shoulder at him with a smile and pointed at the explosion. Jim noticed Sarah standing beside him, also pointing.

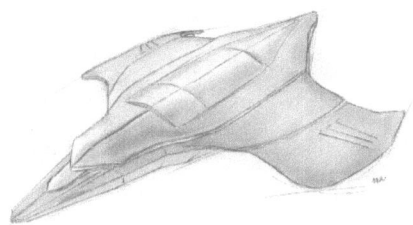

Chapter 22: CLAIRE

Claire St Patrick — when that name was heard, the image of a demure Irish lass with fiery red hair and piercing green eyes came to mind. That was far from reality for Claire. With one look, the simplest description that came to mind was Viking warrior. One look at her face and the description changed to Viking goddess. A tall, muscular woman with reddish-brown, lightly curled hair, mesmerizing blue eyes, and a light splattering of freckles across her nose and cheeks.

Claire had been unlucky in the romance department; she always attracted men who looked at her physical brawn, and lacked the intellectual capacity to stimulate her. Instead of romancing her as a woman, they would challenge her to tests of strength.

The men she was attracted to were intimidated by her size. It didn't help that her beauty made these men think she was out of their league. If someone took the time to talk with her, they soon realized she was very kind, contradictory to the physical presence she commanded, and had a brain as powerful as her body was strong — A catch for any man that treated her the way a woman deserved.

With several degrees in physics under her belt, Claire easily adapted to problems presented to her. This was a major factor that got her a spot on the ship.

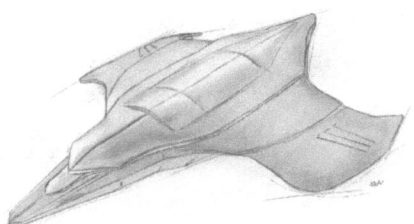

Chapter 23: ALTERNATE HEADINGS?

Jim shot out of bed and slammed his hand on the comm button next to his bed. Captain Dixon was on the bridge and responded, "Bridge here."

Jim hurriedly said, "Begin scans for quantum filaments," as he hurried to get dressed, "I'm on my way to the bridge."

As he ran out the door of his quarters, he heard Scott reply over the intercom "Did you say quantum filaments? What is that?"

Jim did not hear the last of the conversation since he already left the room and bounded across the hall in a quick walk bordering on a jog toward the bridge. When he saw Claire analyzing data at the navigation terminal, he paused in his stride and felt his face flush, remembering the dream. He walked toward her and asked, "What are quantum filaments, and baryon acoustic oscillations, and how can they help us?"

Claire was surprised by the question and said, "Quantum filaments are something made up in science fiction shows." She saw the disappointment on his face and added, "I think you mean the cosmic web. It contains filaments and is believed to be surrounded by baryon acoustic oscillations."

"What are these filaments?"

"The filaments are believed to contain dark matter and are what create the gravity between galaxies and keeps them... connected, if you will."

"What is dark matter?"

Claire explained, "Visible matter is not enough to account for the gravity needed to maintain the orbit of all the celestial bodies we know of, so the terms dark matter and dark energy were invented. The filaments are believed to contain up to eighty-four percent dark matter. The rest is hydrogen gas. Baryon Acoustic Oscillations were formed when the universe was first created in what is called 'The Big Bang'. Matter and dark matter annihilated each other while gravity tried to pull everything together. The two created ripples in gravity and matter known as Baryon Acoustic Oscillations. These oscillations are formed by dense and less dense regions of space. I don't particularly agree with the 'Big Bang Theory', but that's a different subject."

She could tell she lost everyone that turned to listen. She learned it's pretty easy to get blank stares when talking about astrophysics and quantum mechanics so she tried a different approach. "The orbit of the planets are mathematically not correct, because there is not enough known matter to create the gravity needed to keep the planets and everything else on their observed trajectory. Something unknown to us must be making up the difference. That's where dark matter and dark energy come into play. It's believed large concentrations of dark matter are in the filaments, and the oscillations can be pictured as the peaks and valleys of a phonograph record radiating out from the filaments as increased and decreased regions of matter."

Jim said, "I think I understand. Can we detect these filaments, and can the Faraday-Maxwell drive manipulate dark matter?"

Claire raised an eyebrow and thought for a moment. "We can see hydrogen gas in the filaments when it is illuminated by a pulsar, but that's not very common. I'm not that familiar with the drive, but based on what I heard about how it works, if dark matter exists, I don't see why not. But why would you want to?"

"The more matter around the ship, the faster the ship can go and the quicker we get back to Earth."

"Dark matter is only a theory. We don't know for sure if it exists. It's only been proven in mathematical equations. And we don't know what it will do when it comes in contact with normal matter," Claire started to become concerned about where the conversation may lead, or lead the ship. "As far as anyone knows, when matter and dark matter come in contact with each other both are destroyed."

"These oscillations, or the hydrogen you mentioned, are we able to chart where denser pockets of matter are? Or detect where a filament may be near our path? If the Faraday-Maxwell drive can manipulate dark matter, none of it should touch us because the drive moves it over the skin by changing its polarity and does not come in direct contact with it. If I understand the drive correctly."

Claire nervously said, "Yes," and nodded her head. "That is how I understand the engine works, but that's an awfully big risk. The charting of denser regions – I think so, but it will take some time. The hydrogen – we'd need a pulsar, or figure out how a pulsar illuminates hydrogen."

Jim said, "You, Steve Harris, and Samantha, Sam Green are the smartest we've got that are not – for the lack of a better word – sleeping. Can you three get together and look into the feasibility of this? Or something else we are overlooking to get us home faster?"

Claire said, "Absolutely," and asked Steve and Sam to meet her in the cafeteria.

Jim said, "Thank you," and watched Claire as she walked toward the bridge doors.

Scott asked, "How did you come up with that?"

"I didn't. I was dreaming about Sarah and it was something she said."

"Baryon Acoustic Oscillations? You have some weird dreams. I hope it pans out. Otherwise, it looks like we are in for a long flight." He pointed toward the front of the ship indicating the stars have barely moved since they started heading home about 6 hours ago.

"You have no idea," Jim said as he remembered what Claire wore in the dream. "You know the ship will continue to accelerate. How fast we are moving now is just a fraction of how fast we will be moving in a day or week from now. When we do get back to Earth, we will be trying to find ways to slow down. The engine put in reverse will not be enough, unless we start slowing down halfway there, and that will make for a long trip."

Scott said, "This is my second time in space. The first was just a quick up and back during Operation CAMPFIRE. I thought this thing accelerated faster than this."

"Just once? I lost track of how many I did. It must have been every day the brass wanted me to test something different." As he remembered all the flights, he said, "The design of this ship truly got perfected during Operation CAMPFIRE and probably would not be possible without all those trips. It only performed one combat sortie, the one we met on. The rest were just to get its feet wet. Actually, we are accelerating really fast, but it's been on a curve, so our bodies have a hard time feeling it. It doesn't help that the closest objects are so far away, making it look like we're sitting still."

Scott asked, "You mentioned finding ways to slow down, any ideas?"

"I don't know," and shrugged his shoulders. "Hopefully Claire and her team will know the answer to that."

"Could there be something in the computer?"

"Good idea. While we are on bridge duty, let's research that. For now, let's keep it between us. We need to keep the crew's spirits up by focusing on getting home. As far as they are concerned, that is what we are looking in to. I'll ask Claire when we get closer if we don't find anything. Agreed?"

Scott said, "Good call."

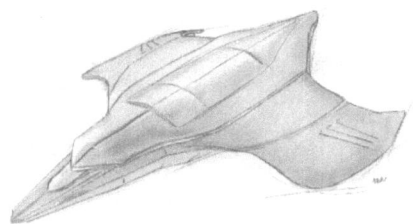

Chapter 24: OPTIONS

Several uneventful hours passed before Jim received a request from Claire to meet with Sam, Steve and herself in the cafeteria. He asked Scott to join him.

On the way to the cafeteria, the two discussed how things were going when Jim heard Dr. Stevens yelling his name. He turned and saw the doctor running to catch up.

Jim asked, "What's going on?"

He was out of breath, and said, "I'm glad I ran into you." He leaned over, put his hands on his knees trying to catch his breath, "Oh, I'm not used to that. I've been doing research on how to make the drugs I need to – whew, give me a second," and put his hand on this left side.

"Will you be alright? Just how far did you run?"

"From the end of the corridor. Now I know why you military types do PT (Physical Training). I'll be alright. Anyway, I don't think I'm capable of making the drugs needed to keep the comas going. It's way too complicated for me and I think we need a chemist."

"Are you sure?"

Dr. Stevens said, "Just to make the ingredients from basic elements is complicated enough. Then combine those at just the right rate and temperature so it doesn't blow up in your face. And that's just for one of the drugs I use."

Jim asked, "Blow up? Just how dangerous is this?"

"It all depends on the quantity being mixed, but whoever does it needs to keep it to small batches."

"Does it pose any risk to the ship?"

Dr. Stevens shrugged his shoulders and shook his head, "I don't know. Probably not in small quantities."

Jim said, "We are going to meet with Claire, Sam and Steve now. If we wake a chemist, one of them will have to be put under."

Scott said, "They are not going to like that."

Jim said, "No they will not. It has not even been a day and each of them has contributed in some way. Is there any other way?"

Dr. Stevens said, "None that I can think of. Unless you know of a pharmacy nearby."

Jim shook this head and said, "Let's get this over with."

When Jim and Scott entered the cafeteria, it was evident a debate had gone on for some time by the crumpled-up papers strewn about and the bewildered looks on the faces of a few crew members who were eating lunch on the other side of the room and casually looking on.

Jim said, "I hope this was productive." He approached the table and took a seat.

Steve started to speak but was quickly hushed by Claire. It was apparent there were a few ruffled feathers between the two. "We are certain we can chart more dense regions of interstellar dust. The probes that were launched – are they capable of looking in the ultraviolet light spectrum, or be reprogrammed to do so?" She paused for a second and glanced at Steve. "Also, we feel it is too big a gamble to try to use a filament and a big waste of time looking for one in this part of space." Steve appeared to deflate a bit and opened his mouth but did not say anything. "With what we know of them, I highly doubt we will find one between here and where we are going."

Jim asked, "I take it the usefulness of the filaments is debatable?"

"Yes," Claire said and glanced at both Steve and Sam, "I feel the best course of action is to chart denser regions of dust and plot the fastest course home. If," Claire stressed the word, "we happen to come across a filament along the way we then deal with it, but for now, we should stick with what is known."

Jim looked at the three and studied their faces. It appeared they were all in agreement with that plan. "Okay, what do we need to do?"

Claire motioned for Sam to explain since this was more in her expertise. "From what Claire described, with the data from the probes, we will be able to make a very good 3-D map of where the dust will be densest – provided the probes are able to be reprogrammed to look in the ultraviolet spectrum of light. To be more specific, we are looking for thermal radiation between the wavelengths of three to one hundred eighty micrometers."

Scott asked, "What happens to the probe when it's reprogrammed? Does it reboot, or what?" The three civilians looked at each other, not sure what the answer was. "If there is any possibility the probes will not come back online and we lose them, can we just program one, make sure it's working, then program the other? That way we don't lose all tracking from the distance they are currently at?"

All three were in agreement with that plan, and Jim was glad Scott thought of it. The farther the probes travel from the ship, the more accurate their mapping will be in the three dimensional plain, allowing them to plot the best route home. The loss of one probe would affect the imagery only slightly since the ship itself was also scanning, but the loss of both probes would set them back to two-dimensional mapping.

Jim asked, "How quickly can it be done?"

Sam said, "Well, first we need to see if the probes will accept reprogramming for what we need. Can I check a probe still on the ship to see its capability? Then download its current program to see what needs to be changed. It shouldn't take long."

"Absolutely, Scott, will you help Sam with that? Get with Chief Besch. He may already have what you need." Jim paused for a bit. He tried to figure out the best way to break the news, then finally decided to just say it. "Doctor Stevens here brought me some bad news."

The three looked at each other wondering '*What now*'?

Jim continued, "In order to maintain the comas, some drugs need to be manufactured and Doctor Stevens does not feel he is qualified to make them. He requested us to find a chemist."

Claire said, "Well that shouldn't be hard – wait a minute. Are you telling me..."

"Yes, one of you will have to take the chemist's place in cryo or coma, wherever he is."

Steve ran through his mind the events that had transpired so far and each of their contributions; Claire had plotted a shorter route to Earth and took charge of the group; Sam was the original nominee to replace a crewman and would work on the reprogramming of the probes to find an even faster route to Earth; him? All he had done was assist the doctor with his tasks. He knew he had to make himself more important or sooner or later, he would find himself in a coma, and he dreaded the thought. Steve figured it couldn't be too hard to make those drugs. Besides, the Doctor had already found the recipes.

Steve said, "I minored in chemistry."

Jim asked, "And you think you can do this?"

"Let me take a look and see what's needed."

"Okay then. You can set up your lab in the room with the

collection equipment. You will find it behind engineering. I guess we can call it 'Steve's lab' now."

Steve smiled and said, "Hmm, I like the sound of that."

Claire said, "If there isn't anything else, I'm going to take a nap. Have sleeping arrangements been assigned yet?"

Jim said, "Not yet. For now, you can use my quarters if you want."

Scott's posture deflated and looked at Jim as if Jim ruined any chances he would have with Claire.

Claire said, "Thank you. If it won't be any bother."

"Help yourself." Jim said, then noticed the look on Scott's face and asked, "What?"

With a quick explanation of their plan, Chief Besch retrieved schematics and confirmed the probes were capable of filtering light to see only the ultraviolet spectrum. The computer also contained the software currently programmed on the probes. Sam went right to work to edit the code. Scott could only sit and watch since he knew nothing about computer programming.

Chief Besch was intrigued by Sam's ability to navigate the probe's systems. He hovered around the workstation she used and occasionally gave suggestions. Eventually, Scott grew bored and started to wander around the engine room, and Chief Besch took his seat next to Sam.

About an hour later Scott and Sam entered the bridge ready to upload the first probe with the new program. Data continued to come in from the probe for a time because of the distance and the delay it caused. A few seconds after the estimated time for the new program to reach the probe, a red light on the control panel lit as the data stream ended.

Sam said, "The probe has shut down, and is now rebooting."

Several agonizing moments passed. The only thing anyone could do was wait for the probe to come back to life. Several minutes later, and nothing but a constant red light on the console. Sam and Claire began to discuss what to do short of launching a replacement probe. Not to mention the time it would take for a replacement probe to reach the same distance, it would have to be reprogrammed beforehand and tested to make sure it worked before launching. If there was a problem with the changes to the software, they wanted it fixed before losing another probe.

Scott noticed the red light begin to blink, pointed at the panel, and tried to get Sam's attention. A few seconds later, data started to stream from the probe. Everyone on the bridge cheered and was full of smiles.

The reboot of the other probe went without delay. It was unclear why the first probe took so long, but this was quickly forgotten as the computer plotted a course home and a new 3-D map was sent to the helm.

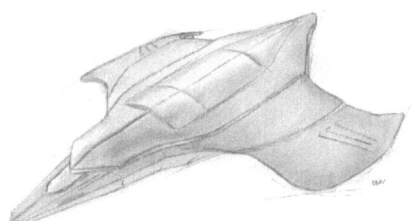

Chapter 25: AGENDA

It took Steve Harris quite a while to get started making the drugs Dr. Stevens needed. He had to scrounge for makeshift beakers, flasks, and a condenser.

A thermometer was strangely difficult to locate. Every thermometer he found was electronic and was no good for what he needed. He eventually found a mercury-filled thermostat in an ammo storage locker he was able to adapt.

A centrifuge and a hot plate were easy to make. He had to change what the ship's drive was collecting so he could create test strips and a few other needed items.

After a few setbacks, he gradually began to produce the drugs needed. It did not take long for him to come up with a routine. Much like a chef timing each part of a meal to be ready all at the same time, Steve reduced the time needed to make the final product.

Despite his efforts, he saw the supply of the coma-inducing drugs was smaller every day. The raw materials the ship's drive collected did not keep up with how much was needed.

He spoke with Chief Besch about the possibility of the ship's engine collecting oxygen instead of all the different chemicals needed to make the drugs.

Chief Besch said, "The problem is not necessarily the lack of oxygen, but the excess carbon dioxide. The scrubbers can only handle so much."

Steve asked, "What if we made more scrubbers?"

"What you're talking about, we would have to more than double our current capacity, and we don't have the equipment for that."

"Could the engine pull CO_2 out of the ship?"

Chief said, "It's not that simple. All the drive coils are aimed away from the ship."

Steve was unable to think of any other solutions and said, "Thanks, Chief."

Considering Claire's opinion, Steve knew his idea of using a filament would be dismissed. He decided to try to help Dr. Stevens on his own. He believed the filaments contained higher quantities of matter and he could get the raw materials faster. He also believed the risk of dark matter was negligible considering the way the ship propelled itself. He ran scans covertly for nearby filaments and planned to divert the ship toward one when the youngest bridge officer was on duty. That was Lt John Anders.

He started his plan by getting on John's good side. He would go to the bridge during his shift to keep him company. John had the night shift when most crewmen were asleep. In space, there was no day or night. To keep their sanity and a routine, the clocks on the ship were set to the time zone they left, Eastern U.S., or as close as they were able to figure.

The hours on the night shift passed by slowly, and John appreciated any company he got. Steve took advantage of John's boredom and would take over bridge duty so John could go to the cafeteria and eat. These were the times Steve performed his covert scans for a filament. He was very careful to be done with his scans before John returned. He made sure all the data screens displayed what was on then before John left. This cut down on the time he was able to scan for a filament but hid what he was doing.

After nearly a month, Steve found what he needed and put his plan in motion. The next night, when John left the bridge to eat, Steve put new coordinates into the helm.

The ship turned so gracefully, no one felt the movement. The change in direction was so slight, and the closest star was so far away, Steve thought it would be a long time before anyone noticed, and hopefully not till the increase in collections would vindicate his actions.

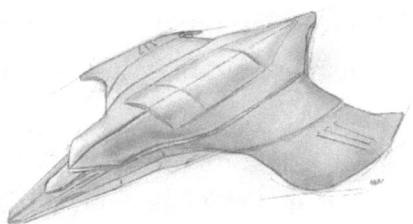

Chapter 26: FILAMENT

Jim and Scott found few insights in the computer on how to slow the ship. They discovered that a planetary body could be used to speed up if they came from behind the planet's orbital path; the gravity of the planet would accelerate the craft two and a half times its original speed. To slow down, they could come at a planet from the front of its orbital path. These maneuvers were called 'gravity assist'. Unfortunately, no data existed on how much this action would slow a craft. Another method, called 'photo-gravitational assist', involved the use of a solar sail. The ship was not designed for such equipment and the size needed could not be fabricated inside the ship.

The progress the ship made was uneventful and went by quicker than expected. Jim decided it was time Scott, Claire, Steve, and Sam got together to discuss slowing the ship for eventual landing on Earth. Jim requested Chief Besch to attend the meeting in case something needed his expertise. To keep it out of earshot of the rest of the crew, Jim decided to have the meeting in his quarters.

Jim started the meeting and said, "With how fast we are currently going, I don't want to wait till the last minute to figure out how we are going to slow down only to find we waited too long and will overshoot Earth. Scott and I have been looking through the computer and have not found much. Gravity assist was the best option we found."

Several ideas were brought up by Claire, Steve and Sam. At this point in human space exploration, acceleration was the primary concern. How to slow a craft had never actually been tested, so all they had were theories. Gravity assist was still their best working option.

Jim was glad he called the meeting. Ideas on how to use the Faraday-Maxwell drive during gravity assist seemed very promising and was not something Scott or himself thought of combining. They all agreed to test different applications of the proposal through simulations before the time came.

The discussion just started to wrap up when, over the intercom, Jim was urgently summoned to the bridge. The entire group followed Jim to see what the problem was.

When the group entered the bridge, John stood and said, "Something is happening with one of the probes. The data coming from it looks garbled and I've been getting trouble alerts from it."

Sam asked, "Can I see what you got?" She reviewed the data John collected. "This is weird — it looks like the probe is corroding, and fast. It won't surprise me if we lose all communication with this probe any minute."

Jim asked, "What would cause that?"

Sam said, "In space? I don't know."

Data from the probe stopped, followed by an explosion recorded from the direction of the probe.

"What the?" Scott said out loud what everyone was thinking.

Chief Besch said, "It must have been the power core. The probes have a miniature version of what's driving this ship and it must have gone critical."

"Scott asked, "But why?"

Claire said, "Bring up the most recent ultraviolet scans from that probe."

Jim asked, "What are you thinking?"

"There are not any filaments along our path and as far as I know they don't move around, but we don't know that much about them." When the scans were available for her to analyze she added, "Just as I feared – we are heading right for one, and the probe got to it first. The drive systems of the probe must have been overwhelmed not knowing what to do, and the dark matter destroyed the probe."

Scott asked, "What do you mean, destroyed the probe?"

Claire said, "What we thought was corrosion was the probe being destroyed as dark matter collided with it. The drive computers are not programmed to deal with dark matter because we do not know exactly what dark matter is. And the drive computer did not know how to manipulate it, so the dark matter impacted the hull, damaging it till the power core was penetrated and blew."

Jim said, "You said we are headed for it. Is that what will happen to us?"

"Unless we figure out what to do with it and program the drive computer, or change direction in time..." with a worried look on her face, Claire said, "Yes."

Scott asked, "How long do we have?"

Claire displayed the most recent 3-D image the computer compiled and applied an ultraviolet filter. The display showed a rope-like structure running at an angle nearly parallel to the ship's course, below and to the right. It was difficult to tell where due to the varied thickness of the filament, but the ship's course appeared to collide with it somewhere in the distance.

Jim ordered, "Send that data to the helm. Scott, take the helm, switch to manual control, and fly between those fingers."

"Yes sir," Scott said as he hurried to take one of the two seats in the forward-most part of the bridge. Scott flew based off the coordinates sent by Sam. "This would be a lot easier if I could see what I'm trying to avoid."

"Engineering to Bridge," came over the internal communications of the ship. "Alarms are starting to go off down here."

Jim replied, "We just switched to manual flight."

"No, not that, it's the drive coils," came over the intercom.

Chief Besch asked, "What about them?"

"A few of them went offline on different parts of the ship," came the reply. "More are shutting down as we speak. It's really weird, it's not a particular series or string but random all over the ship."

Jim asked, "Can an ultraviolet filter be applied to the bridge glass?"

Sam did her magic with the computer and the view completely changed. The colors caused Scott to lose his orientation for a moment and the ship dove and slid to the right closer to the filament. When Scott recovered, the ship pitched up and to the left, then quickly turned to the right again to avoid a thin wisp of bright gold.

"Because of the baryon acoustic oscillations, we may find some eddies of dark matter in rings around the filament," Claire explained and pointed to a large structure now visible on the starboard side of the ship.

With the filter, the filament looked like a mass of golden rope woven loosely together. The mass of it was several hundred times the diameter of the ship and extended farther than could be seen. Several thinner threads shot off in random directions and resembled twine.

Scott navigated around these threads in an attempt to prevent further damage to the ship. He was not completely successful. As time went by, it became easier for him, and he appeared to enjoy feeling like he was in a fighter again.

Thanks to inertia dampeners, the crew did not feel what Scott put the ship through, but one look out the bridge glass caused motion sickness to several people on the bridge along with frazzled nerves.

Jim said, "Claire, you said filaments don't move. I want to know what happened."

Sam said, "I think I have an explanation. It looks like a course change was put in a couple of days ago."

Jim demanded, "What? By who?"

Steve remained silent, knowing the course change could not be traced back to him since passwords and logins were not used on the bridge. This was a military ship, and timing was everything in a fight. Logins slowed access to critical systems in times of need.

Sam said, "The logs only show when, but I could check the video records."

Steve began to sweat, not knowing there were cameras. He glanced around and then saw it above the door to the bridge.

"Do it," Jim ordered. "Claire, are you able to safely analyze the dark matter for the drive computer?"

"I'd love to try," Claire said, excited to work on something no one has ever seen before. "It will take some time. Make sure you steer clear of that thing."

"What do you think I'm doing?" Scott said as the view outside shifted directions at a dizzying speed and the ship turned to avoid another thread.

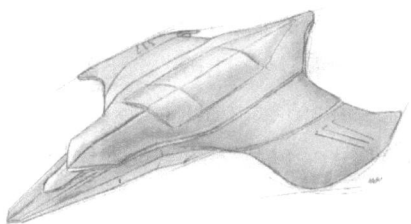

Chapter 27: DEVELOPMENTS

Claire knew the ship could collect samples from space, because the drive coils were already doing that for the doctor. She did not know computer programming and asked Sam to assist her with the computer aspects of the task.

Steve was happy Sam would be busy with Claire for a while. He knew he had to work fast to access the video system and delete the evidence that would incriminate him.

Sam was a wiz when it came to computer programming, but she was at a loss how to tell the computer to attract molecules of something when no one knew what it was. In case they were successful, she asked Chief Besch if his crew could assist with some sort of magnetic containment so the dark matter would not come in contact with anything on the ship.

A magnetic containment box was not difficult to construct, since the ship's drive coils worked on the same principle. The engineering department constructed the box using spare parts and had it completed before Sam and Claire figured out how to collect a sample.

Sam asked, "How do I use the drive coils to direct something to the collection chamber if the drive computer does not know how to manipulate it?"

Claire asked, "How does the drive computer manipulate matter?"

Chief Besch said, "It scans the matter at the atomic level and identifies its magnetic polarity. Then, through negative and positive charges, it attracts the atom to a drive coil."

Claire asked, "Can we get the drive computer to scan dark matter for its polarity?"

Sam said, "It should already do that."

Claire asked, "Then what happened to the probe?"

Sam said, "I think we need a closer look, because we're missing something."

Chief Besch asked, "Does the computer reference a – what is it called? That thing with all the elements."

Sam asked, "The periodic table?"

Chief said, "Yes, that. Does the computer reference that to know how to move atoms?"

Sam did her wizardry and searched the computer. After a few moments she said, "Yes it does, but it didn't originally."

Claire asked, "What?"

Sam said, "It looks like the program was changed at some point. The computer was originally programmed to move whatever it found."

Claire asked, "Why would they change it?"

Chief Besch accidentally said out loud, "Interesting."

Sam asked, "What's interesting?"

Chief Besch said, "Oh I was just thinking, what if we told the computer to collect what's not on that table?"

Claire and Sam looked at each other till Claire asked, "Could it be that simple?"

Sam said, "Let's find out."

The trio asked Scott to fly close to one of the threads to get a scan. The makeup of dark matter was still unknown, but the team felt confident they could safely capture a molecule for further study.

John sat next to Scott and took pointers on how to fly the ship like a fighter. He learned to anticipate the next maneuver before it was needed. This is what made Scott's flying smoother and more fluid.

Sam tried to attract an 'unknown' molecule. It took several close passes to a thread till Sam and Claire were confident they could manipulate what they were looking for.

While Steve made his rounds he accessed a computer terminal and attempted to delete the file showing him entering the course correction. Then he realized this would look suspicious, so he attempted to corrupt the file instead. He opened the file in a text editor. It looked like gibberish to him, but he figured if he deleted a random character here and there, that would corrupt the file enough to prevent it from being viewed.

Chief Besch had a team bring the magnetic containment box to Steve's lab and get ready for the capture of a dark matter molecule.

Upon entering Steve's lab, the team discovered an elaborate setup Steve created to manufacture the coma drugs. The canisters attached to the collection ports containing the raw materials were completely full.

The crewmen only had to connect the box to one of the six collection ports but found it difficult to remove the canister. It was so full, they could not put the lid on it. Thanks to being in a weightless environment, the contents began floating around the room. The powdery substance made it difficult to see as it got in their eyes, and they began to itch where it came in contact with their skin. The powder even made its way under their clothing.

Even though they tried to keep their eyes closed, tears bubbled on their eyes. They itched everywhere and tried not to breathe any of it. They finally completed their task by feel alone and exited the room. "Chief, we're done here. And we're going to the sick bay," one of the crewmen said over the ship's intercom.

Chief asked, "What happened?"

The crewmen explained what happened and Chief heard over the comm channel Dr. Stevens's helping them.

Dr. Stevens said, "Chief, I need to flush their eyes. What were they exposed to?"

Chief said, "I have no idea. Basic elements as far as I know. Steve Harris would have to tell you which ones."

Dr. Stevens said, "If I don't see any complications, I'll release them to their quarters. Whatever it is got under their uniform. They need a shower and change of clothes."

Chief said, "Understood, thanks, Doctor." He then turned to Sam and said, "I'm ready when you are."

Claire was excited and indicated for Scott to fly closer to the nearest thread.

Sam manipulated the drive computer to direct a single molecule of dark matter to the collection chamber.

Claire held her breath for what seemed an eternity till Chief Besch said "Ladies, we have your sample."

Everyone on the bridge, especially Scott, expressed a sigh of relief. Scott made some distance between the ship and the thread he had approached.

Throughout all this, the ship's drive coils suffered more damage but were not at a level of concern. Everyone involved felt a solution would be found before the ship was in danger.

Claire began to analyze the dark matter sample and Sam returned to scour the computer for video evidence.

Sam discovered that the video of the bridge at the time of the event could not be accessed, but this did not deter her. Her knowledge of computer systems gave her tools most people did not know existed. Newer software versions still had embedded old ways to manipulate files, and Sam knew how to exploit that.

Not relying solely on the one file, Sam pulled the video of the hall outside the bridge, which showed the coming and going of personnel. Along with time stamps, Sam was able to establish who was on the bridge. She also discovered, someone tampered with the file she was not able to access. The time stamp on the file did not match when it was created. It was less then an hour ago. She knew someone was trying to prevent being discovered, and parts of the corrupt file could still be recovered and saved it in case it was needed.

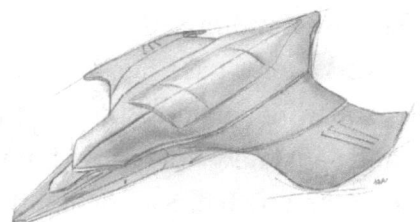

Chapter 28: REPAIRS

Damage to the ship dropped drastically when the drive computer was updated with what Claire learned about dark matter. Because of the volatile nature of dark matter, she was not able to learn much more than how to identify it.

The engineering department prepared for the tedious task of replacing the damaged drive coils. This task was much more complicated with the ship underway, and it required drive coils in sections of the hull shut down to prevent electrocution. If the ship stopped to facilitate the repair, all momentum the ship gained would be lost. This alone would result in months added to the trip.

Two crewmen that knew how to replace drive coils were in the cargo bay preparing for the spacewalk. Chief Besch was on the bridge at the engineering station. Jim took the controls since no one had done anything remotely close to what the crew in the cargo bay would attempt. If anything went wrong, he did not want Scott or John to have it on their conscience.

Jim felt his chair vibrate and knew the cargo ramp had opened. The ship slightly changed course as Chief Besch turned off power to the first section of the ship's skin to be worked on, and Jim compensated for the slight change in direction.

The crewmen worked as fast as they could, knowing their oxygen was limited, but they had to be careful nothing came in contact with other sections of the ship which still had power. Their helmets helped block some of the light caused by the drive system but did not block all of it. This made the areas still powered up visible to them.

A crewman removed a body panel and steadied it to not touch the next section while the other crewman replaced the damaged drive coils. The pair worked together to replace the panel and secure it back to the ship.

"First section complete, moving to zone five," came over the speakers in the bridge.

"Roger that, zone five powered down, you're clear to enter," Chief Besch communicated to the crewmen outside the ship, and Jim had to counter with another course change, then another when the previous section was turned back on.

In order to complete the repairs in one spacewalk, shortcuts were taken. Alignment of the new drive coils was done remotely after the section was powered back on. This reduced the efficiency of the overall system but was enough to continue their journey.

The drive coils were replaced in this manner and almost complete when "Ow, what the hell?" came over the speaker on the bridge from one of the crewmen. Followed shortly by, "Bridge, I'm losing air."

This was immediately followed by the other crewman, "Bridge, blood is coming out of several holes on my suit but I don't feel –" The crewman's voice faded away only to return a few moments later yelling frantically over the communications channel, "Let's get out of here!" The two fought to get back to the cargo ramp before the air completely exited their suits.

Chief Besch demanded, "What's going on out there?"

Claire said, "I think they are getting hit by micrometeorites."

"Well, how come? Isn't the drive system taking care of that?" Chief Besch, concerned about his crew, turned power off to sections in their path to the cargo ramp.

Claire said, "With the power turned off to different sections, the drive computer cannot function in those areas." She became frantic knowing someone was getting injured and she was powerless to help.

Jim said, "I might be able to shield them." He rotated the orientation of the ship to keep the crewmen away from the leading side of the ship. "Keep me informed where they are."

He rotated the ship in a spiral, and other odd orientations to keep the ship between the crewmen and the direction the ship was going. As the crewmen made their way to the cargo ramp, Chief Besch turned sections of drive coils back on behind them so Jim had better control. Jim had to deal with minor bumps in direction as sections were turned on and off. It only took a few bumps for him to anticipate and prepare for the next.

Meanwhile, Dr. Stevens, Scott, and several crewmen waited outside the cargo bay for it to pressurize after the cargo ramp closed. One crewman lost too much blood and died before anyone could get to him. The other suffered severe asphyxiation and two broken bones. He was brought to the medical bay after being stabilized.

All areas were fixed except for one zone which contained two damaged drive coils. Just two coils made little impact, so another spacewalk would not be attempted to replace them.

The loss of another crewman hit Jim as he sat next to the recovering crewman lying on a bed in the medical bay. *'Funeral arrangements'*, he thought. *'Oh God, how do we do that in space'*?

Dr. Stevens assured him the other crewman would survive.

Jim wondered if there was anything he could have done differently. His training told him it was a dangerous job and loss had to be expected. That didn't help him deal with another death under his command and made it sound routine, and it sure didn't make him like it any better.

He was lost in thought when he heard the crewman begin to stir.

"Major, I'm sorry we didn't get all the coils," the crewman said as he woke from the anesthesia, still groggy.

"Doctor," Jim hollered. Then he said soothingly to the crewman, "Don't you worry about that, you did fine. I'm just glad you made it back."

The crewman looked around and saw all the beds in the medical bay empty and asked, "Where is Matt?"

Jim said, "I'm sorry, but he didn't make it. I didn't get a chance to meet everyone yet, and your name is?"

The crewman said, "I'm Henry, sir. Henry Morgan."

"Well, nice to finally meet you, Henry," Jim said as he reached for Henry's hand. "Thank you for the work you did. I can't even imagine what you went through out there."

"Hey, how many enlisted do you know who've done a spacewalk?" Henry said with a smile, "Sir."

Jim said, "You can lose the formalities. It's just the two of us."

Doctor Stevens arrived and began to check Henry over. Henry started to sit up and was stopped by the doctor. "Try not to move," Doctor Stevens said. "Your left ulna and first metatarsal are broke. I have them set and in a temporary cast, so I don't want you moving around."

"My left what and first who?"

"Your left ulna," Doctor Stevens said as he grasped his lower left arm on the side farther away from his body, "and your first metatarsal. That's one of the bones in your foot for your big toe. Also on your left."

Henry looked at his left arm for the first time and winced when he tried to wiggle his toes. The anesthesia began to lose its grip and made Henry more aware of other injuries around his body.

"I had to do a bunch of research on how to treat you, because the body doesn't heal the same in space. Clotting, for one – I had to be creative closing the wounds you received and your bones are going to take a lot longer than usual to heal."

Jim felt the groove in his scalp and asked, "How come?"

"When in gravity, a thin layer of cartilage will form over the break to start the healing process. In space, for a reason that has not been discovered yet, the cartilage has nothing to bond to and does not know what direction to heal."

Henry and Jim asked, "Direction?"

"Space does some weird things to the human body. Don't even get me started on the human eye. I have the chief working on a contraption that will create piezoelectric fields. According to the research, that should help the cartilage bond and know what direction to heal. In the meantime – I don't want you moving around till the chief is done and I replace those casts."

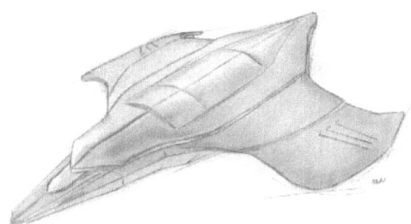

Chapter 29: VOICES

The ship gained an enormous boost in thrust when it entered the filament. Claire's discoveries allowed Sam to program the drive computer of the ship and the remaining probe how to manipulate dark matter. Another probe was launched, which replaced the one that was destroyed. 3-D mapping was still possible, but limited till the new probe reached its apogee.

"What to do with Steve?" Was on everyone's mind after the video record revealed he had entered the course change which put the ship in jeopardy and caused the death of a crewman.

Since the discovery, Steve was locked in the crew's quarters with a guard at the door, since the ship did not have a brig.

Jim, Scott, Claire, and Sam discussed what should be done, and it was decided to hold a trial in the ship's cafeteria with three of them on the panel. Claire requested to excuse herself, since she felt Steve thought she had it in for him after their past differences of opinion.

Despite there being only three civilians not in cryo or coma, Jim preferred to have the majority of the panel civilian. He felt this was necessary to preserve the integrity of the trial and prevent discord. Eventually, after reaching Earth and everyone was revived, he knew everything that happened would have to be explained.

The format for the trial was almost finalized when Jim was summoned to the bridge.

"Déjà vu," Claire said as the group followed Jim.

Strange voices came over the speakers on the bridge when the group entered. It was English, but not a voice that belonged to anyone on the ship, then laughter and more voices.

"Sir," John said as he jumped out of the captain's chair. "We detected this signal on the low band. Ran it through signal filters and had to boost it quite a bit to make it out. I did some checking, and because the signal was so weak, the computer categorized it as cosmic noise and ignored it for several weeks. As we get closer to its source, the signal has been getting stronger, and now it is strong enough for the computer to alert us."

Jim asked, "Where is it coming from?"

John said, "It is coming from somewhere ahead of us, but till one of the probes reaches a strong enough part, of the signal we are unable to accurately directional find its source."

Jim asked, "What is directional find?"

John said, "It's a communications term for finding the source of a signal. Basically, it uses two receivers to triangulate the location of the transmitter.

Scott asked, "What are the odds that English would be coming from anywhere other than Earth?"

Jim said, "It shouldn't even be coming from Earth. Not for another couple hundred years." Jim and Scott suddenly looked at each other, then both turned and looked at Claire. Soon everyone was looking at Claire for answers.

No one asked what was on everyone's mind for a long moment until, "What if we were at the right place but that explosion sent us to the wrong time?" Scott spoke first. "I mean, here we thought we were at the right time but the wrong place. What if the opposite is true?"

"I need a historian," Jim blurted out. "Record those transmissions for later playback and get me a historian. If he is asleep wake him." He ordered.

Sam searched the passenger list on the computer. When she found a historian, she said, "Jim, a historian is in escape pod three."

Jim ordered, "Chief, get a detail to escort Mr. Harris from his quarters to escape pod three."

Chief Besch said, "He'd better not get off that easy."

Jim said, "He won't."

Claire asked, "Jim, are you sure you want to do that without a trial?"

"Steve already cost me one crewman, and he's tying up two more to guard him," Jim said as he pointed at the speaker overhead still playing the transmission they intercepted. "I need a historian; someone has to take his place in cryo or there won't be enough air. Cryo is the best place for him until we can have a trial, and we don't have the time to deal with that now. Unless you know of someone else to take his place."

Claire was surprised to hear that reaction from Jim, and said, "I'm sorry, I thought with the loss of the crewman —"

"I'm sorry for snapping at you. I know it's not your fault and you're trying to help. I'm just getting frustrated. Steve is not going into cryo as punishment. And like I said, he is tying up two crewmen that have other duties."

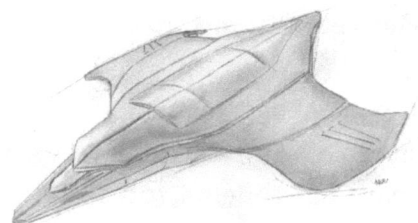

Chapter 30: RADIO

Chief Besch and the crewmen guarding Steve's quarters prepared to escort Steve to escape pod three.

"Just give me an excuse," Chief Besch said to Steve when he came out of his quarters.

Dr. Stevens was already waiting as the four approached, with a gravity lift gurney beside him against the opposite wall from the escape pods.

Dr. Stevens reached for Steve's hand as they approached, took it in both of his hands, and shook it, "Thank you for all your help. I would not have got much sleep over the past few months if it was not for you."

"Touching," Chief Besch said gruffly.

Steve said, "Thanks, Doctor. I hope the extra supplies are enough."

Dr. Stevens asked, "What do you mean? What supplies?"

"I saw you were running low on basic ingredients to keep the comas going. That's what got me in this predicament," Steve replied, pointing at the escape pod.

Chief Besch said, "Oh come off it. You know that's not the entirety of it. Besides, it's just like falling asleep in a field of daisies. *If* you wake up I'll see to it you face justice."

Steve did not like the look Chief Besch gave him and feared he may not wake up. "You're in the military and have to do whatever that man says. I'm a civilian, and I did what I thought was best. That death was not my fault," Steve retorted.

Chief Besch sensed by Steve's posture and the increased volume and tone in his voice that things may go south. He itched to make Steve pay for the death of his crewman but followed procedure and tapped a button on his uniform, which sent a signal to engineering and opened a one-way comm channel with the bridge.

Chief said, "On this ship, regardless of position, you do what you're told. Everyone on board depends on everyone doing their part. If you don't agree, that's just tough. You broke the trust. No one here is behind you."

"I know if I get in that thing I'm not coming out alive," Steve shouted at the chief, which was also being heard on the bridge. "In a few minutes, I'll be nothing more than a – than a piece of luggage."

"Scott, get down there. Stop by the medical bay and grab a sedative," Jim ordered as he sat down in the captain's chair and continued to listen to the commotion going on.

"There is a big difference between you and me," Jim heard Chief Besch say. "I have integrity to stand behind the decisions I make. You went out of your way to cover yours up. In my book, that makes you a coward."

"Yes sir," Scott said as he darted out the bridge door.

Steve said, "How dare you? You know nothing about me."

"From what I know so far, that's enough, thanks," Chief countered.

When Scott arrived at the end of the hall for the port side escape pods, several crew members were already at each end blocking the hall. Chief Besch and Dr. Stevens were near the middle of the hall with Steve in full hysterics about being put to sleep for the rest of the trip home.

Chief Besch noticed Scott at the other end of the hall from where he was with Steve between them. Scott squeezed past the crewmen at his end of the hall and revealed to the chief what was in his hand. Chief nodded and continued his banter with Steve to keep Steve turned toward him. Dr. Stevens was unaware of what was going on since his back faced Scott's approach.

Dr. Stevens looked at Scott when he passed, saw the syringe in his right hand and he reached for Scott's arm. He understood immediately what the syringe was for and took it from Scott and quietly inquired what was in it.

Before Scott could answer, Steve turned and became more agitated seeing Scott there, cornering him against Chief.

It appeared Steve may become violent at any moment. With a subtle signal, Chief and Scott rushed Steve and forced him to the deck as Dr. Stevens immobilized Steve's arm to administer the sedative.

When Steve finally relaxed and fell asleep, Dr. Stevens asked, "What was in that syringe?"

Scott said, "I don't know. The vial said sedative on the label so I grabbed it. Why?"

Dr. Stevens explained, "Depending on what it was and the dosage, we may not be able to put him in cryo now."

"Just great," Scott shook his head. "I left the vial out on the table in your office."

"Crewman," Chief Besch urged one of the crew at the end of the hall to come close. "Go to the medical bay. You will find a vial of medicine left out on a table. Go get it and bring it here. The rest of you, thanks for the help. Now get back to work." Chief smiled so the crewmen knew his last comment was more of a friendly nature than the words implied.

Jim had brought up a camera in the area but did not see the smile and shook his head. He wondered how the chief was so well respected by his crew. Everyone in engineering knew the chief was short on words and shorter on praise. He was fair and would do anything for his people, not to mention gruff and crusty around the edges. He was the kind of man command would prefer not to have around but was glad he was. People like him get the job done right the first time.

When the crewman returned with the vial, Dr. Stevens saw it was Ketamine and instructed, "Make sure he is breathing and keep a close eye on him."

Scott asked, "What's the matter?" as he checked on Steve. "His breathing is shallow, but his pulse is like a racehorse."

Dr. Stevens said, "That's what I was afraid of. Ketamine is supposed to be administered gradually. I gave it to him all at once. We have to wait before we put him in cryo and monitor his breathing till he comes to. Depending on how much was in that syringe we've got five to twenty-five minutes to wait."

Scott asked, "Which one in this pod is the historian?"

Chief Besch answered, "The one on the right wall."

Scott asked, "How do we get him out? Will the others wake when we open the pod?"

Dr. Stevens said, "Not right away, but we don't have much time to waste."

Chief Besch asked, "Then how do we time this? Get him out without waking the others and get Steve in after he comes to and before he starts pissing me off again?"

Scott asked, "Is there something we can give the others in the pod to slow their recovery?"

"I think – let me check something," Dr. Stevens pulled a pad out of his pocket and started scrolling through some data. "I'll be right back. Keep an eye on his breathing. Call me if anything changes."

Scott asked, "Great, now what do we do?"

Chief Besch said, "We wait."

"I hate waiting."

Chief Besch laughed, "Welcome to enlisted life. Hurry up and wait, then wait some more."

Moments later Dr. Stevens returned with a different syringe and vial of liquid, "All we have to do is keep him sedated," Dr. Stevens pointed at Steve still lying on the floor. "Once he is clear of the effects of Ketamine we can keep him sedated with Fentanyl and that will not cause any adverse reaction with the cryo unit."

Chief Besch asked, "Fentanyl. What the hell are you doing with that?"

Dr. Stevens said, "Anesthesiologists have been using it for years."

Chief shook his head and said, "You're the doctor."

The three worked together and kept an eye on Steve while getting the historian, Dr. Paul Bullard, out of the escape pod.

When Steve started to come around, he was quite groggy and docile, so there was no need to restrain him. His breathing was stable, so Dr. Stevens administered a few milligrams of Fentanyl to knock him back out for the time needed to finish the job.

Dr. Paul Bullard was put on the gravity lift gurney to be brought to the medical bay for his recovery while Steve Harris was put inside the escape pod and strapped down. Just as the other occupants of the escape pod started to show signs of movement, the hatch was closed and sealed. The hatch frosted over again and the three were able to breathe a sigh of relief.

Chief Besch and Captain Dixon sat on the floor with their backs on the escape pod to catch their breath.

Dr. Stevens checked over Dr. Paul Bullard rather quickly and said, "Let's get him to medical, he is starting to come around and I want him on a monitor checking his vitals, not out here in the hall." The two got up and the three walked to the medical bay as the gurney floated in front of them.

On the bridge, with the commotion over, Jim returned to

listening to the signal they intercepted. He was certain it originated from Earth, but from what year? And how long did it take to get here? He wondered if they were in danger of running into the very armada they were trying to hide from. He needed answers, and he needed them now.

"Claire, till Doctor Paul Bullard recovers, I need your best guess. How far are we from Earth? Let's assume radio was invented in 1905, how long would it take to reach this far? With that assumption, what year is this?"

Claire started shaking her head, not knowing how long the ship ignored the signal or where they were when they first encountered it. It was impossible to answer his question. Not to mention different astronomical events could speed up or slow down the signal.

He saw the confusion on her face and said, "Just a ballpark. I know what we are hearing was not 1905 but it will give us an idea of what we're dealing with."

"I'll try but it won't be accurate."

"Thanks, Claire. Lieutenant, you have the bridge. I'll be in medical."

In the medical bay, Dr. Paul Bullard, wrapped in several blankets, was dry heaving into the garbage can Scott held. He already threw up what was left in his stomach long ago.

Jim entered the room, surveyed the scene, and asked, "How is our patient doing?"

Dr. Stevens said, "Oh don't worry, this is a common reaction from cryo. He is doing just fine."

"Hmm," mumbled Chief Besch. "Remind me to order more garbage cans when we reach Earth!"

Jim replied, "Or mops."

"Funny guy. If anyone needs me, I'll be planning my vacation."

Chief said as he exited the sick bay and headed back to Engineering.

Jim asked, "Doctor Bullard, has anyone filled you in on what is going on?"

Dr. Bullard replied between heaves, "Something about a signal?"

Jim pushed a comm button for the bridge and asked for the signal they were picking up to be piped through to the medical bay. "Can you tell me what you make of this?" He asked, and they all sat back and listened for a while. Dr. Bullard's queasy stomach subsided considerably, and Scott got him a glass of water.

After listening for quite some time, Dr. Bullard said, "This sounds like commercial radio from the early 1900s. If we listen some more, maybe a news story will come up so I can pin down the date closer."

Scott asked, "1900s? How can that be?"

Jim said, "Your guess is as good as mine, but I'd say that explosion not only sent us to the wrong place but also the wrong time."

Dr. Bullard said, "Major, if we are in the 1900s or later, telescopes on Earth may be able to see us."

Jim said, "I was worried about that. But I don't know what Earth had back then. Scott, get with Chief, Sam, and Claire. Tell them what is going on. We need to brainstorm. Tell them to gather what they need and meet in my quarters in one hour. Doctor Bullard, I hope you will feel up to it. I need you there also, please."

Scott said, "Yes sir."

Dr. Bullard said, "I'm feeling much better already, I'll be there. And please, just Paul – I'm not hung up on formalities."

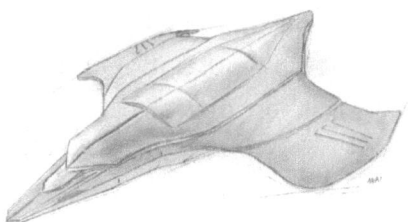

Chapter 31: DON'T LOOK SO HARD

Jim went to his quarters and made himself a hot beverage, one that always helped clear his mind, dark black coffee. Just the smell of it helped at times. He looked out one of the windows in his quarters and deeply inhaled the aroma from his cup, until the liquid inside cooled enough to sip.

Most of the windows were nothing more than round port holes in the ceiling, but there were two larger windows big enough to look out on either side of the room. From the outside of the ship, these windows were located just below the leading edge of the wings.

He stood in front of the starboard window and gazed at the white specks that shot past as the ship's engine pushed and pulled – or pulled then pushed – whatever it could find along the surface of the ship's skin. accelerating the ship as it passed. He wondered how far these little sparks were visible and if it was possible to h de their approach to Earth and still use the engine.

The last thing they wanted to do was let their presence be known. Not only may it alter history, but if the marauders learned what Earth did, Jim, his crew, and all his passengers may be hunted at this very moment.

The 1400s were chosen not only for how easy it would be to hide in the sparse population, but to give more than enough time to build the population back up in Anarbia and develop far superior weapons, to the point that victory was completely ensured. Anarbia was chosen not only as the name of the project but also as the name of the base they would work out of in the Bermuda Triangle.

Anarbia was a name in an obscure Native American text of a mythical futuristic city. The story said the city would appear and disappear at random times. When historians searched, they found no further record of the word, which made the story itself a myth.

The hour passed quickly, the coffee was long gone, and a replacement was steaming on Jim's desk. With no gravity, the steam stayed near the top of the liquid and slowly escaped in all directions. The door chime rang, and Claire was the first to enter when Jim said, "Enter." She was quickly followed by Paul before the door closed.

Jim said, "Please have a seat," pointing to the chairs scattered in front of his desk. "Claire, I'd like to thank you for all the help you have been."

With a smile Claire said, "My pleasure. I learned a lot being on this side of the stars, and I increased our database immensely."

Jim, Claire, and Paul made small talk and answered Paul's questions about what had happened on board the ship since he entered cryo. The other members of the meeting arrived with Chief and Sam bringing up the rear still talking with each other about whatever they were working on in engineering as they came through the door.

After everyone took a seat, Jim started the meeting. "Till an hour ago my main concern was getting us to earth as quickly as possible. Now I fear that may have jeopardized our mission." Jim paused a moment. "Something must have happened during the shot that explosion caused, the extent of which is still unclear. It seems we have been sent about 500 years later than we were supposed to arrive. I'm sure Anarbia has long since passed our level of knowledge and understanding. We might be looked upon as uneducated primitives and have to play catch up when we get there." Jim laughed, "I wonder if they will put this ship in a museum."

Chief joked, "They might put you there as well."

Jim said, "They just might dissect you, try to figure out what species you are."

Sam laughed, "Or bring you to show and tell."

Everyone had a good laugh at the chief's expense.

Jim said, "All joking aside, we might be undoing everything just by being seen." Everyone sitting in the room looked at him with puzzled expressions. "If you are not aware, we recently discovered a radio signal coming from Earth that was originally sent in the early 1900s. Doctor Bullard, I mean Paul, what were people on Earth doing with telescopes in the 1900s?"

Paul cleared his throat and said, "Well, they were cataloging every object they were able to find in space."

"Was that the only thing they were doing?"

"No sir, they were looking for extraterrestrial life and even sent signals hoping for a reply."

Most of the people in the room were shocked to hear that. Those signals may be the very reason they were making this journey.

Claire asked, "Paul, have you been able to narrow down the year?"

"Not exactly. The first national broadcast radio was NBC, which was started in 1926. It was the first radio signal believed to be strong enough to leave Earth. Those signals were so weak, they were being ignored by our computers, and what we are receiving now is from the mid-1960s. The exact year — I'm sorry but I don't know. We are traveling too fast to keep up." Paul threw his hands up in a guessing gesture. "The computer zeros in on a block of the signal then skips ahead. About 20 minutes ago, John F Kennedy was assassinated, which happened in 1963. Then, just before coming in here there was talk about America fighting in Vietnam, which was between 1965 and 1973. Not including the fall of Saigon in 1975 where America still had a limited presence."

Jim said, "Thank you, Paul. Claire, have you been able to pinpoint our current position?"

She said, "We are just under 40 light years from Earth."

"How long would it take a 1960s radio signal to travel 40 light years?"

"Radio signals travel at near light speed in the vacuum of space so about 40 years."

"So right now, on Earth, it is somewhere between 2005 and 2013?"

"That is close, but I'd predict it is a few years earlier. From what Paul said, the computer is skipping large chunks of the transmission, and we may be closer than I estimated. Also, there are anomalies the transmission passed that could have affected its speed. That actually might be why the computer skipped chunks, because it might be all mixed up and got here out of order."

Paul said, "That explains a few things."

Jim said, "Well, the fact remains that we might be – or will be – on someone's telescope as we approach Earth. These sparks the engine is making all over the ship, I fear, are making us visible for anyone that is looking. Paul, the period we're talking about – didn't Earth have space-based telescopes, radio telescopes, and you name it?"

Chief and Sam started whispering with each other and Paul answered, "Yes, they did have all that. They were pretty inquisitive about space back then. In fact, popular culture was loaded with aliens, and large numbers of the population fantasized about it."

Claire said, "You know, we may be able to use that to our

advantage."

Jim noticed Sam and Chief Besch periodically glancing at each other or whispering. Since it was not disruptive to the meeting he did not say anything.

Scott asked, "How so? Wait a minute. How did that alien ship from the general's briefing make it to the moon before being discovered?"

Claire said, "That's partially what I was thinking. I don't know how far the sparks are visible. If they can be seen by a telescope, they will completely obscure what this ship is," Claire was looking at the ceiling as she thought and spoke. "We could head toward the back side of Earth's moon then go dark. They may think we are just a comet or something that impacted the other side of the moon. Then we wait a few days for their attention to move elsewhere and make the final approach to Earth in a region not so populated, like the South Pacific or something. If someone does see us it may be dismissed as a flight of fantasy."

Sam said, "Good idea, but that won't convince anyone watching us now. Naturally occurring objects don't make course changes. And we will change course several times to slow this thing down. We are going way too fast not to use several planets for a gravity assist and to push against using the engine."

Scott asked, "Can we turn the engine off now and only use it when on the opposite side of a planet from Earth? We don't need any more speed and that way we are not making those sparks."

Chief Besch asked, "I'm wondering if we could use the engine to camouflage ourselves?"

Jim asked, "What?"

"Right now, we are attracting material in front of us and throwing it behind us. What if we didn't throw it away?" Chief paused and looked at everyone in the meeting. "We will no longer make the sparks and we might start looking like a big rock."

Jim said, "Yeah but we still have the problem of slowing down and changing directions."

Sam said, "Just wait a minute. Chief and I were talking about an idea of camouflage and I think Chief is on to something. If we made ourselves the same color as the background without any reflection, we will be invisible to whatever might be looking our way."

Claire asked, "Will we still be able to do all the braking maneuvers, use the engines against whatever planet we're at to slow us further, and regain our camouflage as we pull away from the planet on the other side?"

Sam said, "We are not sure. We will have to run simulations, but I think it's doable as long as we can program the targeting computers to do what we're asking."

Scott asked, "What about our probes? Can they be seen?"

Sam said, "We might have to cut them loose. We have enough data to get home, so they are not critical anymore."

Jim said, "Don't get rid of the probes just yet. We may still need them, if for nothing else but to look at ourselves to see if we are invisible. But cut their power so they are not sparking. Let them catch up a bit." He paused a moment, then added, "As far as the simulations and programming, use whatever and whoever you need, but get this done," Jim ordered. "We are out of time." He pushed a comm button and ordered the helm to reduce power and begin coasting. "Lastly, make sure you have good backups before changing any programming. I do not want to be stranded after making it this far."

Chief Besch asked, "Any chance to recover the probes rather than just cut them loose? There is no telling when we can make more. I wonder if they even use them anymore."

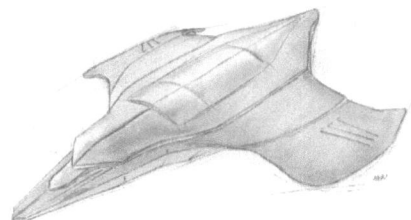

Chapter 32: A TRICK OF LIGHT

The meeting ended with a buzz of ideas on how to hide the ship as they walked toward engineering to test their ideas. Jim felt much better than he did going into the meeting and broke off from the group to go to the bridge.

He checked one of the control panels to ensure the windows surrounding the bridge were no longer tinted. He looked at all parts of the ship he could see to ensure there was no sparking along the skin of the ship.

Hours passed and he got impatient but did not want to disturb the team with update checks or to go to engineering to see for himself, disturbing them even more. That would do nothing but slow them down as they responded to protocol and questions. After the time spent on this ship, he knew his team quite well and trusted they were working as hard as they could.

He did not know Paul personally. Since Paul was not needed for the project in engineering, Jim decided to get to know him and find out what he could about the time period on Earth they were heading into.

Several things had been shot to their new home before the ship was shot, including a massive computer system that contained data on everything humans knew up to this point, including history. That information was not available to Jim at the moment, and he quickly discovered Paul was very knowledgeable about the history of the earth and understood why Paul was selected. Granted that the explosion that caused this mishap was a fluke, there was no guarantee the computer was there or even worked, so Paul may be invaluable.

During this time, the probes closed the distance with the ship. They were about one and a half days behind, above, and below the ship. They were close enough to identify the ship through sensors and optical arrays.

Dr. Stevens continued his rounds. He checked the status of the cryo units in the escape pods, the respiratory levels of those put into a coma, as well as the scrubbers that take carbon dioxide out of the air for those working. The latter was the responsibility of engineering, but since he was checking on all those that had been put to sleep, checking the scrubbers did not take any time out of his day. The numbers on the scrubbers had been going down gradually since they were brought online, which was normal, but they were at such a point that engineering and Jim needed to be made aware. He was unable to get a hold of engineering, and since the entire department had been busy running simulations, he felt it best to notify Jim and request an audience with him.

Jim replied over the intercom, "Doctor, you of all people do not need to schedule an appointment with me. Whatever is on your mind, just come and see me. I'm currently on the bridge."

"Yes sir," Dr. Stevens answered, turned off the comm panel, and headed toward the bridge.

He saw Jim in the captain's chair and approached. "Major," Dr. Stevens said and waited for him to respond. "The CO_2 scrubbers are becoming saturated. I think we have a couple of weeks before they have to be taken offline for servicing."

"Have you spoken with Chief Besch about this?"

"Not yet. He is busy with the project of camouflaging the ship. It's not critical yet, and I didn't want to disturb him."

"A couple weeks you said? Hopefully, we will be on Earth by then."

"We're that close?" Dr. Stevens asked and looked out the bridge glass not seeing anything.

"Close enough that we have to take precautions not to be seen."

"How is that going?"

Jim said, "I honestly don't know. Let's find out. I have not wanted to disturb them, but now seems like a good enough time, and you can pass on the status of those filters to the chief. Care to join me?"

As the two left the bridge, Lieutenant Anders, who sat at the helm, took over the captain's chair and the copilot took over helm control, all without having to be told. The crew had become a cohesive unit after spending so long together. They were able to predict what was needed and when. Jim and others noticed the entire ship ran much more efficiently than when this trip started.

When the two entered engineering Jim saw Chief, Scott, Sam, Claire and several crewmen standing around a large, round hologram projection table, upon which an image of the ship surrounded in speckles was being manipulated as it passed near a planet. Various data was displayed here and there on the table, graphs, and charts, which constantly updated as the ship approached and then departed the planet. Jim had no idea what the data represented or meant.

"I think that's it," Sam said as smiles appeared on everyone's faces.

"Room ten hut," shouted the first crewman who noticed Major Norgas enter the room.

"As you were," Jim said, loud enough for all to hear before anyone had time to snap to attention other than the crewman who first saw him. This journey had taught him why General Long always said that so quickly. It got in the way at times, especially when someone was working on a delicate procedure. He thought about doing away with it for this journey but understood its importance to maintain discipline and distance between officers and the crew.

Including Jim, there were four officers onboard. With such a small pool of people Jim could spend his free time with, he spent more and more time with the civilians the longer the trip took. Along with the bridge officers, Scott, and John, Dr. Stevens held the rank of captain; Sam, Claire, and Steve became the group he spent his free time with. The group routinely came to his quarters for conversation or to play a game. It surprised Jim that he never suspected what Steve was up to.

Claire said, "Jim, you're just in time. We just finished the simulations on the last planet, and Sam programmed the software needed by the drive computers as we went, so we're good to go."

Jim asked, "What do you mean, the last planet?"

Claire said, "Each planet in Earth's solar system has a different composition. Because of that, a different approach vector will have to be used, not only to slow the ship, but to avoid kicking up anything in our wake that may give away our presence. The drive has to be altered slightly for each planet, so the software has been written in packets. As we find out which planet is next, we can upload that packet of the program."

"Which planet is next?" He was amazed they got that far into the details of the project to think about each planet and the wake that may be created.

"Yes," Sam took over and answered Jim's question. "We won't

know till we get closer which planet we will first encounter and where the other planets are in their orbit around the sun. But as we come into the system, we will easily figure out the order of the planets we will pass on the way to Earth, and which ones we will need to use to slow down." She paused, and glanced at the others on the team. "At best guess, we will need three to five planets to slow down, depending on which ones we pass. If we're lucky, Earth will be on the other side of the sun and we won't have to worry about most of this."

"That's not exactly correct," Claire hesitantly added.

Jim asked, "What's wrong?"

She brought up a holographic image of the Milky Way on the table. "As you know, the galaxy is pretty much flat and bulges in the middle. It kind of looks like a hurricane, and we are flying parallel to the plane of the galaxy." Claire set the holographic image to zoom along the path the ship had been flying. "Earth's solar system is flat, like a plate. Sam's explanation is correct, but it makes it sound like we will be entering the solar system from the edge of the plate, but we won't. We will enter Earth's solar system from the top down, looking at the plate full on. We can pick and choose the first planet we use depending on where Earth is."

The holographic image finished its trip and was now displaying Earth's solar system at the angle the ship will be approaching, which was about 60 degrees to the plane of the galaxy.

Jim said, "Looks like that will actually work to our advantage."

Claire said, "Yes, and no. We can use the planet that will slow us the most first and so on. We will not have anything to hide behind till we get to that first planet. Sorry if I stepped on your toes Sam."

Sam said, "No, you didn't."

Jim asked, "So, we could use the sun first?"

"We, hmm..." Sam started, then scratched her head.

Claire helped Sam with the answer, "Earth kept a really close eye on the sun back then. It would not be a good idea if you wanted to remain unnoticed. Besides, the ship does not have enough protection from the radiation we will experience that close to the sun. Saturn or Jupiter would be best for initial braking."

Jim asked, "Speaking of being unnoticed – how are we on the camouflage?"

Scott had a big grin on his face as he started to explain, "Oh, that's the amazing part. As you know, we are able to target space dust on the atomic level. With that, we can either, as you know, use it to push the ship, or hold it near the skin of the ship and," he could barely contain his excitement, "we can even rotate it and aim the light reflecting off of it."

"Oh, come on," Jim said skeptically.

"Show him," Scott said like a kid in a candy store.

Chief Besch said, "It's true. We can bend light around the ship making it invisible."

Jim said, "Wait a minute –"

Sam said, "Not exactly bend light, just reflect it. Think of it like a camera and a display. If you place a camera pointing backward, say behind me. And I held a monitor in front of me displaying what the camera is picking up, you won't see me. You will see what is behind me, making me invisible. By using the reflectivity of the dust, we can do the same thing."

Jim asked, "The ship's drive can do that?"

Claire warned, "Yes, but it has drawbacks."

"Such as?" He was amazed at the possibility of having an invisibility shield.

Sam said, "With our current limitations due to, well, time,

computer power, and so forth –"

Chief Besch said impatiently, "We can't use the engine to move or steer the ship at the same time we do this."

Sam said, "Well to put it bluntly, yes and –"

"We can't make the entire ship invisible," Chief Besch said, which yielded a puzzled look on Jim's face.

Jim's lips started to move to ask "What?" but Sam tried to finish Chief's answer. "We can only make one side of the ship invisible, currently. For example, as we pass by the Earth's moon with the nose of the ship facing Earth, we can make the ship invisible to anyone on Earth, but someone standing on the moon will see us as we pass by."

Jim looked at Chief, who shrugged his shoulders and said, "She's too long-winded."

Sam rolled her eyes and gave Chief a nudge in the ribs with her elbow. Chief gave Jim a sly smile out the corner of his mouth.

Sam said, "This will only make us visually invisible. Some telescopes of the era used thermal or radiographic detection."

Claire said, "Yeah, but those were used to observe specific, known objects. We're more concerned with the backyard astronomer trying to get his name in a book." Everyone agreed with what Claire said.

Jim asked, "When will all this be ready?"

Sam said, "It's ready now."

Jim said, "Wow, you guys, and ladies, did a lot of work, congratulations. Chief, Doc has something important to tell you."

Chief said, "It had better not be another damn kidney stone!"

"What?" Jim said, scrunching his nose and creasing his forehead. "No!"

Everyone in earshot chuckled. Sam, concerned, looked at Chief.

"I'll tell you later," Chief said to Sam.

"Chief," Dr. Stevens said, shaking his head, "It's time for your penicillin shot."

"Doc!" Jim scolded.

Dr. Stevens said, "All right. But he asked for it. And how often do I get an opening like that?" Dr. Stevens smiled, thinking of the possibilities of where this could have gone.

Jim waited a moment and said, "Doctor?"

Dr. Stevens said, "The CO2 scrubbers are getting saturated, and I think we have a couple of weeks before they have to be recharged."

Scott asked, "Recharged? How do we recharge them?"

"We can't do that here," Chief Besch said, shaking his head. "We have to be in an oxygen environment. Doing it on ship will just ruin the air we have left, filling it with CO2. To recharge them, we just pump hot air through them." Chief smirked and looked at Sam, who punched him in the arm.

Jim asked, "Do you have what you need to do this onboard?"

Chief said, "Well, on a normal up and back, we just pump some of the heated air from reentry through them and that takes care of it, but we've never had to flush this much before. By the book, we have to pump air at 400 degrees Fahrenheit at a constant flow rate of seven and a half cubic feet per minute for ten hours. On reentry, we're able to cool the super-heated air enough to get it down to 400 degrees, but that's for just, what –" Chief shrugged his shoulders, "20 to 30 minutes? We are going to have to put it down somewhere and pump some air through the Core to heat it for the amount of time we will need."

Scott asked, "Won't that be radioactive?"

Sam said, "The core does not have that kind of reaction. We will be fine."

"If I remember right," Jim said while glancing at the ceiling trying to remember, "didn't someone say the least populated place on Earth and the best place for us to enter the atmosphere undetected was the South Pacific?"

Claire said, "Yes"

"So where would be a good place to set down while we take care of this?" Jim asked as he walked to a communications terminal to ask for Paul.

"Paul here," quickly came back over the terminal, and Jim asked what he needed. "Pearl and Hermès Atoll," was the answer Paul gave after some careful thought.

"What?" Jim asked, completely puzzled.

Paul asked, "Where are you?" Upon hearing engineering, "I'll be right there."

A few minutes passed till Paul entered engineering and displayed the Hawaiian Islands on the hologram table. He used his hands and zoomed the projection in on a tiny spec southeast of Midway Island. The table displayed a circular reef with possibly enough land above water to land the ship on the eastern edge of a reef.

Paul said, "No one lives there so we won't be seen. But there may be problems flying because there are a lot of birds, and I mean a lot."

Chief Besch said, "That won't be a problem. With this ship's engine, birds just might give us something extra to push against. Besides they just might taste like chicken."

Sam exclaimed, "You wouldn't!"

Chief Besch said, "What? I'm getting tired of that dispenser food. Does anyone else feel like a barbecue?"

Sam protested, "Eugene Samuel Besch! Don't you even think

about it. I know you're from the country and eating unconventional food is just another day to you, but –"

Chief Besch said, "Oh, chicken is okay but some other fowl and you get all squeamish?"

Sam did not know how to respond and just looked at Chief Besch with her mouth open.

Jim asked, "Eugene?"

"Don't start with me, Stinker!"

"Hey, I'm just saying, I've known you for how long? And I never knew your first name?"

Chief Besch said, "It was my grandfather's name."

"Where does Samuel come from?"

"That was my father's name."

"If that's a family tradition, that means your son's name would be Samuel Eugene? When does the second, or third come in?"

Chief Besch looked at Jim and asked, "What?" He thought for a moment and said, "Eugene came from my Mother's side of the family."

Sam said, "That would make his initials either WEB or DEB," Then realized she accidentally let everyone know the chief and her were becoming a couple.

Jim looked at Chief with a raised eyebrow, and Chief said, "Don't start with me, Stinker."

Jim had a smile on his face, began to laugh and shake his head.

Scott asked, "Not to change the subject but, aren't several military installations right near there? We might be seen on whatever sensors they have."

Paul said, "Radar? Yes, Hawaii had several early warning systems in place, and Midway Island is right next door. Midway was usually abandoned but it was used from time to time by the military for training."

Jim asked, "Do you have someplace else?"

"How about..." Paul manipulated the map scrolling across the Pacific Ocean toward the south, "Te Au O Tu?"

Jim asked, "What? If you're testing my geography you won. Who made up these names?"

Paul said, "Well, it was originally named 'Sandwich Island' by Captain Cook. How it got that name," he shrugged his shoulders, "I don't know."

Scott asked, "Sandwich Island? Wait, wasn't the sandwich invented during a poker game? Captain Cook?"

Jim looked at Scott with a *'not now'* look on his face. "Please continue," Jim said toward Paul.

"It is actually two Islands with a shallow reef between them. Manuae to the west and Te Au O Tu to the east. Both are uninhabited. The highest elevation on the two is just 16 feet but with the trees on top of that, it might just hide the ship nicely. Te Au O Tu is what I want you to see. Lake Marecages in the middle, if it is as shallow as the coral surrounding the island, you could set down there and not be seen by any ships or fishermen that happen to come near." He finally found the pair of islands on the hologram table and zoomed in.

Jim said, "Wow, that is in the middle of nowhere." He studied the contours of the islands for a while and slowly nodded his head, "This will do. Let's do it. Eugene, how long will you need?"

Chief said, "Only my mother called me Eugene. And you sure don't look as pretty as her. How do you look in a dress?"

Jim asked, "Should I shave my legs?"

Chief Besch challenged, "Why? She didn't."

Sam started to say something but Chief cut her off, "Don't you even think about it. You're shaving."

Sam said, "Then you don't think about making barbecue out of cute little birds."

Chief Besch knew he was backed into a corner. Reluctantly he relented, "Fine." Then turned his attention back toward Jim, "If you can set the ship down and open the cargo ramp so we're breathing fresh air and not dependent on the scrubbers at all," Chief Besch did some calculations in his head as he spoke. "I'll have to run some hoses since we will be using the core for the heat. If I can get those run before we get there, eleven hours tops."

Jim said, "Sounds good. Everyone, this is coming together, thank you for your hard work."

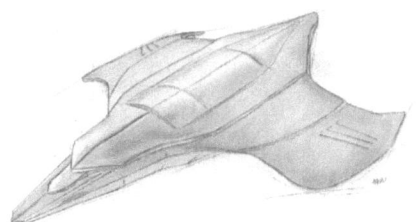

Chapter 33: EARTH IN VIEW

A few days later, with everything ready, the ship slipped into Earth's solar system and put Saturn in the cross-hairs. It was decided Saturn and its moons could be used on several approaches to slow the ship considerably, possibly enough to go directly to Earth from there.

Jim sat in the captain's chair, Scott at the helm with John in the copilot seat.

Claire and Sam monitored the approach to Saturn to ensure nothing from the planet or the rings was kicked up into their wake which could give their position away, yet maximized the effect of the planet to slow the ship. One ran simulations ahead of the ship, the other fed course corrections to the helm.

Jim asked, "How is our camouflage holding?"

"Actually," Sam answered a few words at a time as she continued feeding the data to the helm, "Earth is on the opposite side of the Sun... we don't need it now; the dust we were using... was dumped once we dropped behind the Sun. So now, we can use the engine... to help slow the ship."

Jim asked, "If Earth is on the other side of the Sun, why are you worried about what's picked up in our wake?"

Claire and Sam looked at each other, only now realizing what they did.

Sam said, "Practice." Which caused Claire to smile, and she could barely contain her laugh.

Over the ship's intercom, Jim announced, "All hands, brace yourselves, we may be in for a bumpy ride." Then he asked Scott, "Are you sure you don't want me to take the helm?"

Scott said, "Thanks, but I got this. Actually, this is quite boring. I'm just putting in course corrections that pop up on the panel. You get to enjoy the view."

Jim said in a joking manner, "That's true. Rank does have its privileges, and it's quite lovely."

The ship slowed considerably after using Saturn and several of its moons on consecutive passes. Titan, Rhea, Dione, and Tethys were able to be used on most of the passes. When the ship slowed to the point where it would take mere days to reach Earth, the ship left Saturn and headed towards Earth. The ship's drive picked up a new cloud of interstellar dust and material from Saturn's rings to use as a cloak.

When Earth was finally in view, it was decided to land on the moon to observe and listen to whatever signals they were able to receive. It was quickly apparent they were alone. No signals lit up the normal comm channels. The Bermuda Triangle, where Anarbia was prepared to receive thousands of people, was mysteriously quiet. The Dragons Triangle south of Japan, where China built its base, was equally quiet. Either everyone was hiding, or no other ships made it.

Jim started wondering what happened to Sarah, and, for the first time he could remember, became depressed. He left Scott in charge and locked himself in his quarters.

The crew understood and let him be. Upon hearing the news they may be the only ones that made it, the crew went through their own round of disbelief and depression.

Claire knocked on Jim's door a few hours later and received only silence.

Without the commander around, the depression on the ship had worsened. Scott tried to fill Jim's shoes, but it was not the same.

The next day, Claire tried again. Worried for Jim, she did not stop knocking till he finally answered the door and let her in his quarters.

Two days passed before Jim's voice came over the ship's intercom. "Attention all crew." Every head perked up hearing his voice. "Meet me in the mess hall, now! That will be all."

Everyone was confused by that uncharacteristic announcement, but stopped what they were doing and went to the mess hall. Upon entering, the crew was greeted by a feast spread out almost everywhere they looked.

Jim and Claire said, "Come in, come in."

After everyone was seated and eating, Jim stood and said, "I'm sorry for my absence for the past few days. The weight of realizing we," Jim spread his arms, "might be all that's left, was too much to handle. There is no excuse, but it let me clear my head and come up with a plan on how we should proceed," he paused for a few moments. "These are not orders. I want your input, ideas, and opinions. We will proceed to Anarbia as we have been. Once there, we need to get to work scouring the historical archives for persons with skills we need who will not affect the timeline if they were to suddenly disappear, and recruit them."

Everyone in the room was in disbelief. This went against their number one order: Do not be discovered.

Dr. Paul Bullard stood up and asked, "Do you realize what you're asking us to do?"

Jim started to reply to Paul's question, but everyone started talking at once until, "AT EASE," Chief Besch bellowed. "Major." Chief returned the floor to Jim.

"Best I can figure, right now on Earth it is the year 2005. That puts us three to four hundred years behind where we are supposed to be. Not only is our technology way behind where it should be, but our population should be much higher. We lost all that time to increase both." Jim paused and looked at their faces. "Look, like it or not we are it. I for one do not want to lose this fight before it's begun."

Chief said, "Hear, hear!" He stood and said, "Now which one of you ladies, want some of this?" Only to receive a slap to the stomach by Sam who was sitting next to him. Chief doubled over causing laughter to erupt from everyone in the room.

Paul stood and said, "Truth be told, the chief and Major are right. We do not have enough people to sustain the population. Without inbreeding. Sorry Chief."

Paul's comment caused another round of laughter.

Jim asked, "Think it over, what do we need to do to get back on track? If you have a viable plan, I will happily welcome it. Take your time, finish your meals, and let's get this ship moving in two hours." He sat down and began clearing his plate.

Scott was sitting next to Jim and said, "I was not expecting that. You're right. Short of a miracle, we are way behind."

"So I've got your support?"

"Absolutely, this is going to get interesting."

Jim chuckled a bit and replied, "You said it."

"Is Claire called for?"

"Do we need to revisit how inappropriate that would be?"

Scott smiled and said, "So she is still available. Good to know."

With the meal finished the crew returned to their duty positions and got the ship ready to lift off of the moon for their final approach to Earth.

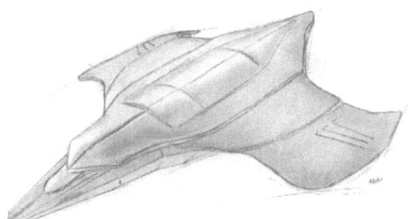

Chapter 34: EARTH

Upon entering the Earth's atmosphere, the ship lost its cloud of dust it picked up from the moon as it made a few orbits to gain speed. The dust had helped camouflage the ship from any prying eyes, but that was no longer possible. The engine was needed to move the air molecules around the ship, not only to slow the descent but also to prevent a fire trail caused by reentry.

Sam monitored radio traffic and nothing unusual was reported. As far as anyone onboard knew, their approach was unnoticed.

The ship started to settle down on Lake Marecages in the center of Te Au O Tu, but it was quickly discovered the lake was much deeper than the coral surrounding the island. Opening the cargo ramp would not allow fresh air in. The ship side-slipped into the atoll of Manuae and gradually settled down on the coral. The creaking of the coral was heard throughout the ship as the coral strained under the weight and soon held the full load of the ship – the first time the ship had touched Earth in months.

Despite the circumstances, it was a joyous occasion. Most of the crew were in the cargo area when Jim arrived. Others leaned over the railings on the second level looking down.

Jim asked, "Chief, do you want the honors?"

Chief pushed a palm sized round button on the side of the railing, and the loading ramp began to open. Most people closed their eyes as they took a long, deep breath of the cool, predawn, salty sea air of the atoll. The smell was like heaven compared to the stale air they had been breathing. The tranquility of the moment was interrupted by a loud slap as the chief killed a mosquito against his neck "Ah, just great!" complained Chief Besch. Soon, several others in the cargo bay were swatting at the nearly invisible, irritating insects, and the ramp was once again closed. "Now what?" asked the chief, looking at Jim for guidance.

"Can you recharge the CO2 scrubbers with the drive coils running?" Jim asked.

Chief said, "Yes, I just need hot air, and pump the exhaust outside."

Jim got on the comm to the bridge and told John to take the ship about a mile out to sea and hover the ship, so that when the loading ramp was lowered it would be about ten feet above the water's surface.

John asked, "Is there anything wrong?"

Jim replied, "Mosquitoes!"

"Mosquitoes?" John spoke to himself, suddenly feeling itchy at the thought of it. "I hate mosquitoes."

The ship was soon in a hover with the loading ramp open once again, this time with no pesky insects trying to gain access to the ship.

Chief took all of the scrubbers offline as the crewmen hurried about the ship connecting the hoses that they had laid in the corridors earlier.

Every once in a while for the next hour, a slap could be heard in different parts of the ship as the remaining mosquitoes were dispatched with extreme prejudice. None of the crew members enjoyed the welcome committee they received upon their return to

Earth.

Several hours into the process of recharging the CO2 scrubbers, Jim was requested to come to the bridge. Upon entering the bridge, Scott and Claire hovered over one of the displays.

Jim asked "What do you have?"

Scott replied, "Sir, a couple of aircraft and one surface vessel are heading this way."

Jim asked, "ETA?" Just as Sam came through the bridge doors.

Scott said, "The aircraft are about five minutes out. The ship looks like a cruiser, about ten minutes."

Jim asked, "What kind of aircraft?"

Sam interrupted, "Sir, I think I can help with those. I noticed them while checking something in engineering. One is unmanned," Sam paused while she brought up some data on a monitor on the starboard side of the bridge. "The other is a fighter jet belonging to the American Navy."

Scott asked, "Don't they fly in pairs? Where is the other?"

Jim ordered, "Keep searching! Sam, how can you help?"

"I can hack into the computers and disrupt their radar, weapons, communications, you name it."

Paul said, "Oh, you better be careful with that."

Sam asked, "Why?"

Paul said, "If they detect your hack it may result in a redesign of the weapon, changing our past. If they don't detect the hack, they may think something is defective and redesign it anyway."

Jim said, "Just great. I'm about to have a few missiles fired at me and I have to worry about changing the past?"

Claire said, "Don't worry about the missiles. The engine can easily deflect them, and any bullets they may fire."

Jim said, "I know all about that."

Claire reminded, "You also know as long as we are using the engine to move, or hover as we are now, we cannot use it to cloak the ship. Detection is our biggest concern."

Paul commented, "I'll agree with that."

"I could make it look like a malfunction," Sam said while thinking. "In some sub-system or something. Like maybe an arming circuit."

Jim said, "Whatever you're going to do, do it fast!" He then said over the ships intercom, "Chief, How much have you got done with the filters? Are we able to submerge the ship for a few days?"

Chief exclaimed, "What? Did I hear —"

Jim said, "Yes Chief, we're going to dive the ship."

Chief argued, "This is an aircraft, spacecraft, not a —"

Jim did not have time to debate, "Chief, do we have enough air?"

Chief said, "It doesn't really work that way, but I'm sure we have a couple days of life left in the scrubbers."

Jim asked, "How long do you need to bring them back online? We need them ASAP."

Chief Besch looked about him and answered into the comm, "Give me eight minutes to clear the cargo ramp and make sure all the vents are sealed. The air we have in the ship will be enough till I can get the system running again."

Jim said, "You got it. Let me know as soon as the ship is ready." He shut the comm link down and joined the others toward the back of the bridge.

Scott asked, "Did I hear, 'dive the ship?'"

Jim said, "I remember one of the designers talking about it. Besides, how else do we get to Anarbia?"

"Ooh, I know," Sam said excitedly. "The drone is being flown remotely. The pilot relies on a video feed from the drone. I can replace the video feed," Sam spoke as she hacked into the communications of both aircraft, "with one from the fighter."

"Video feed from the fighter?" Claire asked.

Scott explained to Claire, "Some Missile systems use video imaging for targeting –"

Claire asked, "How so?"

"Some have images stored internally and compare that image with what a camera is picking up for navigation and to verify the target. The fighter also has cameras to confirm kills and for later review if needed."

Claire asked, "If needed, for what?"

Scott said, "Say a plane got shot down. Cameras from the wingman or other aircraft can verify if the pilot ejected, and possibly where to start a search and rescue. Or confirm a target was destroyed."

"You said to confirm kills. Why do you want to know how many people you killed?"

"It's not for that. After so many kills the pilot becomes an ace, and –" The look on Claire's face made him realize, he was backed into a rabbit hole and was digging himself deeper.

Claire asked, "When you replace the video, won't the pilot notice the difference?"

"Yes," Sam answered as she continued to work. "He may think it is just a glitch in the system and not figure it out till it's all over. In the meantime, he will have a very difficult time flying the drone. Also, the video from the drone of our presence will be lost."

Jim whispered in Scott's ear, "I guess you don't need to worry anymore if she is available."

Scott slumped slightly and shook his head as he glanced at Jim.

Jim asked, "What can you do about the fighter?"

"And the fighter..." Sam dragged out the last syllable as she worked. "Got you. When he tries to feed targeting info to his missiles, a relay will short, preventing the upload from completing, and he will not be able to fire his missiles. If the missiles do fire, they will fly wild, not having a target lock."

"That's great, but what about the video evidence from the fighter?" Jim reworded his question.

"Oh, that." She was satisfied both aircraft had been rendered harmless and forgot the last detail. "The only thing I can do about that is change the resolution that is recorded, making it nearly impossible to get a good image of us. How does two by two sound?"

Jim asked, "What's two by two?"

"The resolution. Two pixels high by two pixels wide."

"Do you mean..."

Sam smiled and nodded her head

Jim laughed and said, "Sounds great. What can you do about the ship?"

"Hmm, not much I'm afraid," Sam said and rested her chin on the palm of her hand as she thought. "Most of their systems are completely internal, which makes it almost impossible to hack into."

Jim asked, "Most, you said? Which ones can you get? Something insignificant might make a big difference."

"Ship to ship, which will be used to give other ships our location and targeting info," Sam began running down the list of possible avenues for electronic warfare against a U.S. Navy Cruiser. "Radar, sonar, engine sensors, GPS positioning, and satellite communications. Not much there."

"You said radar?" Scott asked. "Can you fool it as to our position?"

Sam said, "That's easy! The problem is, that several of their weapons have their own radar linked directly to the weapon. I may not be able to fool them."

Jim asked, "Are those systems transmitting targeting info?"

"No, they are completely self-contained," Paul answered for

Sam, joining in on the conversation.

"Engine sensors," Jim thought out loud and under his breath.

Claire asked, "What was that?"

"Sam!" Jim said in his command voice, startling her. "Can you manipulate the engine sensors? Make it look like they have a fire on board?"

Sam said, "Yes!" Then started to chuckle. "That's sneaky."

Jim asked with a smile, "Switching video feeds isn't?"

Claire asked, "I don't get it. How is a fire alarm going to help? That is a warship."

Jim said, "Fire onboard a ship is the most dangerous thing that can happen. The first thing they will do is stop in their tracks to fight the fire."

Claire asked, "Why don't we just move away from them?"

Eager to redeem himself, Scott explained, "A cruiser usually patrols the outskirts of a large fleet of ships, protecting it. The fleet is possibly playing war games right now. We don't know which direction they might be and just might stumble into the heart of it. The fewer the witnesses to our presence, the better."

The cruiser entered visual range and could be seen out the port side of the bridge. Shortly after, it began to slow as was indicated on the display. Their ruse worked but would not last long.

Jim asked over the communication panel, "Chief, how much longer?"

"Almost there, just waiting on one more... okay, we're good to go, Major," Chief answered as the last indicator on the panel he manipulated switched from red to green. "Have they ever actually tested this thing underwater?"

Jim said, "Only on the scale model. Scott and I meant to but we ran out of time."

Chief said, "Great! Just go easy on her."

Jim said, "We will at first. Make sure you let me know of any problems. I need to know before we get to the Drake Passage that the ship can take it."

Chief asked, "The Drake Passage? What's that?"

"An extremely turbulent region of water separating the Atlantic from the Pacific at the tip of South America," Jim answered, getting the attention of everyone on the bridge.

Chief said, "Great, just great. Move it! Move it! Get those hoses stowed and get the scrubbers online. We are in for a bumpy ride."

Jim said, "Scott, take the helm and submerge the ship. Nice and easy."

Paul asked, "The Drake Passage? Underwater? It's bad enough on the surface, but underwater, is that wise? That area is littered with over 800 sunken ships."

Jim said, "It's quite deep. We won't hit any."

"That's not what I meant. Forty-foot waves, massive underwater mountains, the entire Antarctic Circumpolar Current being funneled through that narrow passage – we will be knocked around like a tin can in a blender."

"I know it will be a bit rough, but the cushion of air created around the ship by the natural function of the engine in a water environment should buffer most of the turbulence. Or so I read."

"Or so you read?" Scott asked nervously.

Paul said, "A bit rough is an understatement. The current circulating around Antarctica in wider areas is only about 4 miles per hour, and over one hundred miles wide. But there, that passage funnels all that water, accelerating it so fast we will get sucked in before we know it. Possibly slamming us into one of those mountains. Not to mention the other currents at work. The more saline-rich water being sucked in with us will be trying to rise, pushing us up, and the cooler water being pushed north while warmer water rushes in to take its place. The region isn't nicknamed 'the washing machine' for nothing." Paul explained what they were in for, getting more concerned as he continued.

In an attempt to calm the historian, Jim said, "Paul, you're scaring the ladies. Besides, we are very limited in our options to get to Anarbia. If we go west we will be going against the current, taking much longer and facing much the same risks. Both canals, Panama and Suez are too shallow to sneak through, and going around Canada or Russia are just way out of the way." Jim ran through all the possibilities, "Flying or being on the surface, we will be spotted, so this is our best option."

Scott said, "I don't know about having the helm through that... Drake Passage."

Jim glanced at Paul, then to Scott, a bit irritated. "When we get there," Jim began, "I'll take the helm, but I want you in the copilot's seat and John, if you will be our extra eyes, I'd appreciate it. For now, let's concentrate on getting this ship underwater and out of here."

Scott said, "You got it."

The ship began to tilt the nose down, still hovering over the water. The engine came online with an audible hum previously never heard and continued to get louder and deeper in pitch. Water started to funnel up and around the ship, which formed a deep pocket of air in the water directly in front of the ship. A fish jumped from one side of the pocket to the other, then another. The drive computer ignored the fish as it created the air pocket the ship would be surrounded in.

Once the ship started moving, anything in its path would be pushed aside molecule by molecule. The engine had never moved so much matter at one time before. Moving through water would be like moving through a solid object for the engine. It would not only have to pull and push to make the ship move forward, but the ship's drive also had to get everything in front of the ship out of the way. Moving through the atmosphere or space was child's play for the engine compared to this.

The skipper on the American cruiser noticed the column of water and the movement of the unidentified object ahead of him. He picked up his binoculars to get a closer look. All of a sudden, the object darted into the waves and disappeared. "Sonar, tell me you got that."

Across the bridge of the cruiser, a sailor stared into a black funnel designed to block light and make it easier to see the screen. He responded, "Sir, it was off the scope almost as soon as it appeared."

A fast attack sub that was closing in on the area suddenly had a collision alarm go off. Before the sub could make any attempt to avoid whatever was in its path, it was gone.

Both Jim and Scott were excited by how fast the ship darted into the water and was propelled forward. It was well known that if you surround an object in a pocket of air underwater, supersonic speeds were possible. Torpedoes had used the technique for years. But to personally experience it, even after everything they had been through, was a thrill.

"Yee-haw," Scott excitedly said as he narrowly steered the ship around the conning tower of the sub they previously did not know was there. "This takes me back to my academy days." Scott beamed.

Jim asked, "But the Drake Passage has you spooked?"

Scott explained, "Being in control of something on the edge is one thing. The way Paul explained that passage is another."

Jim said, "Yeah, I can understand that." He took a seat in the captain's chair and opened a comm channel. "Chief, how do we look?"

"Easy, I said! Give a couple of hotshot pilots a new toy and the first thing they do is try and break it."

Jim said apologetically, "Chief, that couldn't be avoided. Besides, we did not know the ship was going to accelerate the way it did. How is the ship? Any leaks?"

"Alright, well, just pull back on the sticks a little, would ya? Just because Anarbia doesn't have a 'Boom boom room', doesn't mean I don't want to enjoy myself when I get there." Chief Besch said as he calmed down. "Everything is in the green. The core has ramped up a bit and the temperature is holding. The skin, it's weird, I can actually hear the drive coils. I think it's at the max capacity, so just watch it."

Jim asked, "Max depth? We are barely under the surface. Just," Jim paused and glanced over at the control panel in front of Scott in the copilot seat, "we are at 150 feet."

Chief Besch responded, "The depth is not the problem, it's how fast the engine has to work."

"Understood. Record as much data as you can. That's something we will want to take a look at once we get settled and start working on improvements," Jim said, already thinking about the next version of the ship.

"Roger that," came the reply.

Claire listened in and started to record the data she monitored, thinking it may be vital since their new home was on the ocean floor. Anytime a ship entered or exited Anarbia, the engine would be maxed out.

Sam searched for any vessels in the area. Like Claire, she began to record her findings. With her engineering and computer background, she thought she could come up with modifications without having to build a completely new ship.

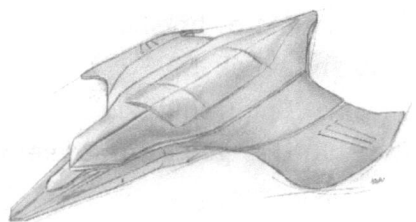

Chapter 35: CALM BEFORE THE STORM

The ship smoothed out at just over eight hundred miles per hour at a depth of two thousand feet. The ship seemed to purr, and Chief was very pleased, for a change.

From where their underwater voyage started, they had roughly 6,700 miles before they entered the Drake Passage.

Jim said, "Scott, I'm going to my quarters to get some rest. Wake me in four hours and I'll let you get some sleep. We will enter the passage in just over eight hours. Give as much of the crew as possible a break to sleep and eat before then. There won't be much of either once in the passage."

Scott said, "Yes sir."

When Jim entered his quarters, the room was aglow from the light caused by the engine that came through the windows on both sides and the ceiling. The entire trip to Earth he had seen it, but it was not this bright. The light was not noticeable while on the bridge, with its glass darkened so the pilot could see what he was doing, but here the windows did not darken. It almost looked like a ball of lightning surrounded the ship. He knew it was a function of the engine, but lightning was the best way to describe it. The light that came through the windows was bright enough that he did not need to turn on any lights to find his way. He thought it was beautiful.

It wasn't till his senior year in high school his family moved to

West Virginia. Before this, he grew up in the Midwest and always liked to watch thunderstorms, even though in the Midwest those storms spawned tornadoes.

Storms in the plains of the Midwest covered the entre sky, where one bolt of lightning most often filled the entire field of view. He thought of lightning as nature's fireworks, and just like fireworks, the louder and brighter, the better the show. That is, until it gets too close.

He remembered one particular night, he was lying in the middle of a field with a date, looking at the stars and other things. Lightning gradually encroached on their location as they enjoyed the show. One particularly loud crack caused both of them to bolt.

Jim had borrowed his buddy's motorcycle, so the two of them had to wait out the storm under a gazebo. The storm continued to worsen with hail and strong winds. His date was not pleased because, in their haste, they had forgotten the blanket in the field, and so she shivered soaking wet.

Jim had found out the next day that a tornado was on the ground just a few miles away.

The lightning that surrounded the ship, however, made ro crack of thunder, just a steady, low, drawling hum as the engine did its work. The hum helped him fall asleep. He did not realize just how tired he was till his head hit the pillow.

Strangely, Jim dreamed of lying on his back on a blanket in a wide-open field. Sarah was lying by his side as they looked at the night sky. Sarah asked, "Did you ever wonder what constellation our sun is in? I mean to an alien, do we look like some sort of alien animal? A flower? Or a warrior?" They watched a distant thunderstorm creep closer. Its tendrils of white-hot light streaked across the sky from horizon to horizon. "One one-thousand, two one-thousand," he heard Sarah count in a whisper. When she got to four the clap of thunder was so loud it shook the earth. "Okay, one mile away, time to leave." Jim heard Sarah say just as the intercom buzzed to life. Jim groaned, wanting to spend more time with her, and the intercom buzzed again.

It was Scott waking him at the four-hour mark. "I'll be right there," Jim said as he jumped out of bed and made a cup of black coffee.

The only person on the bridge was Scott, who sat in the captain's chair. The ship was on autopilot and felt as smooth as riding on a sheet of glass. "Where is everyone?" Jim asked as he took a sip of coffee.

"Claire went to get some rest along with John, both of whom should be here any minute now. Sam just left to get something to eat and then take a nap."

"Did anything happen?"

"No but the autopilot is great. It detected a pod of whales and automatically plotted a new course. Did you know the counter between the pilot and copilot station was a hologram emitter?"

"What? No," Jim answered, puzzled. He piloted a similar ship numerous times during Operation CAMPFIRE, flew how far across the galaxy, and never knew this.

"Yeah, when it detected the whales, it displayed them in real-time as a hologram right here," Scott said and held his hand a few inches over the counter between the pilot and copilot stations. "Then plotted a course around them and altered course."

"Huh, I guess nothing has been in our path before."

"What about that filament?"

"The ship didn't even know that was there. Well, go get some rest. I'll call you in four hours. After your break, if you would, stop by the mess hall and bring me a sandwich or something, please? I was so tired I didn't even think about eating. When you woke me, it felt like I just fell asleep."

"Couldn't sleep?"

"No, I fell asleep as soon as my head hit the pillow."

Scott said, "I've had those nights before. One time I figured I'd just take a nap on a Friday evening and wake up in time to meet my friends to go bar hopping. I woke up in time to go bar hopping the next night, Saturday. I thought it was still Friday till a friend asked where I was last night. And I slept like a baby when I got home that night."

Jim said, "I think you got me beat. The hardest I ever slept was through an air raid siren."

Scott asked, "What?"

"Different time, different place, but my commander was pissed."

"I bet he was. Well, I'll see you in a couple of hours."

Jim sat in the captain's chair, pulled the glass panel out of the arm and started searching the computer for any other hidden gems the ship had. Several minutes later, Claire entered the bridge, and he asked if she knew about anything the designers put into the ship he was unaware of or hadn't used yet.

The conversation went on for a while before John entered the bridge and took his seat at the helm. Later, he turned around and started explaining things he had discovered.

Jim was amazed there were so many things he did not know about the very ship he tested and had flown all this time. Time passed so quickly that he did not realize four hours had passed, and he called Scott when he noticed.

Scott entered the bridge with a nice platter of food and sat in the copilot's seat. John started to get up from the pilot's seat to switch with Scott, but Scott stopped him, saying, "I'll be in this seat in a few minutes anyway, so you may as well stay where you are."

John said, "Yes sir."

Jim opened a communication channel for the entire ship. "Attention crew, in about 20 minutes we will enter an area of very turbulent water. We do not know exactly what to expect. Make whatever preparations you need now – latrine, food, whatever – and secure yourself at your station." With that, several clicks were heard throughout the bridge as seat belts were fastened.

"Lieutenant, let's switch seats," Jim said and sat in the pilot's seat to the left of Scott. He reached over the holographic image and pushed a previously unknown button, which caused a glass control panel to come out of the top of the counter between the hologram area and the windscreen glass.

Jim looked at Scott and said, "There is a lot about this ship we didn't know." With that, he started tapping on the glass panel, and the holographic area between them displayed the terrain ahead overlaid with the ocean's current, with the speed and direction data in contrasting colors.

Scott asked, "Are you kidding me?"

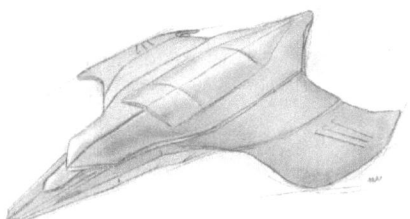

Chapter 36: THE DRAKE PASSAGE

As the ship got closer to the Drake Passage, they were able to see the funneling effect of the area on the holographic display and out the bridge windows from all the silt stirred up.

The Antarctic Circumpolar Current spanned an area over 1240 miles wide along the Pacific Ocean floor. It leisurely puddled along at the slow speed of just two and a half miles per hour, hardly even worth mentioning till all that water was forced into an area less than half that – 559 miles wide with huge mountains rising up from the ocean floor, which made the passage even smaller for all of that water to pass through. Add in the high wind speed pushing the water ever faster from above and chaotic currents as the higher saline content water from the Pacific tried to rise over the water in the Atlantic. Not to mention the different temperatures of the Antarctic water and the warmer water from the north fighting with each other as their buoyancy differences added to the mix. No wonder the area had the unofficial nickname 'The Washing Machine'.

Other colors were added to the display as different directional currents were detected. The position of the most turbulent areas would have been unknown if it were not for this display. The entire passage looked treacherous, but a somewhat smoother course could be plotted with the amount of data collected.

As a precaution, Jim slowed the ship considerably and had to constantly slow the ship as the water sped up and pushed them into the passage ever faster. The engine no longer propelled them forward; it just tried to keep the ship on course.

"All crew," Jim said over the ship's comm, "brace yourselves, we are entering the Drake Passage."

The hum of the engine started to fluctuate, but the ride was relatively smooth. The holographic image showed how the air pocket around the ship shifted as the engine tried to compensate for the turbulent currents.

Suddenly, the YBV-92 dropped a couple of feet and then bounced back up as the autopilot and engine worked together, trying to keep the ship centered in the air pocket surrounding the hull. The sudden increase of power needed by the engine caused the lights throughout the ship to momentarily shut off and then gradually come back on as the power was no longer needed by the engine, only to be followed by another sudden need for power when the ship lurched again. This time to the side, then up. The air pocket not only allowed the YBV-92 to move in the water much faster but also cushioned the turbulence and increased the pressure the hull could withstand.

The Drake Passage was nearly as long as it was wide at 600 miles, every bit of it a constant jolt in a random direction. As they passed the first row of underwater mountains, eddies on the back side of the mountains caused the water to swirl, increasing the discomfort and fear of the crew.

The crew started to envy those who were put in cryo. Those prone to motion sickness who recently had lunch now regretted it, which started a chain reaction of those seat-belted close to each other – a very common occurrence in military cargo planes when passengers were seated shoulder to shoulder, knee to knee, and turbulence was introduced.

Chief increased the output of the core so the lights no longer went out. Even with the lights on, those who were not on the bridge and able to see out wondered if they would make it every time the ship made a sudden jerk up, down, or to the side. Their only clue of what was going on outside the ship was the constant pitch change of the engine as it tried to compensate, followed by a sudden jolt in a random direction.

By listening, they were able to predict when the ship would lunge, but the direction was still unpredictable. The crew in engineering started to make a game of it, betting on which direction next, followed by an impromptu bowling tournament.

Dr. Stevens chose to ride out this part of the voyage with the crew in engineering. He preferred not to be alone for this. For those who chose to unfasten their seat belts to partake in the game, they were lucky Dr. Stevens was there. No one suffered more than a skinned knee or elbow, mostly to the amusement of the rest of the crew, as everyone was laughing by this point.

It seemed like an eternity, but on the bridge, the end was in sight on the hologram. One last underwater mountain chain, and they turned north, east of Argentina, and started heading toward the Falkland Islands.

Jim gave the helm back to John and made a ship-wide announcement, "All hands, we are clear of the passage. Resume normal operation. Smooth waters ahead." He then asked John to plot a course for the Bermuda Triangle.

Claire said, "Jim, at some point we will have to surface." She brought up an image of the air pocket surrounding the ship on her display. "The air surrounding us, among other things, increases our crush depth. The chaos of the Drake Passage caused us to lose about half of the air we had. We do not have a big enough bubble to go deep enough to reach Anarbia"

Jim asked, "Paul, any suggestions on a good place along the way we can surface without being detected?"

Paul had remained on the bridge all throughout the turbulence and still looked a bit green. "The Atlantic features very few uninhabited places, but maybe we can tap into a weather satellite and find a storm or something that might hide us. I don't know how well it will work against radar, but no one should see us unless they are really close."

"Hmm," Jim thought for a moment. "That's a really good idea. I wouldn't have thought of that. Sam?"

Without looking away from the screen in front of her, Sam said, "Already on it boss." A few moments later she found what she was looking for. A tropical storm was making its way across the Atlantic and was a few hundred miles away from their path, just north of the equator.

Jim said, "Good job. John, plot a course. Scott, you got the bridge. I'll be in engineering. I want to check how the ship is doing."

Scott said, "Yes sir."

When he entered engineering, the impromptu bowling tournament was nearing its end. Since the ship was no longer bouncing about, they came up with a way to make it challenging again, or else the scores would not reflect the pain they went through during the passage. Everyone was laughing as they watched the current bowler stumble about dizzy with a makeshift ball in his hand. Jim watched as he tried to figure out what was going on.

"TEN HUT," Someone announced at Jim's presence, which caused the game to stop, to Jim's disappointment.

Jim said, "As you were, please continue." He did not want to end their fun.

Chief Besch started, "Major, I'm sorry, I..."

Jim cut off the chief, "It's all okay Chief, please, enjoy. We need to find ways to unwind when we can." He was happy the crew had time for activities such as this. Lord knows they deserved it. "So, what are the rules?"

Chief explained, "It started while we were in the passage. By the sound of the engine, after a while, we were able to predict when the ship would bounce, but we had no clue which direction. One thing led to another and, well, basically we're bowling. But now that the ship isn't bouncing, we had to come up with a different challenge to finish the game. Now, the bowler keeps his head planted on that pipe and circles it ten times as fast as he can, then bowls. They are just finishing the last few frames." Chief cheered on the current bowler and added, "Care to try?"

"Oh no, maybe next time," and held up his hands. "You were doing this back in the Drake Passage?" He was surprised they were able to stay on their feet, let alone do something like this.

"Well," Chief tried to come up with the words as a smirk crossed his face. "Not directly. It took a while to build up to this, but yeah. We really couldn't perform much maintenance at the time. Had a few scrapes, and the Doc has been here the entire time." Chief looked around the crowd trying to find Dr. Stevens, but he was nowhere to be found. "I guess he left when you announced smooth water."

"Chief, that's fine," Jim said with a reassuring gesture. "I'm just surprised you were able to do anything other than strap yourselves into a chair. I'm glad you found a way to pass the time. Since things settled down, have you had a chance to see if we suffered any damage?"

Chief Besch explained, "The magnetic field relays really had a workout. Several banks went off-line, particularly along the wing tips. They've come back online, but I want to take a look when I get a chance."

"I have every confidence in you, and if you feel checking the relays can wait till after the game, then please do."

"Sir, we have to go outside with that section offline to take a look."

"Oh, right, right," Jim said shaking his head. "I just got a lot on my mind. How is the rest of the ship? Any leaks?"

"No sir. The board shows everything in the green, we're good."

"Good to hear it. We should be inside Anarbia in about 18 hours. Make sure the crew is rested. We'll probably have a lot of work to do when we get there."

Chief said, "Yes sir." Then as Jim turned to leave bellowed, "Room TEN HUT!"

"Carry on," Jim said and left engineering as the laughing started to build again in the room. He continued to walk the ship. He checked on this and that, just to satisfy himself everything was okay. He had every confidence in Chief, but every pilot preferred to see things for themselves. That was ingrained in them by their instructors during flight school.

"Doctor Stevens," Jim said when he noticed the man come around the corner at the other end of the corridor. Dr. Stevens was making his rounds checking on the cryo units and those that were put into comas. "I hear you had a few bumps and bruises to treat in engineering."

"Oh, don't come down on them. They were just having fun and it was nothing a bandage couldn't fix."

"I'm not worried about that," Jim said, shaking his head with a smile. "It looked like fun. Maybe when this trip is finished, and we get Anarbia up and running, we can come up with something similar to unwind." Jim paused for a moment and reflected on the possibilities of having a small Olympics and picnic for everyone. "How is everything?"

"Everything's okay. A couple medical stands got knocked about. One I.V. got pulled out when a stand tipped over, but I caught it in time before the passenger woke up."

Jim laughed, "Passenger, that's funny. This was one hell of a cruise. Get some rest when you can." Jim explained to Dr. Stevens the same thing he explained to Chief Besch about their ETA in Anarbia and how he will be busy waking everyone up.

"About that," Dr. Stevens stopped Jim as he started to leave. "We need to make sure supplies were shot into the past like they were supposed to when we get there, particularly food, before I start waking these people up. It seems nothing else went right with all those time travel calculations and whatnot."

"I'm sure the calculations were right," Jim said slightly defensively, thinking how Sarah spent several nights with no sleep scouring the data worried about that very thing, and had every calculation double checked by Dr. Kovonich. "No one knew that alien ship was so close, or it would have been intercepted long before it had a chance to interfere with our shot."

Dr. Stevens said, "Or our shot might never have happened if they knew."

Jim rhetorically asked, "And where would we be now? I'm sorry, it was a long day. Give me some good news, Doc."

Dr. Stevens suggested, "It's almost over?"

"We can only pray," Jim said as he started walking away. "We can only pray."

Jim finished his rounds and went back to the bridge. He told everyone there to get some rest while he took the controls. Claire decided to stay behind, keep Jim company, and get some rest on the next shift. This was the first opportunity Claire had to be alone with Jim since they left the moon and wanted to talk about what happened.

The rest of the time went by uneventfully. Several ships came near but were of no consequence. A few military vessels were among them, but the YCS-92 was going so fast, no one was able to detect it. If the ship did show on anyone's screen, it was gone on the next sweep and was ignored. One submarine did turn in their direction but quickly lost interest.

Several hours passed, and Scott relieved Jim on the bridge. Jim instructed Scott to surface in the storm only long enough to reform the air bubble around the ship and to wake him when they got near the Bermuda Triangle.

Jim went to his quarters, exhausted, and fell asleep almost as soon as his head hit his pillow.

Jim had a restless sleep. He thought about Sarah again, thanks to the comment Dr. Stevens made about the calculations and the conversation he had with Claire. He dreamed Sarah was sitting on the living room floor with papers spread about her, with calculations and symbols Jim had no clue how to interpret. He only knew that she was building the city Anarbia beneath the ocean floor off the North American Coast in the Bermuda Triangle. Sarah calculated every shot carefully because the shot would create a void in the solid rock and would replace the rock with anything that was on the shot platform. Building materials, supplies, computers, you name it, even the air was transported with the shot.

Prefabricated buildings were considered but decided against to prevent damage. A shot was a spherical shape and anything on the shot pad would end up falling to the base of the sphere when the shot was complete. Because of this, sensitive equipment was very carefully padded prior to being placed on the shot pad.

Mech-Bots were sent ahead of any people to begin the assembly of the structures. They were programmed with schematics to build the city, and when and where to expect subsequent shots of materials and supplies.

Careful planning created the giant diving bell like cavern, fully stocked and ready for its first occupants to arrive.

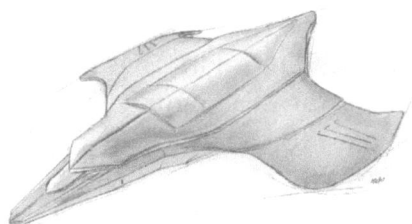

Chapter 37: ARRIVAL

"Major Norgas," came Scott's voice over the intercom next to Jim's bed, waking him.

"Go ahead," Jim said, rubbing his eyes.

Scott said, "We have entered the Bermuda Triangle and are ready to start searching for the entrance."

Jim replied, "Hold position. I'll be right there." He got cleaned up, dressed, and arrived at the bridge doors feeling slightly more refreshed than when he left.

"Claire," Jim said as he entered the bridge, "Search for a strong gravitational pull. As we get closer, our navigation systems may not work right."

Claire said, "Yes, sir. Do you know where I'm looking?"

Jim said, "North of Puerto Rico, you will find a trench that's over 8,000 meters deep. It is somewhere beneath that."

"I see the trench," Claire said, looking at her screen as Jim came up behind her. "Jeez, that has to be almost 500 miles long. How will I —" Claire started to ask when the data on the panel to her right started to change. "Wait a minute." The data changed quicker the longer she looked at it and did not make much sense. North seemed to be in every direction and the computer randomly bounced the ship around in a circle on the map. The more the ship moved, the larger the circle got. "I think I've got what you're looking for."

Jim said, "That's got to be it. John, go deep. We are going down about 25,000 feet."

"Um, Major?" John asked, a bit concerned over the depth he just heard.

"The ship will take it," Jim said. "That is where the entrance is, and the ship was made for this. Sam?" Jim had his apprehensions but did not want the crew to know.

Sam answered, "Yes, the ship will take it."

The ship began going straight down along the trench wall, with the strange gravitational pull directly beneath them. When they reached a depth of 20,000 feet, Jim ordered the nose of the ship to point toward the trench wall and the exterior lights turned on. The crew on the bridge was not able to see far but was able to watch the cliff-like wall rise above them as they sank deeper and deeper.

Strange-looking fish darted past, checking out this new intruder in their space as predators took advantage of the light the ship produced.

"I think I see something," Scott said as he pointed toward the starboard side of the bridge.

John rotated and side-slipped the ship slightly, and an opening in the rock was visible, large enough for the ship to slip through comfortably.

John asked, "Major? Will you take the controls please?"

Jim answered, "I'm sure you can handle it, just go easy."

John eased the ship forward ever so gently into the massive hole that looked like a mouth about to swallow the ship whole. When the entire ship was within the cavern, the walls began to narrow and then abruptly ended in a sheer wall. The holographic image beside John showed the ship had about 100 feet of water on either side, and in front of it.

Jim said, "Take it up. Straight up!"

John eased the ship up nervously, the holographic image showed little of what was above them, and the ceiling of the bridge made it nearly impossible to see straight up, not to mention the lack of light in that direction.

As the YBV-92 ascended, it began to buffet and shake. John stopped the ship and asked, "What did I hit?" He studied the holo image and couldn't see anything.

A deep resonating sound became audible as it increased in volume and pitch. Jim had a puzzled look on his face along with everyone on the bridge. The entire ship began to vibrate, which grew in intensity as the pitch increased.

Chief Besch's voice came over the bridge speakers, "What the hell are you doing to my ship? If you keep this up all the welds will demolecularize. Hell, I already feel my fillings wanting to come out."

Jim jumped out of the captain's chair, and using the holo table, he began looking at the image of the vertical chimney they were in. He told John, "Back us down," just as the glass surrounding the bridge began to vibrate. It visibly moved in waves as the sound increased in frequency. Everyone on the bridge wanted to bolt toward the bridge doors in fear the glass would shatter any second. Then, the sound and all vibrations finally ended.

John asked, "Well, now what?"

Jim asked, "Sam, do you have any ideas?"

Sam and Claire manipulated the holo table and discovered the entrance to Anarbia used a series of Faraday-Maxwell fields to decrease the water pressure exerted on the entrance, so any residents in Anarbia could enjoy the same pressure as on the surface of the planet.

Sam said, "Because John ascended slowly, the two Faraday-Maxwell fields, the one created by the ship and the other across the entrance of the city, fought against each other."

Jim asked, "Okay, what do we do?"

Sam looked at Claire and suggested, "Don't go so slow?"

Claire said, "I have nothing."

Jim told John, "Try again. This time a bit faster, and don't stop."

Scott asked, "Are you sure?"

Jim studied Sam's face and said, "Not really."

John took a deep breath, wiped the sweat off his palms, and said, "Yes, sir. A bit faster and don't stop"

The ship accelerated upward and was buffeted five times as it climbed the chimney. To everyone's relief, the ship passed through the field with only a few rattled nerves.

After ascending a couple of hundred feet, the holographic image began to show an opening above and in front of them. The rock around them became smoother and smoother till it looked polished.

The ship slowly emerged from the water completely silent. Since no water was on the hull, there was no dripping or splashing as the ship rose. The city, however, detected their presence. Red dotted lines on both sides of the ship moved in a line ahead of the ship and curved toward the right. John followed the lights that beckoned him. In the distance a landing pad illuminated. He could tell the landing pad was slightly raised from the rest of the floor, surrounded by a glowing red line with a pulsing red cross in the middle. He centered the ship on the pad and began to bleed off altitude. A solid thump reverberated throughout the ship to confirm their landing. John wiped the sweat off his forehead and palms, looked in the distance, and saw the faint outline of several other pads, all vacant.

"Good job John," Jim said with a nod of his head toward Lt Anders. "Now shut her down." Jim turned to the captain's chair and switched on the ship's intercom for all to hear. "May I have your attention. We are now..." He paused for effect, "Home."

Cheers could be heard throughout the ship, congratulatory slaps on each other's backs, and friendly hugs from fellow coworkers to celebrate.

"Come on," Jim motioned for everyone on the bridge to follow as he walked toward the bridge doors. "Let's take a look."

When Jim entered the cargo bay, it looked like every crew member was present. Jim made his way toward the ramp and said, "Go ahead Chief."

"No sir," Chief Besch defiantly replied. "This one is yours, Major. Besides, remember what happened last time I hit that button?" Chief took one step back, snapped to attention, and commanded, "Hand, Salute!" With that every military member present and some of the civilians snapped to attention and gave Jim a salute.

Jim took the moment in until a tear threatened to spill over the corner of his eye. He knew this was for him getting them here safe. It was a long journey and a struggle at times, but now the real work was to begin. Jim looked around him, returned the salute, and smashed the red button to lower the ramp.

Caught up in the moment, Scott stopped Jim as he was about to walk down the ramp. "Major, we have never given this ship a name."

Jim asked, "Do you have a suggestion?"

Scott answered, "Deliverance." Everyone in the cargo bay looked at each other and nodded their heads.

Jim said, "Very descriptive. Deliverance it is." He walked down the cargo ramp to the landing pad for the ship, 'Deliverance', followed by his entire crew.

Other than the sound created by the crew, the cavern was nearly dead-silent. A faint sound could be heard in the distance of Mech-Bots as they emerged from what they were doing. They tried to see what was happening. Tiny red lights were visible in the distance but seemed to be holding back. One set of lights started to get larger as a single Mech-Bot emerged out of the darkness. The Mech-Bot stopped its approach a few yards from the group, scanned them and the ship, identified the ship, and transmitted data to the rest of the Mech-Bots to bring the city to life. The Mech-Bots in the distance began to leave and started the new task they were given. The Mech-Bot, in a pleasing, mechanical, nonmetallic voice said, "Greetings, welcome to Anarbia. We have expected you for a very long time." It then closed the distance, and a panel in its chest opened to reveal a data terminal.

Jim turned to Sam and said, "You're our computer expert. First thing I need to know is the supply status. Can I start waking our passengers? Then download a schematic of this place. Where are our quarters and such?"

Sam said, "Yes sir." She walked up to the Mech-Bot and began to search the database.

The Mech-Bot identified Jim as the leader of the group and asked, "May we ask your name, sir?"

"Major James Norgas," Jim told the Mech-Bot. "Chief, please get started on checking those relays. I want the ship ready in case we need it for supplies or whatever."

Chief Besch said, "Yes sir. You heard the man, move it. I want every part of this ship checked."

All the Mech-Bots were linked together and in direct communication with the Central Core. The Central Core was a quark-scale computer that controlled all the automated systems in Anarbia. Each Mech-Bot knew instantly what needed to be done and updated the Central Core with constant data streams.

Before the chief could walk to the base of the ramp, Mech-Bots began to emerge and approached the ship. They checked this and that, ran up the ramp, and began to crawl all over the ship. They removed panels and parts hidden beneath. Chief looked like he was about to blow a gasket as he tried to keep up with what was happening to his ship. Pilots thought the crafts they flew was theirs, but they really belonged to the maintenance chief.

The Mech-Bot said, "Major Norgas, we have instructed Mech-Bots to assist the chief. We will have an estimated time of repair for you in a few minutes."

Chief scratched his head and let out a bewildered huff. "Okay, scratch that idea."

"Thank you," Jim said to the Mech-Bot. "Chief, keep an eye on them just in case. I don't want any surprises."

Chief let out a laugh and said, "Yeah right. Keep an eye on them. I don't even know where that part came from." Chief Besch ran after the Mech-Bot to enquire where it was working.

The Mech-Bot said, "Our pleasure, sir. It is not necessary for you to 'keep an eye on us'. The Central Core has a full schematic of this ship. We will bring it back to factory specs and running as the day it came off the assembly line. If there are any modifications that have been made, please let us know. In addition, all data pads we detected on your group, we have uploaded the schematic of the city. We built the city per our instructions. However, we have detected several chambers, not in the plan, beyond the north wall. Please identify."

Jim asked, "What do you mean, chambers?"

The Mech-Bot said, "Sir, years ago, several hollow areas were detected beyond the north wall where previously there were not. Shortly after, there was an earthquake. If the Central Core is correct, the date and time was 11 October 1918 at 10:14 am."

Jim asked, "Sam, what is he talking about?"

Sam described the images she found, "Jim, these chambers appear to have been created by shots. Cylindrical and rounded on the end. How far they go, I don't know; the scans do not go deep enough to see the other end."

Jim was perplexed, and asked, "Shots, in 1918? That's almost 500 years after we were supposed to arrive, so who would have done that? We need to proceed carefully with this. There is no telling what is beyond that wall." He directed his attention toward the Mech-Bot. "What construction was performed and how much noise was created near that wall since you detected those hollow areas?"

The Mech-Bot explained, "Sir, the hollow areas were detected as they were forming while we took measurements for the buildings near that wall. Later we constructed the buildings, which included drilling into the rock floor as close as 20 yards from the wall."

Jim said, "For now, let's stay clear of the area. When we have taken care of our passengers, we will take a look and try to figure it out. Sam, how are we doing on supplies? Can we wake them up yet?"

The Mech-Bot said, "Sir, we have routinely checked on the supplies meant for our human guests. The inventory has all arrived and has remained sealed as required."

Jim asked, "I know this is not part of your normal function, but will you ask your fellow Mech-Bots to set up a seating area and tables in this space?" He pointed to the area in front and to the port side of the newly named Deliverance. "Can you also ask them to start cooking? We are about to have a lot of famished people on our hands."

It took a moment for the Mech-Bot to query the Central Core on how to perform what was asked, and to communicate with the other Mech-Bots their new tasking. "Sir, it will be our pleasure. How many should we cook for?"

Jim said, "Gee, I forgot." He looked around for Dr. Stevens. The last time he saw Dr. Stevens, he was wandering around close to the ship, looking up, trying to figure out how the place was illuminated. "Doc!" Jim said loud enough for Dr. Stevens to hear, then motioned for him to come over. "How many people did we bring with us?" he asked, a bit embarrassed he didn't know.

Dr. Stevens started adding up the number in his head while whispering, "Sixteen in cryo, seventeen in a coma, three civilians awake, the crew, minus one that's in coma." Dr. Stevens nodded his head and said, "Fifty-one sir. Make that fifty, I almost forgot we lost Matt."

Jim closed his eyes a moment upon hearing 'Matt'. He then said to the Mech-Bot, "Fifty." He pondered a moment about what Dr. Stevens said. He was surprised there were that many on the ship, and then he wondered what to do with Steve and asked the Mech-Bot, "Was a brig included in the plans, and is it assembled?"

The Mech-Bot inquired, "Sir, a brig?"

"A jail. Someplace to house a prisoner."

"Sir, no. The archives show examples of several. We can build it."

"Please add that to the list of things I requested, right after cooking."

The Mech-Bot asked, "Sir, where would you like the drawbridge?"

"The what?"

The Mech-Bot displayed an image of an old castle, complete with a moat and drawbridge. "Where would you like the drawbridge?"

"Do you have anything newer?" Images began flashing on the display in the Mech-Bot's chest until a suitable structure was shown. "That one. Can you build that?"

"Yes sir, it will be complete in three days."

Jim said, "Doctor Stevens, you can start waking our passengers. Send them out here when they have recovered enough, and use as many crewmen as you need. Do not wake Steve Harris till I figure out what to do with him."

"Major?" Dr. Stevens asked, not for an answer but as a moral compass.

"Not that – he will have a trial. I'm just trying to figure out what to do with him until the brig is built."

Dr. Stevens said, "There are two others in the escape pod with him. It wouldn't be fair to them not to be received like everyone else while we're set up for it."

Jim said, "You're right. We'll just have to keep him under guard."

The ship's skin plates were pulled off, inspected, and replaced by the Mech-Bots faster than Chief Besch was able to go behind them and ensure the drive relays and the targeting systems worked and were aligned correctly. The systems within the ends of the wings were worked the hardest; Chief particularly wanted the drive components in those areas thoroughly checked. To the extent that he could observe, Chief felt the Mech-Bots did a great job. They not only inspected all the parts but repaired them on the fly, something his crew could not do. His crew would have to remove the part, bring it to engineering to work on, then put the part back under the skin plate, calibrate, and test it. The parts were being repaired so fast, Chief decided to just wait till they were done and then run a full systems check. That seemed a better course of action than to make the Mech-Bots slow down and wait for him.

Chief Besch heard Jim's voice call for him and went to see what he wanted.

"Chief, the Mech-Bots will construct a brig, but it won't be ready for three days. Steve Harris will be taken out of cryo soon. Will you assign a couple crewmen to guard him till the brig is ready?"

Chief said, "Let him rot in cryo."

"Chief!" Jim admonished. "The Doctor reminded me the two in the escape pod with him did nothing wrong. We're taking everyone out at the same time so we can take care of everyone at once."

"Sorry Major, whatever you need. With the way these robots work, the crew won't have much to do." He yelled at a Mech-Bot, "Hey! Put that back!" and bounded its direction.

As the outside of the ship was getting its makeover, the interior was also abuzz as Mech-Bots ran up and down the cargo ramp to fix this, check that, resupply the ship's stores, periodically help a passenger to a chair, and fetch each person's personal belongings.

Considering the circumstances of their departure, each person was allowed to bring one carry-on piece of luggage. Most carried photos or other personal items that could not be replaced. Everyone brought tools of their trade: personally owned scientific instruments, measuring devices, and all sorts of things Jim had no idea where to begin to figure out how to use. It was clear these people were selected from every field of study. Anything needed to be built or invented, this group could figure it out.

It was easy to spot the passengers who were put into comas. They looked a bit more queasy and were selective of what they ate from the buffet-style spread the Mech-Bots prepared. Those who were in cryo ate with blankets wrapped around them and only chose food that was hot – steaming hot. The crew, on the other hand, were not selective in what they ate. They took a bit of everything and went back for seconds. After the rationing that was required on board, they gorged themselves.

When a Mech-Bot helped down the ramp the crewman who volunteered to be put in a chemically induced coma, Sgt. White, his fellow crewmen spotted him almost immediately and directed the Mech-Bot to put him in a spot at their table which was freshly cleared just for him. Extra blankets were gathered by the crew, and whatever Sgt. White wanted to eat or drink, a crewman got it for him.

Everyone wanted to tell Sgt. White their personal account of what happened since they last saw him – about dodging the filaments, coming under fire by navy ships and airplanes, getting chased by submarines, and being attacked by mosquitoes. There was a lot of laughter about the bowling game. All the stories were exaggerated, but everyone had fun. Hearing them tell the stories, it's amazing they even made it.

When Chief Besch noticed what the commotion was about, he stopped what he was doing and joined his crew after he made a plate of food for himself. "Thank you for volunteering. Here is a little something-something to pick you up." Chief slipped Sgt. White his flask, "Keep it quiet though, that's the last of it. Welcome back."

When everyone had their fill, blankets started to come off, and those who were selective about their food started to dive into what they previously avoided. Then, Jim asked for everyone's attention and said, "Ladies and Gentlemen, I'll assume everyone overheard the crew telling their tale about our voyage. But what you may not have heard is 'when' we are. As far as I am able to tell, the year is 2005." Grumbling erupted till Jim was able to quell the group, "I know, it was a shock to me as well. We have a monumental task ahead of us and very little time to do it. All we can do is move forward with the hand we've been dealt. I want everyone to take a two-day break, rest, recover, get your quarters in order, whatever you want to do. The Mech-Bots will help you find your new living quarters. Everyone has a fresh bed tonight." The crew applauded, but the civilians couldn't care less after sleeping for the past few months.

Jim continued, "We have a bit of a mystery. I ask for everyone to stay away from the northern wall." He pointed in the direction beyond the nose of the Deliverance. "After we've rested, we will try to figure it out. Until then, everyone enjoy, and don't forget to pick up a communication pin. We should be able to speak with each other anywhere on the planet using it. Is the cafeteria up and running?" Jim asked a Mech-Bot, who confirmed. "For the time being, we will have meals at the regular times in the base cafeteria. I will post any updates there. We meet back here in two days."

After Jim took his seat, Scott asked, "What's going on?"

Jim said, "The Mech-Bots recorded several areas north of that wall that appear to have been hollowed out by shots."

Scott asked, "What's wrong with that? Maybe they were accidents, just like ours."

Jim replied, "The Mech-Bot maintains it happened in 1918."

Scott asked, "What are you thinking?"

To not be overheard, Jim spoke barely over a whisper, "My first thought is that they didn't come from us. If they did, why almost 400 years late?"

Scott asked, "Then who?"

"Our entire trip, I worried the aliens might figure out what we're doing. Behind that wall might be poison gas, a strike team, who knows what. Whatever it is, we will deal with it in two days."

The emptiness of the vast structure made Jim realize how alone they truly were. It was odd how there were no echoes.

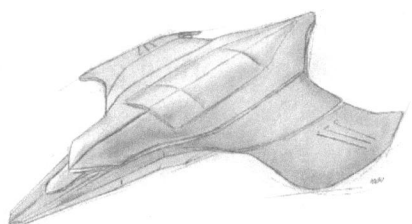

Chapter 38: ANARBIA

Jim woke the next morning and decided to familiarize himself with Anarbia. His quarters were luxuriously furnished. It felt like an extravagant hotel that was way out of his price range. Even the elevator felt like luxury.

A Mech-Bot performing the duties of a doorman asked, "Good morning, Sir. Would you care for a vehicle today?"

Jim asked, "Just how big is this place?"

The Mech-Bot said, "Sir, the building you came out of contains 15 stories, but is not the biggest. That building is 25 stories. We think a few more stories can be added if needed. Shall we build them, sir?

"No, that's okay. What I meant was, how big is this cavern?"

"Sir, we apologize. The cavern covers approximately fifteen square miles. Most of what you need is nearby, but depending on where you are going, you may want to ride."

Jim looked shocked and asked, "Are you kidding?"

"Sir, no sir. Was the schematic not uploaded to your data pad?"

"Yes, but I didn't..."

"Then let us help you, Sir. The area is divided primarily into two areas. The living and research area, where you are now. And the operations area is primarily landing pads and maintenance facilities. Between the two you have a few 'common' buildings, such as hospital, operations, and cafeteria. Where would you like to go?"

Jim said, "To be honest, I just want to take a look around.

"Sir, would you like a vehicle?"

"Yes, please." He noticed a portion of the road changed color. The lane closest to the sidewalk alternated with red and yellow stripes. The color change ended at the entrance to the building he came out of. "What is that?"

The Mech-Bot said, "Sir, that is to warn pedestrians a vehicle is approaching. As the vehicle gets closer, the yellow stripe will fade to orange, then red."

"How?"

"Sir, all surfaces are covered in an electro-chromatic material that can display anything desired. For example, this building looks like a typical luxury hotel. Does it not?"

Jim said, "Well, yes."

"Sir, now what does it look like?"

Jim looked back at the building, but it appeared to be a lush forest. He reached his arm out and hit the building's wall that looked like an empty space between two trees. Suddenly a panther reached up and snapped at Jim's hand, making him jump.

"That is really, wow!" he said, amazed. He thought about the possibilities. "I can see a couple problems with it. For one, people will not know a building is here and walk into it."

The Mech-Bot said, "Sir, this was a demonstration." A knee high stone wall appeared showing the border of the building. "A fence or wall like this could be displayed along with what you desire."

Jim nodded his head and said, "Okay, but if all the buildings show different things, how will I find my way home later?"

"Sir, tell the Central Core where you want to go and directions will be shown on the ground before you."

Jim looked at the street and saw the alternating colors were nearly the same color and saw a vehicle approach. "What happens if where I'm going intersects with someone else and I start following the wrong direction?"

The Mech-Bot said, "Sir, in all the years we have been here, we have not had any complaints."

Jim laughed and got in the car. He asked the Mech-Bot driving the car to take a tour of Anarbia, and a new red line extended ahead of the car. In the distance Jim saw the red line fade to the alternating striped line he saw earlier.

The Operations side contained so many landing pads, Jim gave up counting. Pads, the size the Deliverance landed on, were in rows. Each pad was round and a small pad filled the void between four of the larger pads. Jim figured the small pads were for the fighter sized version of 'Deliverance'.

Jim was in awe of the massive area carved out of the rock and wondered how it was supported. Without a doubt, he knew Anarbia was designed for thousands of people to live and work.

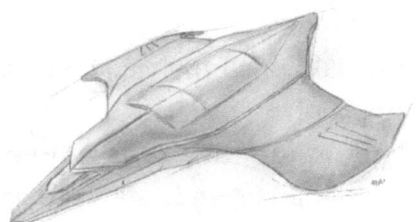

Chapter 39: STRIFE

The next couple of days went by quickly. Impromptu sports games popped up here and there, but mostly, people used the time to rest and personalize their living quarters.

The cafeteria was turned into an unofficial gathering spot for people that just didn't want to be alone or enjoyed a particular conversation that was going on while getting lunch.

Discussions came up which spawned debates among the civilians about various aspects of what should have been done. Consensus had it for the majority of the time, that Jim did the right thing.

However, Jim's hiding in his quarters while the ship was on the moon had some questioning his ability to command.

When Claire caught wind of the conversation, she sat at the table and said, "You have to understand, when we got to the moon and didn't pick up anything coming over the radio frequencies we use, we knew we got here late. This city should have been booming, but nothing. We are all that made it."

The person sitting across from her said, "I'm sure everyone was in shock. That doesn't give him any right to shut himself off when the crew needed his leadership." Around the table, everyone agreed.

Claire said, "That's not fair, it just hit him that his girlfriend – fiancé – what ever she was – he will never find out what happened to her.

The man on her right said, "I hear he let you in, and you comforted him real good."

Laughs arose from the table till Claire slapped the man across his face, nearly knocking him out of his chair. "How dare you!"

The man stood and was about to take a swing when Chief Besch, who was sitting at a nearby table, caught his wrist and said, "You're not thinking about hitting a lady, are you?"

The man tried to take a swing at the chief but found himself lying on his back after the chief swept the man's legs out from under him.

A few crewmen came to the chief's side, and the chief said to the man, "This is over! Isn't it!"

Rubbing the back of his head the man said, "She started it "

Chief Besch said, "Not from what I heard, and I finished it." He then said to the crewmen, "Take him home."

The crewmen said, "You got it, Chief," then picked the man off the floor.

Chief Besch said, "I think he learned his lesson. There's no reason to ruff him up on the way."

The Chief's last statement caused fear on the man's face, not realizing the crew might have done that as two crewmen carried him away.

Chief turned his attention to the remaining people around the table and said, "I've known Major Norgas for a long time. He has earned my deepest respect. If he needed some time to himself, to think, sort things out, or bounce ideas off a colleague, who are we to question it?"

Claire said, "Thanks, Chief."

"Don't mention it." He looked around the table and added, "None of you mention it again. The major has enough to worry about right now without having to deal with this. Understood?"

Everyone at the table shook their head and the chief invited Claire to join him at his table with Sam.

When Chief sat down, Sam said, "My hero, rescuing a damsel in distress. Should I be jealous?"

Chief laughed, "Rescue, yeah right. I think Claire would have cleaned his clock. Good luck keeping this from the major after a medical report. That was one hell of a slap."

Claire smiled, "Thanks, Chief."

Later that night, Jim entered the cafeteria for a late night snack. While preparing his food, he overheard a discussion taking place on the other side of a partition. They were discussing what lay inside the north wall. Jim perked an ear up and listened in. He found no harm in discussing the possibilities.

Soon, a different voice was heard. A familiar voice that did not use singular forms or words to refer to itself. Jim had to see what was going on and discovered a crowd gathered around the front of a Mech-Bot engrossed in watching the video display buried in its chest, which displayed real-time footage of scans taking place by another Mech-Bot at the North wall.

Jim ordered, "Shut it down! I gave explicit orders to stay away from that wall." He looked around at the faces of the six people present and saw Steve Harris in the group. Jim looked around and noticed the two crewmen who were supposed to be guarding Steve, seated on the other side of the cafeteria, oblivious to what was going on. Using his communications pin, he asked for assistance from Chief Besch and Captain Scott.

He made a mental note that he should form a small security detail for possible issues that may arise like this. The people sitting there were all civilians, so to avoid them feeling ganged up on by the military, Jim asked for Claire St Patrick and Samantha Green to also come to the cafeteria right away, using their full names to prevent any familiarity the six may claim. He only wanted some muscle to assist and a few calmer voices to defuse any possible situation.

Steve said, "Major, we were only trying to figure out what is in there."

Jim asked, "And what would you do if you triggered a trap?"

Everyone looked confused by his response and asked questions about what he was talking about. They began to question his mental state when the people Jim called started to filter in. Steve's voice rose above the others, "What trap?" The group started to quiet down as the new arrivals surrounded them, and they allowed Jim to answer.

"Whatever is on the other side of that wall, when did it get there?"

"The early 1900s," Steve shrugged his shoulder. "So what?"

"When were we supposed to get here?"

"The late 1400s? Again, so what?" Steve said sarcastically, which sounded like a teenager talking back to his parents. He looked around at the others gathered, smiling.

Jim asked, "The aliens we fled from – what do you think they will do if they find out what we did?"

Someone in the group said sheepishly, "Try to find us and kill us."

"I'm just a bit suspicious of that!" Jim pointed to the screen in the Mech-Bot's chest, which was now dark but still emphasized what he referred to. "Because we don't know what we're dealing with, before we start poking around I want everyone onboard Deliverance in case something happens.

"I – I – I didn't know," Steve said apologetically.

"You are supposed to be the smartest and best chance for this mission to succeed," Jim said, and for emphasis added, "Now think!" Jim felt like he was scolding children, not grown adults with PhD's and initials after their names.

"We're not trained to think that way," someone in the group said, not even trying to take responsibility for what could have happened.

"Well, you need to start. Whether you like it or not, we are all in survival mode. There are only fifty of us, and the average age of the group is 45. These numbers are not looking good for us to be able to complete our mission. Or did you think we were just escaping?"

Everyone in the small group felt deflated and realized they could have jeopardized everything. Each of them responded one at a time, "No sir."

"Alright," Jim said. "Get out of here and get some sleep."

The group got up and left the cafeteria, apologizing as they went.

"Not you Mr. Harris," Jim said as Steve made his way to the entrance.

"What's he doing here?" Scott asked, coming up behind Jim.

"I don't know what his involvement in this was. It wasn't malicious, but, –" Jim paused till he thought of the words. "Just a couple of people not using their brains."

"Sounds like a pattern," Scott said as he looked at Steve.

Chief Besch said, "Maybe we should assign some of the crewmen for a Security Police detail."

Jim said, "I hear there was a little excitement earlier."

Chief Besch said, "Nothing I couldn't handle. No need to worry yourself about it."

Jim nodded his head looking at Chief Besch, then said, "Speaking of which, there's Steve's guards," pointing at the two still oblivious that anything was going on. "I think you're right, but we should assign someone to the position instead of it being an extra duty."

Chief said, "Excuse me." He got hotter than a tick in a mortuary and headed to the table where the two guards sat.

"I'd hate to be them," Sam said with a grin.

Jim laughed, "That's for sure. Since we are all here, does anyone object to staying for a while to discuss how we should handle the North wall?"

Everyone appeared okay with it but requested to get something to drink first. Jim still had the snack he got earlier and decided to go back and get a big cup of coffee.

When everyone was settled at the large round table near the middle of the eating area, Jim started with the precautions he wanted to take. "I want everyone inside the ship with the engine running in case we need to run." Everyone agreed that was a given necessity. "The Mech-Bots, it seems, are able to scan 25 yards through the rock, and those voids start about 20. Can the ship scan deeper?"

Sam answered, "Not by much, but the ship will have to be right up against the wall. By the way, why do you word your questions to the Mech-Bots as if they are human and have a choice? They are just machines."

Jim said, "I know, but it's my way of ensuring they understand what's needed to be done."

Sam said, "That makes sense."

Jim was not alone in thinking, that bringing the ship close to the wall was a bad idea. With the buildings nearby it would be difficult to maneuver the ship close enough and get out of there in a hurry if needed.

Scott asked, "If we drill a small hole part way through, will that increase the range, or will we have to dig a large area out?"

Sam said, "We only need to drill a big enough hole for the sensor." Then turned toward the Mech-Bot that was still there and asked, "May I see the sensor used for the scans used on the north wall?"

"Absolutely ma'am," the Mech-Bot answered and extended a sensor from its torso that was attached to a short metal rod about seven inches long. The sensor was cylindrical, about one inch across and three inches long.

"Ooh, that will work perfectly," Sam said. "May I remove it?"

The Mech-Bot asked, "Will we get it back?"

Sam looked at Jim with a grin and saw he was smiling. She rolled her eyes and assured the Mech-Bot, "I personally guarantee you will get it back."

The Mech-Bot reached inside its chest cavity, unplugged the sensor, unscrewed it from the rod it was attached to, and handed the sensor to Sam.

Sam explained, "The Mech-Bots can drill a hole with their lasers. I'll attach this to a longer rod, and as it gets closer to the other side it will be able to scan farther as there is less rock in the way."

Scott joked, "Will the Mech-Bot like it being mounted on a longer rod?"

Sam said, "Actually I thought you could hold the rod, I mean, since we have two other capable pilots. How good are you at sticking things in holes?"

Scott glanced around the table and said, "I don't think I should answer that."

Jim asked, "Will the sensor be able to tell us what is in the void without actually breaching it?"

Sam said, "No. All it can tell us is the size and shape of the void and size and shape of any solid objects that are in it. We will be able to make 3-D holo images from the scans."

Scott asked, "So if there is a killer robot in there we will know?"

Jim scowled at Scott and Sam started to laugh. She said, "Yes."

"Hey," Scott defensively raised his hands from around his drink and smiled "I'm just saying."

Jim said, "Alright. You think I'm being overly cautious?"

"No, just having a little fun," Scott said and looked at Jim. "Really! I hope it's nothing and I agree, we have to be careful."

Jim asked, "How do we find out if there are any toxic liquids or gas in the voids without breaching them?"

Chief Besch rejoined the group after a round of wall-to-wall counseling with the two guards. He mumbled under his breath, and as he sat down, he yelled over his shoulder, "I can't hear you!"

"Fifty-one, Fifty-two," shouted the two guards, "Fifty-three."

Sam asked, "How many did you give them?"

"I didn't. I told them I'll let them know," Chief Besch said with a smirk. "I got other guards on the way to take care of Steve. What did I miss?"

Jim said, "We were trying to figure out how to test what is inside those chambers without opening them, and Captain Dixon wants to stick a rod in a hole."

Chief slapped Scott on his back and said, "It's about time. I'm proud of you. Do you need the talk?"

Scott shook his head, glanced at Sam with a slight grin. Sam raised her eyebrows and made a gesture with her hands as if she were asking, '*Well do you*'?

Claire spoke up and said, "To answer your last question, Jim, when we get maybe a yard from breaching the wall, it should be nothing for the ship's drive to analyze the atmosphere."

Jim asked the Mech-Bot, "Will the Mech-Bots help us with this?"

"Yes sir, we agree."

"Sounds like a plan. I want each void tested before proceeding. It might only take one to wipe us out. There's four of them, right?"

"Yes sir," the Mech-Bot answered as Sam turned to retrieve the data but stopped when the answer was given.

"Alright," Jim said, satisfied that they have a plan for tomorrow. "Does anyone have anything they want to add or bring up?"

The group talked about what still needed to be done, and mostly just enjoyed each other's company. This went on for an hour or two till one by one they began to yawn and decided to call it a night.

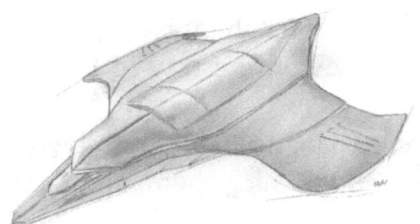

Chapter 40: BREACH A WALL

The next morning, Jim woke with a slight kink in his neck. He was not used to sleeping on a soft bed with an equally soft pillow, but it was very comfortable and reminded him of home. The pillows and mattresses on board Deliverance were the standard military issue, made for durability, not comfort.

He enjoyed a long hot shower since he no longer needed to ration. He had to walk through fog and wipe the condensation off the mirror before he could shave. There were more modern ways to take care of the morning hygiene routine, but he preferred the closeness only a blade could give. He slipped into the crisp uniform he prepared the night before. One last look in the mirror, and he headed to the cafeteria.

He was one of the first to arrive and got himself a tall cup of steaming extra-dark coffee, eggs over medium, crispy bacon, hash browns, and toast with extra butter out of the food dispenser. He sat at the same table his group occupied the night before and started eating. He was joined by Chief Besch, who chose almost the same breakfast. He substituted the toast for grits.

"I never did get a taste for them," Jim said, referring to the grits.

"Oh, you don't know what you're missing. Put some butter and hot sauce in them, mm, reminds me of mother's cooking," Chief said, then savored a mouth full. "Not quite the same coming out of that machine, but close. Hot sauce makes everything taste better."

The cafeteria gradually gained more people. Jim's table filled a bit faster than the rest of the room.

"How is everyone?" Jim asked, making small talk. "Sleep okay?"

Claire said, "Like a baby. Much better than the scratchy sheets on the ship. Um, no offense."

Jim said, "None taken. I had no say-so in that department."

Chief interjected, "What's the matter? Did they chafe?"

"Almost got a rash, care to rub some lotion on?" Claire said as she rubbed her butt, teasing.

"Bare it, honey!" Chief said, daring Claire.

"Hey!" Sam said as she slugged Chief in the upper arm, to everyone's amusement. Chief faked a broken arm. Sam said, "I couldn't sleep. It was like Christmas Eve wondering what's in that wall."

Scott said, "I just hope it's not a sock full of coal."

Jim asked, "Chief, were the repairs to the ship complete?" Seeing Chief nod his head, he added, "How bad was it?"

"A couple banks of relays were offline. The main bus for them fried. Those relays are so small and tightly packed, the next bus took the load no problem. If we would have stayed in that passage longer, more may have blown, but we were in no real danger. The Mech-Bots replaced them with a bus that can take more load, and I will look into the ones that blew to see if they were defective or just what happened."

"Were those the relays in the wing tips?"

"Yes sir. Since they took the brunt of the damage I asked the Mech-Bots to replace the bus in both wings with the upgraded bus."

Jim said, "Good thinking. Thanks, Chief."

The conversation at the table switched to unimportant chitchat as everyone enjoyed their morning breakfast together.

When the room appeared to have everyone present, Jim asked

John to take a head count. Moments later John said, "We have all forty-seven."

Jim corrected, "Forty-seven? We got fifty."

John said, "Mr. Harris and two guards, sir."

Jim asked, "Speaking of guards, how are the two from last night?"

Chief said, "I'd predict their arms feel like wood with a bunch of termites being sought by a woodpecker." He looked around the cafeteria and saw the pair. Both appeared to be in discomfort from merely lifting their fork. This put a smile on Chief's face.

Sam said, "You're incorrigible."

Chief said, "Trust me, they won't make that mistake again."

Dr. Stevens said, "I had two crewmen come into the infirmary last night complaining they outdid themselves in the gym. Is that what it was about?"

Chief said, "Oh they did, did they?"

Sam grabbed the chief's arm and said, "Finish your breakfast."

Chief said, "I was just going to loosen their arms up a bit."

Sam said, "I know what you were going to do. Just let it go. I think they learned their lesson."

Chief Besch said, "Part of the punishment is the pain the next day. They tried to get medical help not to suffer."

Sam said, "Let it go."

Dr. Stevens said, "Don't worry, they will be feeling it, I didn't give them anything."

Chief Besch said, "Thanks Doctor. For them trying to go behind my back and lie about it, I think that dish washing machine needs a break."

Sam said, "Let it go, Chief."

Chief Besch said, "Yes, dear."

Jim waited until everyone was close to finishing their breakfast before he got everyone's attention. "As soon as everyone finishes eating, I would like everybody to board the Deliverance. If you have not heard, we have found several chambers hollowed out beyond the northern wall, and for everyone's safety, I want everyone on board the ship till we find out what is in them."

There was minor disgruntled talk about having to get back on the ship for who knows how long. The thought of being put into cryo or a coma again could be made into a horror movie. Most of the people in the room would avoid watching.

Jim said, "Let me assure you," but no one was listening, and it took a while to get their attention again. "It will not result in anyone being asked to sleep again. Worst case scenario, we find some out-of-the-way place on the surface to live. We will not be on the ship long enough to deplete what air is on board and can be scrubbed. You have my word," he finished to the satisfaction of everyone.

Gradually everyone made their way to the ship. When John reported all were on board, Jim asked, "What about Steve Harris and his guards?"

"They are in the forward-most compartment of the nose."

"Thank you. Close the ramp and let's get started." He asked the Mech-Bot on the bridge, acting as a liaison for the other Mech-Bots, "You can start drilling, but stop if anything happens, and stop one meter from the opposite wall. Do not breach the chambers yet. Okay?"

The Mech-Bot said, "Sir, as you command," and relayed the order to the computer core.

Jim sat in the captain's chair and asked Scott to hover the ship, retract the landing gear, and move closer to the wall.

In no time, Jim saw the drilling lasers cut the holes for the probes, centered on all four chambers. Their progress was displayed on the holographic imaging display next to the helm. It took several minutes, but one by one, each Mech-Bot reached its target drilling point and shut down the laser. The Mech-Bot fitted with the modified sensor moved into position at the first chamber.

Sam had replaced the sensor's metal rod with a long plastic strip, coiled it onto a reel, and fitted it to a Mech-Bot's left arm. The Mech-Bot slowly pushed the sensor into the hole. At the same time, the drive computer of the Deliverance began a chemical analysis of the atmosphere inside the chamber. The process was repeated for all four of the chambers, and the data was shown on the holographic display as they went. Three of the chambers had an oxygen environment with trace elements of pollution. The pollution was similar to the atmosphere of Earth at the time they left. The chambers were approximately 100 yards long. One chamber was filled with seawater and ended in a jagged mass at approximately 65 yards. All were cylindrical in shape with a five-yard diameter. All four chambers had what appeared to be desk-sized boxes evenly spaced along the floor perpendicular to the cylindrical walls.

"What do you make of that?" Scott asked as he turned to look at Jim.

Jim said, "I don't know."

Claire asked Sam, "Can the drive computer analyze a sample of what is inside the closest box?"

Sam said, "If we drill deeper I think so."

Claire told Jim, "Well, the atmosphere in three of the chambers is safe, so I don't see any reason not to drill all the way through."

Jim instructed the Mech-Bot to finish drilling on the closest chamber.

When the drilling was complete, the computer displayed the results of the closest box. The atmosphere was identical to the inside of a cryogenic chamber. Everyone on the bridge was in disbelief. No one said a word for what seemed an eternity.

Sam asked, "Can it be?"

Claire said, "If it's what I'm thinking, they took an awful risk shooting directly here."

Scott said, "When faced with annihilation, people will do anything."

Sam asked, "Why 1918?"

Jim said, "I'm sure we will find all that out and more when we thaw them out."

Scott asked, "Are we certain they are human?"

Jim said, "I thought I was the paranoid one."

Chief said, "I think it's catching."

Jim asked, "You too?" Which caused Chief to raise his hands and shrug his shoulders.

Dr. Stevens said, "If they are medical cryo units, they will have a clear lid, and we will know before we open them."

Jim ordered the Mech-Bot to start tunneling into the air-filled chambers. "What do we do with the one filled with water?" Jim asked Sam. He thought for a moment and said to the Mech-Bot, "Belay that, we need to figure out what we're going to do with that water-filled one before we do anything."

Sam asked, "What are you thinking?"

"Well, if we are careful how we dig into the chambers on both sides of the water-filled one, we might be able to use them in some way to pump out the water," Jim answered, not even sure what he was saying. "Besides, we have to assume it's 100 yards long also, and the other side of that blockage may be filled with air. Not to mention the cryo units in that span."

"We need to be really careful on what we do," Claire joined in as she looked away from her screen. "The Mech-Bot said there was an earthquake; that's how they detected the chambers. Any pressure change may cause another earthquake. Also, if the ceiling there is weak or open to the ocean above, the integrity of this entire structure may be at risk. You know it's essentially just a huge diving bell."

Sam asked. "Why don't we open the one farthest away from the water-filled one and see what we are dealing with?"

Claire said, "That's a good idea, but I suggest the Mech-Bots finish drilling the hole into that one and be ready to plug it if anything happens." She turned to the Mech-Bot and asked, "Are you equipped with airflow sensors and a way to detect pressure changes?"

The Mech-Bot said, "Yes ma'am. We can do what you ask. Continue drilling the one-inch hole in the far left chamber. Verify there is no pressure change or air flow from inside the chamber to the rest of the complex and seal the one-inch hole if there is."

Jim asked, "Can the Deliverance help at all?"

"Just analyze the rock structure above us and those chambers. Get as much data as you can," Claire told Jim as she shifted her focus on the screen to the farthest chamber as the Mech-Bots began moving in that direction.

Jim asked the chief, "Have your crew place probes in a few random areas around Anarbia." And told Scott, "Hold her steady while the ramp is open." He then asked Sam, "Go through the passenger roster for a structural engineer and get him up here, and someone to help run the scanners." He turned to Dr. Stevens and said, "Looks like you will have a lot of patients soon. Gather a team from the passengers to help you.

Claire said, "That was good thinking about the probes."

"Um, Major?" Sam asked for Jim's attention. "Steve Harris is the only structural engineer."

"Great," Scott said as he looked over his shoulder at Jim. "What do you think?"

Chief said, "He still faces charges and I don't trust him."

Scott added, "After last night?"

Jim said, "He was a bit argumentative, and we don't know if he was behind it or was just going along with the discussion. Besides, he might have seen something already that will help." Jim used the ship's intercom and asked the guards to bring Steve Harris to the bridge.

Chief said, "I don't like this. He can't be the only structural engineer we got."

Everyone on the bridge went back to work and managed the tasks they were assigned. The Mech-Bots were almost in position when the bridge doors opened and Steve Harris stepped tentatively through, unsure what to expect. Jim got out of the command chair and walked to the back of the bridge. He offered his hand to Steve as he greeted him. Steve visibly relaxed when he realized this wasn't what he feared, and Jim explained the situation so far.

"You can use the station right there." Jim pointed to a station on the starboard side of the bridge next to Sam, but closer toward the front of the ship.

Jim returned to the captain's chair and Steve went right to work analyzing the integrity of the rock.

Chief kept a very close eye on Steve, which made Steve nervous. That was part of Chief's intent. He leaned over Steve and whispered loud enough for only Steve to hear, "Just give me one excuse, please!"

The probes the crew set up began to come online and flooded Steve's station with data, which included a 3-D rendering of the rock formation above them. Soon, a holographic image of the rock hovered over the table behind Jim's chair and increased in detail as more data was received.

The last crewman outside the ship finally reentered and the ramp was closed.

Claire said, "Just a few seconds and they will be through. Just a little more... and... we're through."

Everyone on the bridge held their breath as they awaited the results. Then, Claire said, "The pressure is stable," and everyone on the bridge cheered and clapped each other on the back.

Several minutes passed till the Mech-Bots were given the okay to start excavating a tunnel into the chamber large enough for a gravity lift gurney to fit through. The cutting with lasers and hauling away of rock took several hours, so most of the bridge crew decided to take a break and have lunch in the ship's cafeteria after landing the ship. John was left in charge of the bridge in case anything happened.

The cafeteria was full; all seats were taken and several people were sitting on the floor leaning against the walls. The room was large enough to hold the entire ship's crew of sixteen and a few extra, but the ship once again held thirty-five passengers and they all wanted to be near each other.

Jim addressed the group and explained what they discovered and what was going on. Everyone was excited at the prospect of more people joining them and eager to help. They remembered all too well what it was like to come out of cryo and decided to have food ready and lots of blankets. Food that would help warm the body – soups and hot beverages.

Someone asked, "How many?"

Jim said, "I don't know."

Sam stepped in and responded, "I'd guess around 300."

"That's a lot of soup," one person said, and another, "We'll need to strip some beds" and the room was abuzz as everyone made plans and organized into groups.

Jim decided to eat in the captain's quarters and invited the bridge crew and any crewmen he could find to join him, to make more room in the cafeteria for the passengers.

After a few hours, Steve Harris, followed by his guards, joined them in the captain's quarters to update Jim on what he found. "The rock over Anarbia is solid and so are most of the chambers," Steve explained. "As for the one filled with water, I am unable to tell if it will continue to flood if we open it."

Jim asked, "Should we open the chambers beside it differently to help with opening that one?"

Steve said, "I'm still thinking about that but want to see the inside of one of them before I finalize anything. And I'd like to move one of the probes to the back of the tube we're opening to scan from."

Jim agreed with his plan and invited Steve to join the group and have some food.

The time passed slowly waiting for the excavation to be complete. Jim called the bridge frequently for updates till finally John called and said, "The Mech-Bots are almost done and should be finished by the time you get there."

Dr. Stevens and Jim were the first to enter the chamber. Everyone else was instructed to wait outside. They were indeed cryo units, tightly spaced. The clear covers were frosted over, preventing Dr. Stevens from looking inside. Jim took a knife from his pocket, scraped the frost where the head of the occupant should be, and was unable to see anything through the internal gasses.

Jim said, "I can't see a thing. Do you have a medical scanner to determine if it's human?"

"You have been watching too many movies."

"Come on Doc!"

"Sorry, we're gonna have to open it to find out."

Jim touched the communication pin, "Chief, I want an armed security detail in here."

"What's going on? Are you in trouble?"

"We're okay. We have to open the cryo unit to find out what is inside."

"Roger that, on the way! I'll also send in a Mech-Bot for backup.

Dr. Stevens asked, "The Mech-Bots are armed?"

Jim said, "Oh yes, and very effective. I take it you were not a field medic in Operation CAMPFIRE."

Dr. Stevens replied, "No, I didn't have the pleasure."

Jim stated, "Fastest way to a promotion is having combat experience."

"Like that matters now," Dr. Stevens said, and Jim agreed as a Mech-Bot entered the chamber and took up position several cryo units over, followed by three crewmen each armed with the latest sub-machine gun.

"You ready for this?" Jim asked, looking around the room at each person there. Dr. Stevens pushed a button near the head of the cryo unit, turning it off. Several clicking sounds were heard and the gasses inside could be seen swirling as they were sucked out of the unit and back into their canisters beneath the bed. Before all the gas was removed, a heavy thunk was heard as the top cover was unlocked. It slid toward the occupant's feet, and the remaining gasses sank to the chamber floor, adding a chill to the area.

The occupant was a young female. What took everyone by surprise was the tattered clothing and dirt smudges on her face, and pretty much all the exposed skin that could be seen. There were abrasions on her knees and hands with dirt embedded under her fingernails.

Dr. Stevens said, "I'd say she is human, or a damn good-looking alien." He used his communication pin and ordered a gravity lift gurney brought in with more standing by. He also asked anyone with medical experience to be ready. "These people got injuries."

Jim asked, "What do you have, Doctor?"

"These are just superficial wounds, but I still want them treated for infection. Who knows what more we might find. The entire crew had self-aid buddy care training. Have them wait outside with disinfectant and bandages. If we come across anything more serious, we will deal with it then."

"You got it," Jim said, then relayed the information to Chief Besch to get his people ready.

Some of the former passengers of the Deliverance had the foresight to stop by the base hospital to get another gravity lift gurney, but no other medical supplies were even thought of being needed. Food and blankets were in abundance. A mad rush for bandages, disinfectant, and pillows had everyone scrambling.

The next cryo unit was opened. The occupant was a male with much the same wounds, but they were slightly deeper, and he appeared malnourished.

The third unit contained two small children. As the two were removed, a third child was found stuffed into the foot of the unit clutching a stuffed animal. The three were in bad condition but would survive.

Jim blurted out, "What the hell. Doc? I hope there is a psychologist in this bunch."

Dr. Stevens said, "Looks like whoever put them in the units grabbed whoever they could find and tried to save as many people as possible. What happened after we left?

Jim said, "I guess we're going to find out."

It took the rest of the day to open the remaining Cryo units in that one chamber, remove the occupants, and get them into the central chamber of Anarbia. Each had their wounds taken care of, wrapped in warm blankets, and brought hot food and liquid. Most were in shock and didn't want to talk, and all were afraid of the Mech-Bots.

Those who would talk, told of the invasion and how the aliens remotely reprogrammed the Mech-Bots and turned them against humans, making them into very efficient killers twenty-four hours a day, seven days a week. The people went underground to hide. Venturing out for food was a death sentence. Thanks to the alien ship that strafed the shot pad, the pad was damaged too badly and had to be rebuilt.

For secrecy, the remaining coils and equipment were dismantled, brought underground, and reassembled, and a plan was put into motion. As many cryo units that could be found were gathered and brought to the base. Safety was no longer a concern, and direct shots were scheduled instead of near-Earth orbit ones. They began carving out the chambers while sending the cryo units at the same time. Many of the selected scientists, engineers, and scholars that were selected to go on other ships were killed in the attacks that followed, so anyone that could be found was put into cryo and shot into the past.

Ninety-four souls were recovered from the 75 cryo units in that chamber. Every one of them had superficial wounds and various stages of malnourishment, but they were alive and would recover.

Jim did not sleep well that night. He kept waking up from a dream involving Sarah, and after each time, it took him forever to get back to sleep. He finally gave up on sleep, got ready for the day, and was in the cafeteria at 0400. He was drinking coffee and deep in his own thoughts when Scott found him there at 0630.

At 0700 pretty much all of the people that came to Anarbia by

Deliverance were in the cafeteria. Everyone had trouble sleeping. Steve Harris and his guards were nowhere to be seen. Jim asked Chief Besch and discovered Steve spent most of the night in the chamber studying it and taking scans. Chief felt that, while he was being guarded, he couldn't make any mischief. "Are you sure?" Jim asked.

Chief said, "Oh, believe me. After the word spread about what happened to the two that night in the cafeteria, it will be a while till anyone makes that mistake again."

Jim said, "I'd say so. I see those two still rubbing their arms once in a while."

"Only their arms?" Chief asked, surprised. "I hear Steve came up with a plan for that flooded chamber and he found out on scans that the back of that chamber was not flooded."

Jim asked, "Really? Are you ready to head over there?"

That day, the other two non-flooded chambers were opened, and the occupants of the cryo units were removed. Eighty-two and eighty-seven souls were recovered from these chambers respectively, totaling 263 people taken out of the three chambers.

A long hose was fabricated, placed underwater at the entrance to Anarbia and fed to the flooded chamber. The one-inch hole was cut the rest of the way through and capped with the hose. Another hole was drilled from the chamber next to it with another hose fed to the Deliverance to pump air into the chamber. This was left to run all night while everyone slept, not only to drain the chamber but to test the integrity of the ceiling. A Mech-Bot kept a constant scan on the inside of the chamber and the pressure inside the central Anarbia chamber. If anything fluctuated, Jim was to be woke and everything shut down.

Even though he was exhausted, it proved to be another night with little sleep for Jim. Again, all he could think about was Sarah.

Scott found him in the cafeteria early in the morning like the day before.

Scott asked, "Major, couldn't sleep? Sarah?"

Jim replied, "Yeah."

"I can't say I know what you're going through, but you have to get some sleep."

"I know. Just one more chamber to go."

"I hope she is there."

"Thanks," Jim said and downed another cup of coffee.

The back of the fourth chamber was opened first, since it was intact and posed the least risk. The pressure inside the front of the chamber held, even after the air pumped in was stopped and it was decided to remove that hose to see what happened. A trickling of water was heard, but the chamber did not fill up. The chamber was opened by drilling through the wall of the adjacent chamber. A cap was made ready for the drilled passage to the main chamber of Anarbia just in case.

All of the cryo units but three were able to be opened. The remaining three were buried under a pile of rock that collapsed from the ceiling. Careful scans by Steve Harris determined one of the remaining cryo units was still intact and, if removed, should not pose a significant risk. The other two were crushed under the pile of rock from the earthquake. Any chance of the occupants surviving, with the seals broken and the gasses escaped, was impossible. The ceiling above them appeared very unstable on scans. No recovery effort would be attempted. The identity of the people inside those cryo units may never be known.

Mech-Bots did the work of removing the debris, opening the one intact cryo unit, and bringing out any occupants. A Mech-Bot waited outside with a plug ready to seal the entrance if anything went wrong. Jim also waited but for a different reason.

After what seemed an eternity, a Mech-Bot brought out the only occupant. Jim recognized him as none other than General Long, Commander of Project Anarbia. He was in bad shape and barely breathing. His skin color was off, and Dr. Stevens identified the symptoms immediately. The cave-in must have done something to his cryo unit and caused a chemical imbalance, similar to what divers call the bends but not as dangerous. The cure, however, was identical, pure oxygen and an IV drip. Dr. Stevens said he would be incoherent for the next couple of days, and he took General Long to the infirmary.

The remaining Mech-Bots in the chamber came out and said, "Sir, all the cryo units that are intact are now empty."

In all, 339 people were taken out of the cryo units, bringing the population of Anarbia to 389. Sarah was not one of them. Everyone that was close to Jim, including Claire, gave their condolences. Jim was beside himself. He wondered who was in the other two cryo units and couldn't wait till General Long was coherent enough to tell him who they were.

Jim was not paying attention to anything, deep in his own thoughts. A rumbling sound came from inside the chamber, and water started to rush out, which brought him back to his senses. "Seal it!" Jim shouted as the Mech-Bots were already in motion sealing the adjacent tunnel and removing the hose from its hole so it could be sealed as well. The final thud made Jim's heart sink.

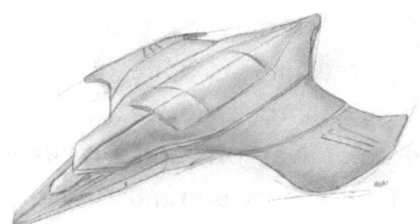

Chapter 41: WHAT HAPPENED?

Over the next few days, Jim spoke with several of the newest residents of Anarbia. They told him about a woman matching Sarah's description who helped an old man do complicated math equations. They did this by hand since access to the larger computers on the base was cut off and the laptops they had were not powerful enough. Together, they calculated shots to send a couple of cryo units at a time directly into the rock surrounding Anarbia in the hopes they would later be discovered.

He was not able to find out who were in the two remaining cryo units or gather any more information about Sarah from the survivors. Was she now entombed in the chambers to the north of Anarbia, or did she stay behind, her fate unknown?

Jim heard the same recurring theme of humans being killed by Mech-Bots wherever they were found, the bodies left to rot where they fell. Everyone took refuge in underground shelters and only ventured out at night to find food and water. Some went out solo to be quieter and not draw the attention of Mech-Bots, while others went in groups.

Domesticated dogs that turned feral and formed packs often attacked these groups as the dogs searched for food. It did not matter how people tried to gather food, fewer and fewer came back, if they came back at all.

All of the survivors taken out of the chambers petitioned for the

Mech-Bots to be disarmed and the children hid from them. The Mech-Bots' lasers had many functions, including the construction of structures and ships. As new ships were developed, it was the Mech-Bots that had the precision and muscle to build the prototypes and later assemble the production models. Without Mech-Bots, the entire mission of Anarbia would be much more difficult.

Jim could not decide what to do about the Mech-Bots and was unable to find out why they had hunted humans. Mech-Bots were used in combat and fought beside humans, but they never attacked their own side. He once heard of a case of 'friendly fire', but it was not just Mech-Bots involved in that incident.

Sam spoke secretly with Jim. She told him she could program into the central computer a 'kill switch', if you will, in the event the Mech-Bots turned against them. As long as the Mech-Bots were still networked, the 'kill switch' could be uploaded to turn them off.

Jim said, "Develop this program on a non-networked computer to prevent being discovered by the Mech-Bots."

Jim checked on General Long twice a day. Each time, he was turned away by Dr. Stevens. Finally on the third day he was allowed to see the general. "It's good to see you, General," Jim said as he entered the room. General Long was lying on a hospital bed chomping at the bit for the doctor to release him.

Dr. Stevens said, "In a few hours I'll draw some blood, and if the results come back the same as they are now, I'll get you out of here in time for supper."

"You better, or I'll draw some of your blood," General Long threatened, then turned to Jim. "With how much that vampire has drawn already, I bet his first name is 'Count'. You better go with him and make sure he's actually testing it."

"He's in one of those moods today," Dr. Stevens said to Jim.

"I can hardly blame him," Jim said. "Three days?"

Dr. Stevens explained, "We had to flush all the chemicals out of his blood, which kept showing back up. I think we finally got it all out." He turned toward General Long and said, "I promise you it won't be much longer."

"So, no more of this slop?" General Long said even though the food came from the same kind of dispenser as those in the cafeteria. And if the stories were true, this food was much better than what he was scrounging before the shot.

"Thanks, Doc," Jim said and waited till Dr. Stevens left the room. "General."

"Oh, yes, Major Norgas." General Long motioned for him to take the chair next to his bed. "The doctor said you had quite the adventure."

Jim said, "Well, I think we managed to break a few records, sir."

The two conversed for several minutes, briefly telling each other what they experienced since last seeing each other, which seemed a lifetime ago for both of them. Finally, Jim could wait no longer and had to ask, "Sir, your cryo unit was partially covered by a cave in. The two units that were on your left had their seals broken, and the occupants were killed. Do you know who was in them?"

"Yes, the Doc told me what happened." General Long thought for a moment as he shook his head. "No, I don't know who they were, some civilians from off base I think." He shrugged and began to yawn. "What's with this Steve Harris character the doctor mentioned?"

Jim said, "We will have to discuss that later. The Mech-Bots constructed a brig, and for the time being he is locked up. What happened to Sarah? Sarah Burnett?"

"Mech-Bots? Here?" General Long became very agitated and

started to rip off the wires attached to him. Dr. Stevens tried to hold the general down while yelling "Orderly!" for assistance. Dr. Stevens and Jim struggled till a sedative was administered and the general fell asleep. "You're going to have to leave," Dr. Stevens said to Jim. "Getting agitated will only prolong his recovery."

It was another two days before Dr. Stevens allowed General Long visitors. Jim was advised not to agitate the general again.

Jim explained to Dr. Stevens, "I'm just trying to figure out what happened. Why did the Mech-Bots turn? And whatever I can about Sarah."

Dr. Stevens said, "I've been talking with the general about that and assured him we have not had any issues."

Jim asked, "But what happened?"

Dr. Stevens said, "I'll let him explain."

Jim entered General Long's room and was motioned by the general to have a seat. General Long said, "I'm sorry about the other day. It's just those damned robots."

"About that, what happened? Why did they attack you?"

"A single alien craft uploaded a virus or something to a communications satellite. It fled before we were able to intercept it. Next thing we knew, we were being exterminated by every networked robot and drone. They were so well organized, we didn't stand a chance."

"How could that happen? Why weren't the central cores taken out?"

General Long explained, "We didn't know what was happening till it was too late. First thing they did was create a defensive perimeter around the cores. Everything we threw at them didn't even make it within a hundred miles of the cores. Any aircraft that made it back were destroyed before they could be refueled. After a week we had nothing left to launch an offensive."

"Incredible," Jim said in disbelief.

General Long continued, "When we were no longer able to put up a fight, they expanded their perimeter, killing everyone they found. We had to hide underground. They were everywhere. Those damn aliens never even had to take us on directly. All they did was flip a switch, and our own technology did it for them."

"What about Project Anarbia? Didn't they —"

"I don't know what they were waiting for or if they were even down there," General Long interrupted, obviously irritated at the situation. "But no, they never helped."

"So we failed."

"Doctor Kovonich kept saying 'paradox' and 'something has to happen before they can do anything'. I told him, 'Whatever the hell it is, they better get off their asses and fight back!' Jim, we're all that's left."

"What happened to Sarah?" Jim cautiously asked.

"Sarah," General Long thought for a moment before continuing, "Sarah was a godsend. She and Doctor Kovonich. They scrounged enough parts together to get us here, and they did as many shots as they were able without weakening the rock formation."

Jim said, "They must have made a mistake, or a shot was off, because it caused an earthquake."

"What are you talking about?" General Long asked as his facial features appeared to be slackening ever so slightly. "I signed off on the plans myself after seeing exactly how much they planned to carve out. I studied the schematics and saw no crack lines anywhere near where they planned. Now, I'll admit the data we were able to get was limited, but the plan was sound." General Long raised his right hand to accent that last bit and dropped it by his side again.

Jim explained, "When we got here, the Mech-Bots said there was an earthquake in 1918 and that is how they detected the chambers."

"Nonsense!" General Long said, a bit agitated. "You can ask Sarah yourself." General Long dwelled on a thought for a moment and his eyes got big as he sat up, "1918? What are you doing here? What year is this?" General Long's speech began having a slight slur to it.

Jim said, "You said ask Sarah. She's not here. Where is she?"

"Damn it Major, I asked what year is this?" General Long said, starting to use his command voice.

"I thought you knew," Jim said, getting frustrated not finding out about Sarah. "Best we can figure, it's 2005."

"My god," General Long said bewildered. "We have been in those damn things almost 100 years? What are you doing here, Major Norgas? You should have died hundreds of years ago!"

Jim said, "Thanks." He did not notice the signs but now realized something was not right with the general. Normally his memory was very sharp and remembered the minutest detail. Now he could not remember what they just discussed. Jim had to risk angering the general and get what information he could about Sarah. "General, you said ask Sarah. Where is she?"

"Oh, Sarah and Doctor Kovonich stayed back to save as many people as they could," General Long said between yawns. "They said after they send me, they will start shots to the supply depot and..." General Long fell asleep, not finishing his sentence.

A chill ran down Jim's spine. He was a bit apprehensive, but with renewed vigor, Jim got up and started to walk out of the general's room when he ran into Dr. Stevens at the door. "Doctor, what is wrong with the general?" Jim asked, concerned the revelation the general just told him may not be true.

Dr. Stevens said, "It's just a side effect of the sedative I gave him."

Jim asked, "What did you do that for? He was just about to tell me what happened to Sarah and fell asleep!"

Dr. Stevens said, "Oh, I'm sorry Jim. But you saw him, I could barely keep him here, if there is still something wrong with his blood he could relapse."

"He said others are at the supply depot," Jim said eagerly. "Is that the sedative talking?"

"What?" Dr. Stevens said, getting excited. "No, no it won't make him say stuff that's not true."

"Doctor, I don't know how many, but we got more cryo units to open," Jim said as he started walking toward the door sideways. "And Sarah might be in one of them." He walked backward, trying to save time and tell Dr. Stevens at the same time, "I'm going to the command center to draw up the plan. Meet me there when you can." He was out the door in a sprint, not wanting to waste any more time.

Via the communications pin, Jim asked his inner circle to meet at the command center, and he requested the historian Dr. Paul Bullard to join them. The command center had not been visited yet aside from a cursory inventory, but he knew it contained everything he needed to plan the mission.

When Jim got to the command center, he asked the computer to display as much detail as it had of the supply depot that was located near Mackinac Island, on the Lake Michigan side of the island. Soon a 3-D holographic image was displayed hovering over the central table in the room. After identifying where the entrance to the depot was, he zoomed the image out to look at the contours and depth of Lake Michigan.

He said to the computer, "Show me all waterways from Anarbia to Lake Michigan with corresponding water depths," and studied what was displayed.

He was thoroughly engrossed in his work and was startled when Scott walked up beside him. "What's going on?" Scott asked as the others surrounded the table.

"I think Sarah might be alive!" Jim exclaimed with a big smile.

"What?" Everyone said in unison.

"General Long said after Sarah and Doctor Kovonich finished as many shots as they could here, they were supposed to start filling up the supply depot," Jim said. He pointed to the area of Lake Michigan where the depot was carved out during the tests. It was decided long ago not to use it as a working base because the lake was shallow, and the risk of being detected was too great. It was used for practice shots before carving out Anarbia. Sarah and Dr. Kovonich were able to perfect their targeting this way, but there was no way to tell if they had the time correct. Both of them decided that if they got the location right, they must have had the time as well, since both time and location worked together.

"How many?" Claire asked excitedly, but deep down she was disappointed. Claire knew Jim's heart belonged to Sarah, but she had hoped to win him over. Seeing the look on his face confirmed she would only be a replacement, even after all the time they spent together.

Jim said, "General Long didn't say. The doctor gave him a sedative, and he fell asleep before he could tell me."

Sam asked, "Did he say Sarah is one of them?"

Jim said, "No, but she has to be."

Scott said, "Just be careful. Don't let your emotions get too high. She might not be there." Everyone around the table nodded in agreement and tried to show Jim their support.

Jim said, "I know, but I've got to believe she is okay til I know otherwise. Thank you for your concern. Really! I appreciate it." Then he asked, "Now, how do we get there?" After a few moments he added, "Those locks are way too shallow to go undetected, and I don't see any other water route. Not to mention most of those lakes are too shallow for Deliverance to stay completely submerged."

Jim studied the contours of the Great Lakes' depth. "What do we do? What do we do?" He said out loud, but more to himself as he picked at his lower lip with his right hand. "Damn, the rivers coming up from the gulf can get us most of the way there, but they're way too shallow."

He turned his attention to those around the table and said, "I don't see how to get there undetected."

Scott asked, "Does it matter if we're detected? It just might play into their UFO phobia."

Jim said, "That's true, but what if it doesn't and they think we are a preemptive strike from a rival country?"

"So what?" Scott shrugged his shoulders. "We can outrun anything they send our way."

"That's not what I meant," Jim said and looked at Scott. "What if they don't send something to intercept us but instead launch a nuke? I thought about going around Canada and entering the Hudson Bay underwater. It's just a short jump from there to this lake. But to America, it might look exactly like an incoming missile, and we just started World War III."

Paul said, "We can't have that!"

Scott replied, "I didn't think of that."

"I might have an idea," Claire said, and switched the view on the holographic table to the weather patterns over the Atlantic. She made the entire area from the western coast of northern Africa to the eastern half of the North American continent visible on the table.

Jim asked, "What are you thinking?"

Claire said, "It won't make us invisible, but I doubt anyone will be looking if we can hide inside a hurricane."

Paul asked, "A hurricane?"

"Sometimes they come up through the gulf and go to the west of these mountains," Claire pointed to the Smoky Mountains, "and might go pretty close to where we need."

To the computer, Claire said, "Show me historical data of the year 2005, hurricanes that went along this path." Her hand passed along where she just described. "I think I found what we want. Computer, show me the path of this storm."

Scott asked, "What do you have?"

Claire said, "Hurricane Katrina. That just might get us most of the way there. I'm not seeing where it went after it was downgraded to a tropical storm though."

"Katrina!" Paul blurted out, "That was a monster, category five, if I remember right."

Jim asked, "Wait, wait, what?"

Paul said, "She wants to bring you into a category five hurricane to hide you from prying eyes."

"Good idea," Jim said as he leaned closer toward the table. "If we come up near the eye we should be shielded from radar outside of the storm and anyone that looks up inside the eye."

Sam added, "Or, we might be taken as debris picked up by the storm."

"Exactly, I like it," Jim replied, approving the idea.

Paul said, "Lunacy, absolute lunacy."

"The ship can take it," Jim said, shrugging his shoulders. "Right Chief?"

Chief Besch said, "It just went through an overhaul. And after how well she performed in that 'washing machine', I don't see why not."

Paul said, "You're all insane. That storm caused almost 2000 deaths and well over 100 billion dollars in damage."

Scott said, "And? That's history. We can't change that, we just want to use it as a blind."

Jim said, "Scott, you're not helping. Paul, we will not put our one and only ship at risk."

Paul said, "I'm not so sure. I saw the look on your face when the general came out instead of your girl."

Jim sat down and began to wonder if he was putting people at risk.

Paul said, "I'm sorry, that was uncalled for."

Jim asked, "Have I been making bad judgement calls?"

Scott said, "No. I'm sure if it was that risky you would find another way to get there."

Jim asked, "Would I?"

Chief Besch said, "If you didn't, I'd make you. Your not taking my ship on some fools errand."

Jim looked at the Chief and said, "Thanks, Chief."

"What about this one?" Paul asked as he read data on the edge of the table and looked at Jim. "Arlene. It goes right over this lake here, Lake Huron. From there you should be able to stay submerged the rest of the way."

Claire said, "Looks like it barely made it on shore before fizzling out."

Paul said, "If all you need is a blind, it spawned tornadoes as far north as Indianapolis. Katrina did not reach that far with anything more than rain. Arlene still caused floods all the way to New York after it merged with another storm here," he pointed at the southern edge of Lake Huron. "Right about where we get off."

Claire said, "Really! I heard about Katrina, but, Arlene?"

Jim said, "Paul, what you said, I know you were just looking out for everyone. Now what do you have?"

"Here," Paul said as he expanded the data he was looking at till a 3-D image of the storm encompassed most of the table. "Take a look."

Jim asked, "What time frame are we looking at?"

"It made landfall..." Claire said, stretching out the last word as she looked for more data on the storm, "– in the afternoon of June 11, just west of Pensacola Florida, and it looks like it took two days to reach Flint Michigan, where it joined up with, yup, another storm."

Paul looked vindicated by the information Claire added to the display and smiled as he nodded his head.

Jim asked, "And what day is it now? Have we ever determined exactly when we are?"

Scott said, "No sir. We have been busy, other than the two days' down-time you gave us."

Jim asked, "So, all these events might have already happened?"

Paul said, "I will do what I can to find out our exact date."

"Get on this. I don't want to miss this window," Jim said to everyone in the room. "Gather a team of who we might need and include two Mech-Bots.

Scott asked, "Major? How will we get out of there and back here undetected?"

Jim took a deep breath and let it out noisily, "One step at a time."

Listening in on commercial radio, Paul was able to determine the date was 2 June 2005. They had just over a week to prepare for the mission they called Operation STORM CHASER.

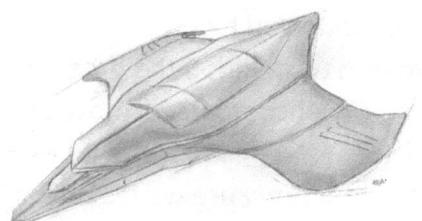

Chapter 42: THE WAIT

Jim appeared outside the infirmary door as soon as he heard General Long would be discharged. "General," he said as the general emerged, "You were telling me about shots to the supply depot."

The two walked toward the cafeteria as they spoke. "Yes, we had about 700 cryo units," General Long said.

Jim looked a bit confused, "Where did they all come from?"

"We found some at the hospital in Hampton, and NASA (National Aeronautics and Space Administration) had a huge stash."

"I have been talking to some of the people we pulled out of the north wall, and it sounded like you were putting your lives in danger just to gather food. How did you move all those cryo units?"

General Long stopped walking, "Major, why don't you ask me what you really want to know?" He paused for a second and looked Jim over. "Sarah planned to get herself and Doctor Kovonich out after sending as many people as they could fit in the supply depot without hollowing out any more rock."

Jim let out a deep breath, "Thank you General. You don't know what that means to me."

"I've got some idea. But you've got to understand, she may not have gotten out and could have been discovered at any time. We did what we could to shield those coils, but they still put out detectable emissions."

"Understood, but as long as there is a chance, I have to hang on to it."

The two reached the cafeteria and got their food, and Jim told the general the plans for Operation STORM CHASER.

General Long said, "I'll leave that in your capable hands," giving Jim the green light to go ahead. "And use whatever resources you need."

"Thank you, sir."

People came and went as they ate their supper. Jim's inner circle joined the two at their table, and they spoke over the next several hours about what had happened since they last saw each other the morning of the shot.

General Long remembered bits and pieces of what Jim told him while he was in the infirmary, but thanks to the medication, he was unsure of most of it. General Long did not like his memory being spotty like this. He prided himself in his ability to remember details.

"So, in short, we are 500 years behind in development and population growth," General Long concluded.

Jim said, "Yes sir."

"Any ideas?"

Jim said hesitantly, "Well, as far as population growth, I have considered selecting from the natural inhabitants."

"Hmm," General Long said, raising both eyebrows. After thinking on it a while he said, "Let's wait till after the rescue. What are we at now?"

"Population? Three hundred and eighty-nine."

"Yeah, we're going to have to. I don't like the idea, but we are way behind the curve. Not to mention the gene pool. Don't we need something like three thousand just to start with?"

"That is something Doctor Stevens will have to answer. I don't have a clue."

General Long started shaking his head. "As far as technological advances, I doubt any of them can help."

Claire, who had been sitting at the table quietly, had to counter the general's skepticism, "General, a lot of scientific ideas are stifled by the dogma of others and not allowed to come to the light of day for fear of ridicule. If we brought some of those scientists and inventors here, the results just might surprise you."

"Go on," General Long said, shifting his attention to Claire.

"Take the speed of light for example. Albert Einstein himself said his theory of relativity was close, but not complete. After his death scientists took his theory as fact and ridiculed anyone who thought differently for years. They thought mass will continue to increase as you get closer to the speed of light, requiring more and more energy to go faster until infinite energy was required to break the speed of light, making it impossible. Well, we proved that one wrong." Claire paused a moment. "And they said transmissions at that speed cannot carry any data. SETI proved that wrong."

General Long asked, "What's your point?"

"I think we should take the scientists who were held back by that environment and encourage them. The ideas they held back just might come out and create a new way of looking at things. Look at the Dark Ages — it was blasphemy to invent anything that went against the current way of thinking. That alone put us hundreds of years behind where we should be."

"Point made. What do you propose so we don't impact the timeline or our past?"

"Well, that's the problem General," Jim stepped in. "We have to find people who are to make no contribution beyond what they already have, who will not be missed if they disappear, and who have the potential of making an impact."

While hearing this, General Long put his elbows on the table, fists together, and rested his chin on his thumbs. After some time he said, "That sounds like a difficult requirement to fill. How? Where do –"

Sam interrupted, "General, if I may."

"Go ahead," General Long said, shaking his head. He raised his left hand in her direction, then put it back under his chin.

"Major Norgas mentioned doing this just before we left the moon," Sam said as the general looked sidelong at Jim. "I've been thinking about it ever since, and the central core computer should have all the data we need to find these people. I can write an algorithm to sift through the data."

"Quite the team you have, Major," General Long congratulated Jim. "Alright, let's see what you come up with. But first, let's get our people back."

Jim said, "Absolutely, and thank you, sir."

The group made small talk for the rest of the evening. Those the general did not already know introduced themselves and told him their fields of study.

General Long always had somewhat of a mean look about him, and his mere presence caused those around him to act on their best behavior. Nevertheless, he genuinely cared about those around him, and even more for those who worked for him.

The next several days, Anarbia was abuzz with people going this way and that, eager to begin work. The Mech-Bots were kept busy finishing the buildings that were not completed and were suddenly needed now that humans lived in the base. Those who arrived by ship asked the Mech-Bots for assistance while the rest avoided them.

The week went by quickly for everyone but Jim. As preparations were made and equipment was stored on Deliverance, everything anyone could think of was put on board including lots of blankets, tables, and chairs. Since everyone in the supply depot was to come out of cryo units, soups, hot beverages, and anything else desired by those who had previously came out of cryo was prepared. Every time Jim had a few minutes to spare, his mind wandered to Sarah. He forced himself to stay busy to make the time go by and to wear himself out so he could sleep at night.

If he was not thinking about Sarah, he caught himself staring at a data pad watching the feed from a weather satellite. He kept an eye on the area around Honduras, where historical data showed the storm first formed.

Finally, on June 8th, Jim started to see the storm form. *'Just three more days'* he thought, *'okay, three days till we leave here, then two long grueling days waiting for the storm to make it all the way to Lake Huron'.* "Come on, grow!" He caught himself saying to the storm on the screen. He noticed people looking at him, so he put the data pad away and found something to keep him busy again to kill more time.

Yet no matter what he did, time crept along. What seemed like an hour was only ten minutes when he checked the time. "I can't stand this," he yelled to no one in particular. He tapped the communication pin and asked for Sam, Scott, and John to meet him at the loading ramp of Deliverance.

He asked Sam, "Can you program the ship's computer a tight course to follow so we can practice? All three of us can fly in a wide-open area, but not in tight confines like the entrance to Anarbia. I'd like to get some practice so we're faster at entering and exiting the base without putting the ship at risk. If you could, please program a course out in the ocean."

Sam said, "I might be able to get the bridge glass to display the boundary of a course. Have it show lines of a road, or a tunnel for you to stay within?"

"That would be great. Can you make it with tight turns and such? Like coming into and out of Anarbia."

"I think I can have something for you in less than an hour. How long a course do you want?"

"For starters how about something simple. You can add on as we get better."

"Care to make a game of it?" Scott asked with raised eyebrows.

Jim asked, "What do you have in mind?"

"Well, Sam programs a course for us to practice. If we stray off-course, the computer takes over and stops the ship. We switch pilots, and all three of us practice." He looked at Jim and John. "We've got, what, three days till we can rescue your girlfriend? How about we practice the next two days and on the last day, we have a timed race?"

John said, "I don't know if that's fair. Both of you have combat experience."

"Dog-fighting is different." Scott assured John, "Besides, there was not much of that going on in Operation CAMPFIRE. And you probably have more stick time on this bird than either of us."

John asked, "Okay – what does the winner get?"

Jim said, "Well, I'd say if you win, a new call sign may be in order. Sorry Scott, but you're stuck with Gumshoe."

Scott came back with, "Ha Ha, Stinker." Jim raised his eyebrows as he turned and walked up the ramp of the ship.

John said, "Stinker? Gumshoe? I don't think I want a call sign."

"Shut up, kid," Scott said as he started to run after Jim and yelled, "So what's the bet?"

"Hey now, wait a minute." John shrugged his shoulders and followed the others into the ship.

Details for the upcoming race were worked out among the four of them, and General Long was brought into the loop for permission. General Long thought it was a great idea. Everyone was new to Anarbia, and no one was in need of a morale boost yet, but something like this just might help everyone bond and get to know each other. Something to increase the skills of the pilots was always encouraged.

The three practiced the course and took turns at the helm, slowly at first, and they gradually increased speed as their confidence built. The bridge glass showed the boundary of the course ahead while the holo image next to the pilot showed the entire course in green. Both displays turned yellow if the ship drifted too near the edge of the course. If any part of the ship crossed the edge of the course, they turned red and the ship shut down.

Sam programmed the route directly into the ship, but she watched and sent course updates from the base command post. She discovered the command post had the ability to project images onto the ceiling of Anarbia. The intent was to simulate day and night to help give the inhabitants a sense of time, but she had the progress of the practice runs displayed larger than life on the ceiling.The initial image surprised everyone. Looking up at the ocean startled them even more till they realized they were not being flooded. Quickly everyone realized what was going on and couldn't look away. They saw an exterior view of the ship and the course ahead of it. In addition, a view of the bridge was displayed so everyone could see who was piloting the ship.

John was the first at the controls and was lightheartedly ribbed the entire course by both Jim and Scott.

Jim said, "Nice bank, is that the fastest you can go?"

Scott said, "The throttle is over there, gramps."

John said, "Gramps? I'm younger than both of you!"

Scott said "Yeah, well you fly like my Grampa drives." In his best old man impersonation he said, "You need some glasses there, sonny?"

Jim said, "If that's the fastest you can go, let one of us show you how it's done."

John replied, "Okay, but you asked for it." He accelerated the ship as fast as he dared to stay within the boundary of the course. Both Jim and Scott nearly lost their footing and began to laugh.

John completed the course with a few close calls but no engine shutdowns.

Each time a different pilot took the helm, Sam altered the course slightly so no one pilot could get an edge on the others by watching their mistakes.

The second pilot that took the helm, Scott, was thrown off by the course change and ran beyond the boundary at the first turn. The engine was taken offline, ending his turn.

"Hey!" exclaimed Scott as he let go of the controls.

"Not so cocky now, huh Gumshoe?" John said mockingly.

Jim took the controls and knew Sam was throwing them some curve balls, so he was prepared for it and finished the course slightly quicker than John.

Each time the three pilots completed another round, the course got harder with tighter and tighter turns.

Scott entered the second round on bottom and was determined to show the others up, but he couldn't quite shake the initial failure and remained in third place.

The pilots were completely unaware that everyone was watching and that a scoring system was being displayed next to their names. When the three decided to end the day's practice flights and head home, Sam turned off the ceiling display by request from General Long to keep the pilots in the dark. The general also made an announcement over the base communication system, "Ladies and Gentlemen, this is General Long. What you have been watching were practice runs leading up to a race in two days. I urge you, please do not let the pilots know we have been watching. I've got something special planned. If you all keep this quiet, it will make the surprise all the better for each of us. Thank you."

After completing the post-flight shut down of the Deliverance, the pilots entered the cafeteria for their evening meal and saw a big poster announcing the race inside the entrance.

Jim said, "I guess the general thinks our little bet will boost morale."

Scott said, "How? It's not like they will be able to watch."

The three noticed more than the usual sidelong glances from people they did not know, but they attributed the looks to the poster and were none the wiser about what was really going on. Even the muffled talk of bets being placed did not tip them off.

General Long sat at the same table as the night before and was joined by Jim and his inner circle. Each enjoyed the little secret that was being kept from the pilots. General Long enjoyed it the most when a whisper was overheard about which pilot was better. He had an idea about the abilities of his pilots but used this info to further rate them. He also enjoyed the uncomfortable feeling it caused the pilots.

Jim thought, *'Only the crew should know anything about the piloting abilities of the three, so where are these people getting their information'?*

General Long used moments like this to gain insight on the men and women that worked under him. He put a slight smirk on his face only those very close to him would notice, none of whom were alive anymore. They passed away years before any of this, and the general was long over it. He made his career his new family.

Nowhere else can camaraderie and teamwork be found like it can in the military. Everyone knew what was expected and did it. Those who didn't quickly found themselves on the outside looking in. No slackers, no showing up to work just to get a paycheck. Everyone pulled their weight and, when needed, chipped in to help each other get the job done. No one worried about "job security." What a stupid concept. In the military, there was no such thing. During training missions, commanders were routinely taken out of the picture to test the unit's ability to adapt without them.

Everyone sat around the table chit-chatting as the night before. Jim began feeling sleepy for a change and thought he would finally get a good night's sleep. He excused himself and went to his quarters. He fell asleep soon after lying down. When morning came, he felt like he had just fallen asleep, but to his surprise, the clock showed eight hours had passed. He did not dream of Sarah last night; the best he could remember, he was flying race courses over and over.

June 9th, two days prior to Hurricane Arlene making landfall. One more day of practice, then the day of the big race. The course progressively got more and more difficult with each attempt. Numerous times, all three pilots breached the boundary of the course and caused the engine to shut down. Each of them became better at piloting in tight spaces, which boosted their confidence whenever they entered or exited Anarbia through the narrow passage. They navigated the ninety-degree turns quicker each time. No longer did they stop and gain altitude before proceeding to the landing pad. Now they flew right through the entrance.

The unofficial scoreboard put Lt Anders in first place, with Major Norgas second and Captain Dixon still unable to move up.

That evening General Long had the Mech-Bots set up chairs

outside the cafeteria while everyone ate their meal. Sam snuck out and headed to the command center.

After the usual chit-chat started, the general gave Sam a head start before he stood and asked everyone to join him outside. The three pilots had no clue what to make of the scene. General Long motioned for everyone to take a seat.

General Long announced, "Owing to everyone's interest, tomorrow will be the First Annual Pilot Skills Challenge. Without the contestants' knowledge, we have kept a close eye on their progress. I'd like to show you what we have been watching – not everything, just the bloopers." Jim, Scott and John looked at each other and the crowd a bit uncomfortably. Jim looked at the general with a '*How could you*' look. General Long tilted his head, tapped his communication pin, and gave Sam the go-ahead.

The ceiling lit up with the image and sound of Captain Dixon saying "Hey!" on the first day of practice, then showed him running off the course, "The throttle is over there, gramps." Captain Dixon's face turned red as everyone laughed, including his fellow pilots.

Their laughter continued as the accidents were shown next. Soon the three pilots got into the spirit of it and enjoyed the rest of the evening, even the push-up challenge to determine who got to go first. Nothing was censored or held back. In the spirit of the evening, General Long asked the Mech-Bots to serve alcohol for all who wanted to partake.

The general noticed many in the audience did not want to be around the Mech-Bots. They felt they were being corralled by the Mech-Bots as they hovered around the outside of the group. This was the most efficient way to serve food and drinks, but many felt it was also an efficient way to kill and kept looking over their shoulders.

He dismissed the Mech-Bots and told everyone, "Help yourself to the refreshments."

As the collection of videos came to a close, he stood and said, "So, now you know tomorrow's race will be shown live for all to see." With a big grin he added, "I hope that doesn't give you any – pressure." The image on the ceiling was replaced by a beautiful golden sunset with a splattering of rippled clouds, and to everyone's surprise, a light breeze wafted through the base.

After the evening's festivities, Sam was inspired to write a permanent safety routine for the Deliverance's computer. She copied from the race programming for the computer to take control of the ship if a collision was imminent. The pilot could override this if needed.

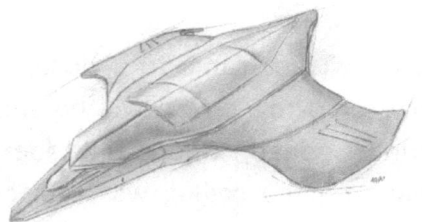

Chapter 43: THE RACE

Jim entered the cafeteria for breakfast on race day and noticed people were betting on the race. Jim and the other pilots started to feel like celebrities with all the attention directed their way.

Everyone lingered around the inside of the cafeteria waiting for General Long to make his announcement to start the race. Most made final bets or just fidgeted.

After what seemed an eternity, especially for the pilots, General Long stood and clinked his knife on the side of a glass to quiet everyone. "Welcome to the First Annual Pilot Skills Challenge," he said to everyone, and then turned his attention toward the pilots. "And I stress the word *'Challenge'*. Sam, did you make the special modifications I requested?"

She nodded her head and gave him a thumbs-up.

"As you all know, for the past couple of days, our pilots have practiced making tight turns and maneuvering in tight spaces. Most of you may not know, but Major Norgas helped with the testing of the Deliverance. So tell us, Major, is the ship taller than it is wide?

Visible confusion crossed Jim's face as he thought, "I think so, yes. Wait, it's wider."

General Long said, "I think you're about to find out." He paused and an evil grin crossed his face. "I highly suggest you plan your course, including which part of the ship goes first for different legs of the race. Samantha Green, will you please go over the race rules?"

Sam stood and explained the following rules:

1) The course will be exactly the same for each pilot.

2) The pilots that have not flown yet are to be kept in a room where they are not able to see or hear anything about the race.

3) Chief Besch will ride in the captain's seat to ensure no cheating. That includes accessing flight logs of the other contestants or any other preflight information gathering. The course will be displayed upon leaving the landing pad.

4) The timer starts when the landing gear leaves the pad and ends when the ship comes to a stop centered over the landing pad.

5) Whenever a course boundary is touched, 10 seconds will be added to the total time. Each second the ship remains touching or breaching the boundary, three seconds will be added to the total time.

6) If the computer takes over flying, the pilot is disqualified.

She finished reading the rules and asked, "Are there any questions?"

Scott raised his hand and asked, "What did you mean, which part of the ship goes first?"

Sam started to explain but was cut off by General Long, "Captain, the three of you have been practicing just going forward. That ship is capable of far more than that. That and your ability to plan ahead will play a key role in completing today's challenge."

Jim and Scott shook their heads, surprised by the announcement. John looked confused.

General Long continued, "If there are no other questions, let's determine who goes first." He produced a cloth bag that contained three tokens with the numbers 1, 2 and 3 written on them. "Major, with R.H.I.P., you get to draw first." Someone called out "What's R.H.I.P.?" and General Long said, "Rank Has Its Privileges." Jim took out the token numbered 3. "Captain, you're next," Scott took out the token with a 1 on it. "Lieutenant, that means you're the second pilot," General Long said as he removed the final token to show it did have a 2 on it.

"Mech-Bots," General Long bellowed toward the two Mech-Bots near him, "Show Major Norgas and Lieutenant Anders to the brig till their turn. Do not allow anyone to see them other than myself till their turn."

The Mech-Bots said, "Sir, as you order." They took the order quite literally and grabbed Jim and John by their collars to lift them from their seats, which caused protests from both and gasps from those who were uneasy being around Mech-Bots.

"Gently," General Long said. "They are not under arrest, just escort them."

"Yes sir," said one Mech-Bot. The other said, "Our apologies sir, we hope we did not injure you," as it started to smooth the wrinkles it caused to John's uniform.

"No, I'm fine," John said, a little shaken.

Scott couldn't help but take his shot. "Have fun in the brig, you two. I might stop by with a book and a nail file for you."

"Ha ha," Jim said. He caught Scott in a headlock and messed up his hair. Then he let go and walked away with John and two Mech-Bots in tow. Scott's hair was less than an inch long, but he still ran his hand through it to straighten it out.

"Chief!" General Long called, "Are you ready to get this started?"

"Yes sir."

"Then let's move this party outside." Everyone funneled out of the cafeteria and took a seat in the chairs still there from the night before. Chief and Captain Dixon made their way to the Deliverance.

The ceiling of Anarbia switched from a morning view of the sky to an exterior view of the Deliverance as the two approached the ship.

A view of the bridge was added to the scene as Scott and Chief Besch took their seats.

When Scott went through his preflight checklist, the canopy painted two green lines on either side of the ship marking the course boundary, leading toward the entrance of Anarbia. From the pilot's perspective, the lines changed to an opaque green box formed around the ship for the pilot to fly through. The holographic image did not reveal any of the course outside of Anarbia yet.

Scott lifted the ship off the landing pad and started moving forward. A timer started counting in the center of the canopy above him, and he goosed the engine a bit. When the ship approached the entrance, he turned the nose down and dove into the water, then brought the ship level when he got to the bottom of the shaft and shot out the other side.

He saw the course laid out before him, which started with a sharp turn to the port side of the ship, then a vertical chimney that got narrower as he went. Scott remembered what General Long said, so he chose which direction he wanted the top of the ship to face for the next turn, which did not appear to be a turn. As the ship approached, he spun the ship 180 degrees on its z-axis, stopped the ship, angled the ship's nose up a bit, and started moving forward again almost in the opposite direction from which he came.

"Good one, General," the audience heard Scott chuckle.

For a while, the course did the usual loops and corkscrews, which Scott was well prepared for, and he put on the speed. He soon realized his mistake when the walls of the final corkscrew closed in and formed a tight box, with barely enough room for the ship to roll on its x-axis. The confining space forced the pilot to finish the corkscrew with the ship at approximately 30 degrees from the ocean floor. This orientation caused the right side of the ship to touch the bottom portion of the box and turn it red. Scott noticed the timer sped up till he was able to correct the attitude of the ship, and the image on the canopy turned green again.

Scott's brush with the course boundary cost him twenty-five seconds. Ten seconds for the initial contact and fifteen for the five seconds it took for him to correct.

He then came to a wall with a side passage going off to both the left and right. "Now what?" Scott asked.

"I'm not allowed to help you, sir," Chief responded, which caused General Long to chuckle as he watched.

Scott said, "Chief, I forgot you were there. I was in the zone, back in my fighter. Just thinking out loud."

Chief said, "This is a lot bigger than a fighter."

Scott said, "Still flies like one." But as they were underwater, he added, "Or whatever."

He stopped the ship and studied what he saw. The holo image was not much help beyond a couple of turns, so Scott got out of his chair and approached the canopy, which showed both paths going off into the distance. He saw the path on the left was mostly straight stretches, with turns and loops going farther than the eye could see. The path on the right was very narrow with switchbacks, side slips, and who knows what else till it exited out the bottom and went back the direction he came. Scott decided to take the path to the left, and he kicked the engine hard to make up for the time lost.

Scott felt he was making really good time, but General Long knew better and could hardly contain his laughter.

The path Scott chose began getting tighter around the ship as it spiraled down, down, down, then ended as the walls of the course nearly touched all sides of the ship. "Damn it General!" he exclaimed, to the general's amusement, and then the audience realized what happened. The path was a decoy. Scott had to go all the way back, either backward or suffer penalty time as he turned the ship around and breached the walls of the course. If the ship completely left the course to do a U-turn, the computer would take over and disqualify him.

After several minutes and quite a bit of penalty time added from scraping the walls, Scott made it back to where the side trip started.

On the path to the right, Scott entered a cube that ended up being a maze with several dead ends and tight passages, which forced the pilot to move the ship every which way, even backward. Finally, Scott found the exit and came across another fork. This time, he studied the paths ahead much closer and switched between the holo and VR to see what was beyond, and he chose the correct path.

The entire course took Scott just over an hour before he breached the surface of the water in Anarbia, hurried over to the landing pad, and centered the ship on the pad to end his time.

General Long was at the bottom of the ramp to congratulate Captain Dixon as he exited the ship. "You are an evil man," Scott said, and he shook the general's hand. The two spoke as they made their way to the audience, who applauded him when he came into view.

John was led by a Mech-Bot who would not allow anyone to speak with him or hand him anything. This was to ensure no one could tip him off about what was to come.

At the first split, John took the path to the right and entered the maze, to Scott's disappointment, but made the wrong choice at the next fork. That mistake cost him even more time than Scott lost. To add to John's frustration, he made another mistake at the third fork. Nevertheless, he continued flying and touched the walls of the course much less than Scott did.

John used his sleeve to remove the sweat from his forehead

several times before finally breaching the surface of the water, so fast it caused the nose of the ship to bounce a few times when he leveled it off, before moving to the landing pad and ended his time of one hour and twenty-two minutes.

General Long again greeted the pilot at the bottom of the ramp, and congratulated him on completing the course. John was also greeted by the audience with applause, and Major Norgas took the helm of Deliverance.

To keep it interesting, Jim's time was not displayed to the audience. They could keep time but would not know if or how much penalty time was added.

Jim did great, till he got to the maze. He scraped the wings on the course walls when he tried to enter a passage above him by going vertical, instead of rotating the ship on its Z axis first. He learned the ship was wider than it is tall. Its stubby, curved wings deceived him. The maze cost him more time than Scott or John.

He started to go down another wrong path, but after several hundred yards, he backed out and went the right way. Both John and Scott were amazed at his ability to back the ship and stay within the boundaries of the course.

Upon completing the race, Jim was greeted the same as the others, first by General Long, who shook his hand at the bottom of the ramp, then by the audience's applause when he came into view.

General Long invited all three pilots to join him in front of the audience. "Before we announce the winner, I'd like to thank everyone for showing your support. I think we all had some fun, including the pilots, who spoke a few choice words directed at yours truly. Don't worry, I won't bring charges, I know it was all in fun. Now first off, Lt John Anders. Even though you did not win this race, from what I saw of your piloting skills, I'd like to take the honor of awarding you with your call sign. While you were flying, Captain Dixon – call sign Gumshoe – and I discussed it. Then on the walk back from the landing pad with Major Norgas – call sign Stirker – he agreed."

Knowing General Long's sense of humor, John dreaded what he may have come up with, and that he would be stuck with for the rest of his life. From the smile on both Gumshoe and Stinker's faces, it must be something off the wall, John thought.

"In light of your ability to turn that ship and double back like you can, I hereby award you with the call sign..." General Long paused to let the tension rise. "From here on, be known as..." and another pause, "Jack-in-the-box."

John closed his eyes and shook his head, deflated. The audience did not know the tradition behind being given a call sign, but applauding felt like the right thing to do.

When John opened his eyes again he saw Jim, Scott, and General Long huddled, talking among themselves. General Long kept looking at John, shaking his head. Jim or Scott would pull his attention back and the three appeared to argue, but John could not hear any of what was being said.

General Long said to the audience, "Excuse us a moment," then rejoined the huddle.

The three began shaking their heads and once again, General Long addressed the audience, "Sorry, I misunderstood. I present to you, Jackknife."

John's eyes lit up as the audience applauded.

After the applause died down General Long said, "Now back to the race. Samantha Green is the one who made all this possible; would you like the honor of announcing the winner?"

Sam joined the general and the three pilots in front of the crowd.

"As we all know, Lt Anders' time was one hour and twenty-two minutes, and was beat by Captain Dixon, who completed the race in one hour and seven minutes. Major Norgas's final score after all penalty time was added in is..." Sam looked around and waited for the general to give her the go-ahead. "One hour and twenty-six minutes."

General Long raised Scott's arm over his head and announced, "Captain Dixon, you are the winner of the First Annual Pilot Skills Challenge."

Everyone in the audience applauded. They did not show it, but most were upset because Dixon was the underdog and they lost their bets. For the pilots, the race started out as practice but ended up being entertainment for everyone and resulted in bragging rights for the winner.

For Jim it meant more. Three days of waiting went by quickly, with only one night and a wake-up to go. And after the grueling race, he knew he would probably have little trouble sleeping that night.

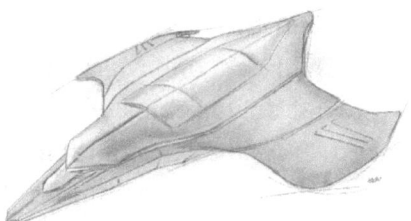

Chapter 44: PREP

The morning of June 11, 2005, Jim woke much the same as any other that involved a mission, early and chomping at the bit to get started. Something was nagging at him this time, and he couldn't quite place it. While getting cleaned up and ready, he went over all the prep they had done so far for this mission: *'medical, food, blankets, and some extra muscle for heavy lifting were all we needed to get everyone out of cryo here. So what am I missing'?*

He found himself walking toward the north wall instead of the cafeteria. Perhaps looking at the caverns where so many people were found in cryo would jog his memory of what he forgot. After peeking in the second cavern, nothing came to mind. He decided to forget it and get some breakfast. When the cafeteria came into view, with all the chairs still set up outside, the feeling came back, but he could not bring the thought to the front of his mind.

Just as he touched the door handle to enter the cafeteria, it dawned on him. He rushed to the ship and asked via his comm pin for Mech-Bots and the chief to meet him there.

Chief Besch asked, "Major, do you know what time it is?"

"Actually, no Chief," Jim answered the groggy question. "Just get over here. We got work to do."

By the time Chief arrived, several Mech-Bots were running in and out of the ship carrying out nearly everything that was not bolted down. Tables and chairs from the cafeteria, beds and furniture from the crew quarters, and even the land vehicles were strewn around the landing pad. When Chief saw one Mech-Bot carrying ammo, he had to query, "Hold it, what do you think you're doing?"

The Mech-Bot replied, "We are lightening the ship, Chief."

Chief asked, "What for?" And why the ammo?"

"We don't know why, Chief, but the ammo adds weight."

"We may need the ammo. Besides, we never send an aircraft up unable to defend herself. Never!"

"Chief, by order of Major Norgas, the ammo is unnecessary extra weight, and we are to remove all of it," and it climbed the ramp for another load.

"You get your metallic ass back over here!" Chief ordered in the way only chiefs can. "You just tell your synthetic counterparts to stop. This is my ship and no one is leaving it defenseless. Till I get to the bottom of this, not one more thing comes off this ship. Got it?" Chief bellowed, "Did you hear me?"

"Yes, Chief. We understand and comply." All the Mech-Bots working on the Deliverance stopped in their tracks to await further instruction.

When the chief reached the top of the ramp and entered the cargo bay, he saw the area was as empty as the day it rolled off the assembly line, which was the last time he noticed the insulation that lined the walls.

Chief said over the ship's comm. "Major! Where are you?"

"I'm on the bridge, Chief, come on up," he heard the major reply.

Upon entering the bridge, the chief saw the major reviewing some data. "What do you think you're doing to my ship, Major?" Chief inquired, "And why are you stripping her ability to defend herself?"

"Your ship?"

"Yes, sir," Chief quickly replied with confidence in his voice. "You may be in command and fly her, but it's the chief of maintenance who's responsible for her. History and tradition makes her *my* ship."

No matter how forceful the pilot may be, if the crew chief says the craft cannot fly, it will not fly. Military history is littered with aircraft taken out of rotation for 'safety reasons' and then, with nothing done to the aircraft itself, suddenly it was safe to fly again due to a signature from maintenance.

Jim said, "You're right, and I'm sorry Chief, I've just got a lot on my mind."

"No problem, Major." Chief returned to his normal tone of voice. "So what's going on, and why the weapons?"

"How many people will this ship hold, Chief?"

"Don't give me that. The ammo is stored in its own lockers."

"Chief," Jim said, slightly irritated, "floor space is not what I'm worried about.

"I'm not sure of the max capacity, but we had fifty-one on board for the shot including crew. You know how that turned out."

"And how many people did we pull out of those tunnels on the north wall?"

Chief asked, "But to take out her weapons?"

"The ship can deal with pretty much anything they throw at us without returning fire, Chief."

Chief nodded his head and said, "That's true. So what's the plan?"

"However many we can fit, for the amount of time they wil be onboard, air shouldn't be a problem. If it is, we can always find some out of the way place and open the ramp for a while. But if there are too many for one trip, I'm thinking we shuttle the rest to the shore and they find some way by land to get to where we can pick them up. That way we don't have to wait for a perfect storm to get them." Jim paused for a bit, thinking. "I don't like it, but I don't want to make multiple trips to the supply depot. That kind of activity might expose us."

"I can understand that. May I suggest that history guy go with them?"

"History guy? Oh, you mean Doctor Bullard, Paul. Good idea. So, how many people, or weight can this ship lift?"

Chief scratched his head for a moment and asked, "Did we ever test that?"

Jim shook his head and said, "Not that I know of."

"So, what's with taking all the furniture out?"

"If we lighten the ship by taking out everything not needed, that gives us space and lifting ability for more people. Hell, the land vehicles alone equal, what, the weight of 15 people? And that might give us the floor space for them. I'm figuring with a skeleton crew and the people we need, such as the doctor, we can fit around two hundred."

"Huh," Chief said while scratching his chin. "That might be pushing it. The ship can handle the weight, but I don't know if we have the room. We should sling oxygen tanks from the ceiling in the hallways. With that many people, it will get smelly and humid real fast."

"You will have to hurry. The storm will make landfall in about twelve hours, and we have to be inside it when it does."

The Chief went to gather a team, including a few Mech-Bots, to fabricate as many tanks as he could. Jim gave final instructions to the Mech-Bots before going to the cafeteria for breakfast.

Jim finished loading his plate, turned around, and saw the general eating his meal. He sat down and said, "Morning, General."

"I hear you have a bit of a problem," General Long said just as Jim filled his mouth.

He needed a moment to clear his mouth and thought, 'how does the general hear this stuff so quick'? Then said, "You could say that, and I can't believe I didn't think of it sooner."

He gave the general the details of his plan. The general was not happy about having a large group of their people out in public, not knowing how to make themselves invisible in a crowd and with only Paul to guide them, but he understood the major's reasoning and decision.

General Long suggested, "If there is a group, why don't you help Paul? Those people will have problems staying inconspicuous, not to mention having PTSD (Post Traumatic Stress Disorder) from what they experienced. And, they may not want to come here."

"May not want to come here? I didn't think of that. Do you think I should bring a couple of people with me for security?"

"That may make it easier to handle our people but will make for a bigger footprint. Besides, you will find help there – Sarah and Doctor Kovonich, just to name a few. I suggest you screen everyone and put the more problematic ones on the ship."

Jim said, "Good idea. I was just thinking of medical screening and sending emergency cases here on the ship. What do we do about local money?"

"We shot precious metals and other items in the event we will have to acquire anything we didn't plan on. How much will you need?"

"That will be something best for Paul to answer. I asked for him to meet me here. He doesn't know yet that he will have to come with us. This won't be as rough, but he didn't enjoy the trip through the Drake Passage."

"This will be interesting, he was pretty green," Scott said as he joined them at the table with a tray full of food. "I hear you're stripping the Deliverance."

Jim asked, "How does everyone hear this stuff so quick?" Then he saw Paul enter the cafeteria and waited for him to join them. Jim explained what was going on to both Paul and Scott. Soon afterward, both Sam and Claire sat down at the table.

Claire asked, "What's going on?"

Scott said, "Major was just explaining the plan for getting our people out of the supply depot."

Sam asked, "Oh? How's that?"

Jim threw his head back and closed his eyes for a moment, then looked at the general.

General Long said, "This is why I have briefings."

Jim said, "Fine." After explaining the plan again, the question finally circled back to Paul. "How much money do we need?"

Paul said, "That all depends on how many people we are talking about. If they are anything like the people that came out of the cryo units here, they will all need clothing. They also need places to stay along the way, transportation, and food."

Sam and Claire both suggested they create as many items of clothing as they could prior to leaving and volunteered to take care of it. They got the designs from entertainment channels they were able to pick up and recruited everyone they could find. For some, it was quite humorous seeing a Mech-Bot sew.

Scott suggested, "We are already bringing food to help warm them and make them comfortable after coming out of cryo. Why don't we bring two days' worth of rations for everyone?"

Jim said, "So that leaves transportation and lodging."

"Two days?" Paul asked, and looked at the faces of everyone there, then asked, "Three?" Getting a bit more of a confident response. "Maybe three to five hundred dollars each. If it's 100 people, then on the high side would be around 50,000 dollars.

General Long asked, "So, what does that relate to in gold?"

"Oh, I'm sorry. I don't know," Paul said, shrugging his shoulders. "Maybe two pounds?"

General Long said, "Take three. I don't want anything getting in the way of this."

Paul said, "Thank you, but you know, there will be a problem. The people of this time will be paranoid about where the gold came from when you start trading in such large quantities."

Scott asked, "What for?"

Paul said, "They'll think we acquired the gold by some illegal means, and may not trade with us."

General Long asked, "What if you spread the gold out into smaller amounts and don't sell it all in one place?"

Paul said, "That might work."

Jim said, "We will drop out of the storm near Flint, Michigan. What if we dropped you off there? You make your way to Lake Michigan, selling the gold along the way. We meet you there two days later?"

Paul said, "Sounds good. But I want to do a bit of research first."

General Long said, "Major, I want you to join Doctor Bullard when he gets off the ship. Get your feet wet if you will."

Jim objected, "But General, Sarah..."

"What will you be able to do that your team can't?" General Long cut Jim off, "The more information you are able to gather about the people of 2005, their customs and behavior, before you have to take care of others, the better." General Long was not cold and knew full well what Sarah meant to Jim. He added, "I know you want to be there for Sarah, I get it. This is already a risky situation, and we don't need any slip-ups this early in the game. If we're discovered, all our efforts will be for nothing."

Scott asked, "General, what if we swap assignments?"

"I appreciate what you're doing, but no," General Long ordered.

"Major Norgas here has experience infiltrating enemy positions from when he was an aggressor, which makes him the right man for the job. You do not have that experience."

Scott said, "Yes sir!"

Jim said, "I don't have much experience."

General Long said, "You have more than Captain Dixon." Then added, "Don't you two defy me," to ensure that, while in the field, the two didn't improvise and switch responsibilities.

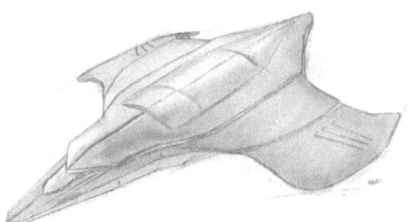

Chapter 45: LANDFALL

The final preparations were made, and everything was onboard when the ramp closed, sealing the Deliverance two hours prior to Hurricane Arlene's landfall near Navarre Beach Florida. Captain Scott "Gumshoe" Dixon was at the helm, with Lt John "Jackknife" Anders in the copilot's seat and Major James "Stinker" Norgas in the captain's seat. Claire St Patrick was toward the rear of the bridge on the port side, monitoring navigation and the storm's position, and Samantha Green sat opposite her on the starboard side of the bridge, monitoring transmissions, military and civilian, and anything else she was able to tap into. The crew was busy stowing and securing all the supplies and making final tweaks to the oxygen tanks that were installed all over the ship.

The Deliverance darted out of the entrance of Anarbia thanks to all the practice over the past couple of days, and then it turned west toward the southern tip of Florida.

As they headed west-northwest into the Gulf of Mexico, the water grew cloudier and thicker with debris the closer they got to the storm. There was not as much debris from man-made structures as expected, but bits of coral were broken off and were churned up by the storm, which scoured the ocean floor and the shallower waters of the gulf. The storm churned up more silt the shallower the water got. Oil wells were spotted in the distance on the holo image, but none were operational, and all were evacuated in preparation for the storm.

As Deliverance drew closer to the Florida Panhandle, Sam discovered all the aircraft from the military installations in the area were removed in preparation for the storm. If the Deliverance were spotted, there would be nothing nearby to attempt an intercept. Jim thought, *'This will be easier than I thought'.*

The Deliverance got within five miles of Navarre and waited for the storm. Jim planned to surface and come ashore hidden just northeast of the eye, where the storm would be the strongest. The storm made landfall just west of Pensacola, so they were in the right position for Jim's plan.

Jim saw his opportunity when the holograph image showed a tornado form just to their east. He ordered the ship to surface and enter the storm. The winds outside the ship were only sixty miles per hour, but they caused the ship to rock and drift every which way, till Scott adapted and started to make the ride smoother.

The hologram area showed the direction of the winds, but was little help near the eye wall. The winds changed direction too quick for Scott to keep up.

After riding through the Drake Passage, this was nothing. Jim noticed the bridge crew still fastened their seat belts.

As they stayed within the storm, the winds slowed considerably, half the speed as before with only gusts reaching full strength. Several funnel clouds were formed directly under the Deliverance, which made the bridge crew wonder if the ship caused them. Since none turned into tornadoes, they were not worried. Later, they decided the Deliverance was not the cause since no more formed, and the rest of the day was uneventful. The Deliverance flew so slowly it felt like they were crawling, but it was necessary to remain hidden in their natural blind.

The next day, June 12th, the storm spawned two tornadoes as the crew watched. The first one was on the ground for over five miles. The holo image displayed its path as it passed over and damaged several buildings. The other tornado, later in the day, luckily touched down before the worst of the storm passed over Indianapolis and caused no structural damage. Sam continued to monitor news updates, and said, "No injuries were reported."

The storm continued its path northerly and kept dissipating, to the point that Jim was worried they'd be discovered.

Then on the next day, June 13th, as the storm passed over Flint Michigan, it started to build again, being fueled by another storm from the west. This helped hide their descent as they prepared to drop off Jim and Paul on the shore of Lake Huron in Saginaw Bay, just east of Bay City.

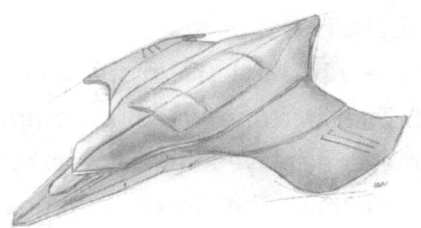

Chapter 46: BAY CITY

Jim and Paul were in the cargo bay waiting for the ship to land, wearing clothes they selected from the ones made for this mission. Jim wore a button-down shirt, slacks, and a wide-brimmed hat. Paul dressed much the same, but with a smaller hat that was crunched down toward the front. To save time, they were actually standing on the ramp with the chief ready to push the button to lower it. Each of them carried one and a half pounds of gold that had been melted into several small decorative ingots, some as small as one gram, to try to help stave off suspicion.

Chief teased, "Well don't you two look pretty? Paul, doesn't that feather in his hat make him look like a pimp?"

Paul said, "Oh geez," and reached for the feather.

Chief said with a laugh, "I guess that makes you his bitch."

Paul pulled the feather out of Jim's hat and threw it at the chief. It did not make it far and fluttered to the floor.

Jim said toward the chief, "I asked the general for you to play that role, and he said we wouldn't make any money."

Chief responded, "Aw shucks." He made kissing sounds as the ship landed with a thunk. The landing struts compressed to cushion the impact, but it still caused Jim and Paul to bounce at the knees, leaving a sinking feeling in their stomachs as the ramp lowered while their knees were extending. The sensation caused both of them to lose their balance for a moment. Chief said, "Make sure you get him home before someone takes a liking to him."

Jim and Scott took one step and were on the soft grass when they heard the chief yell "Go, Go, Go," to the bridge. The ramp started to close as the ship lit back into the air toward the water and then disappeared as it dove into the waves.

Paul asked, "Chief Besch is not all that professional, is he?"

"Oh, he's just having fun. Your lead," Jim said with a motion of his hand. Both of them were getting soaked from the rain. Jim was grateful that the wide rim of his hat kept him dryer than Paul appeared to be.

"Well, the town is this way," Paul pointed toward their west. "Let's find someplace to get out of this rain and sell some of the gold."

"Sounds good to me," Jim replied, and the two set off toward the west.

The two found themselves walking in a field of very well-manicured lawn. Paul realized this must be someone's property and did not want to raise problems with the local authorities. He brought up an aerial image of their location on his data pad "Looks like we are on a golf course. The closest road is to our south. That way." He pointed to their left and headed that direction.

When they made it to the road, Paul used his data pad to guide them toward the downtown area of Bay City, and they stuck to walking along the sides of the roads.

An hour into their walk, the rain slowed to a very light drizzle. Both of them were soaked through to their skin. Even with it being the middle of June, it was none too pleasant being so wet, and with it now getting dark, the two would probably not dry on their own and wanted to find someplace to dry off. All they had seen for the last half hour were run down houses and cars in various states of disrepair. Bags of garbage littered the sidewalk in places. Some of the bags took on a life of their own as rats scurried within. In the distance, they saw a lit-up area, and as they got closer, they saw it was a convenience store.

Paul asked, "Hungry?"

"You know it."

Paul warned, "No fine dining there. Mostly junk food, but it will be sustenance."

"My stomach's been growling for some time now, so I don't care."

"That was yours? And here I thought it was my stomach making all that noise."

When the two entered the store, a small, Asian man from behind the counter yelled, "Paying customers only."

Jim looked at Paul and himself; he thought they looked like two drowned rats. "Don't worry, we have money," he assured the man, and the two wandered the store looking at the snacks on the shelves. When they noticed the restrooms, they both went in and discovered a hot air hand dryer, which they used to dry their clothes. It took so long, the man from the counter started banging on the door. In a thick oriental accent, he demanded they come out. Their clothes were still a bit damp, but the two felt much better, and warmer.

When they exited the restroom, the proprietor kept a close eye on them as they made their food selections. As Jim walked the aisles, he noticed two young males kept glancing at Paul from behind a magazine rack.

When Jim and Paul brought their selections to the counter, the proprietor was surprised neither tried to conceal anything and started scanning each item. "Thirty-two dollar," he said when finished.

Paul took one gold ingot and asked, "Will you take this?"

The proprietor asked "What that?"

"It's gold. Solid gold." The two young males' interest grew hearing what was going on.

"No, only money. You got credit card?"

"Sorry, just this," Paul said and tried to hand the proprietor the ingot. "Are you Mandarin?"

"You get out now before I call cop. You no come back."

Jim said, "Paul, we better get going." Using his peripheral vision, he kept an eye on the two as he led Paul toward the door and left the building.

They walked down the sidewalk heading toward the center of town. Jim asked, "Did you notice the two punks pretending to read the magazines?"

"Yeah, they gave me the creeps."

"Right after we left they watched us a bit, then got into a car and drove off. I got a feeling we might see them again."

Paul started glancing around as he walked, and asked, "What do we do?"

"Nothing, just wait, size up the situation then deal with it. That might be why the proprietor had that butcher's knife."

"What butcher's knife?"

"When he wasn't ringing us up he kept his fingers on it."

Paul was surprised. "Are you serious? Where?"

"You didn't notice? It was under his cash register. I saw the glint from it when he yelled 'Get out'."

"No, I didn't see it."

Suddenly a long dark vehicle came down the alley on their right. It slid to a stop, blocking their path. Three occupants jumped out, leaving only the driver in the vehicle, who was grinning from ear to ear.

Jim and Paul were soon flanked by the three, blocking any escape with the vehicle closing the circle. The shortest of the three grinned and said "So, I hear you have some gold." All four laughed, smiling at each other, obviously proud of themselves. "Hand it over."

Jim recognized the driver and the one that spoke. He heard a click and saw the blade of a small knife come into view. He sized up the three, who were not much more than scrawny juveniles, and replied to the one who demanded the gold, "I don't think so."

The one to Jim's right slid a metal rod with a spike on one side out of his sleeve, and the third popped his knuckles. The driver just sat there laughing. Jim did not want any of them to get away and decided he wanted their car. He reached into the vehicle and slammed the driver's face against the steering wheel, incapacitating him so he could turn his attention toward the other three.

The biggest threat was the one with the metal rod, who took a sideways swing at Jim. Jim leaned back as it narrowly missed the left side of his face. He spun in a tight circle toward his left, catching the assailant's swinging arm in the crook of his elbow. With the assailant's arm trapped, Jim quickly doubled over, causing his attacker to flip over his back, slam into the vehicle, and drop the metal rod. Jim picked up the rod and struck the knife wielder's hand, sending the knife flying and its owner retreating with his injured hand. Knuckle cracker ran off when Jim lunged at him.

Jim turned his attention back to the driver and pulled him out of the vehicle, told Paul to get in, and drove off.

As they drove, Paul looked in the back seat and noticed rolls of money being held together with rubber bands and small plastic bags filled with some kind of substance. "Jim," Paul said, "we need to get out of this car."

"What for?"

"Because I don't think those guys were alone. And we do not want to get caught with this stuff."

"What do you have?"

"Drugs, and lots of it."

"What are you talking about?" Jim asked and looked over his shoulder. "Great. Just great. The general will love this." He made several turns down side streets and watched the mirrors. Not seeing anyone following, he turned south for several miles before he parked on the side of the road. He hoped when the car was discovered, their direction of travel would not be figured out. He knew the odds were against it because of the direction they were walking before the attack, but he had to try.

Jim said, "Let's go, and bring some of that money. We can use it till we sell some of this gold." He got out of the car and opened the trunk to see if there was anything they could use. He discovered several guns and took one. Everything else looked like junk. He hid the gun in his waistband and closed the trunk. The two quickly walked away.

"What now?"

"We get out of here, and now that we've got some money, get something to eat."

"That sounds like a good idea. Hear that, belly?" Paul said jokingly to his stomach.

The two walked for several blocks until they found a restaurant and went inside.

They took their time eating, hoping whoever may be looking for them gave up.

Using his lap, Paul fanned through the money they took and estimated it to be well over a couple thousand. Jim struck up a conversation with the waitress. He acted as if he was a tourist just passing through, and got a couple of leads on where they may be able to buy and sell gold.

With the money they acquired, Paul paid for the food, and asked the cashier to call them some transportation.

While the two waited outside the restaurant, a large white bus pulled up to the doors, and a sizable group of elderly people went into the restaurant. Jim watched as the last person left the bus, the door closed, and the bus parked in a back corner of the parking lot.

Jim said, "Wait here." He walked toward the bus and spoke with the driver for some time before he returned to Paul. "How about we rent a couple of those to get our people to Florida?" he asked with a grin. Paul smiled back and nodded his head, impressed. "The driver said they would take us wherever we needed, then handed me this." He showed Paul a small piece of paper with the company name and phone number on it.

A few moments later, their taxi pulled up, and Jim asked the driver to take them to the "Economy Center."

The driver said, "Buddy, they're closed till morning."

Paul asked, "Do you know a place near there where we can spend the night?"

The driver said, "Sure do, and it's only a few blocks from the Economy Center. But if you ask me, Bay City Discount is better. It's just a little bit farther from the hotel. If you mention my name, they'll treat you right. Sal is the name. If they don't take care of you, just give Ole Sal a call and I'll set them straight."

Sal kept turning this way and that down different streets. Jim saw the meter on the dash going up and up and knew that Ole Sal was taking the long way to wherever he was taking them.

Sal said, "You know, ever since they put all those one-way streets in, it takes forever to get downtown." This was a tactic Sal learned to make his passengers think they were getting a deal when actually he was making the meter go up as much as he could without being obvious. Finally, the taxi turned onto East Main Street and Jim could see a hotel a block down on the left. When Sal brought the taxi to a stop in front of the hotel, he said "That will be fifty bucks, but for the two of you how does thirty-five sound? Just be sure to mention Ole Sal at Bay City Discount so my kickback will make up the difference."

Jim got out of the taxi and Paul said, "Yeah right," and gave Sal the thirty-five he asked for.

Sal acted shocked and asked, "What, no tip?"

"Look Sal," Jim leaned on Sal's arm where it rested outside the driver's door, "I know you were padding that meter of yours –"

Sal said defensively, "Okay, okay, just trying to show you guys the sights."

Jim eased up on Sal's arm, letting him pull it inside the car. Sal rubbed his arm and said, "Damn, guy. You didn't have to do that!" Sal drove off in the direction they came, glaring at Jim as he left. Jim and Paul went inside the Courtyard Hotel.

That night while in their room, Paul tried to make arrangements for two charter buses but ran into an impasse when the person on the other end of the phone required a credit card number. "Stall," Jim said and contacted Sam via his comm pin. Jim did not ask how, but within moments, Paul was able to secure two charter buses with the information Sam gave him.

While Jim was in communication with Sam, he asked how it was going at the supply depot. She replied, "Actually, we just got here. The entrance was covered with silt, and we had to use the engine to move all the dirt out of the way. Wow, there are a lot of cryo units here." Sam exclaimed. "How many people will those buses carry?"

"Sixty!" Paul yelled from across the room, still on the phone,

Sam said, "Sixty? Is that all? He should probably get four buses then."

Jim finished his conversation with Sam, letting her know they will be at the rendezvous point tomorrow night. When Paul set the phone down, Jim asked, "Well, how did we do?"

"We got three luxury coaches and something they call a party bus. They will pick us up in front of the hotel tomorrow at 6:00 pm."

"Good. That will give us all day tomorrow to sell some of this gold and buy some other clothes. I noticed people have been looking. We kind of stand out."

"I've been thinking about that and have an idea. Tell Sam not to use any of the clothes we made."

"What?" Jim asked, a bit puzzled.

"Here in 2005 groups would dress up in weird costumes impersonating a cartoon or movie character, gather together, and act out whatever that character did or reenact certain periods in history."

"So we can just tell anyone that asks we're going to one of those events?"

Paul said, "Exactly.

"All this planning and preparing, I'm not used to things going this easy. Something is bound to go wrong."

"I hope not. So what should we do the rest of the night?" He picked up an advertisement left in the room by the hotel. "Says here the movie '*War of the Worlds*' is showing in the local theaters."

Jim chuckled, "Are you serious? Let me see that." He took the flier from Paul. "Says here it premiered a week ago, starring Tom Cruise. Why not?"

"Maybe we will get an idea of how to beat them!" Paul said jokingly.

The next morning Jim and Paul made their way to Columbus Avenue, where Economy Center was. Not wanting to draw too much attention, Jim sold only two ingots of gold. They then made their way to Washington Avenue, where Bay City Discount was. This time Paul sold two of his ingots. Paul refused to mention Ole Sal's name to the proprietor, despite Jim's ribbing. Between the two of them, they still had quite a few ingots and more than enough cash to finish the mission.

The two wandered around the city, not going too far from the hotel. They checked out the shops here and there and had a very good meal at one of the restaurants next to the hotel. They just finished their drinks when the buses pulled up to the hotel, and Jim quickly made his way to them while Paul paid the bill and followed.

One of the drivers wanted to see a receipt, but since neither Jim nor Paul had anything to verify they were indeed the party the buses were there for, it took a while and several phone calls. After quite some time, they were finally on their way to Wilderness State Park, a trip that took about three hours with time to spare, even with the late start.

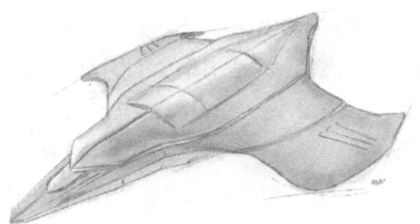

Chapter 47: WILDERNESS PARK

When they got to the park, Jim told the driver to enter on Wilderness Park Drive, turn the buses around on Sturgeon Bay Road, and wait for the rest of their party. The buses' electronic map system said they were on Waugoshance Point Road. The drivers thought this was a bit weird, four empty buses just sitting in the middle of the woods of a state park, but their dispatch warned them ahead of time, and as long as they were being paid, they didn't care.

Paul stayed with the buses while Jim went to meet the Deliverance. He walked north past a sign that read 'Station Point Cabin'. When the cabin came into view, he was relieved it was unoccupied and walked past it to the shore. He used his Comm pin to let Scott know they were in position and left the channel open for Scott to find his exact position.

For Jim, it was agonizing. He paced the shore and watched the waves, waiting for the ship to arrive. He kept going over in his head what he would say when he saw Sarah again. He kicked a few rocks with his shoe, then skipped a few across the water of the lake. He picked another suitable flat rock and gave it a slight spin as it left his hand. The rock skipped several times, about to break his record, when the rock was sent flying high into the air.

The Deliverance silently rose out of the water, moved toward the shore, and positioned itself as close to the water's edge as it could in a steady hover. The ramp lowered, and its precious human cargo started walking down the ramp. Jim looked at every face, waiting to see Sarah. He saw Dr. Kovonich walking down the ramp, nearly the last person in sight.

Jim hollered, "Doctor Kovonich, where is Sarah?"

Dr. Kovonich said "Jim? Good to see you."

"Where's Sarah?" Jim asked again, turning as Dr. Kovonich passed.

"Oh, the doctor – Stevens I think is his name? He is working on her now, and she will be going to Anarbia by ship. She was pretty badly injured and Doctor Stevens wants to keep an eye on her."

"What happened?"

"I don't know. She was fine the last time I saw her. I'm sure she will be okay."

Jim opened a comm channel with Scott, "Why didn't you tell me?"

"I wanted to tell you in person." Jim heard Scott's voice, but not over the comm. Jim turned and saw Scott coming down the ramp.

Jim exclaimed, "Where is Sarah?" He wanted answers he was not getting. "Is she okay?" He knew he was asking what Dr. Kovonich already told him, but he was frustrated he could not be there for Sarah.

Scott said soothingly, "She will be okay. That is one strong woman."

"What happened?" Jim asked, nearly losing his cool.

"Well, turns out she was in the last shot. Apparently, the base was overrun, and she got pretty banged up. The aliens might know what we did."

"What do you mean? How?"

"Sarah said charges to blow the base were set and just before she initiated the shot, she activated the timer for them to blow. But there were Mech-Bots – She said one scanned the shot control panel. They may have had enough time to analyze the display before it blew. If it blew." Scott looked off into the distance before continuing. "You know they are networked together, so if one saw that panel, they all saw it."

"Yeah I know. Did you inform General Long?"

"Not yet. I figured I'd wait till I could do it in person. Besides, I'm sure he will have questions for Sarah, and right now she's in no condition for that. Doctor Stevens has her on some pretty good drugs. Sarah and Doctor Kovonich collected a lot of data for us to analyze."

Jim asked again, "I understand all that and why it should be done in person, but you still have not told me how Sarah is."

"She's banged up pretty bad. Looks like she got caught in some crossfire. Took a blast right in her leg, shattering the bone. Doc is treating her as we speak."

"Thanks, but how did it happen?"

"I'm not sure, but apparently Sarah was all alone. Everyone else was already in the cryo units. She activated the shot, and then it happened. She crawled to her cryo unit and got in by herself, with her leg torn up like that. She asked about you."

Jim asked, "You spoke to her?"

"I did, briefly, before the drugs Doc gave her set in, then what she was saying made no sense. She's a fighter, that one."

"What did you tell her?"

Scott said, "Not much; just that you're okay. I figured you would want to tell her yourself what we've been through."

"Thanks, Scott. So she's okay?"

"Doctor Stevens said she will be. I better get going. I got two more trips to make before I can get Sarah out of there. Oh, one more thing. There are the remains of a Mech-Bot in the depot. Might even be the same one that shot Sarah!"

Jim exclaimed, "What? Don't you think you should have led with that? Especially after hearing what they did!"

"How could I? The only thing on your mind was Sarah. Besides it's completely inert," Scott said defensively. "Sam spotted it from the bridge almost as soon as we got there. I deactivated the power cell just in case, and our Mech-Bots have not left the ship."

"If that thing managed to link with the core or another Mech-Bot, or has sent a homing signal –"

"I know," Scott replied, a bit irritated his superior would state the obvious when he still has so much to do. "Trust me, it is not capable of anything without some major repairs."

Jim said, "Alright, well, you'd better go get the next group."

Scott walked up the ramp as John slowly moved the ship away from the shore. The ramp closed, and the ship, in near silence, slipped beneath the waves. The only sound it made was the sound of a spray of water caused by the propulsion system and the rushing of the water to fill the void left by the ship. Other than a little bit of foam left on the surface of the lake, there was no trace the ship was ever there.

Jim had about a half hour to wait until the Deliverance returned, so he led the group to the waiting buses and returned to the shoreline while Paul took over watching the group.

It took an hour for the last of the survivors going with Jim and Paul to arrive on dry land. The remaining survivors in the supply depot would take a short jump from the Great Lakes, flying close to the treetops to the Hudson Bay, and then remain submerged all the way to Anarbia. Because of the direction the Deliverance would fly, if it was spotted, no one would think it was a preemptive attack and attempt retaliation. The incident would be put in the books as another UFO (Unidentified Flying Object).

Jim led the last of the survivors to the buses, where everyone was sitting in the grass on the side of the road enjoying the cool, fresh air. In somewhat hushed tones so the drivers of the buses could not hear, he tried to brief everyone to stay quiet about who they were and where they came from. Paul gave them the cover story about going to a cosplay convention and explained what that was. The children in the group particularly liked the idea and began running around play-acting.

After Jim and Paul finished explaining what to expect, everyone headed for the buses. Jim took charge of the lead bus, Paul the second, and Dr. Kovonich the fourth bus. Jim did not know anyone else in the group, so Dr. Kovonich took it upon himself to assign one of the parents on the third bus to be in charge. Jim had a few extra comm pins, so he gave one each to Dr. Kovonich and to the parent in charge of bus three, Jose Rivera, with instructions to use them only in an emergency.

When everyone got situated, the bus driver turned to Jim and asked, "Next stop Orlando?"

"Actually, our hotel is in Cocoa Beach. The conference is in Orlando, Disney. We couldn't raise enough money to stay at the hotels there. Way too expensive." Jim pulled from his memory of what Paul taught him to say, and he thought he sounded half-convincing.

"I hear ya brother," the driver said, then turned in his seat, started the engine, which shook the whole bus, closed the door, and started driving. The other three buses followed but kept quite a gap between each one. Jim had a hard time seeing if all four were there until the driver turned to get onto Interstate 75.

"You look as nervous as a trailer park in a hurricane," the driver said over his shoulder.

"Oh, just making sure all the buses are there."

"Don't worry about that. I'm the team captain, and if anything happens to one of the buses, they'll call me on the radio. Go ahead and get some sleep. We will stop for breakfast in about eight hours."

Jim looked at the radio above the driver's head, sat back in his seat, and watched the road for a while till he felt drowsy and decided to sleep for a while.

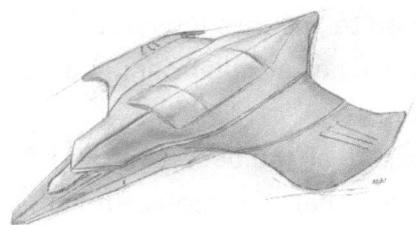

Chapter 48: UP AND OVER

Meanwhile in the supply depot, the remaining survivors piled onboard the Deliverance. Most of them needed medical attention from wounds sustained prior to being put in the cryo units.

When John opened the cryo units, one in particular got his attention. He noticed the occupant was a soldier, lying on his stomach. It did not take long for the retreating gasses to reveal a blood-soaked bandage on the soldier's butt. John yelled, "Doctor, you have to see this."

Dr. Stevens tried to move the bandage to examine what lay beneath, but fresh blood oozed around the bandage as soon as he touched it. "This looks like bite marks. And a bunch of the meat is missing. What did these people go through?" As he continued his examination, dark colored blood began to pulse from the wound. "Get that gurney over here, now," he ordered as he reached around the soldier's neck. "Where is his dog tag?" He then noticed it laced in the soldiers boot. "I need A+ blood."

John asked, "What's going on?"

"His gluteal artery is severed. I need to do immediate surgery."

"His what?"

Dr. Stevens hastily said, "His ass, he's got a severed artery in his ass."

"Well I'm A+."

"Then get to the medical bay. I'm going to need some."

Moments later, Scott closed the ramp and prepared the ship to depart for the fourth and final time. After clearing the entrance to the supply depot, he steered the ship through the deeper waters and headed toward Lake Huron. *'It's a good thing it's dark out'*, Scott thought as he looked up at the moonless night sky. The water was too shallow to fully submerge the ship. He headed for an area called Thirty Thousand Islands, turned the ship north, and silently slipped out of the water, barely missing the tips of the trees along the shoreline at the mouth of French River where it feeds into Lake Huron.

From there, it was nearly a due north jump for 380 miles to the shoreline of the southernmost tip of Hudson Bay, an area where over a dozen rivers emptied into a smaller bay called James Bay. From there, he would follow the Hudson Strait to the Atlantic Ocean, then home to Anarbia.

Most radar systems of the time filtered out "ground clutter." This aided the radar operators so they did not have to see every automobile, motorcycle, or snowmobile the radar picked up, taking their attention away from what they were supposed to be looking for. Even though the Deliverance was nearly invisible on radar, there were other things that gave an aircraft away. Heat, sound, and even the air itself could give away the presence of something moving through it. Measuring the density of the disturbed air would give a clear definition of the aircraft's wake, just as obvious as the ripples a boat made as it moved through the water. Since the Deliverance pulled matter from its surroundings and then threw it in the direction opposite where the pilot wanted to go, its "wake signature" was much larger than the aircraft in use in 2005, even large four-engine propeller-driven aircraft.

Scott knew full well these ripples could give the Deliverance's presence away, especially on a clear calm night like this one. Because of this, he flew the ship so close to the treetops that, if he was flying slow enough, he could see squirrels looking for cover. Luckily, the computer was programmed not to use living matter to push the ship. The squirrels and birds were safe.

Coming over the crest of a hill, Scott had to bank to the right and pull up as Claire yelled, "Watch out!"

"What the?" Scott protested. "Block their radio traffic," he yelled over his shoulder to Sam as he watched the helicopter pass beneath them.

Sam answered, "Already on it. Wow, you really pissed them off," she said as she listened to what the helicopter tried to relay to its base. No one but Sam would ever hear what was said.

Claire asked, "Where did that come from?"

Scott said, "The markings looked like the 16th Wing out of Borden. It must be up here on a training mission. I worked with some of them in Operation CAMPFIRE. Not the brightest bunch, but they got the job done. I never could understand wanting to fly an eggbeater!"

"I heard they don't fly; they beat the air into submission," John joked as he walked onto the bridge and took a seat next to Scott.

Scott said, "Hey, welcome back. There may be some truth to that, if you ever watched them in action." He turned his attention toward Sam and asked, "Sam, did you jam it's radio?"

"Yes, but I'm not going to be able to for much longer," Sam answered with a concerned tone to her voice. "And... I lost it. You might want to alter course."

Scott said, "No need. The only thing that way," he pointed the direction they were flying with his nose since his hands were busy,

328

"is on the other side of the Hudson, and we will already be underwater by the time they get near us." When John took the copilot seat Scott asked, "How is the soldier?"

John said, "I don't know. When Doctor Stevens took the bandage off I nearly lost it. It looked like half his butt had been eaten."

Claire said, "That's awful."

Sam asked, "Eaten? By what?"

John answered, "I don't know. I guess we will have to wait till he wakes up. Here I thought *our* trip was hard. Yeah, I know the people that came out of the north wall looked rough, but this guy? They couldn't even stitch him up before putting him in cryo."

Scott said, "Looks like there is a lot we have not heard about yet."

John said, "Wow, just think. If we didn't make it to Earth, none of them would ever be found and woken up."

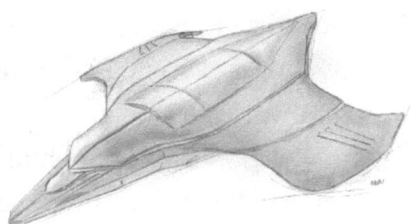

Chapter 49: FLORIDA, HERE WE COME

Jim was startled when he woke, not knowing where he was for a moment. The sky was a lighter shade of black in the predawn mix of black and blue, while everything on the ground was shades of gray covered with slight fog close to the ground that hung to the brush on the sides of the road. There was no sliver of orange on the horizon yet from the sun about to crest, but any moment now the clouds would start to get an orange tinge to their outline.

Jim quickly turned and looked for the other buses.

The bus driver asked, "Someone walk on your grave?"

"What?"

"The way you jumped in your seat when you woke, something startle you? Bad dream?"

"Oh no, no, just forgot where I was for a moment. How are you? Everything okay?"

"Oh, I'm fine. We are actually a little ahead of schedule. We will be at the restaurant for breakfast in about an hour."

"Where are we?" Jim asked, looking around, unfamiliar with this part of the country. "By the way, I never did get your name. I'm Jim."

"Nice to meet you, Jim, I'm Carl. We are on the loop going around Columbus, Ohio. We will stop at the Bob Evans in Lancaster for breakfast. Which is about 50 miles south of us."

"Sounds good, Carl."

An hour later, the four buses pulled into the nearly empty parking lot of the restaurant. The only other vehicles belonged to the morning staff. As everyone piled out of the buses and mingled around, Dr. Kovonich tracked Jim down. Dr. Kovonich was livid and appeared to be quite tired.

"Jim, I cannot ride on that so-called *'party bus'* one more minute. Disco lights and loud music all night long. It was enough to drive me crazy if I wasn't already there," Dr. Kovonich complained. "The younger folk had fun dancing and such but... there was a pole in the middle of the bus, Jim!" Dr. Kovonich was astonished at the things he saw during the bus ride, which caused Jim to chuckle. "I couldn't figure out what the pole was for till I saw some of the younger people gyrating on it. Lord help me, I found a seat on the second floor out of the way, but it didn't help much. The music kept me up all night."

"I don't know what to say, Doctor," Jim said as he tried to keep a straight face.

"You're going to have to find someone else to keep an eye on that bus. I've had it."

"I wouldn't mind switching with you," Jose said, overhearing Dr. Kovonich's dislike of the party bus.

"Oh, thank you. I'll keep an eye on your son for you. Well, if I stay awake."

"That's okay, he'll behave. It's the least I can do for you after the help you gave me in the shelter."

While passing through the scenic mountains of West Virginia, Jim wondered if Sarah's parents had heeded their warning. After hearing the stories from the survivors of the north wall, he wondered if the country was hit as bad as the cities, and how their families fared. He chuckled a bit thinking of them trying to get along.

Several hours later, the buses once again stopped to eat, this time at Cracker Barrel in Mount Airy, North Carolina. Everyone in the group was not sure what to think of the décor but found it quaint. Antiques hung on the walls. Some of it could not be identified.

One table in the group was filled with children. Jim heard one of them ask the waitress, "What is that?" as he pointed to a particular item.

Jim was worried something as simple as that could blow their cover, and he hushed the kids.

The waitress said, "Oh that's alright. I had to learn what some of this stuff was when I started working here. We are always asked what this or that is. It's surprising how much things change." Jim chuckled at the thought.

The group was back on the buses leaving the restaurant at 4 pm when Carl informed Jim they will stop for the night on the south side of Charlotte, about two and a half hours from now. Jim tried to persuade Carl to keep driving but Carl refused. He stated government regulations would not allow it and that they had already driven farther today than they should have. All four of the drivers were getting tired. Jim understood and realized it would be too dangerous to keep going. Besides, they still had over 12 hours to go until their destination.

The next morning, the buses closed their doors and headed toward the interstate at 8 am. They made one more stop for food along the way and finally reached their last stop just after 7 pm, the International Palms Resort & Conference Center in Cocoa Beach Florida.

Jim picked this spot not only for its ability to house everyone in the group but also because just to the north of the resort was a city park right on the waterfront.

He figured, with all the trees, they could walk out of the resort and into the park, where they wouldn't be seen entering the Deliverance once it arrived. It took three trips to get everyone from the supply depot to shore, and so it would also take three trips to pick everyone back up.

He was nervous about doing this right between Cape Canaveral and Patrick Air Force Base. There was no place along the coast that was devoid of military surveillance. He hoped doing the pickups right in the backyard of the base would allow the Deliverance to go unnoticed, thinking, *'who would be so brazen to attempt penetrating the U.S. with this much security'?*

Jim and Paul left the buses to check in to the hotel, which was already paid for when Sam made the reservations. The hotel did not expect this many people and had to make a few changes by adding roll-away beds to several rooms. With how much money the hotel made from this group, they were eager to assist. Jim learned money talked; if you gave enough it spoke loudly.

The team captain of the bus drivers, Carl, pulled Jim aside. "Jim, your group has been respectful and even the children in your group behaved better than I've ever seen. It was kind of weird waiting in that park for your group, but it has been a pleasure driving for you. I don't mean to put you on the spot. but I got a feeling your group is not here for a cosplay convention."

Jim asked, "How so?"

"No one rents this many buses for a one-way trip. We are heading back to Michigan tomorrow morning. How are you getting to the convention? Are you sure you don't want us to stay?"

Jim began to feel uncomfortable, "No, that won't be necessary."

Carl paused for a moment, then said, "Look, I don't know where you guys came from, and the best I can tell, none of you are in trouble with the law. Here, take my number. If you need anything, call me. I'll keep it on the down low."

"The down low?"

"You know, off the books, so the government doesn't find out." The look on Jim's face made Carl think Jim still didn't understand. "Since I won't be paying taxes, I can cut you a deal."

Jim said, "Thank you, Carl." He shook his hand and took the business card Carl handed him.

When Jim entered the hotel lobby Paul asked him, "What was that about?"

"Carl doesn't know what, but he knows something is up."

"Can he be trusted?"

"I think so. He sounded like he wanted to help and he gave me this. He said if I need anything, call him, on the 'down low'."

Paul said, "Interesting, hang on to it. It might come in handy with our population problem."

Jim raised his eyebrows and shook his head.

When everyone was settled, Jim contacted Anarbia to arrange pickup of the first group at midnight. He found out Sarah was doing fine and would make a full recovery; the reconstruction of her leg was a success, and she would have to stay in the infirmary only for a couple of days.

Everyone relaxed around the pool. No one wanted to be indoors. Jim realized this would probably be the last time any of them would ever see the sun again, which was making its descent in the western sky.

Jim wondered how many others were thinking the same thing and if any would balk when it came time to leave. Because of this, He decided to have the families go first. He thought he would let them go last to enjoy the pool and amenities as long as possible, but it would be easier to control individuals, if they got out of line, than a family.

He included Paul and Dr. Kovonich in his plan but excluded Jose Rivera for the same reason. Over drinks on the patio, they consolidated the list of who would go on the first group, and all of them would stay behind to oversee the rest of the exodus.

When eleven o'clock came, the three gathered the first group and led them along the shore to the park just north of the convention center. There was quite a bit of beach between the water and the trees, but this late at night, Jim thought there should be enough cover from the trees to obscure the ship from prying eyes, even with the moon so bright. It was not a full moon but a waxing moon, and he knew it was too much unwanted light when trying to be sneaky.

At midnight, the Deliverance slipped silently from the waves, made its way to the shore, and lowered its ramp as it got closer. Chief Besch descended the ramp as the group ran for the ship from the cover of the trees.

"Hey Chief," Jim said, shaking the man's hand when they got close enough. "How long did it take to get here?"

"Well, we were taking our time. We plotted a bunch of listening devices they've got out there," Chief said as he pointed toward the ocean. "They sure are paranoid."

"That they are. Any trouble?"

"Hell no! This thing is so quiet, they will have better luck listening for a minnow fart. We plotted them just in case though."

Jim laughed and asked, "When can you be back for the second group?"

"I'd say around two and a half hours."

"That will be cutting it close for the last group to get out of here in the dark."

"I'll pass it on," Chief said as the last person in the group started to climb the ramp. "I'll see if we can shave some time off the trips."

The ramp began to close as the ship slid toward deep enough water to submerge, and Jim ran back toward the woods.

He heard the sound of jet engines of an aircraft taking off farther down the beach. It came from the direction of the Air Force base. He stayed near the edge of the woods to watch, but the sound did not get louder, which indicated it was not coming in his direction. With the Deliverance long gone, the aircraft taking off must have been a coincidence. Jim thought the first trip had gone undetected and headed back to the hotel.

The Deliverance departed with the second group a little before 2:30 in the morning – again followed by sounds of aircraft taking off from the base. Jim thought *'with this being the second time, it can't be a coincidence'*. All night, these were the only times he heard the aircraft. He did not wait around to watch this time, and just as he got back to the hotel, a helicopter came racing up the shoreline, followed by another a few seconds later. The pair kept going north, so he did not know what to think.

Finally, the last group waited in the tree line at 5 am. Just under an hour till twilight. Jim told everyone to be ready and to move quickly when he gave the signal.

A half-hour later, the Deliverance was not there. Jim started to wonder what was going on. Everyone in the group sat on the ground or leaned against the trees.

Another fifteen minutes later and still nothing.

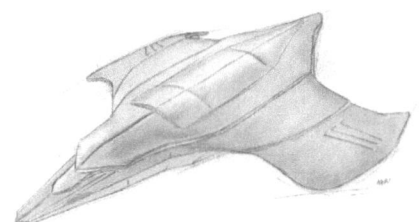

Chapter 50: GOING HOME

"Psst, Hey!" Jim heard someone whisper to his right as he woke. He looked and saw someone motioning for them to come, and out on the beach, he saw the silhouette of the Deliverance and the faint light that emitted from the cargo bay. "Come on!" The person motioned some more.

He hurriedly woke everyone in the group and heard the same engine sounds as before coming from the base again. This was no coincidence. He did his best to hurry the group. They were out of time. He saw a helicopter to his south shining a searchlight back and forth along the beach as it approached. Another was farther in the distance, out over the water doing the same thing.

Everyone ran for the ship, but the last two in the group were lit up by the searchlight just before they ran into the shadow of the Deliverance. The forward portion of the ship was bathed in the helicopter's light.

Jim did not stop running till he entered the bridge two decks up. Paul followed but fell behind. Jim saw the spotlight fighting for dominance with the automatic darkening of the bridge glass. The spotlight was failing. John sat at the helm asking if everyone was on board. Sam and Claire were at their usual consoles. Scott was nowhere to be found.

Jim commanded, "Get us out of here!"

John asked, "Which way? The Navy has a string of ships that

way." He motioned toward the ocean with a nod of his head. "To the north is NASA and the south an Air Force Base. We're kind of hemmed in here."

"Go north. That probably has the least resistance," and he took his seat.

John rotated the Deliverance toward the right, but the helicopter that was searching the water was now blocking their path to the north.

Out of the corner of his eye, Jim saw a flash of light, and the helicopter blocking their path began spiraling toward the waves.

He watched to see what happened as the pilot of the helicopter managed to angle his craft toward the shore. Behind Jim, another flash. The helicopter with the spotlight on them began losing power, and it struggled to land on the beach.

Jim exclaimed, "What is going on?"

Over the bridge speakers, he heard Scott's voice. "Coyote Five – Bomber Two, you just going to sit there?"

Jim watched in disbelief as the fighter variant leveled off in a hover, nose to nose in front of the Deliverance. "What the hell! John, did you know about this?"

"Yes sir, and you will never guess where we got it –"

Over the bridge speakers Scott said, "Hey, you want to get to your old lady or what?"

Jim opened the channel and said, "That's some radio etiquette you got. And you better not let her hear you say that."

Scott said, "Who else is on this channel? No point in sticking with protocol when it's just the two of us."

Jim said, "Good point. So which way to open water?"

Over the radio, Jim and Scott heard General Long clear his throat. They hadn't known he was listening. General Long was concerned how the operation was going.

After a pause, Scott said, "Coyote Five – Bomber Two, your four o'clock has the least resistance."

"Bomber Two – Coyote Five, Roger that. John, make your heading one two zero."

"Yes, sir." He rotated the ship toward the right till the ship was facing east-southeast. John began moving forward with Scott following on their port wing.

Jim noticed beyond the breakwater that a cruiser was right in their path. Suddenly, multiple plumes of smoke were visible across the cruiser's deck as it fired air defense missiles.

A beam of invisible light, beyond the visible spectrum, emitted from the belly of Scott's ship. When the beam impacted with its target, it became a visible, blinding light, instantly burning a hole in anything it touched.

Almost as soon as the missiles left their launchers, they became burning wreckage raining down where they once roosted. Fire ignited on the deck wherever the debris landed.

As the Deliverance got closer, the cruiser began to fire a radar-guided rotary cannon. The projectiles shot wide as the Deliverance's drive computer diverted them. Scott's laser caused the radar above the gun to explode, silencing the gun.

"Bomber two – Coyote Five, I understand the helicopters, that can be written off as engine failure, but the cruiser?" Jim was surprised at the damage Scott caused. He knew full well the interceptor was capable of it, but the paradox and attention it would create went against their orders.

"Coyote Five – Bomber Two, this close to the Bermuda Triangle, General Long said the history of the area might hide our operations. I bet now you wish you didn't take all the ammo out of that thing."

"Bomber Two – Coyote Five, there are other ways to fight." Jim ordered engineering, "Bring the drive coils to full power."

John asked, "Sir, what will that do?"

Jim said, "We're about to find out."

John was nervous about the proximity of the cruiser, so Jim took the controls. The entire skin of the Deliverance began to shimmer in waves of color like the northern lights, but instead of just one color, blues, greens and reds all intertwined. Jim could tell the ship had become more responsive and felt alive to his touch.

Scott watched as the Deliverance's hull took on a life of its own. He thought '*This will be interesting*'.

The Deliverance was so low, its hull scraped the tips of the cruiser's antennae, shorting them out from the massive electrical charge created by the aura of the ship's drive. The Deliverance accelerated with such force that the shock wave caused the cruiser to list in its wake.

Scott, trailing the Deliverance, saw sparks blow out from just above the waterline of the cruiser, which must have been the radio room. "Coyote Five – Bomber Two, impressive. It doesn't look like they will be calling for help any time soon."

"Bomber Two – Coyote Five, I'm surprised. I thought the antennae got hit by lightning all the time and were shielded against that kind of thing."

John said, "Major! Those ships weren't there before."

Jim saw a second row of ships. Each was spraying water high into the air, covering themselves in a fog of mist. "What are they doing?"

Paul said, "That is a Deluge system. It's used to prevent radioactive sea salt from penetrating the ship's armor during a nuclear attack. It was installed on every Navy ship since testing was done in the Bikini Atoll."

Jim said, "Okay? So?"

Paul shook his head, not knowing the significance of the ships doing this.

Sam said, "The Navy tested lasers and found that water vapor, even fog, can make lasers ineffective. Apparently, someone aboard those ships has done some reading."

Jim thought for a moment and asked, "How deep is the water here?"

Claire said, "It's approaching sixty feet."

"Damn it. I need at least one hundred and fifty. Let me know when we got it. Bomber Two – Coyote Five, do not engage any targets till they clear that water system. It may make your laser ineffective."

"Coyote Five – Bomber Two, shouldn't we test that?"

"Bomber Two – Coyote Five, negative, if it actually works, there's no benefit in letting them know they have an effective defense against us."

Claire said, "Sir, I got two fighters approaching."

Jim activated the ship's comms and said, "Everyone strap in, prepare for high-G maneuvers. Bomber Two – Coyote Five, link your controls to mine. I'm going after the bogeys."

"Coyote Five – Bomber Two, how? You're unarmed."

"Bomber Two – Coyote Five, I've got an idea."

"Coyote Five – Bomber Two, am I going to like this?"

"Bomber Two – Coyote Five, I don't know yet."

John looked worried and tightened the straps on his seat as tight as he could get them, along with everyone else on the bridge.

The ship in front of them began to launch its missiles. "Bomber Two – Coyote Five, do not engage. Five, Four, Three, Two..." During his countdown, he programmed the controls to carry out a sequence of maneuvers in case he blacked out. "One," and he initiated the program. Both ships went straight up. The noses of the two craft turned skyward, and immediately gained altitude, losing all forward momentum in the process. They accelerated so fast, they created a series of sonic booms almost as soon as they began to climb. The missiles that were fired at them self-destructed moments later, unable to locate their targets.

"Bomber Two – Coyote Five, status"

"Coyote Five – Bomber Two, all good here. Now I call that ballistic – the altimeter is still trying to catch up. A little warning would have been nice."

"Bomber Two – Coyote Five, now lets take care of these two bogeys."

"Coyote Five – Bomber Two, I'll take the lead."

"Bomber Two – Coyote Five, negative, I got this."

"Coyote Five – Bomber Two, you don't have any weapons. How can you take them on?"

"Bomber Two – Coyote Five, watch and learn, watch and learn." Jim looked over his shoulder and said, "Sam, program the drive computer to collect titanium."

As Sam programmed the computer, she asked, "Where are you going to find titanium up here?"

"From the heart of those engines," Jim said, pointing at the fighters.

The pair of fighters Jim was preparing to engage had lost track of their quarry when he went ballistic. The advantage now belonged to Scott and Jim, who were coming from a higher altitude. With the sun just cresting, Jim was not able to hide in its brightness. All he could do was hide in the bogies' radar gap. "Bomber Two – Coyote Five, stay close, we have a narrow band to fly to stay off their radar."

Jim descended on the rear fighter till the drive computer was close enough to pick its engine apart, atom by atom. The core of the fighter's engine began losing any trace of titanium. A few moments later, the engine tore itself apart. The compressor blades lost their structural integrity and broke off. The centrifugal force caused the blades to rip through the fuselage, tearing the fighter to shreds.

The unsuspecting fighters were unaware they were under attack till the wingman's plane exploded. Both pilot and weapons officer ejected. The remaining fighter began evasive maneuvers.

Jim managed to get behind the fighter and stuck to its tail like a magnetic bond was holding him there.

Scott trailed on Jim's starboard wing. Being the last in the line of aircraft, he did not have to maneuver as much. Scott was amazed at seeing such a large aircraft matching the fighter move for move.

The second fighter succumbed to the same catastrophic engine failure as the first. The drive computer pushed all the debris of its quarry away from the Deliverance.

When the crew ejected, the weapons officer was chewed up as he flew through the shrapnel of the fan blades and was killed instantly. The pilot floated down beneath a silken sheet.

Jim scanned the sky. "Bomber Two – Coyote Five, do you see any more hostiles?"

"Coyote Five – Bomber Two, no sir, looks like we are in the clear. That was some fancy flying, and how did you take out those two?"

"Bomber Two – Coyote Five, thank you, and I'll fill you in later." Throughout his career of working on classified projects, Jim learned not to discuss things like tactics over the radio. He knew no one had the technology to be listening in but it was so ingrained in him, it had become a habit.

Claire said, "Jim, we have enough water beneath us now."

"Bomber Two – Coyote Five, let's take it downstairs."

"Coyote Five – Bomber Two, your lead."

Jim put the ship into a dive and gave the controls back to John, who slowed the ship and dove beneath the waves.

Jim asked, "Lieutenant, where did Captain Dixon's interceptor come from?"

John said, "From the moon. General Long said he had Sarah put a couple there when she was making those chambers on the north wall."

Sam said, "When John and Scott went to get it, I spoke with Sarah about it and –"

"You spoke with Sarah? And you weren't going to tell me?"

"Well, you were so busy since you got on board." Jim closed his eyes and shook his head. "She said the shot pad had to be rebuilt after we left, and to calibrate it, they did test shots to the moon. Since the calculations were already done, General Long decided the moon would be a good place to hide a couple."

"So there are more up there?"

Claire said, "Yes, sir. Sarah said she hid them on the edge of a crater, and I had a tough time finding them."

Jim asked, "You too? So how is she?"

"She is scraped up pretty good but the doctor has her on some pain medication so she's feeling fine. She asked about you."

Jim, slightly concerned, asked, "What did you tell her?"

Claire said, "Oh, you know. Girl talk." Sam and Claire laughed.

Jim shook his head and calmly said, "Just take me home."

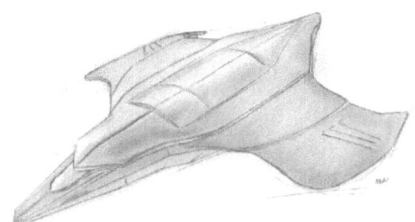

Chapter 51: REUNION

When the Deliverance set down on the landing pad in Anarbia, Jim was already on the descending cargo ramp, not wanting to waste any time to get to the infirmary.

General Long awaited him on the landing pad, "Major Norgas."

The general was cut short by Jim's quick salute and "Sir, can it wait?" Jim was about to break into a run any second.

"By all means," General Long said, and he returned the salute with a grin and watched Jim depart.

"General," Chief Besch said as he descended the ramp.

General Long watched Jim depart, and said, "I hope no one gets in his way, or there will be more people in the infirmary today. Chief, where is Sam?"

"She should be on the bridge."

General Long started to climb the ramp, and said, "Thanks Chief. Still can't salute?"

"Arthritis, sir," and rubbed his left shoulder.

General Long shook his head, and said, "That's your military right, Chief."

Jim shouted "Sarah!" as he burst through the doors to the infirmary, "Sarah!"

Dr. Stevens stepped into the hall to see what the commotion was.

Rushing past Dr. Stevens, Jim asked, "Doc, where is Sarah?"

Dr. Stevens said, "She is in room 118. Be careful with her, she..." his voice drifted off, realizing Jim could no longer hear, and he began to pursue him down the hall.

Dr. Stevens could hear squeals as he approached Sarah's room, then saw Jim lying on the hospital bed beside her, smothering her in kisses.

Sarah half giggled, half said, "Ouch, ow," as Jim accidentally touched a tender spot not yet healed.

Dr. Stevens saw Jim would not aggravate any of her wounds more than he already had, and he turned to leave as he heard Sarah say, "There's my Stinker," followed by a giggle.

Thank you for reading my book. If you enjoyed it, won't you please take a moment to leave me a review? Enjoy this sneak peek into book two of the Anarbia story. It starts out from Sarah's perspective of where Jim's time travel adventure began. Coming soon.

Sneak Peek

Sarah Burnett sat at the control panel and started to prepare for the first time-travel shot of the day. The gravity of the situation had been made abundantly clear a few hours earlier when General Long had held a briefing for everyone involved with Project Anarbia. An alien ship from the approaching armada had been spotted skirting around the moon. The energy could be felt from everyone's sense of urgency, and the threat condition alert status was increased because of the alien ship.

She flipped this switch, adjusted that knob. She tweaked everything on the console as she reviewed her notes, which were double-checked by her mentor Dr. Kovonich. She compared the notes with the displays overhead.

Personnel started to enter the control room as she got near the end of her checklist and finalized the settings for the shot. She had made numerous calculations for previous shots, but those contained only supplies or placeholders for tests. This shot was the first time sending anything alive. Major James Norgas and his ship were to travel back in time to the 1400s, the first of many to come, and Sarah wanted everything perfect.

"Transit One – Anarbia Control, request final approach." Sarah heard Jim's voice from the speaker in the ceiling.

"Anarbia Control – Transit One, permission granted, winds gusting five knots bearing three one five." Came the controller located one floor above the control room.

"Transit One – Anarbia Control, copy that."

She noticed through the control room window that the massive YCS-92 piloted by Jim was approaching the shot pad from the direction of the hangars on Langley AFB to the southeast. She stopped what she was doing to watch him land. Just a few weeks ago, his copilot, Captain Scott Dixon, had crashed while attempting to land. As a result, the landing pad had been made larger and moved farther from the control building since then. Despite the modifications, she was nervous, and the announcement of wind gusts did not help. She did not know how the winds may effect the YCS-92.

It dwarfed the shot pad and required a steady hand to see it down amidst the huge scaffolding. These articulated structures surrounded the pad and held the huge coils that would later be moved into place to surround the ship from all angles.

She could tell from experience when the ship had landed without even seeing the landing gear. The ship nearly stopped its descent, then suddenly dropped a few inches as the landing gear took the full weight of the ship and the pilot shut down the Faraday-Maxwell drive.

News about the alien armada had been leaked and had resulted in a full-blown riot outside the gates of the base that morning. Sarah's car was attacked on the way to work, and she was glad Jim was driving. She remembered screaming when the window behind her shattered from something a rioter threw at the car. Jim was so worried about her. "Are you okay?" he shouted. "Check yourself." At the time she thought it was an odd thing for him to say, but he explained, "With your heightened adrenaline you may not know you're cut."

That's when she saw blood running down his cheek and became concerned. He said, "It's just a scratch," but winced when she dabbed at it with a napkin she pulled from her purse.

He suggested she call her folks and get them moving as was planned. She said into her phone, "Hello Dad? Yes I'm fine, we just made it on base. Everything is crazy. Are you and Mom heading to West Virginia? You tell her you're out of time and leave it behind. I'm sure Jim's parents have one. No Dad, I'm sure I'll be staying on base. Okay, I love you, and tell Mom for me, I love her."

She was lost in thought when she noticed Jim round the rear of the ship doing his preflight check. They exchanged a quick wave at each other, and General Long entered the room in a flurry. She had never seen him like this, and it took her attention away from the window.

General Long announced loudly, "The alien ship spotted last night is headed this way." In his command voice, he ordered, "Make all haste and get that ship sent. We're out of time!"

Sarah turned back to the window and saw Jim come out from under the leading edge of the wing, and she frantically tried to get his attention. She shifted her gaze from him to the sky. The base air raid sirens began to wail with a haunting echo of not being in sync with each other.

She could hear the coils come to life as the scaffolding began its transit over the ship, and blue sparks began surrounding the coils. When a coil got closer to the one beside it, sparks shot between them, and closer yet, the sparks arced across the top of the ship. A dance of electrical energy played across the hull of the ship till reaching the coils closing from the other side.

She knew the coils beneath the pad were also powering up and that Jim needed to get out of there. She motioned frantically for him to get in his ship, but she could no longer find him when she looked in the direction of the shot pad.

She noticed everyone that was heading toward his ship began running every direction, trying to find cover. Nervously under her breath she said, "Jim, where are you?" Not knowing he had already bolted to the loading ramp under the belly of the ship.

The alien ship was chased by two fighters, which were based on the massive ship sitting on the pad. The fighters made a vain attempt to keep the alien away from the base, which caused it to duck and dodge, veering this way and that. It was about to pass over the shot pad when it dove to avoid another volley from its pursuers and plowed right into one of the coils. The impact triggered a cascading effect, and all the coils simultaneously fired as the alien ship exploded, adding to the power build-up surrounding Jim's ship.

The fireball from the explosion expanded and threatened to blind her. She covered her face and ducked. The shock wave from the explosion impacted the building, sending glass shards in every direction. Everything not bolted down was flung against the back wall. Occupants of the room were pinned between the wall and their desks, allowing only their screams to escape.

Sarah was left barely conscious. She heard the distinct sound of the coils winding down after a shot and the sound of the fighters as they rushed past. In their wake, the only sound she could discern was the ringing in her ears that was barely drowned out by the wails of those still alive in the control room.

ABOUT THE AUTHOR

I was born and raised in Green Bay Wisconsin, but finished high school in southern Illinois after my family moved. After graduation I left for Air Force Basic Training. Through my twenty years in the Air Force, I was stationed mostly on the East Coast and in Germany, and I deployed several times to the Middle East. I currently reside in North Carolina.

For as long as I can remember, when I had trouble falling asleep I'd think about this story. It evolved throughout the years and about two years ago a friend suggested I write it down. This is the first of three books I have planned for this story.

I have done a lot of research while writing this book and studied some physics. I found I enjoy astrophysics. I tried to make everything in this book either true or possible, including the engine used in the spaceship. Granted time travel is pretty hard to say is possible, but we have to have some fun.

One of my favorite authors, the way he writes, I see what is going on in my mind as I read. I hope I was able to do that for you.

www.ingramcontent.com/pod-product-compliance
Lightning Source LLC
Chambersburg PA
CBHW050541260626
47157CB00002B/385